The Sea Beach Line

Also by Ben Nadler

Punk in NYC's Lower East Side 1981–1991
(nonfiction monograph, Microcosm Publishing, 2014)

Harvitz, As To War
(novel, Iron Diesel Press, 2011)

The Sea
Beach Line

A NOVEL

Ben
Nadler

FIG TREE
BOOKS

Bedford, New York

Published in the United States by Fig Tree Books LLC, Bedford, New York

www.FigTreeBooks.net

Jacket design by Strick&Williams
Interior design by Neuwirth & Associates, Inc.

Library of Congress Cataloging-in-Publication Data Available Upon Request

ISBN number 978-1-941493-08-3

Printed in the United States
Distributed by Publishers Group West

10 9 8 7 6 5 4 3 2 1

In memory of Newt Johnson.

BOOK 1

The Yeshiva Bocher

IT CAME TO PASS that four sages entered *Pardes*, encountering the divine. Ben Azzai died. Ben Zoma went insane. Akiva emerged with perfect faith. Elisha ben Abuyah "tore out the roots" of the orchard, and emerged with perfect doubt. From that point forward, Elisha's name was blotted out; the rabbis referred to him only as Aher, "the other."

The story, just a few lines long, appears in both the Babylonian and Palestinian Talmuds, but I read it in a photocopied packet of Aggadot and post-rabbinic tales in a Jewish literature class in college. I had taken acid the night before, and when I came to class that morning I was in the posttrip void where colors and logic don't work quite the right way, and you can't sleep no matter how tired you are. I ran my fingers over the lines of the story. The Xerox toner felt thick on the paper.

The story opened up something inside of me. Piety didn't really interest me, but I was fascinated by the path shared by these four sages. They had entered the heavenly garden of *Pardes*, achieving the highest of mystical experiences. Most intriguing was Aher, who found his own individual truth, which led him away from the bonds of his society.

I had been taking hallucinogens regularly and recreationally for five years, since I was sixteen, but once I read the *Pardes* tale during my junior year, hallucinogens took on a ritual importance. They were a way to shake the dust off the world around me, to make the hidden signs on my path glow. My consumption increased dramatically. My mind felt like a local train that had switched to the express track and was picking up speed.

The class soon moved on toward modernism without me. We had briefly discussed Moshe Luzzatto, who heard the voice of a divine messenger in eighteenth-century Italy. I devoted myself to reading his guide, *Mesillat Yesharim*, hoping that if I listened hard enough, and behaved rigorously enough, I could hear the same type of revelation. Despite my lack of piety, I tried to heed Luzzatto's words as best I could, and follow "the path of the upright." I started wearing a kippah, partly out of observance, because one had to live a righteous life before he could receive revelation, and partly because I saw myself as a character in a story and the kippah as part of my costume.

In the university library, I read books by other seekers and tried to find myself in their texts. I learned from Kafka—who learned from the Belzer Hasidim—that everyone had their own door to pass through. It wasn't always an angel or divine messenger who called your name. In Safed, Israel, a rabbi received a letter from Rebbe Nachman—two centuries after the rebbe's death. Then there was Philip K. Dick, who was struck with gnosis in the form of a pink laser beam. In *VALIS*, his sci-fi novel–cum–spiritual memoir, Dick's alter ego learned to thread together hidden narratives from symbols in the everyday world around him. I too believed that messages were waiting for me somewhere. I simply had to find them.

꠵ꠗꠌ

After Oberlin expelled me in the fall of 2004, I went to live with my mother and stepfather in New Mexico. We agreed that I needed to sober up and get healthier—I'd pretty much stopped eating or otherwise caring for myself at school—before I tried to find a job or, my mother emphasized hopefully, reapply to college. I was all for getting sober and healthy; drugs had taken me as far as they were going to, and my brain felt exhausted and bruised.

In the beginning, my mother tried to get me to talk to her. We would go to brunch or a museum while my stepfather was busy with work, and she suggested on several occasions that I attend counseling. Mostly, though, I just spent time alone, walking through the arroyos. It rained every afternoon for the first month that I was there. In the evenings, the sun set over the mountains, painting an image of fire on the sky. Late at night, the coyotes howled like demons. I slept facing east so the sun would wake me.

Then, after two months in New Mexico, I received two signs. The first was a postcard from my father. Alojzy had not sent a postcard, or communicated with me in any manner, for several years. This postcard had been mailed three weeks earlier but had only just been forwarded from our old address on Long Island.

The postcard depicted a pinup-style tattooed mermaid with the words "CONEY ISLAND" in big block letters. On the back Alojzy had sketched a cargo ship, a heavy freighter set against a New York City skyline. Each cargo container, smokestack, and antenna was detailed, though it wasn't clear what flag the ship sailed under. The rough waters carried down to the bottom of the card, and the ship's wake bled off the left edge. Skyscrapers twisted together in the background, forming a latticework. Other than my name and old address, and Alojzy's signature—which stretched across the starboard side of the ship, where the ship's name would be—there were no words. A Brooklyn, NY, postmark was printed by the American flag stamp.

Two days after I received Alojzy's postcard, the second sign, a note-card from a Semyon Goldov of Brooklyn, arrived. It was addressed to my mother and folded into a small envelope:

Dear Mrs. Ruth Edel—
    I am writing you to sadly inform you that Alojzy Edel is missing, and can only be presumed dead.

I have known the Alojzy for many years, and this is a great tragedy.

I thought you may want to know of this occurrence, both for the sake of sentimentality as you were once his wife, and also for the fact that there may be issues of estate or outstanding debts or accounts which you feel obligated to settle.

Do not hesitate to write to me if you have questions on these issues.

Yours and truly,

Mr. Semyon Goldov

The arrival of the two cards in the same week couldn't just be some sad coincidence. There was more to the messages than what I could see on the paper. Was Alojzy telling me that no matter what I heard, he was still alive? Was he saying good-bye? Was he calling for me? One way or another, I was being summoned to Brooklyn, my path lit by two signs. I called my sister, Becca, in Manhattan to ask if I could stay with her, and bought a one-way plane ticket to New York City.

I I I ■

Two weeks later, I found myself back in Alojzy's world. The Q train stalled at the Brighton Beach station, and rather than wait—I had waited long enough—I got off and walked through my father's old stomping grounds.

I stepped down the station's green metal staircase and onto the Brooklyn pavement, where people with angry and haunted faces pushed through me like I was invisible, a ghost. The majority of the people on the sidewalk were fifty or older, and many leaned on canes or folding shopping carts. Some people closer to my age filtered through the throng as well.

Brighton Beach Avenue was disorienting, blocked off from the sun by the elevated train tracks. Businesses refused to be contained by their doors, and merchandise tables, carts, and crates tumbled out onto the sidewalk. Cars and motorcycles wove past each other in the street, occasionally clipping one another, or popping up onto the curb. Though I could read a bit of Russian, it had been a long time since I'd seen so many non-English signs, and I was struck by the sight. Many of the signs were just English words like "food stamps" written in Cyrillic letters. The mixed languages confused my mind.

I didn't remember how the street numbering worked—Brighton Beach has a completely separate grid from Coney Island, where I was headed—but the area is not that large, and I soon found my way to the boardwalk. The ocean on my left, I headed west past the aquarium and along into Coney Island, all the way up to the old fishing pier. No one was crabbing off the pier. But it was late in the day, and early in the year.

I turned off the boardwalk at West Eighteenth Street and continued north through the more desolate streets of Coney Island, where everything was covered in a layer of sand and grime. Everyone's heard of the boardwalk side—Nathan's, the Cyclone, the Parachute Jump—but the neighborhood side is more neglected, unseen except by the immigrants and other poor families in public housing, the desperate souls praying at the storefront churches, and the police officers who patrol the area. Most things in the world are like that: they have a visible side and an invisible side.

A public home for seniors occupied the block closest to the water. Old people, abandoned by their families and forced down to the very edge of the city, milled outside with their walkers. Across the street from the senior home was a somewhat neglected community garden. The tips of green stalks were just beginning to emerge from beds bounded with salvaged two-by-fours or truck tires. A rooster emerged from a doghouse. He puffed up his chest and paraded back and forth on top of his black-feathered boots.

On the next block, I passed a boarded-up bait and tackle shop where my dad used to buy his crab traps and line. The store had been destroyed in a fire, and the bricks were blackened, the giant striped bass on the store's sign now barely perceptible on the warped metal. I wondered what had happened to the older Chinese couple who had owned the store.

Farther up the street, heroin and crack addicts loitered outside a padlocked Christian mission whose walls were painted with anchors and crosses. They were the undead, their bodies wasted away to skeletons. On the corner of Surf and West Eighteenth Street, a group of teenage boys stood outside a deli. Like many of the businesses on Surf, the deli announced its name and offerings in Spanish on a hand-painted sign decorated with palm trees.

"You looking for something?" one of the teenagers, a tall, skinny kid wearing a basketball jersey, asked me. I shook my head. I was looking for something down here, but it wasn't dope.

2871 West Eighteenth Street was in the middle of the block. I double-checked the return address on the envelope in my pocket, but there was really no need; I'd read Semyon Goldov's notecard so many times that I knew the entire thing by heart, including the address.

The building had clearly been a tenement house once, but the windows were now bricked over, and the whole structure painted black. Above the door was bolted a hand-lettered sign that read, "The R. Galuth Museum." I'd pictured the encounter many times over the past few weeks, and expected that the building would be a residence of some sort, or maybe a shoe repair shop with pocketknives and refurbished radios in the window. Certainly not a museum.

I climbed the two cement steps, took a deep breath, and rang the doorbell. No response. I rang it again. Disappointed, I stood helplessly on the doorstep. Then I heard footsteps and heavy breathing through the closed door and could feel myself being scrutinized through the peephole. The door opened.

"Welcome to the Galuth Museum!" The pale skin of my greeter's wrinkled face—wrinkled, you could tell, more from worry and torment than from age—was overshadowed by the orange and purple streaks of his acrylic sweater. The few words he'd spoken were enough for me to hear a strong Russian accent, which matched the syntax of the notecard. This was the right man, Goldov. He stepped aside so I could enter.

The interior walls had been knocked out so that the bottom floor was one wide-open space. White paint had been applied directly to the bricks, and the shape of each one could be made out. There were no windows, and the electric track lights were not quite adequate to properly illuminate the framed pictures that circled the room at eye level. A wooden bench in the middle of the room reminded me of the ornamental stone benches sometimes found at grave sites. In fact, the whole room felt more like a tomb or shrine than an art gallery.

Goldov drew my attention to a plexiglass box mounted next to the door, marked "Museum Donations." Next to that box was a smaller, tin box that said "Tzedakah"—charity, or righteous act—in Hebrew, and "Glupsk Yeshiva Fund" in English. I put a five-dollar bill in the "Museum Donations" box, to get off on the right foot.

We started our tour to the right of the donation boxes, with an old black-and-white snapshot that had been blown up beyond recognition and set behind plexiglass.

"This, here," Goldov said, "is the only known photograph of R. Galuth." I squinted. It was a picture of a slim young man, wearing a suit and hat. "Very little is known of the life of Galuth, one of the most illustrious painters of the 1930s." He seemed to be reciting a memorized script. "We know that he arrived in New York City in the mid-1920s, from Ukraine by way of Paris. He apparently returned to Europe in 1937. Nothing more was heard from him. Presumably, like so many great artists, he was killed by the Nazis.

"His home, for the earlier part of the period he spent in America, was this very house, though he later became a fixture in bohemian Greenwich Village. Very few of his paintings have survived, but almost all of the ones that have are collected in this museum. On occasion, another Galuth painting surfaces, in which case we do our best to acquire it. So our collection continues to be growing. We have been very lucky that an anonymous benefactor subsidizes our work.

"Over here, we have one such painting." I followed my guide down the wall. "Some consider it Galuth's masterpiece. It depicts an unfortunate but true-to-life incident, in which goons were hired by the Sea Beach Railway to eject fare evaders. They murdered innocent passengers by throwing them from an elevated portion of the line."

"It's a very beautiful painting," I said. It was a New York street scene, a whole world in one intersection. The old elevated tracks slashed across a purple evening sky. Cruel faces peered from the open windows of the stalled, rust-colored train car. A young woman, tangled in her long green skirt and half-unraveled braid, hovered in the air. She had an angelic quality, and you hoped that she was ascending, but the force of gravity in the painting was too strong to ignore.

The individuals in the gathered crowd—each one a full portrait—looked upward, unable to save her. Their long backs stretched up from the bottom of the canvas, and as a viewer I became one of them, fighting to push myself forward through the crowd, to get a better view of the girl in that last moment before she died. A boy in knickers picked a man's overcoat pocket, but the personal victory did not exempt him from his share of the collective pain.

"Yes," Goldov agreed. "Very beautiful. If you notice, even the expression on the face of this goon, this murderer, is masterful. If you will look at his eyes . . ." I looked into the man's eyes. Truthfully, they reminded me of Alojzy's. That wasn't so far-fetched, that the goons were men like Alojzy and his friends. Rough men who did as they pleased. Would Alojzy throw an innocent person from a train? I had been entranced by the picture, but was now jolted back to my purpose.

"Listen," I interrupted. "Thank you for showing me this, but I didn't come down here to see the museum. I actually came for something else. You see, Mr. Goldov . . ." He tightened up at the mention of his name. I saw his hands become fists at his side. I smiled, to show him that I came in good faith. "My name is Izzy—Izzy Edel." I stuck out my hand, but he did not reach to shake it. I took it back. "My mother received a letter from you. About my father. Alojzy Edel."

"You? A slim thing like you? You, coming into my museum in your fancy shirt and your yarmulke, are the son of Ally Edel? Is that not a thing!" I didn't think my shirt was particularly fancy, but it was true that button-down oxfords weren't Alojzy's style. And though my path was taking a different turn, I still wore the kippah out of habit.

"Well, now," I said to Goldov, "I've lived a different life than he's led . . ." Alojzy never had time for hallucinations or revelations. He was a practical man who spent every day fighting and hustling, a man who'd already been through everything and achieved perfect doubt.

"This I can believe," Goldov said. We stared at each other. "You know, Ally stole from me eight thousand dollars, once. Restitution has not yet been made." I had been half expecting something like this, considering the tone of Goldov's note. "I thought your family might want to tie up loose ends."

"I'm very sorry," I said. "But I'm afraid that's not a debt I myself will be able to make up to you. In fact, I'm sure if you added up all the child support he still owes for my sister and me . . ." This was a popular refrain of my mother's. The man waved away my comments with his right hand, then waved me up the stairs with his left.

"Come. Let's talk."

There were far more canvases upstairs than in the gallery. They were stacked all around, leaning together in both orderly and not so orderly piles. One mostly blank canvas rested on an easel by the window. Empty paint tubes littered every surface, and brushes stood upright in jars of turpentine. This was Goldov's studio. In the corner was a small bed with a metal frame.

"*Govarish po Rusky?*" he asked hopefully as he turned on his electric teakettle, which sat on the windowsill next to a hotplate and a small radio, all three of which were connected to the same rat's nest of an electrical outlet. "I assume not. I always chatted with your father *v'Rusky*. He spoke it quite well, for a Pole."

"*Da*," I said. "*Govaroo chut chut.*" I'd only started studying Russian because my college didn't offer Polish, and my three and a half semesters' worth were totally insufficient for the conversation I wanted to have. When Goldov spoke next, to offer me a seat, he did so in English.

"These are your paintings?" I asked him, feeling that I had to say something about them. Abstract expressionist in style, almost to the point of parody, they surrounded us. The disordered thoughts of a frustrated man congealed into acrylic globs. I surmised that the materials were chosen because the old man could not afford oil paints in the quantities he desired. The paintings might not have appeared so terrible to me if the Galuth painting weren't still haunting my mind, creating an unfavorable comparison.

"Yes, yes. My life's work. You know, in Soviet Union, all I ever wanted was to be free to be an artist. I was dismissed from the academy in Leningrad for 'abstractions indicative of a bourgeois nature.' And I always knew . . . if I would make it to the West, my creativity would flower. Such a scene I would make. I come here, I learn: they let you do whatever you want, because it's nobody that will care." It seemed like he wanted me to feel sorry for him.

The timer on the kettle buzzed. Goldov stood up and placed tea bags in two glasses, which he then filled with water.

"Would you like jam for your tea? I'm sorry I have no lemon." He pulled a half-full plastic tray from a box of orange cream cookies and placed it on the table. "I don't entertain so often."

"No, thank you. It's fine like this." He shrugged, then sat down and began to spoon jam into his own glass. "My father studied art as well," I continued. Though Alojzy never talked very much about his life in Poland before he moved to Israel, he had said he was expelled from the art academy in Warsaw in 1968. He'd implied it was because he was Jewish, but I didn't know if there were other contributing factors. In a way, my getting kicked out of college placed me in my father's footsteps.

"Yes, your father studied art under communism also. We both possessed solid appreciation of art, despite having had solid socialist art education inflicted on us. We were both expelled. Though I must say, the Academy of Fine Arts in Warsaw is not as respected as the one in Leningrad. You know, that was a typical move on Al's part, to be born a Jew in Poland, after the war. A Russian Jew in New York, that's nothing special. *Kak sebak ni rieznih.* But to be a Jew from Poland, in modern times . . . typical Edel. Always had to do things the wiseass way."

"What is your connection to Alojzy, exactly?" I asked. Presumably they had had some sort of friendly relationship before Alojzy allegedly robbed him.

"Business partners. We sold art books, on the street in Manhattan. He sold other books also—and other *things* besides books as well." I didn't know what he was insinuating, other than that Alojzy was a hustler who would buy and sell stolen goods, which I already knew.

"But art books, there is money in that. Art books are not cheap. People in lower Manhattan are mostly not poor. There was plenty of business. It was a profitable endeavor, until he stole our money and left town." Goldov's face contorted into something ugly.

"I'm very sorry that happened," I said. Alojzy surely had his own side of the story, but I didn't want to anger the man. He didn't acknowledge my comment.

"I don't hear from him again for almost two years after that. The next thing I do hear, he's in jail in Las Vegas. Passing bad checks, I believe. He described it as just misunderstanding. He needed bail money." The old painter sighed, then chased the sigh with a gulp of tea. "I sent it."

"Why did you do that? If you say he'd already robbed you?"

"I wish I knew. I didn't want to, but he persuaded me. Thing is, your father was, to me, like a drug. A bad habit. I could never shake him. Besides, I thought maybe he'd still pay me back someday. He always made promises to pay my money. With interest." I raised my tea to my lips, but it was still too hot to drink. "Well, he's shook now, apparently. They say he's gone for good."

"But who says he's gone for good?" I demanded. "Was it reported somewhere?"

"I heard it only as a rumor. But these rumors are most often true." It occurred to me that Alojzy could have started the rumor himself, if he believed someone was after him. If Goldov was in on it, he could be spreading the tale for Alojzy. If this was the case, I needed to press Goldov until he came across with the truth. On the other hand, considering this apparent bad blood between them, Alojzy might have specifically wanted Goldov to believe the story.

"I remembered your mother's name—lucky she didn't change it when she remarried—and the lady at the library helped me find her on the Internet. We found her crafts Internet page—the candles she makes look very nice, by the way, though I have also seen nicer—and I sent a postcard to the address listed on the page." My mother actually had changed her last name, to Bernie's name, Fischer. But I guess she did business under her old name. "I felt I should let your family know." He looked up at me. "My condolences," he added, without conviction.

"Thank you," I said. "But I really don't know if they're necessary. Your letter is the only indication I've had that he's dead. And you don't know this for sure, do you? You haven't seen any evidence?"

"Only rumor. But I don't have a reason to doubt, either." The man held up his arms in a gesture of helplessness. "You could have written in regard to settling matters. You did not need to come down here for so little."

"But since I did, isn't there anything else you could maybe tell me about my father's life? What he may have been doing. Or be doing now? I haven't seen him since I was in high school."

"He's doing nothing now," Goldov said, setting his glass down on the table with a small thud. "Sleeping in the dirt." I didn't move. Goldov sighed. "Fine. After our partnership dissolved, he ended up selling books again by himself. Not so much the fine art books, more the cheap paperbacks. More time was spent chasing women than working. He could charm any woman. I saw him one time chatting up a nun. She blushed, but she listened." He seemed to be getting away from useful information, but I enjoyed hearing about my father and didn't interrupt. "People didn't walk away from Ally Edel. He carried himself fearsomely sometimes . . . he could be very intimidating. It was good to have a man like that with me on the street. He was not a guy who took any guff." Yes, that was Alojzy. He was a truly tough man. I hoped to become tough too. "It really was a loss, his death."

"If he *is* dead," I said. "His body must be somewhere." As long as there was no body, Alojzy was alive. The rabbis said that you should not mourn for someone when they were merely missing; you needed confirmation of their death from a witness.

"In potter's field on Hart Island, I imagine. That's where I'll be going. An unmarked grave, no words above it."

"Yes, I guess so." Who would hold a funeral for these men? "Do you know where he's been living?"

"No. Now and then, I did see him, but there was the money problem between us, always, so that kept a distance between us. The last time I saw him, he called me up, said he wanted to talk about the money he owed me, maybe paying some of it back." Goldov had far more information about Alojzy owing him money than about Alojzy dying. He could be using the rumor of Alojzy's death to try to squeeze me. Or he could have made up the story himself, as a plan to scam money from our family. "When we met up, well, of course he didn't have the money. All he had was excuses. I don't know what it was he wanted from that meeting. He didn't have to call me in first place. I left him there on the bench." He shook his head. "No, I'm sorry. I got nothing else for you."

"Fine," I said. "Can you think of anyone who might know more? Anyone who can verify his death, or trace the rumor? Or at least provide details about his life before that? Maybe I should check with the police or hospitals or something, see if they have records about him." I wasn't going to accept Goldov's account alone.

"No, I would not recommend going to authorities. Go if you want. But Edel lived . . . under radar. If he ever went to the hospital, it would be under fake name."

"Please. You have to give me something. I've come all this way. I can't leave without something. I really can't." Goldov looked at me with annoyance and disdain. He slurped up the rest of his tea, then finally spoke.

"*Ladno*. There is another bookseller, Mendy, who maybe knows something more about where he was living, or his business. He could be the one I first heard the rumor from. Maybe there are still some assets you can sell off, to settle the estate. Go harass him."

"Thank you. Is there a telephone number where I could reach him, this Mendy? Or an address maybe?"

"No." Goldov shook his head. "No telephone. And I'm not knowing his address. But he sells on West Fourth Street in Manhattan, by the southeast corner of the park there. He's out on the street most days, providing it doesn't rain.

"Thank you." He waved me off.

"Come back to me if you learn anything about Alojzy's finances."

2

MY NEXT DESTINATION AFTER Coney Island was Sheepshead Bay, Alojzy's old neighborhood. For the past few years, I had done my best to
avoid thinking about Alojzy too much. He was out there somewhere,
and he was my father. I was safer because he was in the world. But
he wasn't around, and it was easier to push him to the back of my
mind. Now, since receiving his postcard, he had been pulled back to
the surface. Images of him filled my mind as I left the museum, but
I couldn't be sure how much of those were my own memories, and
how much were me assimilating Goldov's memories. I didn't want
to mix up my own image of Alojzy with one painted by the failed
artist. My own memories were so fragile, I didn't know how much
cross-contamination they could withstand. Visiting the neighborhood
where so many of my happy memories of Alojzy were situated would
help me ground them.

As I walked back up the boardwalk, two freighters passed by. I
pulled out Alojzy's postcard, which I kept in the same envelope as
Goldov's note, and held the picture up against the ocean. The view
didn't line up. Alojzy hadn't drawn the picture in Coney Island. I

stayed on the boardwalk until it ended. Passing up through Brighton, I bought two pirozhki stuffed with *kapusta* off a folding table outside a grocery store. The smell of cabbage and grease reminded me of days spent with Alojzy. I followed below the train tracks at first, but as I got closer to the bay, my memory of the local geography began to return. Walking up West End Avenue, I noticed strange bits of steel and brick sticking out of the trees down past the flat end of the bay. I couldn't figure out what they could be. Brooklyn was full of things that did not make sense and were not explained; this was part of the reason it had been such a source of wonder to me as a kid.

When I got close to the trees, I realized I was looking at the Holocaust Memorial Park. The monument had not been completed when my father lived down here. The local Jews were still arguing then about the details of its construction. My father had agreed with a popular sentiment in the neighborhood: it was wrong for the city to try to include the Roma in the monument's lengthy text. Why should the Jews be disgraced by having to share their history with some damn Gypsies? All in all, though, Alojzy was not impressed with the whole idea of the monument. He found the American Jewish obsession with the Holocaust sentimental and indulgent.

I walked through a row of trees and entered the park. Dozens of rough-hewn gravestones were scattered through the park's center, each one bearing the story of some atrocity or death camp or partisan leader, in whichever language—English, Hebrew, Russian, or Yiddish—the donor had felt most comfortable. Little round stones rested on some of the gravestones. Around the top of the column, the word "remember" was written in all four languages. In the center, oversized strands of fake razor wire threaded around a spiraled column. The column was made to look like the bombed-out ruins of something old and brick, but was clearly one molded, red cement piece. Alojzy had seen real bombed ruins as an Israeli soldier during the War of Attrition. And though he never spoke of it, Warsaw must have still been full of rubble from World War II when he was a child. It was no surprise he had so little patience for such a fabrication, which contained the narrative but not the pain.

Two old men sat on a park bench arguing in Russian. These were the types of men Alojzy sat and chatted with. They spoke slowly, considering their positions, and I was able to make out the gist of the discussion, a debate about the likelihood of the city filling the bay in with cement. Their paranoid fantasy was completely real to them.

Emmons Avenue led me along the bay. The bay was connected to the ocean, and the whole wide world of adventure and chaos, but as it was squared off against the avenue, it still held the safety and domestic comfort of a residential block. It seemed as if the bay was once just another street, but on a whim a miracle worker had turned it into a body of water. Moses had turned the Nile to blood. Surely some lesser prophet could turn pavement to brackish water. Boats sailed in from the ocean, and anchored parallel to the cars double-parked on Emmons. Once they got out past Breezy Point, nothing stood between the sailboats and the coasts of Morocco and Andalusia. A wooden footbridge curved over the bay. On the far side were the mafia castles of Manhattan Beach, with their columns and towers.

Beside and below me, ducks and swans swam together. There was plenty of food for all, even though most of the food was just garbage. A fisherman sat in a low beach chair, drinking from a carton of orange juice. He had three fishing rods—two big ocean rods and a little five-foot freshwater rod—propped against the railing, their lines stretched taut out into the water.

| I I ▪

I remembered the first time I visited Sheepshead Bay, when I was eleven. My mother, sister, and I had been out in Nassau County for about a year and a half. It had been two years since we last saw Alojzy, at our old apartment on East Ninety-Second Street. Neither my mother nor my sister mentioned Alojzy, and so I didn't either.

Alojzy had sent my sister and me a few postcards from places like St. Louis and Las Vegas when we still lived in Manhattan. He was never much for writing, and aside from a few words here and there, he mainly filled the backs of the cards with little sketches of him and

us, or of the places he was writing from. We hadn't received any since
moving out of the city, and it didn't seem that the old postcards had
survived the move. Maybe he didn't know our new address. We had
Bernie, who was childless until we came along, and was more attentive than many actual fathers. He was more consistently attentive than
Alojzy had ever been, in fact, so we didn't feel a glaring absence. But
I still missed Alojzy.

People where we lived liked to talk about Israel a lot. It was some
sort of fantasy world, not quite real, but terribly important, where
they were a stronger and purer type of people. The word was spoken
with slow reverence, and conversation ceased when the region was
mentioned on the news. People walked around fearlessly in their green
Israel Defense Forces T-shirts, as if the thin fabric were bulletproof.
They stuffed cash into preprinted envelopes in the belief that it would
blossom into trees as soon as it arrived in *Eretz Yisrael*.

When I heard the word "Israel," I saw my father, because he had
actually lived and even fought in a war there. He was the only real
thing I could associate with the place. But I couldn't be sure he wasn't
part of the fantasy too.

Bernie called my sister and me into the dining room. We came in
to find him and my mother sitting at the table. We ate there on hol-
idays or when we had company; otherwise we sat at the table in the
kitchen. The only person who used the room on a regular basis was
Bernie, who would spread the files he brought home from the office
out on the table in the evening. My mother warned Becca and me
against entering the room when Bernie had his files out, for fear that
we would disturb one of his carefully sorted piles. She would shout at
us if we even made too much noise in another room of the house while
he was working, but he himself never complained. He just smiled half
a smile, without looking up from the screen of his laptop or the sheets
of numbers in front of him.

When Becca and I came into the dining room that day, though,
nothing was on the table except my mother's mug of tea, and a paper
towel to protect the finish of the wood from the tea's heat. The mug
was still full to the brim, and the paper towel was shredded into little

pieces. Becca and I sat down facing our parents. Were we in trouble? We must have been, because my mother was silent. But I hadn't done anything.

"Your mother," started Bernie—we looked at her, but her grinding fury was terrifying, and we looked back at Bernie—"and I have been in touch with your father. I should say, he's gotten in touch with us. He's back in New York now, in Brooklyn, and he would like to see you kids."

"You don't have to see him," my mother interjected. "Don't feel bad if you don't want to. There's nothing he's done for you that you need to feel obligated."

"No," said Bernie, "you don't need to feel obligated. You needn't feel obligated one way or the other. This is a decision you have to make for yourselves. He's invited you to spend next weekend with him. If you need some time to think about it—"

"I don't want to go," said Becca, who was fifteen and getting pretty good at saying things with indifferent confidence. "I'd rather spend the weekend with my friends. It's Sarah's party, and you said I could—"

"That's fine," said Bernie.

"I think you made the right decision," said my mom. "There's no reason, considering how well you guys have adjusted, that you need to—"

"I'd like to go," I said. I didn't know if this was true or not. I missed Alojzy, and going alone without Becca seemed scary. But they were dangling something in front of me—something they didn't really want me to have—and I had to snatch at it. "I'd like to see him." Becca glared at me, like I'd said it just to spite her. My mother frowned, but nodded in acceptance. Bernie smiled his usual distant smile behind his round glasses and neatly clipped beard.

Bernie was going to drive me to Brooklyn the following weekend, but he got called in to work. Alojzy didn't have a car at the time. My mom made different excuses for why she couldn't take me. In the end, Bernie and Alojzy worked it out that I would take the Long Island Rail Road into Brooklyn.

No one was waiting for me when I got off the train at Atlantic Terminal. I leaned against a pole and listened to a hip-hop radio station on my headphones, trying my best to look cool and tough so no one would bother me.

Nearly an hour passed, and I became afraid, then sure, that Alojzy wouldn't come. Maybe if Becca were with me, because he couldn't leave his *królewna* alone at night. But he wouldn't come just for me. He had better things to do. Business that came up, that he had to take care of. Maybe he'd never meant to come. Maybe he wasn't even in the city. Maybe Bernie had misunderstood. Maybe I had misunderstood.

Just as I was beginning to despair, and considered calling my mother, a body flew at me from the shadow. I stuck out my arms in defense, but failed to block the hard jab to my side.

"Getting big, eh there, fella?" My father jabbed me again in the side with his right, faked a third right, then landed a light left to my chest.

"I was afraid you weren't coming," I said, still not believing it was really him.

"Why would you think this? Never doubt me, boychik." His voice was strong and true. I wouldn't doubt him.

"Come on, now, fella." He put his arm around me, and we walked off toward the subway. Still shaken from his greeting, I chafed from the tightness of his arm around my neck, but did not want him to let go. I was proud to be walking down the street in Brooklyn with him. Of course he had come.

We didn't talk too much on the train. He asked me how I was doing, how my sister and mother were doing. They were fine, I told him. I was struggling hard to remember that he was my father, the same man who had once lived with us, danced with my mother to the radio in the kitchen, and taken us all to Greenpoint on Sundays to eat cheese dumplings and potato pancakes.

He wasn't part of a Middle Eastern fantasy. He was a real man, with strong arms and a little potbelly. He tucked in to the *Daily News*, and I pulled a schoolbook from my backpack.

We picked up a pepperoni pizza and a two-liter bottle of Coke on the way to his apartment from the train station. Alojzy placed the pizza on the coffee table, the only table in his one-bedroom apartment, and we ate straight from the box. We washed our pizza down with mugs of Coke. Alojzy poured arak into his, and the sweet licorice smell filled the room as we ate. Above the couch was a large black poster, bearing the coat of arms–like logo of the rock band Queen. The only other decorations on the wall were a plastic Israeli flag and an old snapshot of the four of us in Central Park, when I was about six and my sister maybe ten. Like the flag, the photo was held on the wall by bits of black electrical tape. When I went into the bathroom to pee, I saw a faded pink bra hanging on the shower curtain rod.

The apartment felt very small at first. It was not really much smaller than our old two-bedroom in Manhattan, but living on Long Island had already warped my sense of scale. There was hardly any furniture besides the coffee table and couch in the main room, and the bed in his bedroom. The rest of the space was packed full of cardboard boxes and stacks of books. They were mostly large hardcovers, in piles so dense and tall I thought of them as integral structures, not stacks of individual objects. I asked Alojzy if these were all books that he had read.

"No, no," he said. "In my life I've left behind two entire libraries. I wouldn't risk another. I read a book and let it go."

"So what's all this?"

"Merchandise. Got to make money, kiddo. You'll learn that sometime. Hey, take a look at this." He pulled out an old leather-bound atlas from the middle of a stack and showed me the various places he had lived. I could locate Israel by myself, but wasn't quite sure where Poland was. It turned out it was tucked in the shadow of the USSR.

My father had a small TV, which sat on one of the stacks of books, and we watched the TGIF lineup of sitcoms on ABC. I followed the plots, while my father made comments about the teenage actresses.

"Your girlfriend look anything like that?"

"I don't have a girlfriend."

"A good-looking guy like you? Not even one girlfriend? I find that very hard to believe. You got your papa's charm. You must drive the girls crazy." After a few shows, and a few more araks for my father, he turned off the TV.

"Look, I know I ain't been around lately, buddy."

"Okay." I wished the TV was still on.

"No, it's not okay. It's gonna change. Because I'm your papa. But listen: It's never been that I don't love. I'm father, of course I love. It's just, I've had my life. You see, I am the wandering Jew of Europe." He saw my confusion. "It's an old story about a curse. But it's a true story, about the life I've had to lead." I didn't say anything. I was only eleven and didn't know how to respond to a whole life. "Izzy, buddy," he said. "We're friends?"

"Sure we're friends." I didn't want him to doubt me.

"Becca couldn't come with you?"

"No," I said, worried he would see through the lie. "She wanted to. She had a school thing she couldn't miss."

"Oh. Well. Tell her what I tell you."

"Sure." I knew I wouldn't, but I wanted to please him.

"But you and me, fella, we're friends."

"Yes." We were. He knew it and I knew it. He clicked the TV back on.

"I was thinking," he said a few minutes later, "in the morning we could go crabbing?"

"What's crabbing?"

"Like fishing. You know. But for crabs instead."

"Okay. Sure." I still didn't exactly understand what we'd be doing, but other boys' fathers took them fishing. "That sounds fun."

| | | ∎

Leaving the bay now, I headed up Shore Parkway, passing a sushi restaurant that had not been there before and an Irish pub that had always been there. Just under the exit ramp from Shore Parkway was a small side street, also called Shore Parkway. This was where my father had lived, all those years ago. I had spent a lot of time here. Becca didn't come with me very often. It had been an obligation for her, but for me it had been a refuge.

The street I turned down did not match my memories. Everything looked different. Had I forgotten which block Alojzy lived on? No, this was the right address, and the exit ramp was in the right position in relation to where I stood. Alojzy's building was gone. In its place was a new building, a box coated in lumpy plaster, with blue trim and shiny railings on the narrow balconies that faced the ramp.

I stared at the new building, half hoping that time would run backward if I waited long enough. That the new building would be torn down, my father's old building rebuilt with a wrecking ball. I pictured the boards falling off the third-floor window and the light flicking on and off, then Alojzy pushing open the front door and inviting me in.

I remembered waking up in my father's apartment that first morning, after I fell asleep watching TV with him, how normal it had felt. Waking up on my father's couch in Brooklyn felt far more natural than waking up in my own bed out on Long Island.

|| ▮

For breakfast, my father put out slices of black bread. This bread was far denser than the bread I was used to eating, and though it seemed a little stale, he didn't offer to toast it. I vaguely remembered eating bread like this when I was younger, but I'd grown used to eating fluffy grocery store wheat bread. I smeared on lots of butter—at home we were only allowed margarine—and used all the muscles in my throat to choke the morsels down.

When we were ready to go, Alojzy hoisted an army surplus pack full of gear onto his back, and handed me an empty cooler to carry.

"What about the rods?" I asked.

"Rods?"

"We're going, like, fishing. Right?"

"No rods, fella. For crabs you use traps." He tapped his pack.

We walked down the Coney Island boardwalk. I'd been there a few times with my family, but only in the afternoon. Families didn't hang around Coney after dark back then. Now, in the early morning, it was pretty much deserted, aside from a few old Russian women who looked like they were rushing even though they were strolling, a shirtless man drinking a tall can of beer, and some homeless people who'd crawled out from under the boardwalk, squinting at the sunlight.

We turned off the boardwalk and up the T-shaped fishing pier that stretched much farther out into the Atlantic Ocean than I could swim. A pile of break rocks extended out from the shore, parallel to the pier, and we stopped just across from where they ended.

"Here," said Al, kneeling down to reach into his backpack. He pulled out two hooped wire baskets and a greasy brown paper bag.

"What's in there?"

"Chicken necks." He showed me the yellow-gray mottled lump before he began fastening it to the bottom of one of the baskets with a piece of twine.

"Those are the real necks of chickens?"

"Of course."

"Where did you get them?"

"Butcher shop. Where else? It's good crab bait. Cheap meat. Crabs are bottom feeders. They love this kind of meat." He scored the necks with his pocketknife, so that the yellow skin separated and the pink flesh was exposed.

"Do people eat them?"

"Sure, if they're hungry. You eat chicken, don't you?"

"Yeah, chicken wings. Not chicken necks. People cook them up like chicken wings?"

"No, there's not so much meat for that. It's more for a stew. Listen, trust me, if you're hungry enough, you'd be happy to eat chicken-neck stew. Maybe today you'll find this out, if we don't catch any crabs." My face must have betrayed my fear, because Alojzy let out a deep laugh.

He tied the baskets onto some braided lines, and tied the other ends of the line onto the railing of the pier. The rail was full of grooves worn by similar lines, which made me think that what we were doing wasn't so strange.

Alojzy showed me how to toss the trap out over the water like a Frisbee. The baskets opened fully in the air, then fell straight into the water. We gave it a couple minutes to give the crabs time to smell the bait. When we finally pulled the baskets up, I was sure that I felt the weight of crabs in mine, but as soon as the basket rose into the air, I realized it had just been the pressure of the water.

We threw the baskets back in. In the distance was a big boat, stacked high with different-colored shipping containers. Beyond that, I could make out a distant coastline.

"What's that out there?"

"There? A boat."

"No, not that, the land." I could make out a mass in the distance. "Is that New Jersey?"

"No. Staten Island. Still New York City."

"Oh. So can you swim there?"

"Me? Sure I can."

We pulled the traps in again, and to my delight a crab was in one of them. I hadn't actually believed that we would catch anything. It was a terrible thing we caught, with wart-like growths and splotches of mud across its uneven shell.

"Look! Dad! I caught one!" I usually referred to him as "Alojzy," or "my father," but when I was speaking to him the word "Dad" came smoothly and affectionately from my lips.

"Yeah, so I see. Or maybe it caught you? But it's just a spider crab. No good for eating." He took the trap from me and turned it upside down, shaking it until the crab fell back into the ocean. I felt a little cheated of my catch, but at the same time was happy to see the thing gone.

Next throw, we pulled up a couple spider crabs each. Alojzy dumped them on the pier and kicked them hard, so that they skidded across to the other side. He walked over and kicked them again, booting them far out into the water. I understood why he did it. They were ugly, and deserved to be kicked.

"We don't want them on same side as us," he told me. "They'll keep coming back now that they know about the bait."

We moved farther out on the pier, and our luck changed. My father pulled in two rock crabs. They were about the same size as the smaller of the spider crabs but had smoother backs and looked altogether more sanitary. After that, we started pulling them in left and right.

"This is the spot," my father said. We threw back four because they were too small, and one because it was pregnant. You could see its bloated egg sac hanging from its underside. In the end, we came away with thirteen crabs, five of which I had hauled in myself. Not bad.

My father had been sipping from his thermos all morning, so he needed to take a piss in the restroom on the boardwalk before we headed out. He left me to watch our crabs. Now that we had moved farther out on the pier, we were close to the old men who had been fishing when we arrived. Two of them sat across the pier from me on plastic crates, and passed a small bottle of something purplish back and forth. Their long fishing poles were propped up against the railing. I wondered how they would know if there were a fish on the line. One of the men caught me watching. He gave me what would have been a toothy grin if he'd had any teeth, and raised his bottle in a mocking toast. A lengthy filet knife was tucked in his belt. It looked like a fearsome dagger that could cut me wide-open. I was scared, but then I remembered that my father would be coming back any moment.

On the ride back to his apartment, I sat with the Styrofoam container on my lap. I couldn't believe that I had a box full of wild sea creatures with me on the train, and I kept lifting the lid to look at them, until my father told me to stop.

When we got home, he took the cooler from me and dumped the crabs into his empty bathtub. A few of them landed on their backs. Alojzy found a flathead screwdriver on the windowsill, and flipped them right side up. A few more adventurous crabs scuttled across the floor of the bathtub. The rest sat where they landed, flicking their little mouths and occasionally flexing their pinchers. One didn't seem to be moving at all. My father jabbed it with the screwdriver. Its little mouth moved, and some bubbles flitted through the little bit of stagnant water pooled in the bathtub. They were alive. Life was the opposite of death. That they were really alive meant that we were really going to make them dead. A stream of liquid trailed behind one of the scuttlers.

"What's that?" I asked.

"It's shit. You don't know shit when you see it? That's something you're going to have to learn, you want to get by in this world."

Alojzy turned on the faucet, washing the shit and sand down the drain. When they were clean, he grabbed them one by one by the back legs and tossed them into a paper grocery bag. We went into the kitchen, where he put the bag into the freezer.

Alojzy put his one pot on the stove, and twisted together a long tinfoil spiral.

"What's that?"

"A rack. To hold the crabs."

He cracked a twenty-four-ounce beer from the fridge, took a good long swig, then poured some into the pot.

"Why did you pour that in there?" I asked.

"We're going to steam the crabs in the lager." Lager meant beer? Would I get drunk from eating beer crabs?

"I'm just a kid, I can't have beer."

"Feh. When I was your age, already I was drinking beer. That's the way in Poland." I tried to picture him at my age, and saw a tough little boy with scars, stubble, and gold chains drinking beer. "Besides, the alcohol boils off."

"Oh. So can I have a sip of the beer?" I held my hand out for the can.

"No." He took a swig.

He took the bag of crabs out of the freezer, and dumped them into the pot. I peeked in. They weren't moving.

"Are they dead?" I asked nervously. Had I helped kill something without even realizing it?

"No, no. You can't cook dead crab. Bacterias. They are just stunned, slowed down from the freezing."

"So we're going to eat them alive?"

"No, of course not. They will die in the steam."

"I don't think I want to eat a crab."

"What? We go to the trouble of catching nice crabs all morning, and you don't even want to eat them?"

"I don't . . . I don't think so." I had been interested in the crabs as bounty, but the idea of eating whatever was inside these rough shells was physically repellent to me.

"Look at the rich American boy, so soft, so picky. So *pachech*." At home, there were no foreign words in conversation, only English.

When Alojzy spoke I always understood what he meant, even if I couldn't always define the words or their language of origin. "Maybe you'd prefer lobster? Well, fine then, more crab for me."

"Listen, I don't want lobster either." I reached for any justification other than the fact that I was a pussy. "People can't eat shellfish."

"Oh, can't they?"

"I mean, shouldn't. It's wrong."

"Where did you hear that?"

"At the synagogue." They had warned us about pepperoni too, but shellfish seemed far more serious.

"What synagogue? Who took you to the synagogue?"

"Bernie." Since we'd moved in with Bernie, he'd started taking us to shul with him every Friday evening. He and my mother also sent me to a religious instruction class on Saturday mornings and to a Hebrew class on Wednesday evenings. Alojzy had no time for such institutions.

"Who's Bernie. Nu?" I wasn't sure how to answer this question. It felt as if Alojzy and Bernie existed in two completely different worlds, and there would be no way to explain one to the other.

"You know who Bernie is. My stepfather."

"No. Wrong. Stepfather? What's that? He's your mother's husband." He turned on the burner. "I'm the only kind of father you got."

"I know." I nodded my head in affirmation.

"Good. It's good that you know." The beer began to boil. Soon the crabs would die a hard death in the pot. I took a deep breath. It was okay. I went into the cabinet, found some plates and silverware, and began to set the table.

The crabs were surely dying now. Soon they would be dead and cooked. My father and I would crack them open with butter knives and eat their flesh with dessert forks. The meat would be the richest thing I'd ever had in my stomach, and bits of sand we had not managed to wash off would grind down my teeth. The crabs were dead, but I was alive and my father was alive, and we were together.

॥▮■

I had started on a path with Alojzy that day, then later diverged from it. There was a lot more I could have learned if I had stuck with him. He knew secrets of the streets that a thousand years in college couldn't teach me. He knew the difference between the real stories and the sentimental fabrications. Now I needed to find him, or at least the path he had left for me.

I caught a Manhattan-bound express train at the Sheepshead Bay station, and watched southern Brooklyn intently from the elevated tracks. A man stood on a rooftop, swinging an orange safety flag on the end of a stick. White pigeons circled above him as he called them home to their coop. On the way down to Coney Island, I'd been too busy anticipating my meeting with Goldov to pay attention to the outside world.

In college I knew several kids from Park Slope, and other parts of brownstone Brooklyn, who liked to talk about how much their neighborhoods had changed. But southern Brooklyn was a different world from theirs, and it moved at a slower speed. The area had not changed all that much in the past ten years, aside from the scattered newer condo buildings. Even some of the billboards and faded graffiti on the old rooftops was the same. My fingers remembered tracing the letters on the train window when I was twelve years old.

Kings Highway was the last elevated stop in southern Brooklyn. I looked down on the crowded business district. People lounged in front of stores, while others dashed back and forth across the wide street with plastic shopping bags. Alojzy had spent a lot of time here. He had been right at home on this strip where Hebrew, Yiddish, Russian, Turkish, and other languages blended together.

For a while, Alojzy had a girlfriend named Karla who sold jewelry in a little stand in the front of a clothing store on Kings Highway and East Thirteenth Street where Orthodox women shopped. The giant jewels on the broaches Karla sold were impressive, though in retrospect they must have been fake. Cut glass, or even plastic. But her smile had been genuine when she saw Alojzy walk into the store. Karla would close her stand, and Alojzy would take us to eat at a kosher deli owned by a family of Egyptian Muslims, who had bought the restaurant when the original owner retired to Florida. Alojzy would joke with the countermen in his limited Arabic and they would give us free knishes.

The train rumbled on past Kings Highway. I was conscious of the rolling of the steel wheels as they followed their tracks. The train went down to street level at Newkirk Avenue, and then into the tunnel after Prospect Park. Brooklyn disappeared, leaving me in darkness.

3

IT WAS GETTING ON toward evening by the time I made it back from Coney Island to the Upper East Side. I got off the subway at Eighty-Sixth Street and walked down Lexington Avenue for a few blocks, then turned back in the other direction. The building where the four of us lived as a family before Alojzy left was only about twelve blocks from Becca's apartment, but I hadn't gone up there since being back in the area. In fact, I wasn't sure if I'd been to the old block, Nine-ty-Second between Second and First Avenues, even once since we left. After we moved to Long Island, we didn't return to visit. I wondered if Becca ever passed by the block, or if she avoided it.

As a kindergartener, the address had been drilled into my ahead, along with our phone number and the phone number of our next-door neighbor, Mrs. Almanzar. After my experience with Alojzy's building in Sheepshead Bay, I was afraid that this one would be gone too. But it was there, just as I remembered it. Six stories of bright red bricks. The details around the windows had recently been painted green, and the black paint on the stoop's handrail was freshly touched up. Those were the only changes. The stoop looked just as it had fifteen years ago, when Alojzy would sit on it holding a beer in a brown paper bag, and tell Becca and me stories about bandits and goblins. I sat down in his old spot.

The Stanley M. Isaacs Houses began across the street, and continued down to the river. I wondered if their presence had helped preserve the block, as housing projects scared away transplants. A cab pulled up in front of the building. A thirtysomething couple in business clothes got out and walked up the stairs, swinging their briefcases. I said hello, but they ignored me. Maybe things had changed here, after all. These people were young professionals like Becca and Andrew. Becca hadn't turned her back on where she came from; the city had changed and she'd changed with it.

Becca lived in a newer, doorman building down in the Eighties. It was only a ten-minute walk from our old building, but it felt very foreign to me. It was all glass and steel, with no brick in sight. Getting through my adolescent years on Long Island had always felt like something of a trick; I spent eight years waiting for everyone to figure out I didn't belong. Becca's building aroused in me an even more concentrated version of the same feeling. When I entered that evening, I tried my best to adhere to the shibboleth of saying hello to the gold-epauletted doorman in a superior tone. It was important to always speak in a way that betrayed no weakness. I held my head up high as I walked to the elevator, for fear that if my shoulders slouched for a moment I would feel his hands on them.

I had been back in New York City for the better part of a week. Speaking with Goldov had been my first priority, but I had put it off for several days getting settled, reacquainting myself with the city, and then spending time with Becca and her fiancé, Andrew, who I'd only met a few times before. They held hands when we went places, and Andrew would kiss my sister when he thought I wasn't looking. It was awkward to be around them, but he seemed to make her happy.

Becca and I hadn't lived in the same house since she'd gone to college, but she was very welcoming in letting me stay at her home indefinitely. She thought I'd come to New York solely to find a job and had no idea I was looking for Alojzy.

Really, I had put off going to Coney Island because I was scared. What if Goldov had provided proof that Alojzy was dead? I wouldn't have known what to do with that knowledge. A book would have snapped shut on my fingers. But Goldov had only muddled things, and raised more questions. My search had begun, and I needed to keep going. First thing in the morning, I would go downtown to find this man Mendy.

My sister and Andrew generally worked pretty late into the evening—she was a junior executive at a credit-card company, and he managed a hedge fund—so I had the apartment to myself for a while. I was still getting used to the luxury unit Becca lived in. The old walk-up on Ninety-Second Street hadn't been renovated since probably the '50s. Bernie's house on Long Island had been much nicer, though sparse. He had lived there with his first wife, who died long before he met my mother. Even that had felt like a place I didn't belong in. I once accidentally smashed a window, messing around, and was scared for a week that Bernie would throw us out because I had damaged his nice house. This was no reflection on Bernie; he'd never done anything to give the impression that he didn't want Becca and me around. It was just that I always felt I belonged in a walk-up apartment with uneven floorboards, not in a big suburban house. And certainly not in a luxury apartment in a doorman building, with marble counters and floor-to-ceiling windows. Ninety square feet of glass I had to be careful not to break.

It was a bit past six so I decided to make myself macaroni salad for dinner. Having been so caught up in memories, I wanted a physical task to occupy myself as much as I wanted something to eat. While the macaroni boiled, I grated the carrots and chopped the pickles and red pepper. When the macaroni was nice and soft, I drained it in the colander, then poured it into a bowl. I put mayonnaise in fast, so the macaroni didn't clump up, mixed in the vegetables, and poured in some pickle juice, making sure to leave enough brine in the jar so that the remaining pickles didn't dry out. The pickles were Becca's. I didn't know how long I'd be staying with her, and I felt like a mooch living in her apartment for any amount of time, so I'd made sure to stock up on my own supply of pasta, peppers, and carrots. She told me several times that I was welcome to any food in the house, but I wanted to maintain some minimal sense of self-sufficiency. It was okay, by my rules, to use her pickles and mayonnaise, though, because that was just using some condiments from a jar. It wasn't really eating her food.

After I ate, I made a cup of tea (my teabags, her honey), settled into Becca's big leather armchair, and tucked into a paperback I had borrowed from Bernie's shelf before I left New Mexico. The cover picture of a young man with a kippah and *payis*, swinging a scimitar above his head, had caught my eye. Once colorful, the cover had been rubbed down over time. The book itself was thin, owing more to the quality of the yellow pages than to the story's length. *The Yeshiva Bocher*, the cover read, *The Rediscovered Treasure of Benjamin IV*.

When I asked Bernie if it was worth reading, he had shrugged and said, "It's a book. I suppose it's on my shelf for a reason. Before Benjamin IV was Benjamin III, but that was just a character." I didn't try to get anything else out of him. Bernie hardly spoke at all anymore, unless prompted. It wasn't that he was depressed, or unfriendly, just that he was retreating deeper and deeper into his world of numbers and written words. He didn't need the world of the living. This frustrated my mother, who was more full of life than she'd ever been, at least within my memory. During the day Bernie worked in his home office, dissecting files for clients back in New York. Evenings, he sat on the back patio and read books of American or Jewish history, or occasionally a mystery novel from his childhood or before. My mom mostly did her own thing—like running around to workshops and gallery openings with her art collector friends—but she and Bernie seemed happy enough together. Weekends, Bernie obliged my mother by driving her to craft fairs in yuppie-hippie towns throughout the Southwest where she sold her candles.

The paperback was a 1963 Jewish Publication Society translation from the original Yiddish. According to the blurb on the back, the author—whose real identity was unknown—published three books in Warsaw under the pen name of Benjamin IV, between 1926 and 1938. *The Yeshiva Bocher* was the only one that survived.

It told the story of a cocky young yeshiva student who spends a Shabbos dinner at the home of his rabbi. The rabbi has another guest, a visiting Torah master. The student drinks too much wine and steps outside to relieve himself. On his way back to the house, the tsar's army sweeps him up and takes him off to fight in the Crimean War. He serves for several years, becoming an expert rifleman. He kills twenty Englishmen, and just as many Frenchmen, though some of those may have actually been Sardinians. By the time he has killed his fifth man, he has forgotten every word of Aramaic. By the time he has killed his tenth man, he has forgotten every word of Hebrew. By the time he has killed his twentieth man, he has forgotten every word of Yiddish.

On the journey back to Russia, Black Sea privateers capture him and sell him to the Turks as a slave. He works his way up from the quarry to a position in the palace, where he seduces an Ottoman princess, who frees him so he can become her husband. A woman like that cannot be trusted, though. She betrays him in their sixth year of marriage, and plots with her Azeri lover to kill him.

At the last moment, he escapes by switching his poisoned wine for his wife's untainted glass and then takes to wandering. The onetime yeshiva bocher, now well into his fourth decade, was walking down the road toward Isfahan when I heard the key in the lock. I glanced at the digital display on Becca's DVD player. Nine thirty-three p.m. I turned to the kitchen counter to make sure I'd finished cleaning up. Becca was proud of her marble counters and said even water could stain them disastrously. Her house, her conception of reality. Luckily, I had remembered to clean up.

It was Andrew, not my sister, who came through the door. He had a place of his own down in Hell's Kitchen, but slept over here with Becca most nights, so it wasn't a surprise to see him. He'd taken off his tie, and the collar of his striped shirt was unbuttoned. There was something slightly sweaty and crumpled about him, but it was hard to pin down because he walked in the door standing up straight, like always. The man had a confident posture and a strong physique, which his closely tailored suits made clear. He blinked twice when he saw me, then grinned.

"Hey there, Edel the Kid." He called me that because I was Becca's kid brother and because I'd been kicked out of school for illegal activities. He meant it in a friendly way, and to be honest, I liked the outlaw sound of the nickname. It wasn't really a joke. Toward the end of my drug use, I had crossed the line from mischief and experimentation to actual crimes. I was lucky not to have been caught in possession and sent to jail. I was glad that hadn't happened, but didn't regret my actions.

"Hi, Andrew," I said. He had said his buddies all called him Wolfie—his last name was Wolfson—and I should too, but I couldn't bring myself to call him anything but Andrew. He swung his briefcase and a black plastic bag up onto the kitchen counter, and extracted a six-pack of imported beer from the latter.

"Brew?" He tipped a bottle my way.

"Sure, why not." He tossed me the beer, which I caught with two hands. My catch was overwrought and embarrassing, and Andrew grimaced. Maybe I had closed my eyes. I just didn't want to drop it, and get beer and broken glass all over Becca's freshly waxed parquet floor.

Andrew became aware of his grimace, and forced it back to a grin. He wasn't a bad guy. He tried his best. The same traits he found alluring in Becca—a slight, boyish frame, soft brown eyes that never met anyone else's, a general refusal to laugh at good-natured jokes—he found simply off-putting in me. Still, he tried to treat me in a big-brotherly way, because I was his girl's little brother.

"How was work?" I asked him. The beer was a nice gesture, and I wanted to meet it with one of my own.

"Rough."

"Yeah?"

"Some of these guys are really gunning for me. It's a cutthroat business." I wasn't exactly sure what business he was in. A hedge fund involved funds. So finance, I guessed. But not stocks. Something different. "But I can hold my own."

"Sure you can, man."

"Yeah. Yes, sir. It's a lot of stone-cold bastards out there, though."

"It's true. I see them everywhere I go."

Andrew coughed out a chuckle. It was genuine, but I couldn't tell if it was directed at me or at the bastards.

"Yeah, I bet you do."

He picked up the remote and turned on the TV. Some cartoon characters were sitting around a bar, drinking bottles of beer and telling jokes.

"This okay?" he asked.

"Fine by me."

We watched for a little while until Becca came in the door. She looked tired, but she smiled when she saw us sitting together on the couch.

"I see how it is," she teased. "The boys were sitting around drinking beer while I was slaving away at the office."

"Nah, babe," Andrew said, grinning and standing up to give her a kiss. "I just got in myself. Kicking back with a cold one after a long day. I'm gonna grab another. You want one?"

"No," she said, "I'm okay." She wasn't much of a drinker.

"Edel?"

"No, thanks. I'm actually going to hit the hay in a minute." Drinking five or six more beers sounded good, actually, but I wanted Becca to see I was being responsible and doing my best to stay sober and sane. I couldn't keep going around in circles. I took my empty bottle and teacup into the kitchen and rinsed them out. "I have an early morning." There was no way of knowing when Mendy would be on the street, but I figured I should get down as early as I could.

"Oh yeah?" Becca said. "You have a job interview?" I had considered telling Becca about my encounter with Goldov, and the few things I'd learned about Alojzy, but I decided to keep them to myself until I knew what it all meant. Becca would probably just tell me that Goldov sounded shady, and I should stay away from people like that.

"Yeah. Something like that. An appointment, actually; I'm going to talk to a guy down by NYU."

"Okay." Becca looked skeptical, but didn't press it.

"Knock 'em dead, kid." Andrew said.

"Thanks. Night, guys."

I headed into the alcove where I slept beside Becca's elliptical machine. She'd offered me the couch when I arrived, but it was too soft for me. I also didn't want to force myself into the middle of Becca's space. It was better to be tucked out of the way in my sleeping bag, on the hardwood floor, braced between the walls.

When you smoke weed every day, you don't dream. Sober now, my head filled with stories and dancing images every night. I closed my eyes and waited for them to come. That night the freighter from Alojzy's last postcard appeared. It came unmoored from the paper, and began to float off. The lines that Alojzy had used to draw the waves rearranged themselves into letters. Latin letters, Hebrew letters, Cyrillic letters. Diacritic marks. The ship sailed away from me, and I found myself pitched forward, thrashing in this Sea of Babble, struggling toward a life raft up ahead.

| | ■

The sounds of Becca and Andrew getting ready for work woke me up at seven thirty the next morning. The pressure in my bladder was uncomfortable, but I would rather suffer a little discomfort than face my sister's wrath if I got in the way in the morning. It was wisest to stay hidden as they put on their war paint and chomped their energy bars.

Finally, I heard Becca's exasperated, "Are you coming or not? I'm late. I can't wait," and the answer of Andrew's galloping loafers. I gave it a minute after the door slammed to make sure they weren't coming back for anything, then made my way to the bathroom. Religious Jews said some prayer about being glad that all your pipes were in working order. I didn't know the words, but was thankful I had been given another day on earth and eager to make the most of it. I was not great at making the most of my days. But now I had a purpose.

I looked out my sister's huge living room windows, at the newly risen sun over the East River. It had been sunny for days. The booksellers would probably be getting out on the street around now. I was not up and out as early as the booksellers, or Becca for that matter.

She had inherited more of Alojzy's hustle than I had. It was something I needed to work on, to cultivate.

I wanted to lie down on the couch and sleep some more. After I stopped going to classes, I'd gotten into the habit of sleeping until noon or later. My time in New Mexico had helped break that habit. Even Solomon was rebuked for sleeping late, with the key to the Great Temple under his pillow.

Some Adderall or Dexedrine would have provided a good jump-start, but I was relying on myself now, on my own will and motivation. I put the teakettle on the stove to boil, and turned on the TV with no sound. The movement of the colors on the screen helped get me into a more mobile mind-set. I drank my tea and headed downtown.

4

AS SOON AS I turned the corner from Broadway onto West Fourth Street, I saw the booksellers. They were a feral element in the landscape, contrasting with the purple New York University flags and the attendant crowds of clean students. The booksellers were a black mold growing through the new paint. I admired the defiant role they played in the cityscape. Unlike all the people rushing off to offices—Becca and Andrew, for instance—these street vendors interacted with the metropolis on their own terms.

At the first table, a man wearing an old military jacket and a black beret was taking science-fiction paperbacks out of a Poland Spring box and arranging them on the edge of an already crowded card table. He lined the books up evenly with each other, letting as much of each one hang off the edge as he could without it falling onto the sidewalk.

"Excuse me," I said. He looked up and shook his head. "No," I said, "I just wanted to—" The man shook his head again, and pointed to another man, who had long black dreadlocks with pieces of seashell and wire tied into them, and wore a long coat that seemed too heavy for the tail end of a warm winter. He leaned against a large cement planter in which nothing grew, bent over in a halfhearted attempt to hide the wad of cash he was counting. A cigarette dangled from his mouth, but he neither drew nor ashed, and I waited to see if his bouncing dreadlocks would catch on fire. As I watched, a gust of wind dispersed the quarter inch of gray ash into the air.

"Excuse me," I said.

"Yeah? Could I help you? Could I?" His pupils—bits of charcoal floating in a glass of dirty water—darted up toward me for a moment before he resumed counting his money. It wasn't a huge sum of money, but he kept getting confused and starting over.

"I was just wondering if you knew if there was a bookseller around here named Mendy?" The man stopped counting and looked up.

"Mendy? Mendy, Mendy. Mendy? There might be." He turned and shouted at the man with the beret. "He wants to know is there a Mendy around here?" The man with the beret smiled warily, and clutched his box of books tighter. "Yeah, there's a Mendy around here. What do you want with that asshole?"

"Nothing, it's just that somebody told me I should talk to him."

"Okay, okay." He put his money in his pocket so he could gesture with his hands. "But look: if you got some textbooks to sell, you might as well go ahead and bring them to me first. Because I, frankly, will give you a better deal than that bastard."

"No," I said. "I don't think . . ."

"What do you mean, 'no'? You can ask anybody out here on this street. It's the truth. I can give you a better deal on your books. Don't get me wrong, I can't make you rich. Used books are worth very little. But compared to that stinker down there, well, let's just say that he will not treat you so good as I will treat you."

"No. I mean, I'll keep that in mind." I held out my empty hands, to show I didn't have anything to sell. "It's not about books, though, it's about something personal."

"Aw, hell. I don't care about nothing like that. Mendy's down that way." He jerked his thumb over his shoulder. This man was a hustler, and if I wasn't buying or selling, he had no use for me.

"Where?" I asked.

"Down there at the corner where the park starts. Old guy with a beard. That is to say, older than me, with a bigger beard than mine." Our interview concluded, he went back to peering at his bills through his thick glasses.

I passed two more tables before I came to Mendy's. His setup was by far the most expansive on the block, stretching along the sidewalk for a good twenty feet. Sheets of plywood spanned several card tables, and on top of them the books were packed tight in long, snaky rows, held at the end by the T-shaped metal bookends librarians use. Between the rows, other books stood upright, some encased in plastic slipcovers.

Debris was strewn underneath and behind the tables. Empty water boxes. The red-and-white woven plastic bags sold in Chinatown, weighted down with two-by-fours. A box of tissues. A shiny handcart. Stacks of books. Always, more books.

The whole setup gave me the impression of a kid's clubhouse. I peeked, half expecting to find a twelve-year-old sneaking a smoke under the table. Someone was indeed hiding there, but he was a grown man well into his sixties. Though he was hunched down, busily cleaning book covers with rubbing alcohol and tissues, I had a clear profile view. There was something Hasidic in his lean face and long cloudy beard, but his soiled wifebeater and sinewy arms—surprisingly muscled for so old a man—betrayed more than a passing familiarity with the material world. He caught me staring and rose to an upright position. His eyes stayed locked on mine, as if he'd just discovered me inside his house, and couldn't decide if I was a harmless sleepwalker or a burglar.

"Were you looking for something particular? Something I could maybe help you with?" Each word was a testing jab.

"No, I'm not looking for . . . I'm just looking."

I picked up a thin book called *The ABC of Anarchism* and made myself read a few pages. The author was trying to convince somebody about something.

"The guy who wrote that"—he gestured at the book in my hand with the one he held in his—"Berkman. He's the one who shot Frick."

I didn't know who Frick was, but the old graybeard sounded like he was happy Frick got shot. "During the Carnegie Steel strike. He was Emma Goldman's lover."

"Yeah."

"You're familiar?"

"Not really." My ex-girlfriend, Mariam, had sewn an Emma Goldman patch on her messenger bag, but that was the extent of my knowledge. "Is your name Mendy?"

"Yeah. It is. So?"

"My name is Izzy. Izzy Edel. I'm Alojzy Edel's son."

"Oh, I see. Jesus." He took off his glasses, and rubbed his palm over his eyes and face and beard. "Ally, Ally, Ally. I didn't even know he had a son. A daughter he'd mentioned, a few times . . ."

"Yeah, that's my sister. Becca."

"Sure. Right. Hey. Listen." He put his glasses back on and stuck out his hand. "It's nice to meet you . . . Izzy, was it?" We shook hands. His grip was very strong.

"I heard that he died. I'm very sorry. For whatever that's worth."

"Thank you for your concern, but . . . I'm not sure if he's dead or not. It's not been confirmed yet."

"Oh. I see. I'm not optimistic, but of course I hope you're right. We could sit and talk a minute, if you'd like?" He led me across the wide sidewalk to a short stone ledge extended off the NYU library.

"Had you been in touch?" he asked me once we'd sat down. "With your father?"

"No. Not in a long time. Years."

"I can't say that surprises me. He never struck me as a family man. So how did you find your way here, then, if you don't mind me asking?"

"We only found out about my father's . . . disappearance because we got a note from a man named Goldov. I met him yesterday. He mentioned your name."

"Goldov? Sure. Sure. Excuse me." Mendy turned to shout to a potential customer holding up a volume of Greek myths. "The price is on the front page. No, that's the cover. I said the front page. That's right. There. What it says. Three dollars." The customer came over with a ten-dollar bill, and Mendy made change from the fanny pack around his waist.

"When my own father died," he said to me, "I felt him around. I kept thinking he was just in the next room. Which was sort of funny, because it was not like I was used to him being around, ever actually being in the next room. I mean, there were years, as an adult, where I hardly saw my parents at all. It was mostly like that, more years that were like that than not. I always would think of him, but in a distanced way. Then he died, and all of a sudden, and for months, I kept thinking of him, in a much closer way. Like death made him more present." It was true that Alojzy felt more present to me recently, but I didn't think that was because he was dead. I thought it was because he had reached out to me. If I sensed him in the world, it was because he *was* in the world. Mendy saw the skepticism on my face.

"That's neither here nor there. You said you think Al is only missing, not dead?"

"Well, Goldov said Alojzy was missing and *believed* dead. And you said you *heard* he was. But I don't know anything for sure. Do you know any details?"

"No, I'm afraid I don't. He'd been away from the street for a week or so, which wasn't so strange, but then I heard about his death. Maybe it was from Goldov, actually, that I heard it first? I think it was, though I wouldn't swear to it." This brought me back to the idea that the story of Alojzy's death had been purposefully crafted, by either Goldov or Alojzy. "Then everyone was talking about it. But that was all anyone seemed to know, that he was dead.

"Let me be clear," Mendy said. "I'm only telling you what I know. I can't tell you for sure he's dead. I can only tell you that he disappeared from the street. But my opinion is, to be perfectly honest with you, I wouldn't hold my breath waiting for him to come back. I'm sorry to say."

"Excuse me!" A man in a jacket and tie jabbed a stack of books at us.

"No," said Mendy. "Excuse me, I'm having a conversation here."

"Sure, I just wanted to make a purchase, if you can imagine that."

"Listen, I don't care what you want to do. I told you I'm having a conversation."

"Are you serious? Is this the way to run a business?"

"No, I don't think this is any way to run a business. You're right about that, pal." The man started to say something else, but couldn't think what and shook his head instead. He tossed the books onto the table and stomped off.

"My father," I said. "What can you tell me for sure? You worked on this street together? What do you know about his life?"

"Your father. He sold down here, off and on, for years. Everybody down here knew him. He was, I don't know, he brought something out in people. Women especially. There were always women looking for him." Mendy smiled. I imagined my father and this man exchanging little jokes about women's bodies, in a streetwise male language I'd never quite learned. "But he could talk to anyone. He would just as soon stay quiet, he wasn't one to run his mouth for no reason, but he was capable of talking to anyone. The gift of gab, I guess they call it. He spoke like six languages."

"Six? English and Polish and Hebrew . . ."

"Some Arabic. Some Russian."

"That's right."

"A little Yiddish too, I found out. He had a girlfriend who was teaching him Spanish, for a while." Mendy looked at his fingers. "Now we're up to seven. He had all that up on me. I got English, scraps of high school German, and some house Yiddish. That's about it, for me. It all adds up to just English, really. My parents never let me learn Yiddish proper, because they didn't want I should have an accent. Better I should speak like an American. They came from Poland too. But before the war. When there were Jews in Poland, still. Lots of them. I talked to Al about that, sometimes."

"About . . .?" I had lost the thread of what Mendy was saying.

"About Poland, and the Jews who lived there. The history of it."

"Oh. Okay. Is there anything else you can tell me about him, though? I mean, him personally?" I needed clues.

"Personally? He is—was—a rough person. But kind. He had *ziskeit*. You know the word? There's no other word for it. I know he did some things. I know he hurt Goldov. I know he hurt some girlfriends. I imagine he hurt others. Maybe he hurt you . . . if I might be so bold, as to interpret the look on your face. He was involved in I don't know all what. But I always thought of him as kind.

"I remember—I had a van for a while—I told Al he could borrow it one time, when he needed to move some books. He was shocked. He said, 'Mendy, you're really trusting me with your van?' I said, 'Al, is there a reason I shouldn't trust you?'"

"I see." I remembered a van of his own that Al had owned when I was in high school. It was a white Astro van, and was always dirty and packed full of boxes. "Do you know . . . do you know where he'd been living?"

"I don't know if you could say he lived at any fixed place, exactly. But his, you could say, base of operations, where he kept his books, was a storage space down past SoHo. Where I do believe he slept sometimes, though he was very private about things like that. Very guarded.

"His space is in the same facility as mine, just down the hall. It's the only facility downtown with twenty-four-hour access. I guess that's another reason I think he died. It wouldn't be like him to just abandon his stuff, to not try to sell it off or something before he left."

"So his stuff is still there? You don't think it's been cleaned out?"

"No. No one's been by to clean it out. I keep my eyes open."

"They don't throw stuff out, when a person dies? Or disappears?"

"They throw stuff out—or sell it, if they can—when someone stops paying the bill. Not that it's my business, but I believe a man named Timur, who your father knew, took care of those details. He's a rich guy . . . kind of a benefactor. I guess it's paid up, because they haven't cut the lock yet.

"Matter of fact, I got the spare key to that lock in my own space there. Al had me hold on to a copy in a neighborly sort of way, in case of emergencies. If you come back with me in the evening, I can let you in."

❙❙■■

I spent the rest of the day with Mendy. He said I could meet him down on Varick Street in the evening, but I wanted to see how Alojzy spent many of his days. Maybe I would meet someone who knew something about his disappearance. I wanted to know how it felt to work out on the street all day long, and see what the street looked like from this side of the table. *The Yeshiva Bocher* was in my pocket, but I was more interested in the street life than in a book.

The book table was both part of and an oasis from the crowded sidewalk. Foot traffic passed by indifferently for the most part, but sometimes people detached themselves from the herd to come look at the books. Sometimes they browsed. Other times they looked for a specific title. Often, though, they seemed to be hungrily searching for something specific, but they didn't know what it was. I watched their faces as they picked books up and responded to them with curiosity, confusion, disappointment, and excitement.

I helped Mendy clean old price tags off newly acquired books. If they were left on, people would try to get the price on the tag, not the price Mendy had penciled in on the first page. He showed me how to clean the tags. First, you dissolved the glue by putting a drop of lighter fluid onto the tag, then you scraped the tag off with a razor blade. When that was done, you wiped off the tag residue, and any other grime, with a tissue and bit of rubbing alcohol. You had to be careful you didn't use too much alcohol, or you'd end up wiping off the ink from the cover picture. I did this a couple times with old paperbacks, but Mendy didn't seem to care too much.

"This," he said, "is why I am not in the antique business."

When Asher, the dreadlocked bookseller I'd spoken to earlier, saw me sticking around, he came by and introduced himself properly. I was also introduced to Hafid, a skinny Moroccan guy who set up next to Mendy and spent his day quietly reading Sufi books underneath a sun umbrella, and Robertson, a rare-book man who did his selling on the Internet, but hung around the block to talk shop and see if any interesting volumes surfaced. They nodded with respect when they heard who my father was. I didn't press them all with questions, but I made sure they knew I was curious about Alojzy's life, whereabouts, and fate.

Around one o'clock, customers descended like a wave. The socializing stopped, and everyone went back to his own table to focus on making money.

"The lunchtime rush," Mendy explained. I helped out by packing peoples' purchases into old Gristedes grocery bags while Mendy tallied the prices. He ran up and down the length of the table, connecting with each and every customer who was interested in making a purchase. After a customer left, I straightened out the books they'd disturbed. The people who didn't buy anything seemed to leave the biggest messes. I referred most questions to Mendy, but after a while I was able to point a few people in the right direction on my own.

After business slowed down, I bought a quart of macaroni salad and a Diet Coke from the deli and ate it in the park. When I returned, Mendy asked if I would cover the table while he used the restroom and got some food. He handed me a bankroll from his fanny pack of cash to make change with. It seemed strange that he trusted me with his cash, but then I remembered the story about my father and the van. If he could trust Alojzy, he could trust me.

I sold a couple books and wrote down the names so I could tell Mendy what they were. An NYU coed with sweet brown dates for eyes thumbed through an anthology of d.a. levy's work. She was looking at the collages, and asked me if I knew him and was he a good poet. I said he was, and told her about the love poem he wrote to the fifteen-year-old girl who turned him into the "subversive squad" of the Cleveland Police Department. The woman went away without buying the book.

Another wave came down on us at five o'clock, dropping off just at the end of dusk. It got colder as the sun went down, and Mendy put on a big green sweater he pulled from one of his many bags. The sky was hardening, closing in. Between the sky, the pavement, and the brick buildings along the square, I had the strange feeling that this wasn't the outside, just a giant room.

Mendy sat down beside me on the curb. "This is the dinnertime lull. There'll be one more chance to make some good money, starting around eight o'clock or so, then we'll pack it in."

The whole world felt calmer than it had half an hour before. The people had gone off the street into homes and restaurants, or else down into the subway. The air was thicker and lazier. The cabs that had rushed by earlier were now on some other block. Mendy, for his part, was no longer running up and down the length of the table, and had taken out a yogurt container and a metal spoon.

"So what do you do with yourself, Izzy?" he asked between slurps. "You in college or something?"

"No. I was there for a while. It didn't really work out."

"Sure. College wasn't for me either. I felt—this was in the '60s, early '60s, maybe things are different now—they didn't have anything I wanted. I always think of that scene in *Casablanca*. The guy says, What brings you to Casablanca? And the other guy, the Humphrey Bogart character, Rick, I think, says, I came for the waters. But, Rick, the guy says, there's no waters. Oh, he says, I was misinformed. That's how I felt about the university."

"I'm not sure I follow."

"I was misinformed."

"Ah. Yeah. I get you. Before the semester, they give you a little magazine, informing you about the classes, and they were straight with me. I chose the classes I wanted, and I read a lot of books, even if I didn't write all the papers. I maybe read too many books. But yeah, it wasn't where I was supposed to be." I kicked an empty coffee cup away from my foot. "I had to leave, because they threw me out. But it was time for me to go anyway. I'd gotten all I could from a place like that. When they told me to leave, I said, 'fine.'" Thinking back on it now, I should have left as soon as I read the *Pardes* story. That was all they had to give me.

"Was it brawling?" Mendy asked. "You get into some fistfights?"

"No, nothing like that. It was drugs, actually. I hooked some kids up with some acid and when one of them got in trouble he turned me in." I was a little surprised to find myself being so open about all this, but Mendy had been honest with me about Al, and I felt I should be honest with him in return.

"Life's rough like that," Mendy said. "You try to be a nice guy, and help another guy out. And then that's what you get in return."

"That's what you get, all right."

"Still, you're lucky you're a free man. A friend of mine got in some trouble like that once . . . they gave him ten years for two sheets of blotter acid. This was back in the '70s. It was the '80s by the time they let him out." Mendy was quiet for a minute. "He was real different then."

"Well, this wasn't that much. Just a few tabs. I was just trying to help some guys out, you know? I wasn't a drug dealer or anything. But I was tripping daily, so I kept a good supply, and people knew I was always sure to have something on hand. Or at least could always get something."

I hadn't been on any one thing in particular. I wasn't a dope fiend or an addict, just a seeker. Most of the things I was into aren't even addictive. But I always had to have something to put me in the dream world: acid, mushrooms, morning-glory-seed oil, whatever. At least some Adderall or Benzedrine to elevate things. Some good bud to help me ease away from the physical world's illusions. It was better to buy in bulk than to run dry, and the only way I could afford to do that was by selling off half of every bulk purchase. People started coming to me, and the bulk purchases got bigger and bigger.

"Still, just for hooking the guy up, I was scared there was going to be some serious police problems. My stepfather got involved and smoothed things over as best he could. I agreed to withdraw from the school voluntarily, to save everyone the headache."

The story was slightly more complicated than that, but that was the gist. There had been a couple minor incidents, then the one serious situation where the kid took some stuff he couldn't handle and freaked out. He had to go to a mental asylum for a couple weeks, where they pumped him full of Risperdal. His father and his father's lawyers got involved, and made the kid out to be a victim. He gave me up as the "campus source," even though I was only buying from another guy on campus, who had connections up in Cleveland.

Campus security searched my dorm room and threatened me, but I wasn't going to drag anyone else down with me. Besides, all they found were a few pills and residue-covered bags. I was lucky that they didn't come earlier or later. When I broke the kid off, I had had a whole sheet of blotter acid, but in the interim it had all been sold off or consumed. I'd been making arrangements to buy a vial of liquid LSD the week after the search. One hundred doses for four hundred bucks was a good deal. If the school had found that, they would have called the police. Possession of more than fifty doses is considered a third-degree felony in Ohio; I would not have come away with anything less than nine months of jail time, and I would have done my time rather than snitch on my source.

The circumstantial evidence wasn't really enough to get the police involved. It was just the other kid's story against mine. But the school interviewed a bunch of other students, and then it was all of their stories against mine. I had thought some of them were my friends. Apparently not. I was failing out anyway, and it was clear to everyone that I was out of my mind on drugs. When they interrogated me, my answers didn't make any sense. They didn't even pertain to the issue at hand. The school just wanted me to go away, and Bernie and my mother came to a quiet agreement with them. My mother was still pretty mad about the whole situation.

"When I left school," I told Mendy, "I went and stayed with my parents in New Mexico, where they live now, to get my head straight."

"Your parents?" Mendy was confused; the only parent of mine he knew was Alojzy.

"My mother and my stepfather. They sort of retired down there, I guess." Bernie was a few years older than my mother. "The climate's good for my stepfather's asthma. I mean, he still works, but from there. There wasn't really any reason for me to be there. I'm staying with my sister here in the city now."

"I see."

"It's where I'm from originally. I guess I feel more at home here."

"Me too. I'm the same way." I took a look at Mendy. I really couldn't see him existing anywhere else except a New York City street.

"Hey, why did you guess it was fighting they kicked me out for?"

"I thought maybe you had that part of your father in you." It made me happy that he thought that.

"He got in a lot of fights out here?"

"Well, look: he was always a nice guy to me, and everyone else who treated him nice, but if someone crossed him, oh boy, it was on." Mendy finished his last bite of yogurt, and put the empty container down on the curb. "His face, the shape of his face, could physically change. It was terrifying. He had a thing about respect. If you were respectful to him, fine. But if he felt disrespected . . .

"This one time, he forgot his heavy jacket out on the street by mistake, his own mistake, after he'd packed up for the night. He comes back the next day, and asks Eye—a guy, a street guy, who hangs out around here—if he's seen the jacket. Eye says yeah, right after Al left, this guy who passes by here walking a little white dog every morning and every evening, he came by and picked up the jacket.

"So Al, he waits until the guy comes by on his morning walk and approaches him. He says, 'Excuse me, did you pick up a jacket from here yesterday night?' The guy says, 'No. I didn't.' And Al says, 'Oh really, that surprises me, because you know, my long-term acquaintance Eye, who's never steered me wrong on any factual matters, says you picked up my jacket that I forgot.' The guy says, 'Fine, so what if I did, what I find is mine. It's none of your business what I pick up off the street.' Al, I could tell he's on the verge, he says, 'Maybe you didn't realize it was my jacket. But it is, and I'd like it back.' The guy says, 'No, fuck you, it's my jacket now.'

"Al looks at him calmly. So calmly the guy thought maybe he'd won, but the thing is, your father at his calmest was your father at his most frightening. So he looks at the guy and says—his tone just as friendly as could be—he says, 'That's fine. I just want you to understand, though, that after I finish beating the shit out of you, I'm going to beat the shit out of your dog.'

"The guy went right on home and got the jacket and brought it back.

"Later, I said to him, 'Damn, Al, that was something.' He says, 'What do you mean?' I said, 'Al, I mean, you were really going to beat up a little doggy?' He says, 'Look, Mendy, I knew by the fact he's every day taking this little dog for walks in the fresh air, that he really loves that animal. If people cross you, then you have to hurt what they love.'" I liked hearing this story. Alojzy was strong, unyielding. People showed him respect.

"But at the same time," Mendy said, "Al wasn't petty. I'm not saying that your father was going to hurt the little dog because he was petty about the fucking jacket. You asked him for a fucking jacket, he'd give it to you. Matter of fact, this sweater I'm wearing right now . . ." Mendy tugged on the green fabric hanging loosely from his frame . . . "he gave it to me."

As the last rush was dying off, we started packing up. The sun was long gone, the moon barely a sliver, but there were enough electric lights for us to see. Mendy had a whole system worked out. The books came off the table in order, row by row, and went into specific, numbered boxes. His handcart folded out into a long four-wheeled cart, and each of the boxes, folded tables, pieces of wood, and plastic bags had their own set places. We were tying the whole rig up with rope when a man built like a scarecrow sidled up to us.

"Mendy. Mendy, my man."

"Oh, how you doing, Eye." Eye was tall and lanky, though his oversized sweatshirt obscured the exact shape of his frame. The most noticeable thing about him was his thin, black, horseshoe mustache. His dark brown skin seemed like it had been weathered by centuries, but I guessed he was about Alojzy's age.

"You need some help with the cart tonight?" he asked Mendy.

"Nah. Thanks, but I already got this guy here. He's been helping me all day; I think I'll just let him see it through."

"This squirt here? Who the hell is he?" Something was off about Eye's gaze; it seemed like he was eyeballing me, but only one eyeball was actually fixed on me. Then I understood what it was: his left eye was glass.

"Oh, sorry. This is Izzy. Izzy, that's Eye." I nodded at Eye. He blinked his good eye back at me.

"He's Al's son," explained Mendy.

"Al? Al Edel? That Russian fuck?"

"Polish," I said, as if there was some pride in the word for me.

"What the fuck I care what kind of Russian your daddy is, boy?"

"I'll talk to you later, Eye," Mendy told him.

I pushed the cart from behind, while Mendy pulled from the front, steering with a little length of rope. Mendy had an established route that he followed. We walked down the middle of the street, out of necessity. I knew that the city streets sloped down on the sides for drainage, but I had never realized how extreme of an arch it was until I had to keep a moving cart from tipping over. We pissed off more than one cab driver, and hearing the honks and shouts right behind me made me nervous. Mendy didn't seem to notice them at all. He calmly snapped down the mirrors of parked cars threatening to clip us, and maneuvered us around potholes with hardly a glance at the ground. The cart was heavy on the uphill blocks. I wasn't used to this kind of work.

At the very end of the route we had to cross Varick Street. It was well past what I thought of as rush hour, but the street was still fully inhabited by the caravan of commuters trying to find their way back to suburban New Jersey through the Holland Tunnel. The idling cars spilled through the intersection. Mendy forced a way across for us, staring drivers down or banging on their hoods until they backed up enough to let us through.

We cut through a parking lot. Cars were parked four stories high on metal girders, and I couldn't make sense of the system that raised them up there. Mendy nodded at the parking attendant, who nodded back from his little booth, and we came to the back door of the New York Mini Storage, where two women were arguing in Russian. The only word I could make out was "*dengi*." Money. The woman doing most of the shouting was older, about fifty, and had bleached blonde hair. The other woman was about my age, and had black hair. She started to argue back against the older woman, waving her finger in her face, and the older woman slapped her twice, knocking the girl to her knees with the second blow. The older woman took a drag on her cigarette, making the ember at the end glow red, then flicked the cigarette at the girl's face.

I stopped pushing the cart, but Mendy shook his head.

"Not our business," he said. "Besides, you don't want to mess with Zoya. Let's get inside." He swiped a magnetic key fob against a panel to unlock the door, and guided the cart through.

It took us a few tries to get the cart into Mendy's storage space. There was just enough space between the boxes to fit it in, and we kept getting in at a bad angle, and having to pull back out and try again. When we finally got in, I let myself sink down to the ground. I sat there and sweated. I still hadn't caught my breath from the walk over.

Mendy counted out some money from his fanny pack and held it out to me.

"Here you go," he said.

"What's this?"

"Sixty-four dollars. It's what I figure is fair, considering how long you worked, and what I made, and what I can pay."

"I wasn't doing it to get paid . . ."

"Well, you earned it. If you weren't helping me, I would have had to get Eye to help me push the cart. He would have been doing it to get paid. I'm giving you the same rate I give him. It was most of your day. It made my day easier. Take it, or I won't feel right. I don't need one more thing to keep me up at night." I took the money and put it in my pocket. It felt good to hold a wad of cash that I'd earned through an honest day's work.

"Now." He snapped his fingers. "That other thing." He extracted a shoebox from his cluttered storage space, and rummaged through it until he pulled out a key ring. He lifted his glasses and pulled the keys close to his eye. Satisfied he had the right ring, he tossed it to me.

"That's the key to your father's space. It makes more sense for you to have it than me. The number written on the keychain should be

Timur's . . . I was supposed to call it if your father got jammed up or something. I guess maybe he did. You can sort things out with Timur yourself. That little fob on the ring gets you into the building.

"Well, there it is," he said, pointing to another unit down the same aisle. "Your family legacy. I'll say good night now, and leave you to it."

5

WHEN I OPENED THE metal door, I found a cart stacked high with water boxes. The rig was tied up with bungee cords, ready to hit the street. Alojzy had been planning on coming back here. Beyond the cart were stacks and stacks of water boxes, labeled in shaky Sharpie. "HC Mysteries." "20th Cent. Art." "Photog." "Catchers in the Ryes."

Based on the outer metal wall, the space extended quite a bit to the left, past the stacks of boxes. I climbed up over the cart and onto the stacks to see what was there. In the little light that filtered in from the fluorescent tubes on the corridor ceiling, I could make out a field of books, with a clearing in the middle. When my eyes adjusted, I saw that the clearing was an inflatable camping mattress. This was my father's bedroom. I jumped down onto the mattress, the only place I could safely land. Luckily, it didn't pop. Next to it, a camping lantern sat on an upturned milk crate. I switched the lantern on. It was bright enough to give me a fairly full view of the space.

I lay down on my father's narrow mattress. With the sleeping bag and army blankets he had laid out on top of it, the mattress was comfortable enough to sleep on. I was a lot skinnier than him, though, and if he tossed and turned at night—as he always had, during his violent nightmares—he must have butted up against the collapsing stacks of books. When I laid my head back on the pillow, something hard knocked against my skull. I moved the pillow aside to reveal a gun of sorts. It had started life as a bolt action .22, not unlike the rifles we'd fired prone at the summer camp I attended in the Catskills when I was in junior high. The barrel of this one had been dramatically shortened and the stock sawed off altogether, so the gun could be held and fired more or less like a pistol. The magazine extended straight down, longer than the tape-wrapped grip.

I climbed back over the boxes and pulled the door shut. The storage-unit doors were made to only lock from the outside, but Alojzy had rigged up a chain and a deadbolt to hold the door closed from the inside. I fastened them both.

The gun did not surprise me. I had handled a gun of my father's once before, about a year after he'd given up the apartment in Sheepshead Bay. He was gone for ten months after that, during which time I received four postcards from him, three from Nevada and one from California. Back then, I just accepted postcards as signs that Alojzy was thinking of me; I hadn't known to try to parse whatever he was telling me through the drawings.

When he came back, he moved into a residential hotel up in Ridgewood. Most of the other rooms seemed to be occupied by twitchy Serbian men—war criminals, I imagined, on forged passports. Between the Serbs and the fact that we were in Queens, I got the impression that my father was hiding out. It didn't help matters when he showed me the revolver he kept under his mattress.

"Is it real?" I asked.

"Of course."

"Is it loaded?"

"What good would it be, a pistol with no bullets?" He let me hold it, making sure that I kept my finger off the trigger and away from the hammer. It was heavy, and I kept thinking it would go off or even explode in my hand.

My most instructive interaction with guns came on a trip to Israel I'd taken with my synagogue youth group the summer between my junior and senior years of high school. I kept a precise mental log of everything I saw on that trip, so I could talk to my father about it when I saw him again. We spent a day and a half on an IDF base, a desert outpost in the south, where we got to shoot Galils with the soldiers. The unfired shells were as long as my middle finger. So much power erupted from the barrel, and yet I barely felt any kickback against my shoulder.

My father had served in the IDF in the pre-Galil era. He once told me that the first rifle he was issued wasn't an M16, but a twenty-year-old Czech Mauser. These guns had been built for the Germans, but remained undelivered at the end of World War II, and the fledging Israeli army had bought them from the Czechoslovakian government wholesale. The outline of a swastika was still visible in the stain of his gun's butt, he told me, underneath the riveted-on IDF insignia.

They tried to sell us on joining the IDF as overseas enlistees after high school, and I considered it, but not seriously enough. Instead I enrolled in Oberlin on Bernie's dime and observed the world from a smug distance. I attended a couple meetings of the campus chapter of Jews Against the Occupation, read Edward Said's *Orientalism* in class, and dated a Lebanese girl, Mariam. She was from a Christian family. I think her dad had been in one of the militias. She liked to talk about her Arab American identity and denounce the murderous Zionist state, because it made her feel less guilty about the fact that her father had probably murdered Palestinians himself.

We broke up after three months, not because of religion or politics, but because I would always get anxious halfway through sex and lose my hard-on. I came maybe six times during those three months I was with her, and only two of those times when I was actually inside her. I was already smoking a lot of weed and messing around heavily with drugs, especially pills, but I don't think that had much to do with it. I think I just wasn't that good at sex. After I broke up with Mariam, I started doing a lot more hallucinogens. I didn't have any other girl-friends after her.

I pulled open the bolt of Al's sawed-off. An unfired round ejected, and another one popped up at an angle, ready to be slammed forward into the chamber. I'd never been alone with a loaded gun before, and wasn't entirely comfortable with the feeling, so I started to eject the rounds one by one. There had to be a simpler way to do this, by removing the entire magazine from the bottom, but I didn't know how to do that. And as much as I didn't want to leave a loaded gun around, the feeling of loading each round into the chamber before I ejected it was satisfying. For a moment, I let my finger rest on the trigger. If I wanted to, I could shoot a round off into the concrete floor. Taking my finger off the trigger, I ejected the round. Then I loaded and ejected until there were eleven shells on the floor and none in the gun.

I collected the shells, and lined them up in the grooves of the plastic crate, next to the lantern. Leaving the bolt open, I placed the gun down on a pile of books. It looked wrong—too casual—so I picked it back up and leaned it against the metal wall, next to a gallon jug half full of water, which I then drank from. Water ran down my cheeks, and I flinched from the cold. My father had drunk this same water. It probably tasted less stale then. He wouldn't have minded the coldness, though. Three or four pint bottles of Mr. Boston blackberry brandy were piled on the floor. Nothing was cleaned out. It was like he'd just stepped out, and would be coming back any minute. One of the brandy bottles had a little left in it, so I finished it off.

So many books were packed into the small space; it was hard to see them as anything but one oozing mass. As I became acquainted with the unit, I figured out the vague order to the piles. Paperbacks. Hardcovers. Fiction. Nonfiction. One pile of books caught my eye as being altogether different from the others. They were sketchbooks, not published books, and they had color newspaper photos of what appeared to be bombing scenes, maybe in Iraq or Pakistan, scotch-taped to the fake leather covers. A mosque burned in full color. A market lay in ruins.

The same type of images, only hand drawn, filled the inside of the book. Smoke. Flames. Smaller flames bursting from the barrels of guns. The crying faces of children with Middle Eastern features.

Their bodies writhed and burned. Details of Israeli insignia appeared through the smoke. Guns were rendered in full detail, while bodies faded away into abstraction.

Alojzy had drawn with multiple thicknesses of black pen. Faces were sketched with long, mournful strokes from felt-tipped pens, while guns and insignia were drawn in minute detail with thinner ballpoints. Smoke and flames were made with thick streaks of Sharpie, which poured over everything else. There was not always white space, or even clear delineation, between one scene and the next. Bodies tumbled into one another. The living shared space with the dead.

I flipped through the pages quickly, afraid if I dwelled too long on any one page I'd be sucked into its horror. A third of the way through the sketchbook, the horror ebbed, and the foreign faces gave way to faces I recognized. My mother and my sister. Me. There were neighbors I remembered from our old building on East Ninety-Second Street. The olive trees were replaced with the foliage of Central Park. My mother was so beautiful. I hoped Becca and I had really once been as small and sweet as my father portrayed us.

By and by, these few happy scenes faded into smoke themselves. New York burned slowly. Our Upper East Side sidewalk smoldered. The destruction carried into the next sketchbook, which began with smoke. But then the curves straightened, the lines became thicker and darker, and began to bound controlled hash marks. There was a narrower street, and ragged, blocky buildings. One—a cross between a birthday cake and a prison—loomed above the rest. Another page showed a close-up of the interior of a streetcar. The picture seemed to focus on one tired, middle-aged couple who sat close together, looking out the window. All the severely Slavic faces seemed to be staring at them. Their faces were drawn in more detail than the others. The man had an unmistakably Jewish nose, wore a cap low over his eyes, and looked sort of like my father—as did the little boy sitting beside them. Was the boy my father? Was the older couple my grandparents?

I picked up the next book. There were sketches of Goldov at his easel, and sketches of the Galuth Museum. For some reason, in a couple sketches Hasidim were lighting candles in the gallery. There were studies of some of the Galuth paintings, including the one where the girl was thrown from the train. There were detail studies of the people's faces, including the falling woman. Goldov and his museum were apparently important in my father's life, though the man himself made me nervous. I didn't like the bitter way he talked about my father, nor how he had tried to weasel my mother for money. He had probably just sent me to Mendy to get me out of his hair; if he knew Alojzy had this full storage space, he would have come to Mendy himself and tried to get the key, so he could loot anything of value.

Alojzy's drawings were nothing like Goldov's paintings. While Goldov's work was pure artifice and contained no meaning, Alojzy's drawings were packed full of emotion and information. If anything, they were closer to Galuth's paintings. They seemed to depict the same world, in some ways, though Al's drawings were more brutal, less full of hope. But then, black ink is a harsher medium than oil paint.

A significant portion of this book was devoted to sketches of West Fourth Street, clearly made from behind Alojzy's table. There were the book tables, Mendy and the other booksellers, and all the pretty girls passing by. Then West Fourth Street became Jaffa Road in Jerusalem, and the book tables were replaced with the stalls of the *shuk*. Then the *shuk* was in ruins, as bombs exploded and left body parts on the street. Then the explosions were in the desert, and the bodies wore helmets. An Arab girl lay dead in the sand. Then a beautiful woman with long dark hair lay naked—but very much alive—on a couch in an apartment. There were pages and pages of sketches of her.

In the next book, there were more soldiers, and men in suits carrying the same guns as the soldiers. One dead soldier's face appeared over and over. He had appeared sporadically in the previous books, but filled up nearly half of this one. He was in his thirties or forties, with a narrow face, a sharp nose, tight black curls, and, in some pictures, a thin mustache. Because he wore an IDF uniform in many of the pictures, I assumed he was Jewish, but he looked very Middle Eastern, and was probably Mizrahi. In other pictures, he wore flashy civilian clothes. Sometimes he was in the desert. Sometimes he lay on a dock. Always, he was dead. His eyes never opened, even when he was standing upright in a scene with living people.

The last several pages of this book were blank.

Earlier, I thought the postcard drawing might lead me to my father. Now I had found hundreds more of his drawings. Surely the answers I wanted were all in here. Alojzy had put down the keys to his whole life, his whole history. I just needed to make sense of it. He hadn't made it easy. People and things that should be in Israel were in New York, and vice versa. Everything seeped into everything else. Some pictures had detailed backgrounds—I thought of how I'd tried, and failed, to place the freighter picture the day before—but other drawings floated in white space, or were bounded by indistinct hash marks, for purely compositional reasons. Looking through the sketchbooks was exhausting and overwhelming.

I sat in the quiet storage space, an interstitial zone between the painful—and hopefully revelatory—world of the sketchbooks and the outside world where people went about their business. Occasional footsteps and clattering sounds broke through to me. At one point, the clattering was in the same row as my space, and shook my walls. I heard a protracted, hollered exchange in a language I didn't recognize. It seemed that each of the two voices was coming from behind a different one of my walls. There was a crash, and then some laughter.

I wondered if maybe the facility had employees patrolling. This thought made me nervous, although I supposed I had a claim to the contents of the space, if not the space itself, and therefore had some sort of right to be in there. If Alojzy was "presumed dead," I was a "presumed" legal heir. But then again, my father was probably not supposed to be sleeping in a storage unit in the first place. Was his bill paid up? Maybe he skipped town owing money, or a new bill had accumulated since he left. People were probably doing shadier things than I was in this place, late at night, but that was not actually the most comforting of thoughts. Keeping a loaded gun at hand might not be a bad idea after all. My father had it here for a reason. Maybe because he knew dangerous people were looking for him.

I fumbled with the magazine, but still couldn't figure out how to get it off. The latch I thought was a release wouldn't budge. I didn't want to force it, in case it wasn't the release. In the end, I just inserted one bullet directly into the chamber with my fingers, and slammed the bolt closed. The safety had been left in the "fire" position. I clicked it to "safe."

Sitting back down on the bed, I placed my father's gun across my lap. He couldn't really be dead, could he? I felt his presence too strongly for that to be true. Two old men I'd just met believed he was dead, but what did they know? Goldov would clearly say anything to squeeze money out of our family. Mendy came off as better intentioned, but his world was confined primarily to one street, and his knowledge was built on little more than the rumors that circulated in that street. In fact, Mendy had said that he heard the rumor from Goldov. So where had Goldov heard it in the first place, if he hadn't made it up? Did he have some other angle or motivation I couldn't see, besides his simple greed? Did he have a reason to lie? Or did he have information about Alojzy's fate he couldn't share?

My mother believed the postcard easily enough, but she had cut Alojzy out of her life long ago. Becca, I assumed, felt the same way.

I knew this: three times Alojzy had left me, and twice he'd returned. There should be a third return, to even out the balance. There was never any way to know when Alojzy would and would not appear. There were lots of times he had been gone when he was supposed to be around, and that was a big part of why my mother had divorced him. But then there were other times—like my bar mitzvah—where Alojzy had appeared unexpectedly.

I I I ▪

Alojzy had actually helped me prepare for my bar mitzvah, on my Sheepshead Bay visits. Growing up under communism, he hadn't had much religious education himself, but he was fluent in Hebrew, having gone through the military ulpan and lived in Israel for seven years.

Modern Hebrew and Biblical Hebrew are not so different from each other as people will tell you. Hebrew is Hebrew. My mom had agreed to let me bring him an invitation, but he knew as well as I did she didn't want him there, and none of us really pictured him showing up to a family event on Long Island.

My Torah portion was Exodus 30:11–16, *Parshat Shekalim*. It deals with the taking of a census, and how many shekels each person should pay as a tax (it's one-half of a shekel). The portion is about obligations, Bernie told me. Responsibilities. The corresponding haftarah passage is 1 Kings 1:1–17. There's more exciting stuff in there. It tells of Moab's army facing off against Elijah the Tishbite. At Elijah's behest, fire comes down from heaven and consumes one hundred and two enemies of Israel.

"I also," Alojzy told me during one of these tutoring sessions, a few weeks before the bar mitzvah, "have seen fire come down from heaven and consume enemies of Israel."

"What do you mean?" I asked. "This was Bible times."

"Bible times, sure, also Bible land. In Israel, such things continue to happen. 1973, I was called back up and sent up to the Golan. We called in an air strike against the Syrians. I watched through binoculars. It is a horrible thing to see. They should have written that in the book, as well." I recalled times when he woke up shouting in the middle of the night. Crying out names in Hebrew, moaning in pain. This must be why. He didn't say anything else about the war, and we went back to trying to scratch a passably fricative *chet* sound out of my smooth American throat.

When the big day arrived, I chanted my way through the portion without any great embarrassment. As I stood on the bimah and took that first sip of wine from my shiny new kiddush cup, I caught a glimpse of Alojzy sneaking out the side. I hoped our eyes would meet and he would wink, but he didn't look back. His eyes were focused on the door. The important thing was, he'd come. He'd been there.

|▐ ▐ ▪

All these years later, I still found myself half expecting to catch a glimpse of Alojzy sneaking away. Now I was in his space, very close to him, surrounded by his books and drawings, and yet he still didn't show himself. I couldn't be sure the footsteps I heard passing by the locked storage-unit door weren't his.

The stock half of the space, closer to the door, packed full with boxes of books, contrasted sharply with the hidden living space. The living space felt more like a tiny apartment, but had plenty of books too. Some were probably excess stock that had spilled over from the other side. There were the sketchbooks, of course. A half dozen crime novels by people like David Goodis sat right next to the lantern, and were evidently Alojzy's nighttime reading. Two tall stacks of damaged books also sat by the bed, and there were supplies—X-Acto knives, glue, and so one—on top of them, so presumably Alojzy did some repair work while sitting in bed.

Several radios, two intact and the others in pieces, were piled in the corner, next to a set of screwdrivers. Did he use the radios to listen to the weather? Did he listen to the news at night? Alojzy had always been a keen follower of international events. He had to be, having been at their whim so many times. I tried to imagine his evenings in here as best I could. How long had he been living here? If I'd come six months earlier, instead of sitting in my dorm room, would I have found him here, fiddling with a radio antenna?

Behind the mattress was a plastic chest. Inside were clothing and blankets. I was cold, and pulled out one of his sweaters to wear. Wherever Alojzy had gone, he wasn't able to take all of his clothes. Maybe he'd only been able to take a suitcase or backpack with him. Maybe he thought he'd be back soon and that was all he'd need.

ı ı ▪

I'd seen Alojzy leave New York in a hurry before, back when he had a van. It was the last time I saw him, and a shameful memory, at that, because I'd failed him. This was three and a half years after my bar mitzvah, when I was sixteen. Alojzy had called, and said he wanted to come see me in person. He didn't mind driving out to Long Island, but he didn't want to run into my mother at the house. I told him it was okay, I would be the only one around. My mom and Bernie would be gone all day.

He pulled up in his white van. The inside of that van was a lot like the inside of the storage space. He got out of the van and leaned against the side, waiting for me to come to him. He was wearing a Yankees cap, and all his gold chains. When I made it across the lawn to him, he gave me a manly hug.

"This is the house?" He looked over my shoulder with apprehension. He had never been there before. I think the house was bigger than he expected.

"Yeah. We live here. You want to come inside?"

"No. I don't want to go in there." His family had been taken from him, and relocated to this suburban house. Of course he didn't want to go inside.

"I think they have some Sam Adams in the fridge." I knew they did, because I'd been pilfering them all day. "If you want a beer?"

"No, not right now. You doing all right, boychik?"

"Sure." I was confused. Had he driven all the way out into the suburbs just to check up on me? It felt strange to be standing beside him on a green lawn. I associated him with pavement.

"How is Becca?"

"She's good. She's still up at school, until May."

"Yes. I know. Boston. Boston College."

"Boston University." I felt bad correcting him. There was no reason he should know the difference between the schools.

"Yes. Boston University. She is doing well in her studies?"

"I don't know. I guess so." She always got good grades. She was competitive, and it was important to her to do better than the other kids.

"She has a field of study?"

"A major? Marketing, I think."

"Marketing? Ah. Advertising. Selling. Smart. She is like her papa.

"Listen. *Takhlis*: I have something going on, out West. Something big. I'm going out there now." I didn't know what "something going on" meant exactly. He never told me too much about his hustles. All I really knew was that he made "deals" from time to time, and that he would be flush with cash afterward.

"Right now?"

"Yes. It is sudden. But the situation out there." It was only later that I realized I never even asked where "out there" was. I knew he went west, but I didn't know what state. "And the situation here. You know, I could use a partner."

"A partner?"

"*Tak*, road partner, business partner. You interested?"

"You want me to help you?" How could I help him?

"Sure. Who else would I turn to, buddy, except my own flesh and blood?"

"I don't know. I'd like to."

"Nu?" He needed an answer. Did I want to man up, and head out into the world? "I can't just go," I said. "I mean, I have school . . ." It was very sunny out. A man was watering his lawn across the street. He eyed the Astro van suspiciously. I really felt as if I couldn't go. Packing my backpack and getting in the van seemed impossible.

"What's that Jew prick looking at?" Alojzy said. He gave the neighbor a hard look. The neighbor turned off the hose and went inside his garage. Alojzy turned back to me and sighed.

He looked sad. Something bigger than the trip was slipping away—a whole part of what I could do and who I could be—but I was scared to grab it. I thought about the moment many times over the years, and that was the only explanation I could ever come back to: fear. The moment passed completely, the two of us standing there silent, and then it was gone.

"Of course," Alojzy said. "Of course. You should be in school. You are a real good fella. Study hard. Go to Boston University."

"I'll see you before then." I was sure I would.

"Of course. I'll see you soon."

"Maybe I could go with you, if, just in a couple days. If I talked to Mom—" I was already regretting the scene, even as it was still unfolding.

"No. You're right. It was just a thought I had. You should be in school. You don't need to get mixed up in my endeavors." It was clear to me even then that he didn't believe this, that he was just giving me an easy way to punk out and still save face. But I took it.

We talked a little more. He didn't want to stick around the house for too long, for fear of seeing my mother. We ended up going to the Dairy Queen for sloppy joes, and then he dropped me back at the house. We didn't talk too much while we ate, though at one point he said that if anyone ever came asking about him, it would be best if I just told them that my father was dead.

|▮▮▮

I hadn't seen Alojzy since then. For the first year or so, I received postcards off and on. Then they stopped. He was gone from my life until his most recent postcard brought him back. Now I was being told by Goldov that he was gone for good and I would never see him again. I hoped this wasn't true, that this was just another of Alojzy's disappearances and he was lying low somewhere. Surely he would come back once more, and I'd have a second chance to prove I was a worthy son.

What would my life be like if I'd gone with Alojzy that day? Surely, I'd be stronger and tougher. Not so confused. I would never have wasted time in college and would have seen more of life. Maybe I'd be a hustler myself, in business with Alojzy.

It occurred to me that even though Alojzy wasn't here, I could still go into business with him, selling his books. The cart was just sitting there, waiting for me to come take it out. Goldov's comment about "selling off assets" might have been somewhere in the back of my mind, but I had no intention of giving that man a dime.

I had enjoyed spending the day working with Mendy, and wouldn't mind spending more days on the street. As I spent more time on Alojzy's turf, around people he knew, I would find out more about him. Maybe someone even knew where he was, or could get a message to him. Maybe that wouldn't end up being necessary. Assuming Alojzy was hiding out somewhere, he was bound to return when things blew over. When he did, he would find me here, working. I would save the money I made from his stock for him, and I would be able to show him that I was capable of taking care of business.

6

I WOKE UP TO the sounds of street vendors beginning their days. Unoiled wheels creaked as heavy carts rolled over the concrete floors. Carts banged against metal doors. Someone was tossing boxes from a ladder to the ground, and each landed with a heavy thump. People argued in different shades of English and French. Occasionally I heard a burst of Russian, and the same language I hadn't been able to identify at night. It sounded South Asian. Maybe Urdu or Bengali? It hadn't occurred to me that a storage facility would be filled with so much activity. While the upper stories housed regular long-term personal storage, the majority of the ground-floor units were occupied by street vendors.

I took a drink from the plastic water jug, hid the gun under the air mattress, and stumbled over Alojzy's boxes to the door. In the corridor, three Russian girls were arguing over a stack of T-shirts. I recognized one of them as the black-haired girl I'd seen get smacked the night before. If her face had been bruised, her makeup concealed it. A shirt fell to the ground as I passed by, and I picked it up. The shirt had an image of a woman with her finger to her lips. "*Nee Boltaee*," she said—no gossiping. Handing it to the girl closest to me, I pictured my father flirting with these girls and wondered if his Polish schoolboy innuendos translated smoothly into Russian, if the girls giggled and blushed. A dreadlocked woman pushing a cart piled high with African wood carvings came up behind me and yelled at me for blocking the aisle.

I used the men's room and bought a Diet Coke from the vending machine in the lobby, then went over to the pay phone to call the number Mendy had given me.

"*Allo?*" demanded a Russian voice. I could hear that the word had been shaped in a square jaw.

"Yes, hello. Is this Timur?"

"No. Is not. Do not call again." The line went dead. Had I made a mistake? The man didn't say I had a wrong number, he just said he wasn't Timur. The number was all I had so I tried again, afraid the man would just let it ring, but he picked up again.

"Didn't I tell you not to call again? Who the hell are you?"

"Wait!" I said. "Listen. My name is Izzy Edel. I've been looking for my father. I was given this number . . ." The man on the other end of the line was quiet for a moment, but he didn't hang up. Cars pulled in and out of the parking lot.

"You are the son of Alojzy Edel?"

"Yes."

"How did you get this number?"

"First, I talked to a man named Semyon Goldov, and then I got the number from a man named Mendy. I don't know his last name."

"I know who they are. Why are you calling?"

"I don't know if you know, but my father's missing . . ." I was hoping this would get some response, but it didn't, so I kept going. "I was told that Mr. Timur had paid the rental bill—but you're not Timur?"

"No. I am not. That person does not speak on the telephone."

"Oh. So how do I speak to him?"

"You don't. You speak to me. But do not waste my time."

"Fine. I'll be quick. First of all, I just wanted to touch base about the status of the storage-center bill, to make sure my father's stuff doesn't need to be moved out immediately, or anything like that. But more importantly, I'm trying to locate my father, and I'm trying to talk to anyone who might know where he is or what happened to him."

"All right. I will call you back on this number in five minutes."

While I stood waiting next to the phone, a man approached and asked if I was done. I told him no. He picked up the receiver anyway and proceeded to argue in a mixture of French and some West African language for the next six minutes. My father would have made him get off the phone, but I didn't know how to do that. Finally, the guy hung up. I waited another five minutes, but the phone didn't ring. Maybe Timur's man had called back and got a busy signal. But it was also possible that he wasn't ready yet, and would just be annoyed if I called back. He didn't sound like a man I wanted to annoy. After debating for three minutes, I decided to go for it.

"*Allo?*"

"Yeah, this is Izzy—"

"Yes. Edel. I told you I would call you back."

"I know, but I hadn't heard from you and—"

"That is because you didn't tell me you were calling from a pay phone. Where the hell did you even find a pay phone? No, I can make guess: it's the pay phone at that rotten storage space. Don't you know a pay phone cannot accept incoming calls?"

"No. I didn't know that." A straggling street vendor rolled out of the door with her cart, and I flattened myself against the wall so she could pass.

"Well, now you are knowing," the man said. "It's because of the gangbangers and their pagers."

"Oh."

"Yes. It was very clever, to make an innovation of technology used only by doctors, so as to facilitate untraceable communication for drug deals."

"Sure."

"Still, I do not have time to be calling a phone which will not ring."

"I'm sorry." Who was this guy? He was angry that I wasted his time, and yet he had time to give me a history lesson about crack dealers? Or was this a roundabout way of making sure that I knew he was a gangster and should be treated with fear and respect? Well, I didn't think Alojzy's storage space was paid for by the Hebrew Immigrant Aid Society.

"Forget it," the man said. "Now, Timur and I would very much like to speak with you in person about your father. Do you drive a car?"

"No."

"Fine. Take the Q or B train to Brighton Beach. I will meet you on the southwest corner of Brighton Beach Avenue and Brighton Sixth Street. Six p.m."

"Okay. Sounds good."

"Hasta la vista, baby."

Back in the storage space, I grabbed my backpack, a few of Alojzy's sketchbooks, and a Yankees cap hanging on the wall. The day was sunny, but I also felt awkward walking around visibly wearing my kippah. The kippah had seemed right when I was in my own internal world in Ohio and New Mexico, but in New York City a kippah came with the obligation to talk to religious Jews. I didn't want old men on the train to keep interrogating me about my employment or marital status, or asking me to join their minyans. The kippah also gave a certain sense about me to non-Jewish and non-Orthodox strangers, and I'd look a bit tougher and more street-smart with the cap on. Taking the kippah off altogether would have been easier, but it also would have felt like a renunciation, an erasing of the pages that had brought me to this place. Aher never took off his kippah and talis, even after he'd been excommunicated for heresy.

The street vendors were already out all along Spring Street as I walked across SoHo to catch the 6 train. Several painters displayed canvases not much different from Goldov's work. Artisans wore their own creations: T-shirts covered with sequins and puffy paint, heavy necklaces garnished with dyed feathers. There were T-shirts silk-screened with bootleg Andy Warhol images—Elvis with his pistol drawn—and there were more T-shirts silk-screened with old Soviet slogans. There were booksellers here too, selling big coffee table books with color plates in them, and smaller, square books about younger artists, which had soft covers, with French flaps to make them feel more substantial. This was the art-book trade Goldov had spoken of.

Up at Becca's place, I took a long, hot shower and put on some clean clothes. Afterward, I laid the sketchbooks out on the coffee table. It was easier to study them in the bright apartment than in the storage space with the dim light of the electric lantern. I spent a good hour drifting through the pages, then went back though to study each book page by page, image by image. There might be practical clues to Alojzy's disappearance in here. On a piece of scrap paper, I tried to write names and descriptions for each repeated figure. "Alojzy." "Me." "Becca." "Ruth." "Mendy." "Goldov." "Man in suit #1." "Man in suit #2." "The dead soldier." "The naked woman with the long dark hair." "The street." "The museum." "Galuth's paintings." The process was like music-history class, when we listened for the leitmotifs in Wagner's *Ring* cycle. "Sleep." "Wotan's spear." "Renunciation of love."

The phone rang while I was making myself a cup of tea. I was going to let it go on ringing, even after I saw the New Mexico number on the caller ID, but something got the better of me and I picked up.

"Hi, Mom."

"How do you know it's me?"

"Becca's phone has caller ID."

"Of course, of course, I always forget about that thing." Flipping to Alojzy's sketch of her, with wide eyes and mischievous smile, I tried to connect the drawing to the voice.

"How are you, Mom?"

"Oh, I'm all right, I suppose. I've been fighting with your uncle Howard on the phone all morning."

"About what?" They had fought before, and gone for as long as a year at a time without speaking. Howard had not liked Alojzy, and he and my mother had gotten closer again once my mother was divorced and remarried. But they still had their spats.

"My mother's papercuts. She made these beautiful papercuts. He got all that stuff when they cleaned out Bubbe's apartment."

"That was, like, six years ago."

"I know, I know. But I've had so much to deal with. Now, I finally feel like I have the time, and I want to get out those papercuts that your grandmother made and take a look. Maybe do something with them? But your uncle is giving me a hard time, saying he's too busy with work to deal with this." Her tirade was hypocritical. After Alojzy's latest postcard had arrived in New Mexico, I'd searched the garage for the old postcards he'd sent me in high school. Unable to find them, I asked my mother, who said she'd thrown them out, not realizing I would want those "useless old papers." She knew what she was doing.

"Howard might be busy," I said, taking her brother's side out of spite. "He is a lawyer."

"I know he's a lawyer. I know he works hard. I'm very proud of what he's accomplished. But honestly, this shifty way he's acting, it makes me think he's just thrown everything away and doesn't want to come clean about it."

"I don't understand what it is you're talking about, exactly. Papercuts?"

"Yes. Papercuts. The intricate art of cutting designs into paper. Don't you know?"

"Like the snowflakes we'd make in grade school?"

"Snowflakes? Like snowflakes? No, not like snowflakes, thank you very much, for Christmastime. Traditional Jewish papercuts I'm talking about here. Like they used to use for ketubot? To frame and hang on the wall?"

"I can't picture them. It's not calligraphy?"

"No. Wouldn't I say 'calligraphy' if I meant calligraphy? It's papercuts. Cut paper. Carved paper. You go to school and study all this modern art. Then, when you were here, you borrowed books from Bernie about Hasidism and *tzadikim*, *Nineteen Gated Mystics* or whatever, to read when you were stoned from smoking your dope in my house."

"Mom." It was true that I smoked a little weed that I bought off her neighbor's boyfriend now and then, but I was sober for the most part, and had stayed away from pills and hallucinogens.

"And yet, you don't even recognize a basic Jewish folk art when it's described to you?"

"Mom."

"It's okay. I don't really mind about the dope." This meant she did mind. "I know you were finding yourself. Although, there comes a time when you need to stop finding yourself and start finding a career. But you're thinking about going back to school now, I hear?"

"Mom."

"Yes, my darling?"

"The papercuts?"

"Yes. The papercuts. Your grandmother made these beautiful papercuts. Beautiful little things. The whole time I was growing up."

"I don't remember."

"Well, she had to stop on account of her arthritis."

"Oh."

"Yes. It really was quite a shame. But she had made so many beautiful things, and saved them in a box. Now that I'm semiretired, and for the first time able to do crafts—Bernie says I can say art, but it's not art to me; maybe arts and crafts—I want to go back and look at my mother's work. And Howard has prevented me from doing this."

"They'll turn up." I remembered my tea and took a sip. It had cooled considerably, and was not pleasurable to drink.

"How do you know they'll turn up? Maybe they won't. And you didn't answer my question."

"What question?"

"You're looking at going back to school?"

"What? No, they didn't want me back."

"Not there. I know. But I talked to Becca this morning. I thought she said you had an interview at NYU?"

"Huh? Oh, no, that was something different."

"So you're not going to apply to NYU?"

"Are you serious? There's no way they'd let me into NYU."

"Well, no, it might be a reach. But there are other schools. I went to Hunter, you know, in the city. It's not such a bad school."

"I know."

"Well. So what are you doing? Have you been looking for work? You're not sitting around smoking dope all day are you?" I wouldn't have minded a joint, actually, after this conversation. My mother was always on my case about drugs because she regretted spending her early adult life as a bohemian, partying in the East Village and marrying my father. She didn't want Becca and me to end up like Alojzy and the other people they had known, and became obsessed with raising us as middle-class, college-bound Jewish children. When I arrived in New Mexico, she told me my expulsion had "devastated" her.

"No, no. I'm doing things, I was just on my way out the door."

"Oh, to where?"

"To talk to a guy. A friend of Dad's."

"One of Bernie's friends?" I didn't know why she'd think that. I sometimes called my mom and Bernie my "parents" as collective shorthand, but I never referred to Bernie as "Dad," or really as anything other than "Bernie." "Who? Oh, did you finally call that Mr. Clybourne, like Bernie suggested? I'm sure he could help you find a job."

"No, not Bernie. Alojzy. A guy who knows Alojzy."

"Oh. Ah."

"Yeah."

"Isaac. Isaac Edel. I don't think that's the best kind of person for you to be spending your time around. The kind of life your father led . . . it was attractive to me, when I was very young. He led me down a lot of roads I wouldn't have gone down otherwise." Her voice grew soft, dreamy. We both noticed it, and she didn't speak for a moment. I heard her sigh, build herself back up so she could tear him down. "Well, alleys, maybe. But there were dark places down there. There were reasons I had to get away from him. There were reasons I got you kids away from him."

"He was always good to me."

"What? Good to you? Are you serious, Izzy? When he abandoned you—for the second time!—when you were a teenager, it broke your heart."

"Broke my heart? I don't think I was heartbroken."

"You didn't smile for six months."

"So? I was a teenager."

"And that's when you started to go off the wrong track, and get involved with the drugs. That was his fault too. Look what came from that."

"No, that had nothing to do with him." People did drugs because they wanted to. It was no one else's fault. Drugs—and drug culture—had been attractive to me for as long as I could remember. "Listen, Mom. I'm trying to figure out what happened. I talked to that guy, Goldov."

"Who?"

"The guy who sent the note about Dad being missing."

"Oh. Yes. He said your father was dead."

"He seems to think so. But did you hear anything else? From anyone? I mean, how do we know for sure he's dead?"

"We don't know, for *sure*."

"Didn't you say Bernie was going to check it out?"

"He looked into it. He couldn't find any record either way, to show that he was dead, or deported, or in the hospital, or in prison. Nothing. But your father used so many fake names, it doesn't really prove anything. He was in the country illegally until he married me, you know. He had a stolen green card. And Bernie is a forensic accountant, not a CIA analyst."

"So we don't know."

"No, we don't know for sure. But I'm sorry, sweetheart, he's likely dead. It's amazing he didn't die years and years ago. You're lucky he lived long enough to have you children! He was your father, it's true, but he wasn't a very good one, and now he's gone. Let him go. I let him go a long time ago. There's no use chasing down any alleys for something that isn't there."

"Mom, I have to go."

"Where, to hang out with Alojzy's hoodlum friend?"

"Mom."

"Lie to me. Tell me another. Tell me you're going to speak to an admissions counselor at Hunter. Or you have an interview for an internship. At the very least, an informational interview."

"Bye, Mom."

FOR THE SECOND TIME in three days, I took the Q train from Manhattan to Brighton Beach. I leaned against the pole of the elevated tracks, hoping I bore enough of a resemblance to Alojzy that Timur's man would recognize me.

"Izzy Edel." I turned around. The man facing me was a few inches shorter than me, but built like a weight lifter. Under his black blazer he wore a silk shirt with the top third of the buttons undone. Probably the shirt had popped open when he flexed his muscles. How strange, I thought, to see a short, balding, middle-aged man with such virility. Moving up from his torso to his face, I recognized him. He was man in suit #1, from the list I'd made that afternoon. Would Timur be man in suit #2?

"You're the man I spoke to on the phone?" I asked.

"Yes. I am Roman." We shook hands. "Come." He put a hand on my back, and we started walking. "You came alone?" he asked.

"Yes."

"And you came on your own behalf?"

"What do you mean?" I asked.

"Nobody sent you?"

"Who would send me?"

"People making an inquiry into where Alojzy went. Police. Maybe your family has an investigator?" This surprised me. Why would anyone investigate Alojzy's disappearance? Why would Roman even suspect that?

"Nobody cares about Alojzy except me," I said. Roman didn't respond. He led me down a side street to a restaurant that looked closed.

"Arms up," he commanded.

"What?" I said. What had I been brought down here for?

"Pat down. Standard precaution."

After a quick search, Roman seemed satisfied I wasn't carrying a recording device or weapon. Next, he demanded my ID, ostensibly to verify that I was really an Edel. He inspected my expired driver's license, nodded, and handed it back. A young Hasidic man exited the restaurant's curtained front door. Roman caught the door before it closed, and gestured for me to walk in ahead of him.

Though no light had escaped through the blacked-out window, the restaurant itself was brightly lit. Turkic warriors rushed heroically across the wall toward death. On a muted flat-screen TV mounted up by the ceiling, girls with long black hair twirled against computerized backdrops while men waited for them, leaning on their Mercedes. It was odd that an Orthodox Jew had been inside what was clearly a nonkosher restaurant, but I shrugged it off. That was Brooklyn for you. Besides, if I didn't have the Yankees cap over my kippah, someone could have made the same comment about me.

At a small table against the sidewall, a man with a long white beard and another with a short black beard were drinking tea. The only other occupied table was set in the back corner. A tall, elegant-looking man was seated at this table with his back to the wall, sipping mineral water and scrolling through e-mails on his BlackBerry. He rose as I came in. Yes, he was man in suit #2 from the sketchbook. Things were lining up.

"Isaac! Welcome!" He came around the table and gave me a hearty handshake. "Alojzy Edel is like a brother to me. His son is like a nephew to me." After Roman's suspicion and interrogation, Timur's warm greeting was welcome, if disorienting. I had introduced myself to Roman as Izzy. Did Timur know me as Isaac from talking to Alojzy? Timur was clearly a different breed than Roman. He wore a tailored suit and silk tie with a diamond tiepin. His formality probably didn't allow for nicknames. I had met men like Roman before—Alojzy was a man like Roman, in some ways—but I didn't think I had ever met a man like Timur.

We sat down, and the table was soon filled with platters of kebabs, eggplant and cucumber salads, big loaves of flat bread, and a pot of tea. I had rarely seen so much food outside of a wedding or a funeral. Was this all on my account? Why would Timur need to impress me? Most likely Timur was just a big roller, who spent lavishly and excessively every day of his life. Impressed though I was, I also felt uneasy, like a crab staring at a pile of chicken necks and unable to see the wire trap around it. Forcing the feeling down, I decided I was done retreating out of fear.

"Please, Isaac," Timur urged me. "Eat. No, no, take more. You are my guest. First food, then business. Enjoy this food! Even in Tashkent, you don't find better shashlik. Sayyid here will be insulted if you don't partake of his cooking." The white beard looked up from his tea and nodded in our direction. "As will I," said Timur, placing his hand over his heart like he was pledging allegiance.

The food was delicious. I hardly ever ate meat, except a kosher hot dog now and then, and hadn't known I'd been missing anything until my teeth tore through the tender cubes of lamb. The kebabs were served over beds of juice-drenched onion, as good as the meat itself, which I scooped up with slabs of bread. Roman—who had produced a bottle of vodka from somewhere—advised me to pour vinegar on everything, to bring out the sweetness of the food with a bit of the bitter.

"Listen, Mr. Timur—"

"Just Timur. You didn't try the veal kebabs." Another tray of kebabs appeared on the table. Unlike Roman, Timur didn't have a strong Russian accent. Nor did he sound like an American. His speech was precise and stateless. It was clear that phone calls, pat-downs, and other petty or unpleasant tasks were handled by Roman because Timur was above all that.

"Oh, thank you, I'm stuffed."

"Nonsense. Sayyid will be offended. Here, take."

"Thank you." I accepted some veal on my plate. "And, Timur, thank you very much for your hospitality here."

"It is my pleasure."

"But the reason I called you . . ." I wanted to ask my questions about my father, but I was overwhelmed and intimidated by the hospitality.

"The storage bill, you said?" Roman asked.

"Yes, I'd like to address that," I said. "But more generally, do you know anything about my father's current whereabouts? People are saying he's dead. But I don't believe it."

"That's good," Timur said. "Because I don't believe it either." So I wasn't the only one who doubted the rumors of Alojzy's death. Someone with much more authority than Goldov or Mendy felt the same way. This was comforting. "It is true Edel has disappeared. But he must have had his *reasons* for doing so." The way he said the word "reasons" made me think he knew what some of them were—and made me think I wasn't supposed to inquire further. "Tell me, do you know much of what your father does?"

"What he does for you?" Despite the intimacy of the dinner, I still didn't know who Timur was, or what he did. Roman's cagey demeanor on the phone and in the street had only raised questions. What was Timur's relationship to my father, and why did he have me come all the way down here and treat me so well?

"Yes. For me, and for himself. What I mean is, do you know much of your father's enterprises?"

"I know about the books he sells."

"Other than that?"

"No, I'm afraid I don't about anything else." I didn't want to sound naïve—there was clearly something criminal in Alojzy's relationship to these men—but I really didn't know what was at play here.

"I see." Timur seemed relieved, though it was hard to read his reactions. "That is just as well. I'm sure you do know that your father is involved in some sensitive business. It is not good to ask a lot of questions. Interfering, trying to find people or facts that don't want to be found." Timur sounded like he was welcoming me and threatening me at the same time. "I'm sure we can trust you, based on your parentage?"

"You can," I said.

"Good. But you must understand that for us to have an honest conversation, and relationship, I need to be able to count on your discretion in *all* matters. It wouldn't do for me to find out you had been speaking about me, or about things I tell you, to other people."

"I understand that. I understand discretion. And I don't want to . . . overstep with my questions. I only wanted to know a few things." I was lost, but I needed to push forward. "A few pragmatic things. About the storage space, as Roman said. I didn't know how long the bill was covered for, and I was just afraid that the unit would get evicted before Alojzy returns. I don't want him to lose his stuff. So I didn't know when I'd have to pick up the bill to keep that from happening?"

"Don't worry about that. It is an annual payment, so it is fine until the end of the year. Perhaps your father will be back by then?"

"Perhaps, yes. Thank you."

"Of course. Your father has done a great many favors for me. It's the least I can do." More platters of food appeared. Glasses were refilled.

"So, Isaac," Timur asked, "are you employed?"

"Not currently. I've just come back to the city recently. But I was thinking, actually, that I might handle Alojzy's bookselling business until he returns."

"Very good. I'm sure he will be proud when he sees that. And personally, I like having friends on the street, who can keep their eyes open for me. We will be friends?"

"Absolutely." I wanted to have friends like Timur. What's more, I needed to be in his confidence if I was going to find Alojzy.

"Good. Have you done work like this before?"

"No, it's new to me. I was a student, until very recently."

"Ah, you've been to university. Excellent. What did you study?"

"Some philosophy. Some Jewish studies. Some literature, and art history. Different things." These were just classes I had taken. In two and a half years, I had never actually declared a major.

"Excellent. Excellent. Art history . . . so you know something about paintings?"

"A bit." I pictured Hieronymus Bosch's *Hell* and *The Flood*. The scorched ground and fiery sky of hell. The lounging demons. The ark resting on the mountaintop.

"Your father studied art. He knows a good bit about paintings. A man of many talents. You take after him?"

"Yes, I suppose so," I said. "I do take after him." I hoped that saying it would make it true.

"Perhaps you could do one thing for me, as you will be going back to the storage center?"

"Of course." I would never again make the mistake I'd made when I was sixteen of turning down an opportunity to be part of something real. These were my father's peers, and I wanted to hold my own with them, to belong with them.

"Do you know who Zoya is?" I recalled the argument the night before, and the girls folding the shirts in the morning.

"She's in charge of the girls who sell Soviet T-shirts?"

"Exactly. I have been meaning to get up to see her, and give her something, but perhaps you could bring it to her for me?"

"Absolutely. No problem." I was happy to be trusted with a concrete task. Roman passed me an envelope, which I tucked into my jacket. It was thin, like it held only one or two sheets of folded paper. Probably the errand was of no great importance and Timur only wanted to test my reliability. I would make sure to pass the test and gain his trust so I could learn more about Alojzy's activities. Of course, I didn't know that I could trust them either. But trust was a two-way street, and I would do my part to establish it between us.

"Let us drink," said Roman, who refilled our water glasses with vodka. We raised them up. "To your father's health." I drank it down in one gulp. These men were clearly deeper into my father's world than anyone else I had met. If they believed he was alive, he had to be, and I would find him, sooner or later.

‖‖■

On the train ride back to Manhattan, I finished reading *The Yeshiva Bocher*. The student has grown old by the end of the last chapter. He has lived a hard life and is dying in the poorhouse in Baghdad. As he takes his last gasping breaths, he notices three letters traced in the thick dust by another dying old man. Hebrew letters, letters from the beautiful aleph-bet he forgot long ago on the battlefields. A beth, a shin, and a taw. From those three letters, he puts the whole alphabet back together in his mind, and from that he is able to assemble the whole of the Torah he studied long ago in his youth.

With all his strength, he pulls himself to his feet. He takes one step and finds himself stepping back into the Shabbos dinner in Poland he had been stolen from so many decades before. In the time it had taken him to live his life, only one minute has passed at the rabbi's table. The traveling master winks at him, and pours him a small schnapps to settle his nerves.

‖‖■

When I entered Becca's apartment, she and Andrew were sitting on the couch watching a movie. On the screen, a man and a woman sat across from each other on a train, arguing. Becca and Andrew were giggling. They didn't seem to be paying attention to the movie. Becca wasn't normally someone who giggled, but Andrew had a strong effect on her.

"Oh, hey," Becca said. She held a glass of white wine in her hand.

"Hey," said Andrew.

"Hi," I said. "How are you guys doing?"

"Not too bad," Becca said. "We were both off work early, and we went for Thai food. I was hoping you could get dinner with us tonight. But of course we had no way to get ahold of you. I got you some veggie pad Thai. I know you like noodle-veggie dishes."

"I do. Thanks. I had dinner with some people in Brooklyn, so I'm stuffed. But I'll have that for lunch tomorrow."

"Cool." She muted the television, but didn't turn it off. "But you really should get a cell phone. It's kind of ridiculous you don't have one."

"Yeah. I should. I'm going to get one," I lied. When I lost my last phone, it was month to month so I just let it go. Honestly, I liked not carrying around a machine that could buzz and suddenly take me away from my own thoughts. I liked walking around feeling untethered, like I could just drift above the earth. This train of thought reminded me of the Galuth painting, how the woman only appeared to be rising.

"What do you put on résumés?" Becca asked.

"What?"

"Aren't you applying for jobs? What phone number do you put so they can call you back for an interview?"

"Oh, just the landline here, for now."

"Okay. You have been applying for jobs, right?" She meant this conversationally, but it felt like an interrogation.

"Yeah, sure, jobs. Absolutely, jobs." I had no intention of getting any kind of straight job that would require a résumé, but knew not to tell Becca that.

"Are you drunk?" She looked at me with reproach.

"No, but I was drinking . . . I was drinking with these guys . . . don't worry about it. It's okay. I'm good to talk." The truth was I was still a little drunk from all the vodka, but was starting to sober up after the long train ride. That process, mixed with the meat in my stomach, was making me feel sick, dehydrated, and light-headed. I went over to the kitchen and drank a glass of water.

"Okay," Becca said, "whatever." She chewed her lip for a second. "Look, Izzy, I'm happy to have you here. I really am. As long as you want to stay." She meant it earnestly. "I'm not trying to hassle you. But when you said you wanted to come out here, you said you wanted to get your life going."

"Get the story of my life going. Yeah." I still hadn't told her that my primary reason for coming East was to find Alojzy, who she didn't like talking about, but she was right. I had also traveled out here to change my life.

"Right. Whatever. So any help you need doing that, I'm here."

"We're here," said Andrew.

"I know," Becca continued, "it's hard in this city. Especially with the economy these days. And especially with you not having a degree. Not having a degree *yet*. And it sucks to say, even though I have a good job now, I don't love what I do. And I loved it even less when I was still an assistant, let alone an intern." Becca had gotten through college in three years, and had started at her company as a full-time intern when she was still twenty-one. "But that's the way it is. I have a good position now. I have this apartment."

"Becca," I pleaded. My sister's lectures were even worse than my mom's.

"Look, dude, I'm not trying to nag you. But I had to figure all this stuff out myself. Mom wasn't . . . super helpful. She was encouraging—a driving force—but not helpful in any practical way. I'm trying to help you. You need to get a start somewhere."

"Well, actually," I said, "I might have something going on downtown, a job opportunity."

"Doing what?"

"Selling books. But I haven't officially started yet." I struggled to put my experiences into acceptable language without lying. "I went down yesterday and had a paid training session. I'm going to have a full trial run tomorrow, to see what it's like, make sure it'll work out. It might not be anything real."

"That's the problem, isn't it?" I heard Becca's voice beginning to switch, the way it did. The way Alojzy's voice switched when he got angry. "You don't seem to know what's real and what's not real."

"Come on, Becca," Andrew said. He heard the switch too. "Lay off the guy. Let him see if the job works out first."

"Stay out of this, Andrew. I'm trying to help my brother."

"I know you are, babe. He knows you are. But look, how about this: I'll take Edel the Kid out Friday night, when I meet up with the guys. The kid clearly needs to blow off some steam. Am I right, Izzy? And it would be good for him to meet those guys. They have connections, you know? I'll tell them he's looking for career experience, so they can see if they hear of anything."

"Sure," I said. "Sounds good. Thanks."

"Okay," said Becca. "It might be good for Izzy to spend some time with you and your friends. I just want to make sure, Izzy, that staying here is helping you get on the right track. I'd feel better about you staying here if I knew you had a position, or some structure."

8

I TOOK ALOJZY'S BOOKS out onto the street the next morning. His handcart was smaller than Mendy's rig, but it was still a lot to maneuver by myself. At the perfect angle the weight of the boxes was balanced on the wheels, so the cart required hardly any force to push forward, assuming I didn't encounter any cracks or uneven pavement. The problem was, when the cart was angled that far back, it increased the weight on my arms. I toggled back and forth the whole way to West Fourth Street. By the time I got my books set up, I had completely sweated through a nice button-down shirt. I decided that from then on I would just work in an undershirt. If it got cold in the afternoon, I'd put on one of Alojzy's big sweaters. Luckily, he had a couple packed in the supplies bag on the rig.

Not wanting to step on anyone's toes, I asked Mendy, who was already on the corner where Washington Square East dead-ended at West Fourth Street, where it was okay to set up. He said that if I stayed off the corner, he and I would stay friends. He also said I probably shouldn't set up directly to the west of him, because that was

Hafid's preferred spot, but directly east of him—which was actually where Alojzy had usually set up—should be fine. Asher and the others mostly set up farther east, toward Mercer Street, so I wouldn't be encroaching on anyone's territory.

Alojzy's rig had eight water boxes and two three-foot-long card tables on it. I later learned to space the tables out and fill the gaps with plywood, to get the legal maximum of eight feet, but for my first day six feet was more than enough. The boxes were labeled by category: two "Fiction," two "History," one "Drama," one "Philosophy/theory/religion," one "Art and oversize," and one "Misc." Except for the hardbacks in "Art and oversize," and a stack of mass-market thrillers in one of the "Fiction" boxes, Alojzy seemed to focus primarily on trade paperbacks.

As expected, the supplies bag held a stack of sheet-metal bookends. Following the way I'd seen Mendy arrange his table, I put fiction and drama in the first rows, closer to the sidewalk traffic, and put history and "Philosophy/theory/religion" farther back, where more rigorous searchers could find them. Within each category, the books were alphabetized by the author's last name, and I maintained that order. The rows of different-colored spines looked beautiful, like a mosaic, and I was proud of the setup. To improve the display, I scattered some of the "Art and oversize" books around the table.

It wasn't difficult for me to interact with the customers. I had always felt comfortable discussing books. Many of the customers were college students, and I had been one recently enough to know what they needed.

"Is there more than one *Norton Anthology of English Literature?*" a student in a zipped-up fleece asked. "Because this doesn't look right."

"Yes. What class do you need it for?"

"English."

"I figured . . . but what are you studying?"

"Oh, eighteenth-century lit. Which is what this is supposed to be. But why isn't Blake in here?" I smiled. English literature didn't speak to me, generally, but I could understand Blake's visions.

"He's in the next one, the Romantic one, not the Restoration one."

"Do you have that one?"

"No. But I have *Blake's Complete Poetry & Prose*. That should have what you need in it . . ."

It went on like that for the rest of the day. Even though I felt like an imposter, someone pretending to be a street vendor, customers treated me like the real thing, so I ran with it. Alojzy had penciled prices onto the first pages of his books—this seemed to be standard on West Fourth Street—so I knew what to charge. I tried to make a record of everything I sold, like Mendy did, as well as the prices to get a sense of what would needed replenishing and how to price books in the future.

The day followed the same ebb and flow as the day I'd spent with Mendy. The slow uptick of the morning followed by the lunchtime rush, the afternoon lull, and then the after-work rush. The other booksellers were accustomed to this flow, and planned their days accordingly.

Working a table on my own for the first time was no small task, and I was already tired by the time the lunchtime rush ended, and exhausted after the after-work crowd. In just six hours, I'd made sixty-two dollars. Since I didn't know how much Alojzy had paid for the books, I couldn't know how much was profit. Still, it had been a good day, and I'd be back soon.

⊪∎

Andrew came by Becca's apartment the next evening, and we walked down to a lounge on Second Avenue. We got there before his friends and ordered a couple of craft beers. Andrew handed his credit card to the bartender when he came back.

"On me," he said.

"Thanks." We sipped in silence for a couple minutes. Down on the other end of the bar, three women in their midtwenties were laughing and drinking martinis. Their clothes and hair were done up for the night. They looked good.

"How the New York City girls treating you so far?" Andrew asked me.

"I haven't really been out socializing much since I've been here. I've been taking care of things. Family stuff, and business stuff."

"Yeah, I understand that," he said, though I could tell my vagueness was frustrating him. He tried again. "Becca said you had a girlfriend at school? Not still pining after her, are you?"

"Mariam? No. I mean, I liked her a lot, but we'd been broken up for a while when I left school. I've been through a lot since then. I don't think I was in love with her or anything. Though sometimes I do miss spending time with her." I didn't realize I'd missed her at all until I started talking. Even then, it was more nostalgia than ache. Time was twisted around in my mind, and I felt as if I'd seen Alojzy more recently than I'd seen Mariam. "She lived off campus, and we'd spend whole weekends in her room, smoking weed and listening to records. She was into all this old indie rock and drone stuff."

"Doesn't sound like too bad of a way to spend a weekend."

"It wasn't. But it was silly, just a college kid thing. Anyway, it seems like you and Becca are pretty happy."

"Yeah, man. I love your sister." He smiled. "I'm going to marry that girl." He finished his beer. "You and I are going to be brothers-in-law." He raised his beer, and we clinked glasses. "So you said 'business' stuff. Is it that thing you mentioned last night? What kind of a job was it?" It was true, we were going to be brothers, under the law. We were going to be family. He was making an effort to reach out to me, and I should reciprocate.

"It's more of a gig than a job. Pretty informal. But I'll be selling books downtown in the Village." It felt good to say that out loud, but I also knew I had to follow through, and really try my hand at running Alojzy's business. The two days I'd spent on the street so far were just a start.

"Like at one of the Barnes and Nobles?" he asked.

"No, used books."

"Ah, gotcha. You don't mind doing retail work?"

"No," I said, though I hadn't really thought of street vending as retail. It was, in a way, but I associated retail work with a shift and a manager. Selling on the street was more direct and independent than that. "It's honest," I said. "A straightforward transaction. I appreciate that."

"I used to work at my dad's hardware shop on Long Island, when I was in high school." This didn't quite fit with my image of Andrew.

"Your dad owns a hardware store? I thought he was a dentist or something."

"That's my stepdad. He's an orthodontist in Westchester. My dad owned a hardware store. Two locations, actually. My grandfather started the business. It got bought out by Home Depot a few years ago." He looked pensive for a moment, but then his usual goofy grin returned. "But I'll take what I do now over that kind of honest work any day. Even if they are working me to death. And even if it's not as honest.

"I didn't mean that as a dig . . ." He held up a hand.

"Look, I'm not stupid. We had to read Marx at Binghamton. I get it. The hardware—the hammers and screwdrivers and power tools—someone made all that somewhere, with labor. Taiwan, Vietnam, wherever. At the hardware store, we did add fictional value on top of that—it was capitalism—but you could still see the labor.

"What I do now, with these funds, is so divorced from any labor. It's mystical, it's black magic. It's not tied to anything. There's no labor. There are no hammers. Maybe these financial products started out as hammers a long time ago, but that's ancient history by the time they get to me. And sometimes . . . sometimes I have to push things even further. Abstract them further than is expected." I didn't quite know what Andrew meant by the last statement, but his tone made it sound like a personal admission of some kind.

"My dad, after he had to sell his store, he ended up getting hired by the Home Depot as an assistant manager. He thinks it's great. He got some money off the sale, his house in Great Neck is paid off, and now he gets a salary and benefits. But damn, he's sixty-three and selling hammers. He wears a nametag. I don't want to sell hammers on Long Island. Especially not for Home Depot. I want to do black magic and wear a dope suit and live in the clouds." I wondered how to take Andrew's use of the term "black magic." It seemed like he knew exactly what he was saying, and that he had made his bargain.

"Wolfie!" The shout from the door let us know that one of Andrew's friends had arrived. There would be no more talk of Marx or black magic.

"Sup, gentlemen?" the guy said, slapping Andrew five. He wore a similar polo shirt to Andrew's, but his was salmon instead of navy. He had a lot of gel in his hair.

"Hey, DC!" Andrew said. "This is Becca's brother, Izzy. Izzy, this is DC."

"Like the comic books," DC said. "Short for Dylan Cohen. But call me DC."

"Nice to meet you, DC," I said.

"Likewise, my man." He slapped me five too. "Let's order some shots." We all drank some Jägermeister.

"What do you do, Izzy?" DC asked. That was the reason I was here, at least in Becca's mind: to talk about my career and future with these guys.

"Izzy's starting a job as a bookseller," Andrew said, answering for me. "But like I mentioned yesterday, he's keeping his eye out for other stuff. Entry level in a good line."

"Right," DC said. "Bookseller? Is that like a bookie? I'll put two hundred on the Giants." He slapped me on the back. "But seriously, sales, that's good. You know, I can always use sales guys."

"What business are you in?" I asked. "What do you sell?" I wondered how abstracted it was, whether he was in the world of hammers or the world of derivatives.

"Real estate. The only real industry in New York." He took a big gulp of the beer that he had ordered to chase the Jäger. "The agency I'm with has a lot of properties in the East Village. That whole area was developed fifteen years ago, but that didn't quite go all the way to Avenue D, because people were scared to live by the projects. I get it; the projects are scary. I get scared there, late at night. But things are calmer now. There's more police, which is good, and everything is pretty safe." I was disgusted by the combination of privilege and weakness in this statement. Alojzy had always made it clear that if there were two sides, the police and anyone else, you sided against the police. Police were for people who were soft, who possessed property but couldn't protect themselves.

"So we've been buying up these places that were subsidized housing run by these shady nonprofits—halfway houses, single-room-occupancy-type places—and renovating them. We're not even messing with too many leases. We just get an interior decorator and furnish them ourselves. Then, we can rent them out short-term to people coming from overseas, or who are just in the city for an internship or something. It's good money. We can always use a sales agent."

"Thanks," I said. "But I'm not a licensed real estate agent or anything." I wondered where all the old men from the subsidized buildings went. All the men like Alojzy and Mendy, who lived alone and scraped by on their hustles.

"Oh, that's not hard. You just have to sit through a forty-hour class on ethics and stuff. Blah blah blah. Just a formality. And you can actually start working without your pocket card. We just call you an 'apartment shower' instead of an agent, and don't let you touch the contracts. And pay you less! Let me know."

DC's entrepreneurial hustle was inherited from the same type of Lower East Side street hustlers he was displacing. Just as Andrew's mystical moneymaking abilities, though purely materialistic in their aims, were descended from the skills of ascetic Talmud masters. Everything contained its opposite. Everything devoured itself. I wanted out of the cycle, but didn't see an exit. One thing was sure, though: I didn't want to take a job where I helped rich interns move into an evicted SRO.

Two more of Andrew's friends showed up. Jason was at the same investment firm as Andrew, Haber Simson Assets Management, and Allan was a friend of his who had just graduated from law school and moved to the city to start a job with a big firm. Someone ordered another round of drinks, and we moved to a booth in the back of a bar. DC showed off a new watch and everyone admired it. The watch did look cool. Solid gold, clean lines. The conversation turned to the luxury cars their bosses kept at their weekend houses, and my mind drifted off. I pored over Alojzy's sketchbooks in my mind.

"How about you, Izzy?" Allan asked me, abruptly trying to engage me in conversation.

"What's that?"

"What do you think of the Islanders' chances this year?"

"I . . . I don't know. I don't really follow sports."

"Oh, okay." He glanced at my Yankees cap and shrugged. I had failed to relate. He turned back to his friends. I leaned back in the booth and watched the four men joke and jostle each other. They had an easy banter between them, and I had trouble catching the rhythm of it. These guys were the group I was expected to be part of, but had never been able to fit into. My high school on Long Island had been full of guys like this. For years, I'd felt out of step, felt a burn of exclusion. I didn't know if it was their fault or mine. Maybe it was no one's fault, and I was just in the wrong place.

Now something was beginning to change in me, and I felt relief at not being one of the guys. Generations of struggle and study had resulted in what? More bankers, lawyers, and landlords? What did you get for all that effort and work? A gold watch? I finished my drink. More had appeared on the table. Andrew might become my brother, but I would not become like these guys. I would become something from an older time, when Jews were fiercer, gangsters like Benya Krik. Tough guys like Alojzy. If there was devouring to be done, I would devour myself. I was getting pretty drunk—the Jägermeister had hit me hard—but I knew my perspective was not merely alcohol induced. I didn't want to get a position at a firm of any stripe but to find my own way, in the streets.

"Hey," DC announced. "This place is kind of dead. Let's head downtown and find some action." Allan had to get home to his fiancée, but the rest of us piled into a cab. I let myself be swept along into the car.

DC knew a spot on the Bowery. In the old novels I read, the Bowery was bleak, full of the down and out. It had changed since then, but not as completely as I expected. Dark silhouettes milled about as we passed the illuminated windows of the Bowery Mission. We got out of the cab near a group of bundled-up men sleeping on cardboard on the sidewalk. A man in a filthy army jacket and knit cap approached DC, who still held his wallet after paying the cabbie.

"Hey, my man? Can you spare a couple bucks so as I could get something to eat?"

"Get lost, you damn bum," DC said, shoving his wallet into his pocket. "I work for this money." Andrew grinned. I wasn't sure if it was out of awkwardness, or if he was entertained by DC's cruelty. I was embarrassed by the situation, but I didn't say anything, and followed DC, Andrew, and Jason in through the door.

Inside the club, everything was new and shiny. Everyone was young, good-looking, and well dressed. I suddenly understood the phrase, "You look like a million bucks." Colored lights flashed. Bass thumped from the speakers. Laughter echoed off the walls. A drink appeared in my hand, and I stood in a corner and sipped it.

A woman in a sleeveless green dress danced up next to me. Her hair didn't move as she shook.

"Hey," she said. "You're Andrew and Jason's friend?" She gestured back to them at the bar.

"Hey. Yeah. You know them?"

"Sure do. I went to b-school with Jason. Stern." I knew that Stern was NYU's business school; their building faced West Fourth Street. "Are you in finance too?"

"No." She looked me up and down.

"Still in school?"

"No." I hesitated, then said, "I'm a street vendor."

"Okay. Neat." She looked at me like I was about forty bucks, and danced away.

I decided I needed to leave. This was the wrong place for me to be. I didn't have any animosity toward Andrew and his friends, except maybe DC, but that wasn't the issue. I was figuring out where I needed to go, what I needed to do. Following Alojzy's path, not these guys' paths. There was no point in hanging around and pretending just to placate Andrew and Becca, or my own conditioned sense of obligation.

Following that track, out of fear, had caused me to fail Alojzy when I was sixteen.

I put my empty glass on the bar. DC was busy flirting with a girl from Wisconsin, telling her he could help her find an apartment in the city.

"Harlem is totally safe now," he told her. "There's lots of great renovations up there." She looked skeptical.

Andrew and Jason were arguing about something at the bar. I was surprised at the intensity of the exchange, but I figured they were never not working, even when they were hanging out. I couldn't tell what the issue was because their discussion consisted of more numbers than words. At one point, I heard Jason shout, "The numbers don't add up, Andrew. They just don't add up."

"Hey man," I said, putting my hand on Andrew's arm. "I have to cut out. Thanks for the drinks. This was fun."

"Huh?" he shouted, overcompensating for the din of the room. "Where you headed? Aren't you coming back uptown with me?"

"No," I said. "I have to be somewhere else. I'll talk to you later."

Becca had told me I needed a job or structure to stay at her apartment. That was fair enough. But I didn't need to stay at her apartment. I belonged in my father's house. We were pretty far downtown. It would only be about a half-hour walk across town to the storage space. I could use the walk, and the fresh air, to sober me up.

After making sure I still had the key ring, I walked across Chinatown, stopping to buy a wax paper bag of greasy vegetable egg rolls from a late-night stand. A couple people were hanging around in the parking lot outside the storage facility, but no one was in the facility's hallways.

Entering Alojzy's unit, I locked the door behind me and lay down on the mattress. I thought about my evening with Andrew and DC, who were probably still drinking at the same club, or at yet another bar. I was supposed to be here, in the cold room with the mattress on the floor, alone with the books.

BOOK 2

Knickerbocker Avenue

9

THE NEXT DAY I left a voice mail for Becca, telling her that I was going to be working downtown full-time and crashing at an apartment in the back of the bookstore. It was essentially the truth, and I didn't want her or my mother to worry. Sleeping in the storage unit felt right. The simple living arrangement helped me feel ordered and undistracted. I had found Alojzy's world, even if I hadn't found him yet.

It was useful to wake up in the storage space on days when I was selling Alojzy's books. There wasn't really any money to be made in the morning hours, but it was necessary to get out early and get set up in your spot, so you'd be positioned for later in the day. My second day of selling Alojzy's books went as smoothly as the first. I stayed out for a good ten hours, packing up when Mendy did in the evening. The third day went the same way.

That night, I heard Zoya shouting at her girls in the corridor, and came out of my space to give her the envelope. It was still sealed; I hadn't looked inside it. Some messages were meant for me, and some weren't. I would have discipline. It had occurred to me that the note could actually be about me, asking Zoya to confirm that I had delivered an envelope as promised and unopened.

"Excuse me?" I said. "Ms. Zoya?"

"*Shto*? What? What do you want?" I held up the envelope.

"This is from Timur."

"Okay. Very good." She snatched the envelope from me, and didn't say anything else. She went back to supervising her girls sorting their T-shirts, but I was confident she would report back to Timur that I'd done as asked.

After that, the Russian girls looked at me with recognition, and were slightly less rude when I passed them in the corridor. I don't know if Zoya said anything about me, or if they just treated anyone who dealt with their boss with some measure of respect. Of course, she also could have told them to keep an eye on me, so she could report back to Timur about my behavior. Until I found out what happened to Alojzy, I couldn't trust anyone.

I went out every day, to establish myself on West Fourth Street. Soon I wasn't counting the days. It was like road hypnosis: I'd wake up, take out the cart, set up my table, and sell all day long, following the ebb and flow of foot traffic. Before I knew it, I was waking up the next morning, getting ready for another day.

I got to know the other booksellers on the street. There was Asher, who I'd met the first day, and his silent friend, Milton. They set up next to Roberto, who liked to play psychedelic rock on a tape deck and smoke weed out of a one-hitter under his table. There was Steve Lesser, a proud Vietnam vet. Milton was a vet too, a Marine apparently, because Steve Lesser referred to him as "that stupid jarhead." There was the other Steve, who drove in from Jersey. All of the booksellers knew my father and treated me with respect, not like I was some green college chump, or an interloper in the trade. Most of these men appeared in Alojzy's sketchbooks, and as I met them, it felt like the books were coming to life.

I asked each of the booksellers about Alojzy. They all had stories about him, generally of the type that Mendy had told me. He sounded tough in all of them, even like a hero in some. Once, he saved a woman from a purse snatcher. Another time, he found a fifty-dollar bill inside a book he'd bought for fifty cents from a homeless man; unable to find the man to pay him back, he bought two cases of beer for all the homeless guys and street vendors. In other stories, he sounded like a bully. He'd apparently once roughed up Asher for setting up in his spot. The booksellers all called Alojzy "Al," and I started to think of him that way too.

None of them knew anything about where he'd gone. This wasn't to say they didn't have ideas.

"He went to California," Steve Lesser said. This made sense; Alojzy had sent postcards from out there, and often spoke of going "west."

"Florida. I'm sure it was Florida," the other Steve said. "But he got hurt down there. Maybe he died down there."

Hafid just said, "He went away."

"Poof," Roberto agreed, "Al was gone without a word. I don't know where. Did you talk to Mendy?"

I got to know some of the other park fixtures as well. The hot dog vendors, the pot dealers, the homeless people. Some of the homeless people, like a sweet middle-aged woman name Sonya who had once been a chef, were cool, but just had substance issues that kept them on the street. Others were so crazy they couldn't string a full sentence together. They all knew us though, and we knew all of them. They'd pause in the middle of their rants to nod hello.

The area was heavily policed. There were beat cops all over the place, and even some undercover cops, running around playing their spy games. Mendy said they had to justify all the Homeland Security money they'd received. There were guys who acted more like undercover cops than the undercover cops, but were actually only plain-clothes NYU security guards. Even though NYU was in the middle of the city, not in the middle of nowhere like Oberlin, the administration wanted to form a bubble of safety for the students.

A rotating cast of musicians, acrobats, and dancers performed in the park for tips from tourists. One lean old man played a tenor saxophone in the northeast corner of the park, Broadway tunes over a prerecorded string backing. He reminded me of my father's friend

Kurban Vileshchay, who used to play on the Q and N trains. Kurban had been on my mind recently because he appeared in one of Alojzy's sketchbooks.

The first time I met Kurban was when he pushed his way from the previous subway car into the one where my father and I were sitting. Back then, people passed between cars all the time; it wasn't a big deal. The police had only just started to give out tickets for stuff like that. With one hand, Kurban pulled a luggage cart behind him, which held a Casio keyboard blasting an auto beat and chord progression. With his other hand, he held a large wooden flute to his lips. The music was already playing when Kurban came through the doors; there must have been a moment when he was playing in the space between cars, for nobody except the tunnels to hear.

When Kurban saw my father, he nodded in recognition, but he kept playing, and didn't come greet us until the song was finished and he had collected his hat-full of dollar bills and coins.

My father introduced me proudly to Kurban as his son.

"What kind of instrument is that, Mr. Vileshchay?" I asked.

"This, my young friend, is a balaban. I carved it myself from a single piece of mulberry wood."

"I know mulberry," I said. "There is a big mulberry tree on Kings Highway." The branches were too high for me to reach, but my father had lifted me up on his shoulders, and I had eaten until I was sick.

"Yes," said Kurban, "I know that tree well. It has white berries."

"Yeah!"

"The white berries are much more delicious than the red ones. Well, gentlemen, I bid you a safe journey." The little man tipped his cap, and crossed through the door into the next car. Through the windows, we could see Kurban playing his song, but we couldn't hear him. Then he moved forward and we couldn't see him anymore either.

I wanted to hear Kurban's balaban again. I wanted to taste mulberries, especially the sweet white ones. Mulberries would be in season in a couple months, sometime in May. I hoped I would find Al by then.

|▌▐■

During the first week or so of selling, I gave in when people would ask for discounts. My patience was soon expended. I asked myself if Al would let these people take money from his pocket, and the answer was hell no. If they were going to waste my time, and tear me away from my reading, the least they could do was pay full price. By the beginning of my second week on the street, I was done providing discounts. They could take my price or leave it.

Over this time, I gradually adapted to spending my days out on the street. I was like an abandoned house cat learning to hunt and feed himself. It was a different way of interacting with the world, to claim part of the curb and sidewalk as your personal space, rather than just passing through it. When Becca and I moved to Long Island, the suburban kids made fun of our city kid habit of referring to the ground as "the floor." I never really lost the habit, and it made even more sense here, where the cement ground was the floor of my business, the place where I set my table. The buildings felt like flat walls. I was very conscious of the fact that customers were stepping onto my patch of the earth. I'd had a few jobs in high school and college—retail or library work—but in those situations I'd been standing in someone else's space, and hadn't claimed ownership of or responsibility for the work environment.

I not only became more conscious of the ground, but of the sky and air as well. When it would be light and when it would get dark. How gray the clouds had to be before I should worry. It was a pleasure to sit on the curb for an hour at a time, during the afternoon lull, and watch the clouds above the tops of the buildings. It wasn't like I was in the countryside, though. The exhaust from cars and trucks clogged the street. It was warm on my face and thick in my lungs. After a while, I began to think I could see the plumes of exhaust swirling off the blacktop.

Though I wasn't making any immediate progress in finding Al, I was on the right track. Not everything came quickly. Akiva didn't make it to *Pardes* until very late in his life's journey. He spent his younger life as a shepherd, before going away to study for twenty-four years. I was studying, in a way. I was gaining an understanding of how

Al experienced the world. I was sticking to the path he'd cut. I was maintaining his presence on the street. Maybe these were my shepherd days. Either way, it felt right.

Sometimes I felt more like Akiva's wife, Rachel. I could often see myself on both sides of the same story. Rachel had given up luxury and class position to marry Akiva, because she believed in him when no one else did. The whole time he was studying, she waited for him to come down the road. When he finally came home after twelve years, because he missed her, he overheard her telling a neighbor she wouldn't mind if he spent another twelve years studying, if that's what he needed to do. Akiva turned right back around, and studied for twelve more years. I imagined that Al might visit West Fourth Street, but not be able to show himself. Maybe he already had. It was important that he see me holding our position on the street, even if I didn't see him.

Still, I found myself looking longingly down the street for a familiar face. I put off calling Becca, but half hoped she would wander by one day and find me working. She would see me differently, out on the street. A girl I'd gone to high school with stopped and bought a book from me one day. Something by Ayn Rand, I think. The girl, who was going to college in the city, looked at me like she thought she knew me, then shook her head. Context clouded her recognition. Every day, I began to recognize more and more of the people coming down the street. Regular customers, regular browsers, regular passersby. Other street vendors and street people. But I was still watching and waiting.

| ▮ ▮ ▮

I tried to make sense of when and how Al had gotten involved with selling books. He had been selling out here consistently for a while. West Fourth Street appeared in all but one of the sketchbooks. That one featured the dead soldier, the docks, and many scenes of war.

It was hard to get a clear account from the other booksellers of when Al had come down to the street, but he was there before Hafid, who had been selling for about three years. Mendy had known Al for at least six or seven years, possibly more, but he had met him when he was selling art books with Goldov. They primarily sold down in SoHo, so Mendy wasn't sure when Al had actually started selling on West Fourth Street. And of course, Al came and went at different times. All I knew for sure was that he had sold art books with Goldov for a while, then gradually ended up selling his own paperbacks on West Fourth Street. He must have dabbled with bookselling long before that, though, because I remembered the boxes of hardcovers in his Sheepshead Bay apartment. Was he already in business with Goldov then? I didn't think I'd ever met the man as a kid.

Al's Sheepshead Bay apartment had been filled with boxes of other things besides books. Cigarette cartons. Knicks jerseys that were clearly counterfeit, even to my inexperienced eye. A crate of etrogs one autumn, each one carefully wrapped in newspaper. Whenever I asked what something was, the answer was "merchandise." One time, he had a plastic postal crate filled halfway to the top with subway tokens. This was during the interstitial time, when MetroCards existed but turnstiles still took tokens. They were gold, with five-sided holes cut out of the middle. There must have been a thousand tokens in the crate. It was like a treasure chest.

Even when Al lived with us on the Upper East Side, he'd occasionally bring "merchandise" home to the house. He often had a straight, if temporary, job, and when he did he kept the hustles to a minimum. He was good with his hands, and worked on and off as a house painter, mover, and welder. I wondered if I should—or could—learn to weld. Reshaping metal at will seemed magical. It was also a good, solid way to make money. Al never got a steady welding job—he blamed it on the nepotism and cronyism of American unions, a view that also made him skeptical of the Solidarity movement in Poland—but he'd get on a project now and again. He worked on the subway tracks one year, though it was as an outside contractor, not an MTA employee.

Between jobs, Al would get up to his hustles, and bring things into the apartment. One time he brought home two bronze eagles. They were over a foot tall, perched with their wings half spread. They looked just like the eagle on the quarter. My mother flipped out when she saw them, screaming at him to get them out of the house.

In retrospect, Al—or someone he knew—had stolen them from a flag-pole base in Central Park with a hacksaw. This was an egregious and stupid theft of city property. Then, I was only five or six, and was under the impression that the birds had flown away from the park and come to live with us. Becca and I bickered over what to name them, eventually settling on the compromise that we each got to name one. She named hers Joey, and I named mine Sinbad. Al warned us not to mention the birds to anyone, and after a few days they were gone. Becca told me they had flown south for the winter. Thinking back on it, I wondered if Al sold them for scrap, or to a collector who valued them for what they were.

| ▮ ■

Toward the end of the second week I was out selling, I bought a bag of weed off a Rasta in the park named Malachi. I knew enough by then to know that he was an actual pot dealer and not an undercover cop. Sonya and her boyfriend Lionel bought from him. They were mainly drunks, but they would get messed up on anything that didn't require a needle. When he wasn't selling drugs to NYU students and teenagers who came off the PATH train, Malachi would stand around and extoll the virtues of an all-raw diet. I hadn't gotten high since I'd been in New York. I didn't really have a desire to smoke, but getting high had been a central habit for a quarter of my life, and I felt weird not getting high for this long.

Because I was a recognized bookseller, Malachi offered me a twenty sack for fifteen, which sounded like a good deal. "The man in the street must look out for the man in the street," he said, "no?" I gave the old dread my three fives, expecting him to hand me a baggie in return. Instead, he nodded at a kid on a bike, who took off toward Sixth Avenue. I asked what was up, but Malachi said, "Have patience now." A few minutes later, the cyclist returned. "Ah," said Malachi, "here is Merlin now." I shook hands with Merlin, and he slipped the baggie into my hand.

I smoked some of the weed in the storage space that night, out of a Diet Coke can, after stuffing the gap under the door with rags. Expecting it to be shit weed, I smoked a couple bowls in quick succession. It wasn't bad weed at all, just slow and creeping, and twenty minutes after I smoked up, I was tweaking out and becoming very paranoid. The fear was physical. It constricted and twisted my skull. I deeply regretted the decision to smoke, and wished that the feelings would end. I felt like I was peaking higher than marijuana alone could account for. Maybe the acid thoughts that had been receding to the back of my mind had trailed out under the influence of the weed. The ditch weed I'd smoked in New Mexico hadn't affected me like this, but the combination of stronger, chemmy weed and being in the pressurized environment of New York City pushed things to another level.

I convinced myself that the facility staff had smelled the weed through the vent, and had called the cops to come get me. They would throw all Al's stuff in the street; when he came back, he would be angry that I had gotten all his property destroyed. It occurred to me that, as it was, when Al did come back, instead of being proud of me, he might be angry that I had taken over his business. Then I started thinking, out of nowhere, that some men my father had robbed would come looking for him, and kill me when they found me in his place. I stayed up all night, cowering in the corner of the storage space with Al's sawed-off rifle in my arms. After locating and oiling the stiff release latch, I managed to remove and load the magazine.

I finally came down and passed out around five a.m. When I woke up it was close to nine, which was much later than I went out selling. Rushing to get the rig together, I kept mixing up the boxes and tying the knots wrong. Finally, I gave up, and crawled back into bed. In the afternoon, I flushed the rest of the weed down the toilet. I was done with that shit. It hadn't been fun, and even if it had been, it couldn't cost me any more days of selling. Selling books was my job now. Al was no saint, not by a long shot, but his hustle didn't allow room for this kind of nonsense and wasted time. I needed to stop fucking around.

❘❚❚■

I stopped by Becca's apartment to take care of a few things: picking up my belongings, showering, e-mailing my mother. Knowing I'd be gone before Becca returned in the early evening, I went in the late afternoon and left her a note telling her I stopped by and thanking her for letting me crash there. Even so, I felt like a burglar, moving through her empty, luxurious apartment. I didn't belong there, and I left quickly. From then on, I settled for washing up in the industrial sink at the storage facility, at night when no one was around.

As the days and weeks rolled on, I got deeper into my selling routine. It was best to leave the storage space at seven thirty a.m., because that got me through the streets just before rush hour, and gave me time to set up before the sidewalk got crowded with people heading to work and class. From the diagrams in Al's sketchbooks, I learned the best way to set up my table. These sketchbook details contained a lot of information. Al's arrangement was generally maintained in my setup, but I focused on fiction more heavily than he had. It was important to keep a box of duplicates and second-line stock open under the table, so I could fill gaps right after I made a sale. There was no value in empty table space. I determined how to make the most of the flow of the day; I knew when to straighten up and when to wait, when to make sure I had change, when I could take a bathroom break, and when there was money to be made.

I started to get a sense of the flow of the week as well, and discovered that Thursdays are the best weekdays to sell. They're the last full day of NYU classes, so the students are up and about and need schoolbooks, but it's the end of their week so they're more impulsive with their spending. Fridays are the worst; the students are hungover, and the weekend tourists and brunchers haven't rolled in yet. My selling days were often decided by the weather forecast, but if there was a chance to go out on a Thursday or on the weekend, I didn't miss it.

The longer I spent on the street, and the more I started learning how to make money out there, the more I began to see that buying was as much a part of the game as selling was. You had to constantly replace the stock you sold with similar material, so you didn't lose sales due to a lack of inventory. If I wanted to succeed in this hustle—and I did, if only to show Al that I could—I needed to be working both ends. I wanted to contribute, so Al would find that his business had thrived, not been depleted in a closeout sale.

Over the course of two weeks, I looked through all of Al's boxes and took notes, so I had a pretty good idea of what he had in back stock. During this inventory, I found Al's cash stash, which was about sixteen hundred dollars. Wondering why he hadn't taken it with him when he fled, I initially took this as a troubling sign. But knowing Al, he probably had multiple cash stashes. I used the money to buy books from people who approached me on the street. These were just loans for working capital; as soon as I recouped the money, I paid it back to Al's shoebox bank. Pretty soon, I had my own small bank too.

The booksellers were generally pretty protective of their wholesale sources, and I didn't try to develop my own connection. I didn't have room to both bring in a whole big haul of books and keep living in the storage space. Besides, I didn't know how long I'd be doing this; hopefully Al would reappear, or I'd at least get a lead on him, soon enough. So I stuck with smaller street buys.

The first person I bought from was Eye. He approached me after I'd been selling for a couple weeks.

"Hey, Baby Edel," he said, dropping a bag of books at my feet.

"What do you want, Eye?" I didn't appreciate his condescension.

"I got some stuff here I would normally sell Edel. Thought you might buy it instead." He showed me a bag of books, all of which fit in the general "Philosophy/theory/religion" category.

I had no idea where he got them from, but most of them were titles I had been selling.

"I know who buys what," Eye said, noting my surprise at the relevance and quality of the books. "And these here are Edel books."

"Okay," I said. "What do you want for them?"

"Your pops gives me two bucks apiece for these."

"No he doesn't. Fifty cents apiece." Some of the books would sell for as little as three or four dollars, and I doubted Al's markup was less than fifty percent. The sales had to be profitable enough to make up for all the time you worked, on the street and in storage, without making sales.

"Hey now," Eye said. "Hey now." We settled on a dollar per book.

Eye was a semiprofessional—books were one of his established hustles, along with helping unload newspapers for newsstands, selling MetroCard swipes at the West Fourth Street subway station, and a few other things—but other street people would come by with random books. A lot of them were junkies. They'd find books in the trash, boost them from Barnes and Noble, or sneak them off of coffee shop tables, and bring them by Fourth Street. The asking price was always based on the cost of a bag of dope in the projects on Avenue D—the dealers in Washington Square Park didn't really mess with heroin or crack—never the actual value of the book, so you could occasionally come away with a good deal. That being said, nine times out of ten it was a waste of time, because junkies are irrational and because they would usually only come around with three or four books at a time, sometimes only one or two.

A few days after I first bought books from Eye, a tall junkie in a formless blue polo shirt three sizes too big for him flipped out on me when I wouldn't give him twenty bucks for a shoebox full of Louis L'Amour books. I tried to explain that people didn't really read cowboy books in New York, so I didn't want them, and even if they were better titles I couldn't pay more than five dollars for a small box of mass-market paperbacks. I could only charge about two fifty for most mass-market crime and romance novels.

"Do you think I'm some kind of hick?" he asked. "I been in these streets for years. Years and years." He started ripping handfuls of pages out of the Louis L'Amour books and throwing the pages in the air. I was disoriented by the paper fluttering back down, and afraid that after he was done tearing the books apart, he'd turn on me. In the end, he lost interest and tromped off in search of a fix.

||■

Wednesday of my third week on the street was spent preparing stock. I sorted the boxes—checking which categories were low and what common titles were missing, and replenishing them from books in storage—as well as newly purchased stock. After restocking the street boxes, I went ahead and loaded and tied up the cart, so when I woke up at seven on Thursday morning, all I had to do was hit the can and get dressed, and I was ready to go.

Mendy was already on the street when I arrived. After setting up my card table and asking Mendy to keep an eye on it, I ran over to a deli on Broadway and bought hot tea and a butter roll for breakfast, macaroni salad and a Diet Coke for lunch, and a cream soda for Mendy. He hadn't asked for the soda, but the sugar was about all that kept him going through the day, and it was the only nice thing I knew how to do for him.

When I returned, there was another table next to mine.

"Whose stuff is this?" I asked Mendy, handing him the can.

"Thanks. It's Asher's. NYU is having some sort of event out in front of Stern, and security kicked him out of his usual spot. He threw a fit about it, but he gave up and now he's shifting down here for the day."

Asher soon came down the street with the rest of his boxes and set up, slamming his books on the table with fury.

"What's your name, kid?" he demanded. I didn't answer. Asher and I had spoken several times. It wasn't my problem that he was too far gone to remember me from one interaction to the next. His permanently dilated eyes made it clear that he'd done a lot more acid in his life than I had. He made me glad I was done with hallucinogens.

"That's Izzy, Asher," Mendy said. "You know that. Al's kid."

"Right. Right. Yeah. Listen, Izzy, I'm going to tell you just what I told Mendy: these NYU security forces, they have a three-month plan to drive all of us off the street. One by one. Inch by inch. You see how today, they drove me down here. Eventually, they'll drive us all into the river. Or lock us up on trumped-up charges. We lower the property value. That drives down tuition, everything." He was waving his arms. His voice was getting louder and louder. "They waited until I didn't have Milton with me, 'cause they know Milton was forward recon—a trained killer—and they're scared of him. He had to go to the VA hospital today. But now that we've ceded space, we'll never get it back. They have us over a barrel. Jackbooted bastards. They're gonna replace us all with vending machines." Some of what Asher said made sense, and some of it seemed insane. It was difficult to sort through it.

Midmorning, Asher put a heavy arm around my shoulder and directed my attention to a police car parked on Washington Square East, halfway up to Washington Place.

"You see how they're watching me there?" The cops were facing away from us. I couldn't see the one on the passenger side from where we were standing, but the one in the driver's seat was eating a large sandwich.

"I don't know," I said. "I guess they could be." The morning had been pretty good so far. I made a few early sales, and an NYU student who'd just been expelled—he didn't say for what, but he reminded me of myself a few months earlier—sold me a whole crate of good books for twenty-five bucks. He didn't try to negotiate. They were mostly staples, Hegel and Locke and the like, and all in mint condition. You could tell he'd never opened any of them. I wished him luck.

"You're damn right they could be!" Asher shouted. "In fact, they are. They always got their eyes on me, those bastards. Like this one time I was walking right down here by Sheridan Square when this cop starts following me on his little scooter.

"I had a kitchen knife on my belt, in a sheath I made for it. The cop says, 'What you got there?' I say, 'You know what I got here. You don't protect me so I protect myself.' He starts grabbing at my knife and manages to pull it out. I say, 'You got what you wanted, now why don't you leave me alone now?' But he did not. He grabbed me, slammed me against the wall, handcuffed me."

"Damn," I said. Asher ignored me and kept talking, his eyes focused on a larger, invisible audience.

"I seen him the other day when I stepped out of the hotel where I live. He says, 'You got any more knives for me, Asher?' I say, 'I'm watching you, you bastard. I know what you are doing, and I will burn your ass.'"

Asher started up again during the lunchtime rush, when an NYU security guard approached the table. It pissed me off, not just because it was annoying to me personally, but because I was afraid he would drive away customers. I wondered how Roberto and the Steves put up with this every day. Though, to be fair, Asher usually seemed more calm and coherent. Being displaced from his spot had disturbed him.

The guard that set him off, Chalbi, wasn't even a bad guy. A lot of the guards were assholes, wannabe cops, and got off on harassing homeless people and booksellers, but Chalbi wasn't like that. Mendy had introduced us a couple weeks back. He only worked as a security guard so he could take NYU classes for free, and when he came by it wasn't to bother us, just to check out what books we had.

"Lay off of Chalbi, Asher," Mendy pleaded, "he's just looking at the books."

"Yes, lay off me, please," Chalbi said. "I'm not even on duty."

"No, no, no." Asher slammed his fists down on his table, knocking some books to the ground. The one person browsing at his table backed away. "They are all, always, on duty. 'Off duty' is just a trick. They were on duty this morning, when they wanted to evict me from my spot. But when they come down to spy, suddenly they're 'off duty.' Well, I'm always on duty. So they better not fuck with me again. One day, I will burn all their assess. All of them!"

Chalbi shook his head and walked off. I sold a customer a Chuck Palahniuk book. The guy had his shirt collar up over the collar of his blazer. He rolled his eyes toward Asher as I gave him his change, grinning at the nut. I didn't know what to do. I didn't want to side with Asher's paranoid tirades, but I didn't want to enter into a secret alliance with a yuppie against another street vendor.

"It's in my blood," Asher shouted. "You go over to Warsaw, you'll see there's a big statue of the underground who killed collaborationist police during the war. That was my relatives! There should be a statue of me like that. In fact, there will be, after I sue the city and the university. They'll have to put one up. Solid marble. It'll say: Asher will burn your ass."

Spending the day next to Asher disturbed me, not just because he was loud and annoying, but because he seemed like a parody of Al. I didn't think Al would deal well with being forced out of his spot. He had his own stories of arguing with the police. Of talking his way out of open-container and parking tickets. Of decking a cop in a pizza place in Canarsie and not getting arrested. He never carried a kitchen knife, but I remembered him sitting on a bench uptown, flicking a straight razor open and closed. It was a cherished memory. I wanted to be confident and fearless, sitting in the city with a weapon in my hand. But until I heard Asher ranting, it had never occurred to me to wonder why Al was holding a razor in his hand.

Al had his own tales of the Polish resistance too. He didn't talk much about his own childhood in Poland, but he spoke proudly of Mordechai Anielewicz and the *Żydowska Organizacja Bojowa*. He spoke of how easy it was to make petrol bombs, and how people should not be afraid to defend themselves. I hoped that when I saw Al again, he would seem dignified, and not absurd like Asher.

By two thirty, the lunchtime rush had ended and Asher had tired himself out. The block was peaceful. I took out my macaroni salad and a plastic fork and began to eat. The few students walking down the street were all far away. They didn't want anything from us. There was a bit of breeze, strong enough to soothe, but not so strong it chilled you.

While I was eating, a girl appeared at the table. Her long black skirt billowed, and I had the feeling the wind had blown her up against the table, like it did with plastic bags and other refuse sometimes. She looked down at the table, but her eyes didn't focus on any book. She looked familiar to me. Maybe I'd seen her around the street. No, I would've remembered more distinctly if I had, I thought, because there was something very striking about her. She was beautiful, actually, though not in a contemporary way. Sort of like a picture of Sarah

Bernhardt in a book I hadn't managed to sell. Not because she looked like Sarah Bernhardt but because she looked like a black-and-white photograph.

From her gaunt face, long black sleeves, and nervous demeanor I figured she was a junkie working up the nerve to sell me something. But this girl wasn't holding anything to sell. She looked more like a ghost than a junkie, truth be told.

It came to me. The girl didn't just look like a black-and-white photograph; she looked like a black ink drawing on white paper. The girl was somewhere in Al's sketchbooks. Had Al just seen her on the street before? Or was she connected to him in some way? I tried to remember where in the sketchbooks she had appeared.

As I studied her, her stomach growled audibly. I grinned. She blushed with genuine embarrassment, and tried to hide her face in a delicate hand.

"Are you hungry?" I asked her. It was an unusually direct thing for me to ask a stranger, but I had to engage her if I was going to find out what she had to do with Al.

"Yes. It seems so." She spoke each word deliberately. She didn't sound like a junkie.

"Would you like some of my food?" I held out my plastic container of macaroni salad.

"Oh, no, I couldn't."

"It's okay, I have more than enough."

"That's kind of you. But no, my stomach . . ."

"It's only macaroni salad. I don't eat rich foods. It's good. Just macaroni, prepared as a salad with shredded vegetables."

"I could eat something like that, I think. Is it kosher?" The question took me aback. "Not that it matters, really," she said. "I just wondered because you have a beard and a yarmulke." I'd taken my baseball cap off earlier in the morning since it wasn't very sunny, and after a few weeks of street life, my beard was pretty full. "Surely you don't eat treif food?"

"It's not certified kosher, there's no *hechsher*. But it's vegetarian. So it's not treif either. Have some."

She ate the whole container, thanked me, and then, before I realized it, she was gone. I cursed myself for letting her disappear without asking her anything.

When I returned to the storage unit that night, I searched through the sketchbooks looking for the girl's picture. She wasn't in any of the West Fourth Street scenes. I found her in Al's study of Galuth's masterpiece. The girl on the street was the same girl who'd been thrown from the tracks of the Sea Beach Railway in the 1920s.

All sorts of ideas went through my mind. Was the girl actually a ghost? Or maybe she'd never lived before, was conjured from imagination by R. Galuth, and had just now walked out of the painting? Did such things happen? Had I finally had a mystical experience, and encountered someone from the other side?

Of course, there were other explanations. My father could have seen the girl on West Fourth Street, as I'd first suspected, and then grafted her face onto the study. Or it could just be a coincidence. But no, I knew there were no coincidences. All things meant something, even if the meanings were hidden.

10

TIME PASSED QUICKLY ON the street. I blinked the third day, and when I opened my eyes again I'd been selling for almost a month. I felt badly for not seeing Becca, but before coming to New York, we hadn't talked more than once every month or two anyway. Had it been like this for Al these past years? He'd think of sending a postcard, but then months and years of work would pass without him doing it? I was afraid that if I wasn't careful, five years would pass, and I'd still be on the street, unable to remember how or why I came down here.

Although I enjoyed frequent downtime on the street itself, the long days, manual labor, and responsibility of managing every aspect of the small business were physically and mentally exhausting. I had never worked so hard in my life. My muscles grew from pushing the cart and lifting the boxes. If I had extra time at night, I read a bit of one of the crime novels stacked by the bed. These books were lighter than the texts I'd been reading before, and easier for my tired mind to keep up with. I was also intrigued because they were evidently what Al read. They were his entertainment, but they also related to his code, to his worldview. I read a couple short ones, then tucked into a tome called

Knickerbocker Avenue, by Sal Di Conte. According to the foreword of a newer reprint I later found, Di Conte was the pen name of a woman named Leah Schkolnik, who also wrote private detective books under the name Ricky O'Banion.

Knickerbocker Avenue was an epic about the rise of a Brooklyn gangster named Arturo Costa. At the beginning of the book, Arturo is a poor, good-hearted kid—a former altar boy, in fact—growing up in Bushwick, Brooklyn, in the '60s. His father is killed in an accident at the Fresh Pond Freight Yard when Arturo is young, and as soon as he's old enough Arturo drops out of high school to help support his mother and sisters. He gets a job at a bakery, rising early six days a week to knead bread and cannoli dough.

Despite being surrounded by books, I actually read less than I used to. Most nights I was so tired from working that I only got through a few pages before I lay down and closed my eyes. As I fell asleep, my mind flipped through the lists of sold stock, and my hands imagined they were placing books on the table.

Of course, becoming a bookseller was not supposed to be an end in itself, but a means to connect with Al. On the days I didn't go out on the street because of the weather, I looked through his sketchbooks, trying to make some sense of his life and disappearance by studying the images. It was like scripture to me. I could see the simple level, the *peshat*, for myself. The more I looked, the more I began to see the *remez*, the hinted meanings. Some things made more sense in context. That was called the *deresh*, and the more time I spent in the streets the more I would understand the context and references. What I was really after was the *sod*, the hidden meaning. The secrets. I had no idea how to get at that.

There were some clues, though, like the woman from the Galuth painting who'd appeared on West Fourth Street. When I asked around, no one knew who she was. I was afraid that I wouldn't see her again, and that I had missed an opportunity. I kept my eye out for her on the street.

Goldov appeared in the sketchbooks a surprising number of times. Apparently he and Alojzy were deeply involved. I didn't know how

much of Goldov's importance was tied to his connection to Galuth, or
vice versa. My father had spent a long time creating detailed studies
of Galuth's paintings, especially the "masterpiece," where the poor
young woman was thrown from the train tracks. Goldov appeared
outside of the gallery too, though. There were times when Goldov also
appeared with Roman and Timur, and even one time when the dead
soldier appeared with all three of them.

The dead soldier was obviously key. He appeared in the sketchbook
more than anyone else, with the exception of my mother, and in every
setting and situation. Since he appeared in both Israel and New York,
I wondered where Al had met him.

On closer inspection, I discovered Hebrew words worked into the
background texture around one of the images of the dead soldier.
The picture also included Timur and Roman. The soldier stood next
to them on the dock, upright but clearly dead. In the wood of the
dock itself were the words אני מצטער. I was used to the book form
of Hebrew, not curving script, but I made out the letters. The first
word meant "I," but I had to check the adjective in a Hebrew–English
dictionary. "Sorry." "I am sorry." Had the dead man committed some
transgression or error? Was Al sorry for what had happened to the
man? Or for something Al himself had done to the man? I went back
to other images of the dead soldier, and found the same words in three
or four drawings.

The dead soldier appeared in the notebook alongside Roman and
Timur in three different places, including the dock picture, so he had
to be connected to them in some way. They appeared several times
without him too. Roman and Timur were clearly important figures
in Al's life, and I had to learn more from them. They were holders of
secrets. I had to study them like a text to try to find the *remez* and the
sod beneath their statements and assignments.

Around this time, Zoya, the T-shirt tsarina, knocked on the door of
my storage unit. She held a cell phone in her hand.

"*Malchik*," she said. "You can do for me a favor." I didn't hear a
question mark at the end of the sentence.

"What kind of favor?" I asked. She handed me the phone.

"Hello?" I said.

"Izzy. Roman. You are well?"

"I'm fine. Yourself?"

"*Slushai*. I mean, listen." He had been talking to Zoya in Russian, and was grinding back into English. "There are some boxes in Zoya's possession which need storing. It is not prudent for her to hold them in her unit. Perhaps you could hold them in yours for few days?"

"Absolutely. I'm happy to help."

"Great." The phone went dead. Grabbing a luggage dolly, I followed Zoya back to her unit. Zoya wielded tremendous power over her girls, and I thought of her as a witch, but that was none of my business. I was happy to be able to help Roman and Timur, and work my way closer to the truth. There were three bankers boxes, taped up with packing tape. From the way the contents shifted when I loaded them on the dolly, it felt like they were full of paper files, like you'd find at a doctor's or lawyer's office.

I took them back to my unit and stacked them without looking inside, though I wondered what they held. Most likely it was evidence that needed to be hidden while the police searched a business connected to some crime, like Medicaid fraud. Or maybe they were stolen files being used to blackmail someone, or sink a lawsuit. It was exciting to participate in the hustle, but I needed to mind my business, to show Timur and Roman they could trust me. Even if I resealed the boxes, Zoya might be able to somehow tell that I had looked inside them. I didn't want Timur to have any reason not to trust me. A few days later, Zoya and a young Russian guy came and picked them up.

| | ∎

I kept watch for the girl from the Galuth painting, and when I saw her on the sidewalk, five days after her first visit, I was ready.

"Hey," I called, turning my back on the customer I'd been speaking with, and trying not to show how excited I was. She gave me a shy little wave, but kept walking.

"Come on over," I said. After a moment's hesitation, she complied.

"Hello again," she said warily.

"I was just about to eat lunch. Did you want to join me?"

"No, you don't have to keep—"

"It's no problem. You'd be doing me a kindness. I'd rather not eat alone."

"All right." She smiled, and came around the table to sit with me. "Thank you. I've been walking all day."

"To where?" I asked.

"Nowhere. Just around." I couldn't mention the picture in the notebook to her. If there was some hidden, even supernatural connection, I needed to figure it out before I spoke about it. And whether it really was something hidden or something mundane and coincidental, I didn't want to come on too strong and drive her off. As a result, we barely spoke after our initial exchange. After eating and sitting for a while, she abruptly rose to leave.

"Come see me again soon," I said. "When you want to sit and rest for a while."

She returned the very next day. On this visit, she told me her name was Rayna.

"The other men," she said, "they call you Izzy." She had heard me speaking with Mendy and Hafid.

"Yes."

"Is that your real name?"

"It's short for Isaac."

"Isaac is a better name. I will call you Isaac." I liked hearing her say my name.

She started coming by often, and sitting for longer and longer before she'd disappear. I rarely saw her leave, just like I rarely saw her approach. It was more that she'd fade into the air when I turned my back. I started buying extra food in the morning, just in case she'd show up. She liked bread and bananas.

I wanted to maintain a connection to her, in case she knew something about Al, or could lead me to someone who knew something. She was also very pretty. The drugs had killed my libido, but it was returning, and this was the first time since Mariam I'd found myself so strongly attracted to a woman. But I also just wanted to help her out; she didn't seem to have anywhere to go, or any way to support herself.

Rayna didn't speak much at first, other than to ask if she could help with anything. I showed her how to clean the books and straighten them on the table. Gradually, she got over her shyness, and she became more talkative. Her voice possessed a tinge that was familiar but from across a great distance. A perfume they didn't make anymore. It somehow reminded me of my mother's mother, who had died when I was a kid. As she started speaking more, I realized what it was: despite being so young, she had a slight Yiddish accent.

"Do you enjoy being around all of these books?" Rayna asked me one day, while she cleaned brown smoke off of book spines with rubbing alcohol.

"Yeah. I like them okay. They're my dad's, not mine, mostly. I'm selling them for him until he gets back. Have you ever met my father?" I'd been waiting for days to ask the question.

"He sold in this spot before me?"

"No." She shook her head. "The first time I saw you was the first time I came here." If Rayna had never been to West Fourth Street when Al was selling, he couldn't have sketched her face on the street. Maybe she really was the girl from Galuth's painting.

"Well, they're his books. I have to sell them for him until he gets back. I'm not attached to them. But I do like them."

"By my dad were a lot of books too." She had never mentioned anything about her background before.

"Yeah? Like these?"

"No. They weren't so colorful. And none had paper covers."

"What kind of covers did they have?"

"Black and leather mostly," she said. "Some of them were red, or green. But black mostly, brown and black."

"Were they novels?"

"I don't know."

"I mean, were they storybooks? Or scientific books? Did they have pictures?" Normally, I didn't ask so many questions, worried she would disappear if I said the wrong thing, but she intrigued me. I wanted to know more about her and where she came from.

"No. No stories. No science. No pictures. Law." Was her father a lawyer or judge, maybe? Between her Yiddish accent, her long sleeves, and her reluctance to eat treif meat, I gathered she was from an Orthodox household. So maybe law meant Talmud, and he was a rabbi. I wanted to ask more, but was interrupted by a customer interested in buying a fifteen-dollar Dalí book. Over the course of the past few weeks, I'd decided to make a go at the business and turn a profit, not just for Al's sake but so I could finally support myself. The guy didn't buy the book, and when I turned back around, Rayna was gone.

⁞ ❚ ▮

It rained the following day, so I didn't go out, and instead took care of a few things in the storage unit. I wondered about Rayna and hoped she wasn't out in the rain, although it wasn't my concern. Everyone had to look after himself. My mother and Becca barely knew where I was.

When the rain let up, I went out and ran a few errands. It had been a couple weeks since my brief conversation with Roman on Zoya's phone, and I didn't want to let Roman and Timur forget about me, so on my way back into the storage space I called Roman on the pay phone.

"Izzy," Roman said, curtly but not unkindly. "What can I do for you?"

"Nothing. I just wanted to check in. See, you know, if you'd heard anything about Alojzy."

"I am afraid not. But from Zoya I heard good things about you."

"I'm glad. If you ever need me for anything else . . ." I wanted Roman and Timur to see me as valuable and trustworthy so I could learn more from them.

"You would be willing to do some more serious tasks for us?"

"If you need me." I wanted him to understand I was serious about following in Al's footsteps.

"Very good. I will keep this in mind."

"And if you do hear anything about Alojzy . . ."

"Of course." He hung up. I was taken aback by the shortness of the call, and couldn't shake the feeling that Roman was obstructing me. But he had taken my call, and not rejected my offer outright. Roman was clearly the underling, Timur's lieutenant or aide, but I had to work my way up the hierarchy. How did Al fit into their dynamic? Was he a henchman like Roman? No, he was no one's dog. He was more independent than Roman. There were so many questions. But I needed to be patient, and keep working. Akiva studied for twenty-four years, but I had only been down on the street for twenty-four days. Answers would come. I would find Al.

I sat on the loading dock and read more *Knickerbocker Avenue*. Arturo idolizes the bakery's owner, the local mafia boss, Don Niccolo. He dreams of having the flashy life of Niccolo and his associates. What's more, he is enamored with Don Niccolo's daughter, Isabella. Niccolo takes a shine to Arturo, but advises him to stay on the straight path, so he can one day became a legitimate business owner, instead of a wise guy. Before Arturo decides what to do, he is drafted into the army, and sent to Vietnam in 1967.

| ▮ ▮

The rain lasted for two days. Rayna came by West Fourth Street the first day I was back out selling. She had been caught in the rain and now had a cold. I bought her a cup of chicken noodle soup, and gave her one of Al's old sweaters.

Her visits soon became a daily occurrence. She'd usually show up in the afternoon, after the lunchtime rush, and help me straighten and restock the table. We'd eat a late lunch on the curb, and she'd tell me the strangest and most wondrous things she'd seen in the city that day. Always, she focused on the present day, never again mentioning her father or speaking of things from her past.

Though I couldn't stop wondering about her past or her connection to the Galuth painting, her visits were about more than that. I hadn't realized how lonely I was, how badly I needed someone to talk to. It wasn't that I didn't have others in my life. Mendy was always kind to me, I'd shared many jokes with the other street vendors, and if need be Becca was just a subway ride away. Still, nothing compared to spending time with Rayna. At night, I kicked myself for not interrogating her about her connection to the sketchbooks, but when I was with her, those concerns disappeared. I was happy. Her visits were the highlight of my day, and I wasn't going to jeopardize them.

Rayna was only one of many faces in the sketchbooks, and I needed to find more of them. Waiting for them to appear on the street like Rayna had wasn't going to work. I'd been debating whether or not I should show anyone Al's sketches. They were his private thoughts and experiences, and when he returned, he might be upset to find out people had seen them. At the same time, the drawings contained clues to his disappearance, and showing them to people who might recognize something could help me find him.

Not wanting to lay Al's whole inner world bare, I chose one representative drawing, the picture of the dead soldier standing with Roman and Timur. The dead soldier was central and most recognizable in this picture. Having him in context with Roman and Timur might also prove helpful.

One morning, after we had set up, I showed Mendy a photocopy of the drawing. He studied it for a long time, taking off his glasses and holding the picture close to his face, but ultimately shook his head.

"No. I'm afraid I don't know him. Roman and Timur I've seen with your father, of course, but never that guy with the closed eyes."

"What you got there?" Eye asked, coming up behind us with a stack of books. Business had been good, and Eye was helping Mendy out frequently. I decided I might as well show him the picture too, since he was already looking at it, and because he seemed to know my father and most of the players in the street.

"A drawing of someone I'm curious about. Have you ever seen this guy?" I tapped my finger on the dead soldier. Eye scanned the drawing with his one functional eye, then turned away.

"Nope. Never seen any one of them."

"Now, Eye," said Mendy. "That ain't so. I know you've at least seen Roman, with Al at storage."

"I make it a point not to see anything that doesn't concern me," Eye said. It seemed that this was a sincere philosophy, not an oblique reference to any information. Eye, like many people on the street, was resigned to his condition. His life was hard, but the only alternatives he could imagine were worse. He'd been out here for years, and he didn't want to tempt fate by pursuing anything outside of his limited world.

  ‖ ∎

That Friday was extra slow, mainly because Steve Lesser, who set up at the corner by LaGuardia Place, was clearing out his stock. He was moving out to California, which was great for him, but he was selling all his paperbacks at two bucks a pop, or three for five, and undercutting everyone else's business. I had nothing to do but sit and read volume four of Ginzberg's *Fantasies of the Jews* and wonder if old Moses would have been better off marrying a Jewish girl, and, speaking of Jewish girls, when I'd see Rayna again. Hopefully she was okay. I hadn't seen her in four days and was getting worried. Normally no more than a day or two went by without her coming by the street.

Then, just as I was thinking about her, Rayna appeared at my table, like I had conjured her myself. She looked more disheveled than usual. Her blouse was wet with sweat, and there were dark circles under her eyes. Instead of greeting me, she asked, "Do you stay out here all night, with your books?"

"No," I said. "I pack the books up and take them to a storage space."

"What kind of place is a storage space?" This happened often, that she didn't seem familiar with a common term.

"It's a big closet, with a lock on the door. Inside a big warehouse."

"And you sleep there, too? With your books?"

"Yes, I have a little mattress, and I sleep on the floor, next to the books."

"Next to the books?" she asked. "Like you yourself are a book on a shelf?" Rayna was across from me, on the customer side of the table. It seemed like she wanted the barrier between us. Her questions were spoken eagerly, not conversationally, and I was becoming concerned.

"I never thought of it like that. But I suppose so."

"That sounds safe."

"It is safe. The walls are made of metal, and there are three locks on the inside of the door. Where do you sleep?" I had been wondering this for a while. She only had a few garments of clothing, and seemed to spend the whole day wandering the city. She shrugged and looked away. "You have somewhere to sleep, don't you?"

"Well, I sleep in a tree."

"A tree?" What did that mean?

"Yes, a tree. In the park, down there." She pointed east, toward Tompkins Square.

"There is a big branch that crooks downward, and has room enough for me inside it. I climb up after dark, and no one would know I was there. The police lock the gates, and I'm safe."

"How long have you been doing this, Rayna?"

"I've been out here about a month. I . . . I couldn't stay at my father's house."

"Where is your father's house?" I was afraid to push too hard, but it seemed like she wanted to talk.

"Boro Park. I lived in that house my whole life. But I couldn't live there any longer. It is a large house, almost like a mansion, and my whole family lives there. It is a *frum* and pious home. But there are secrets." She was speaking quickly, almost frantically. "It wasn't . . . it wasn't always nice there. I didn't want to live there anymore. I couldn't. I got on the D train, and rode until I crossed the bridge and came to Manhattan."

"I understand," I said. I didn't entirely follow why she had left home, and didn't necessarily need to know details she didn't want to share. But it was clear that she had run away from a bad situation, and didn't want to go back. I wondered if Al had seen her in Brooklyn; he had spent time in various parts of the borough. Or maybe the Jewish communities of Brooklyn were so inbred that the same faces appeared over and over. But then again, her account of her home was so strange, tortured, and timeless. The story didn't disprove any ideas I had about Rayna's origins, and her connection to Galuth's painting. Who knew when she'd run away, how long she'd been wandering?

"I'm sort of a runaway too," I said. Rayna smiled inquisitively at me.

"I thought your father was the runaway, and you are waiting here for him?"

"That's true too," I said. "It's my sister's house I ran away from." Rayna and I sat down on the curb, and I told her about Andrew and Becca uptown, and my mother and Bernie in New Mexico, and how I preferred to stay downtown by myself. I told her that I hadn't spoken to them for a while, but I was doing fine on my own. Rayna's mood lightened. She stuck around for the rest of the day.

I wasn't really a runaway, not in the way Rayna was. Though I kept meaning to call Becca or e-mail her from an Internet café, everything outside of my downtown world and search for Al had faded into the distance. The least I could do was send a postcard. I picked two out from the newsstand on West Third and Sullivan and wrote them both quick notes, explaining that I was fine but working a lot and didn't have a phone yet. I left the return address sections blank.

｜ ❙ ■

Rayna was quieter during her next visit. She had talked herself out the last time she was here. I didn't mind; it was nice to spend time with her, even if we weren't talking. I had sold a lot of books during lunchtime, and she helped me straighten up the table. In the afternoon, we split a bottle of lemon seltzer and some almond cookies. She didn't seem to want to leave, and stayed to help me through the evening rush.

When I started the slow process of packing up, Rayna became agitated. She pulled at her long hair, like she was trying to rip it out, and wrapped her arms around herself.

"It will be time for you to leave soon," she said.

"Yes. I'm afraid so." She looked scared. "You don't want to be by yourself, do you?"

"No." She shook her head. "It's not that I don't want to be alone. But I can't go back to the park tonight. I don't mind sleeping in the tree. But now there's a man who comes over the gate in the nighttime. He is too fat to climb the tree, but he stands at the bottom and grins up at me. It is a wicked grin. The past two nights he has done this. If he catches me, I'm done. If he tries to touch me . . . I'll . . . I'll . . ."

"It's okay," I said. I thought that I should give her a hug, but it didn't seem like she wanted to be touched by anyone just then.

"You don't have anywhere else to go?"

"No. Last night I didn't sleep at all. I walked around all night. Quickly, so no one could catch me. I'm very tired now. I can't walk around so quickly for another whole night. I know people sleep on the subway train, but I'm afraid."

"You think someone will bother you down there too?"

"No. Yes, I do, but it's not that. The subway is underground, and makes twists and turns. I know it's silly, but I feel that if I fall asleep, and don't see where I'm going, the train might go on a different track and carry me down to Sheol."

"Yes, I know. I often think the same thing."

"Don't tease." She looked wounded.

"I don't. I'm not. I can't see who's driving the train. It could be a devil. The ground could open up further, they've already opened it too far." The story we were telling each other was childish, but the fear was real, and this was the only way we could talk about it. But then, for all I knew, Rayna really was the ghost of a girl who died in 1920. Maybe her story was even worse than that. Who knew what terrible things had happened in her home. Maybe she really did run from demons who wanted to drag her down to the underworld. It didn't matter. Real or not, man or demon, I wouldn't stand by and let anyone take her.

"Come stay in my space," I said. "You'll be safe there." Saying these words made me nervous. Of course I wanted to protect Rayna. She was dear to me, and I wouldn't mind spending the evening with her.

But I'd never tried to protect anyone before, to take care of them and keep them safe, even for one night, which is what I was promising now. Al was a protector, not me.

"I don't know," Rayna said. I knew she liked spending time with me too, but that didn't mean she completely trusted me. Maybe she was right to be wary; if I was being honest with myself, I saw an opportunity here to learn more about Rayna, and her presence in the notebook.

"You see me," I said. "You know me." She was quiet for a moment, exploring my face with her eyes. Then she nodded.

"I need my bag," she said.

"Where is it?"

"Hidden in the tree branch."

"Go and get it. The fat man won't be there?"

"No. He comes very late. When it's very dark. It's safe in the evening still."

"Are you sure? I can pay Eye to watch the table, and go with you." She considered it for a moment, then shook her head.

"No, it's okay. It's only dusk. It's midnight that I'm afraid of."

"Fine. Then go and get your bag and come right back. And here." I handed her a twenty from my bankroll. "Go and get us some food. Some bread and good things for us to have for supper. Then come back here, and I'll have finished packing up. And you'll come back to my storage space with me and the books. I'll lock the door from the inside, and we'll be safe, and you can sleep."

Rayna was nervous when we first got into the storage space, looking over her shoulder and jumping at every sound, and I assumed it was because she was alone in private with me, a man she didn't really know very well. On the way back to the storage space, she told me she had shared a room with her sisters in Boro Park but had never been alone with any men other than male relatives or schoolteachers. I tried to give her as much space as I could, but as it turned out, she became calmer once I fastened the locks and came to sit beside her.

We shared a simple dinner off an upturned milk crate by lantern light, eating the bread, cheese, and hardboiled eggs she'd bought from the Korean green grocer, washing everything down with Al's brandy.

"Thank you for your hospitality," she said, after dinner.

"It's my pleasure. You're the first guest I've had here."

"It does feel safe here, like you said."

"It is. But I'm sorry it's so crowded. Are you comfortable?"

She didn't respond but closed her eyes and drifted across the bed. I was tired too. It was warm and stuffy in the storage unit. Normally, I slept in my underwear, but I left it on, not wanting Rayna to think I was taking advantage of her. As I squeezed my way onto the mattress, she snapped up with a start, then recognized me and lay warily back down.

11

FOR OVER A MONTH, I had slept alone in a locked metal box. Between midnight, when the front desk closed, and dawn, when vendors and other people who used storage units for work purposes started arriving, I was just about the only person in the building. The sounds of people stopping by to retrieve something would wake me up—who knows what kinds of things were stashed in a twenty-four-hour storage facility—and I noticed a few other vendors who occasionally napped or crashed in a storage unit. But if the building had any other permanent residents, they stayed well hidden.

I thought it would be strange to sleep with another person in my space, but it felt perfectly natural. With Rayna beside me, I slept peacefully through the whole night.

She shook me awake in the morning. "Isaac!" she pleaded. "Isaac, wake up!"

"What is it, Rayna? Are you okay?"

"What is going on? Such a din! Like stones against metal, from all directions!"

"Huh? Oh, don't worry about all that. It's just other street vendors starting their days. Getting their carts out. I'm used to it, now."

"I see. This makes sense. But I guess I thought . . . maybe it was pursuers."

"No. Just street vendors. There are no pursuers." I was stiff with morning wood, and strained against the pants I'd slept in. "I'm going to lie here a little longer." I didn't want her to see my erection. She might be creeped out. Or she wouldn't be, and I would be embarrassed. I hoped it hadn't brushed or pushed against her in the bed. I didn't want her to think that I was a pursuer. "There's water in the electric kettle; you can plug it in out in the hallway, and make tea if you want."

"Don't you have to bring your own pushcart out today?" What was today? Saturday. I was planning to go out, as a matter of fact, because Saturday was a good day to make money. Tourists came down to the Village from their Midtown hotels. You could sell them every Kerouac and Ken Kesey book you had, and name your own price. If the forecast held, the day would be sunny. But I wanted to spend more time alone with Rayna.

"No," I told her. "Not today." I felt happy being alone with her, and I didn't want that feeling to go away. It also seemed like a good opportunity to get to know her more, to find out what she was running from and whether it had anything to do with Al. I didn't want to say all this, of course, and struggled for an explanation.

"It's Shabbos," I said. "There's no need to work on Shabbos." I clearly wasn't running a religious business. In fact, Rayna had seen me working on a Saturday before. But in a way, I was actually serious. Shabbos was a way to set aside a day and elevate it. Inviting Rayna into my solitary cell, and sharing a meal in here, had made the space feel special. I wanted to make the day feel special too. Why not call the day what it was supposed to be?

"Really?" Rayna asked, incredulous. "Your street cart is *shomer Shabbos*?"

"Yes," I said, suppressing a grin. "I am a halachic street vendor."

"But you pushed the cart home well after dark last night." I couldn't tell how seriously she was taking me.

"Yes. It's true. It was an infraction. It was wrong of me. But Shabbos is one-sixtieth of paradise. We can still salvage at least an eightieth of paradise, I think, or a hundredth. One percent of paradise. That's something."

I recalled another story about Aher, long after he visited *Pardes*. One Shabbos evening, he was walking with his former student, Rabbi Meir. The two men were deep in conversation, and when they reached the *techum Shabbos* boundary, Aher had to stop Meir. He explained that he was going to keep going, but he wouldn't be responsible for Meir breaking Shabbos.

The lights in the storage facility were all motion activated, which was annoying when I was sitting still, working on my stock, but meant that I didn't have to further break Shabbos in front of Rayna by turning on any light switches. Later in the morning, when we stopped by the green grocer to buy a picnic feast, I realized I had to handle money. I apologized but Rayna just laughed.

"I'm glad you aren't working today, so you can spend the whole day with me"—apparently I wasn't as slick as I thought I was—"but the rules don't really matter. I don't live in my father's house anymore." She chose pickles, hardboiled eggs, plums, three chocolate bars, and a liter bottle of Fanta. I chose a big container of macaroni salad, an equally large container of a different kind of pasta salad with pesto, a wedge of brie, a loaf of crusty bread, and a bottle of wine. The food would have been cheaper at a grocery store, but I didn't know that either of us could handle being in a place like that, with the lights and people and aisles.

We went to Washington Square Park and sat in the far northwest corner so none of the other booksellers would see us. Malachi the drug dealer noticed me, but he just nodded, and went about his business. We spread an army blanket we'd brought from the storage space, and laid out our bounty.

"So, Rayna," I said, after we'd eaten. "You were talking about your family's house before. In Boro Park? I still don't know much about you, or where you come from."

"That's true." Her face clouded, and she didn't say anything else for a long while. I had pushed too hard, as I had with Roman and

Timur. I kept asking questions, when I needed to wait for answers to come. It had been so nice spending time with Rayna, and I'd ruined it. We chewed our food in silence. Squirrels and pigeons came too close. They were not afraid of people, and they wanted a bite of our food.

"I'll tell you a story," Rayna said, carefully. "From my family's neighborhood."

"Yeah?" I said, wanting to encourage her without pushing.

"There was a family who lived down the street from my family," Rayna said. "The father ran a nice business selling hats. The Hat King, they called him. The Hat King's oldest son was a fine young man, and the family hoped that the son would grow up and take over the business. But then, the boy somehow got it into his head that he was a pigeon." I sat, enthralled. I didn't think Rayna was going to tell me anything, and now words were pouring forth. Clearly, she was repeating a story she had heard—perhaps even told—many times before. Still, I was happy she was telling it to me.

"Why did he think that?" I asked, to encourage her to keep going.

"I don't know," she said. "Who knows where people get ideas? Maybe something happened to him that made him feel he wasn't a human. Well, for whatever reason, all day long he would hang out in the park with the other pigeons, with no clothes on, not even a hat, pecking around. There are stone tables in the park there? With chess-boards for tabletops? Where old men play?" I nodded.

"There are some in this park too," I said, pointing down to the southwest corner, where men played chess every day. They weren't a part of my scene—I didn't come to the west side of the park very often—but they were part of the park life, just like the drug dealers, the street musicians, and us booksellers. Washington Square chess was not recreational. These chess hustlers played all takers, for two or three dollars a game. Al was a pretty good chess player but probably wouldn't play them unless he knew he'd win.

"Oh, yes," Rayna said. "I've seen them there. Just like that. So the son would go around and around the bases of the tables, all day long. He would eat chips that children dropped on the ground. It was very embarrassing to his family. In Boro Park, everyone is always watching

everyone else. Judging. His siblings were able to get him back home
at night, but only by shooing him out of the park with a broom. He'd
coo at his mother—whom he'd always loved—and eat the challah she
baked, so long as she ripped it into little pieces and tossed them under
the table.

"The Hat King and his wife tried everything. They brought in the
boy's old friends from yeshiva to visit, but he didn't seem to recognize
them. They brought in rabbis, gypsy hypnotists, doctors with theories.
What do you call them? Analysts? But none of them could convince
him. He wouldn't respond but with a peck and a flapping of his wings.
Arms." Rayna paused to sip her wine, and a park pigeon cocked his
head, as if waiting for Rayna to resume. "He knew the truth, that he
was a pigeon, and didn't understand why everyone wanted to convince him otherwise.

"What could the family do? They kept on as best they could. They
built a nice big coop on the front porch for the boy to sleep in, and
threw scraps from their nice meals on the ground. They had to get rid
of the family cat, because who could bear to watch their son chased
around the house by a little pussycat?" Rayna looked genuinely
shamed at the thought of a boy being tormented by a cat.

"Then, one day, a stranger appeared in the park. The Hat King's
son found the man crawling around under the tables, without any
clothes, making cooing sounds. Pecking around. The son waddled up
to him and said, 'What in the world are you doing?'

"And the stranger said, 'What do you mean what am I doing? I'm
a pigeon, like you, anyone can see that. I'm pecking at crumbs, like I
always do.'

"'Well, listen, pal,' the boy said, 'you don't look like any pigeon I've
ever seen.'

"'Well, you don't look like any pigeon I've ever seen either. But
if you say you are, you are. I guess we're both of us just a couple
of pigeons.' The son wasn't sure what to make of this. Because the
stranger looked like a human to him. But it was nice to have another
pigeon that was his size, and understood his language. The other
pigeons in the park didn't talk to him, and he'd been very lonely.

What's more, he knew what it was like to have people say you weren't a pigeon. That they knew you better than you knew yourself. So he decided to believe the man.

"'I guess we are both pigeons,' he said, with a shrug of his shoulders. Is it called a shoulder, for a bird too? In any case, the two pigeons became close. The Hat King's son invited the new pigeon home to share his coop with him at night. It was large enough for two. In the day, they went out to walk in circles together."

"What about the Hat King and his family?" I asked.

"They didn't understand. They couldn't help. They just sat back and watched. I think they were embarrassed.

"After a few days, the man went out to the park with clothes on. Pants, shirt, jacket, hat. The Hat King's son took special note of the hat, which was a very fine one. Black, with a wide brim. Wider than is normal in the neighborhood.

"'Say,' said the son, 'I've never seen a pigeon wearing human clothes. You are sure you're a pigeon?'

"'Coo!' said the man. 'You know me, friend. Of course I'm a pigeon. Is there a rule that says a pigeon can't wear clothes if he wants to? Can't we pigeons do anything we want? What kind of pigeon would be so unsure of himself he would think that wearing clothes made him less of a pigeon?' The son was skeptical, but he had to admit the man had a point. And the clothes didn't keep the man from pecking around under the table. He stayed focused on his pigeon tasks, even as he wore holes in the knees of his trousers. When the days grew colder, the Hat King's son eventually pulled on some clothes himself. Why not? He could put on all the clothes he wanted. It wouldn't change who he was." I sat there, in Al's sweater and baseball cap, and listened to Rayna's story.

"Then, one morning, the man sat at the table and ate breakfast with the rest of the family, instead of eating his bread crumbs under the table. Again, the son confronted him, questioned his pigeon-ness. But again, the man argued back, saying, 'Is there a rule a pigeon can't sit at a table? Maybe it's a more comfortable way for a pigeon to enjoy his meal. And maybe he wants to eat something more than crumbs. Maybe he wants to feast on cheese and blueberry blintzes.' The son badly wanted to eat at the table, but had convinced himself he couldn't. Now he pulled himself up into a chair for the first time in over a year.

"With every new action, the man convinced the Hat King's son with the same argument. 'Is there a rule a pigeon can't drink wine, if he likes the taste of it? And is there a rule a pigeon can't converse with humans, if he has something to add to the conversation?' And so on." She stopped, as if she'd come to the end of the tale.

"The son was cured?" I asked. "He became who he was supposed to be?"

"No." Rayna shook her head. "He was never 'cured.' Some people are . . . hurt so badly they can never be healed." She looked very sad, and I realized she included herself on that list.

"He never stopped believing that he was a pigeon. But he did come to believe that he was a very clever pigeon, and that it was all right for a clever pigeon to run a very successful hat company, making money off the humans. And he acted like he was supposed to. Eventually, he married and took over the family business."

"Was he happier?" I asked.

"I don't know. He'd been sad when he was a pigeon without any pigeon friends. But I think he was still sad when he was a pigeon in the human world. I think he was happiest when he first made friends with the other man, when he had someone to share his coop with."

"When he had a friend," I said.

"Yes."

"And what happened to his friend?"

"He was just gone, one day," Rayna said. "The friendship had to end, when the story was done. The Hat King's son became the new Hat King. The store is still there, on Thirteenth Avenue. He had a wife, and human friends. The man wasn't one of them. Sometimes people come into your life. And sometimes people go away. You are grateful, but . . . you don't hold too tight."

Rayna seemed to be delivering a warning about our situation, but I wasn't clear if she was telling herself or me not to hold on too tight.

Was she saying she expected me to desert her after I'd grown tired of helping? Or was she warning me that she'd be gone one day, with no explanation, when our story was over? Maybe she was just tying up the story, this tale she'd told me to pass the time and avoid talking about herself. Was it just a local legend, or something she'd really observed? She sounded very serious. Either way, every word didn't have meaning to glean.

I poured us each some wine. The police liked to give people a hard time about open containers in the park, especially when they were trying to hit a ticket quota, so we kept the wine bottle in a paper bag, and drank out of coffee cups. We lay in the grass very near each other and sipped our wine. How could I be sure Rayna was real? That we were really here together and the ground itself was solid? I couldn't be sure I wasn't a pigeon or a squirrel who just thought he was a human man. It felt nice to sit in the grass with Rayna and drink wine. I knew that much. After a good night's sleep, a good meal, and a few drinks, Rayna no longer looked so tortured. She looked bright, and alive.

I leaned forward, and tried to kiss her. She pulled back. Her face tightened with pain, and she wrapped her arms around herself. Her skin turned pale.

"I'm sorry!" I told her. "I didn't mean anything by it. You just looked very pretty." I was afraid that I had broken the spell.

She was very quiet for an unbearably long minute, and then she said, "It's fine. I know you only meant to be nice. But it scared me." The wind blew her long hair in her face, but she didn't push it away.

"I'll tell you a story, then," I said. I didn't want us to lapse into silence again. All the stories that came to mind were about Al, so I picked one he told Becca and me as kids. "A story my father told me."

"Please," Rayna said, brightening again. Stories were apparently a more comfortable way for us to interact with one another.

"Well, when my father was a little boy he lived in a big new postwar apartment building in Warsaw. A prefab, concrete, communist apartment block. The father of one of his friends was a building engineer, and he told the boys that the cellar of the original apartment building—which had been destroyed by bombs during the war—was still there, underneath the new basement. All of the boys were interested, and they made plans to go down and explore. Who knew what was down there? Maybe treasure. Maybe rifles the Jewish partisans had buried. Maybe the skeletons of people who were killed by the Germans, or who swallowed poison to avoid capture." I didn't remember exactly what details Al had given when he told the story, but these sounded right. Rayna seemed interested.

"When they actually opened the cellar door, all the boys were too scared to crawl down into the dark subcellar. They all dared each other to go first, but only my father stepped forward." Al had in fact grown up in Warsaw, and as far as I knew the story was true so far. As a kid, I'd believed the entire story was true, until Becca convinced me otherwise. But I didn't know at what point the fiction began. Maybe Becca was right, and the whole story was made up. Or maybe she was completely wrong, and the whole story was true. Or maybe it was true, but it was someone else's story Al had taken for his own. "He thought the others would follow him, but they were all scared and ran off. My father found himself alone in the dark cellar.

"All of a sudden, something jumped out at him from the darkness!"

"What was it?" asked Rayna, with genuine concern.

"A devil!"

"Oh no!" She put her hand over her mouth.

"Yes. My father was scared at first too, but then he saw that it was just a little devil, and not a very strong one at that. He was an inch or two taller than my father, but nowhere near as tall as a grown man. He was very, very thin, and his ribs stuck out through his blotchy red skin. My father wrestled at school, so it only took him a couple minutes to overpower the devil and grab him by the toe.

"My father held the devil upside down, and said, 'I expected more of a fight from a devil!' 'Well,' the devil said, 'twenty-five years ago, things would have gone a good bit differently! I can tell you that! But you see, a Jewish devil like me feeds off the fears and doubts of Jews. In the good old days, there was a whole building and a whole court-yard full of religious Jews here. They were full of fear and doubt. The more pious they were, the more doubt. But then, it came to pass that there were no Jews here at all. I nearly starved to death.'" I had never told the story before and tried to imitate as much of Al's phrasing and delivery as I could, but it had been a long time. I filled in the gaps. My version had more religion in it than Al's.

"'I am very grateful for this new housing project the government has made. There are no religious people left, but there are a few Jews tucked here and there, in one apartment or another, even if they don't all know they are Jews, and there are bits of faith—and bits of doubt—tucked in all of their hearts. There is enough sustenance for me to survive, at least.'

"'Now,' said the devil, 'how about letting me go?'

"'What's in it for me?' asked my father.

"'If you set me free,' said the devil, 'then I'll be your slave and do your bidding. I will do all your chores and all of your homework for three years.' So my father set the devil free, and never had to do one page of homework, or carry any trash or coal, the rest of the time he was in grammar school."

"Your father is a man who consorts and makes deals with devils?" Rayna asked me, frightened.

"Yes, but only little ones," I said, though I didn't really know what kind of devils my father might have made deals with. I didn't know what he was involved in, what kinds of deals he'd made, or how far into darkness he'd descended. For that matter, I wondered what kind of devils I was prepared to make deals with.

᛫᛫᛫᛫

I never asked Rayna to move into the storage unit, and she never asked if she could. We both just understood she would stay. She came home with me from the park that afternoon, and she went out on the street with me Sunday morning. We weren't together every minute; she went on walks by herself almost every day, but she always came back to the storage space. It was difficult to remember that I'd had an ulterior motive in befriending Rayna. My whole life I'd just been trying to move forward, toward something else, toward some goal.

With Rayna living with me, I was enjoying the present. The days on the calendar followed one after the other, but I felt like I was floating, suspended in time, enchanted.

Rayna didn't have anywhere else to go, but she also seemed happy to spend her days with me. We'd both been lonely. To my surprise, I completely stopped longing for drugs, partly because of my bad experience with Malachi's weed but partly because Rayna was herself intoxicating.

At first, I considered telling Roman and Timur that Rayna was staying in the space, but it was my life and my home, not theirs. Zoya and her girls could tell Timur, if they cared to. When I called Roman again to check in, I didn't mention Rayna, and he had nothing to report about Al. Maybe he and Timur didn't know much more about Al than I did. Maybe no one knew what had happened to him.

Because of what happened in the park, I was nervous to try to kiss Rayna again. But after a few days, when we were settled and Rayna was more comfortable, she started giving me little kisses on the cheek when we were alone in storage. I would kiss her back, but didn't push things further than that because I didn't want to make her uncomfortable again. The outer world was a scary place for her already. I was content holding hands, trading kisses, and sharing my little world with her.

The only woman I'd ever spent so much time with was my ex-girlfriend, Mariam. I was crazy about Mariam, but it was just a schoolkid romance. Just a game: let's play at being lovers. Nothing was really at stake. Though I hadn't known Rayna long, and we weren't as physically intimate, our connection felt much more serious. Our lives were in each other's hands. We needed each other.

Aside from what I got from Rayna's presence personally, she became a big help to me in the business. The books and the money were hard to keep track of on my own, and she was good with figures. Her practicality made her seem less otherworldly.

Still, as much as I enjoyed Rayna's presence, I couldn't ignore the question of her origins, and appearance in the sketchbook. She had the right to a new story for herself, just like anyone else, but if she had some connection to Al, I had to discover it.

"Rayna," I finally said, after she'd been with me for four or five days, "I need to show you something." Taking out the notebook that focused on the Galuth Museum, I turned to the study in question. "Look. I saw this picture first, in my father's sketchbook, and I didn't know what to make of it when I met you." She studied the picture in silence for a minute or so.

"What do you mean?" she asked. I'd expected shock, not indifference.

"Don't you think the woman in the picture looks like you?" I looked from the image in the book to the woman in front of me. There was no question about it. They were one and the same.

"Like me?" She bit her lip as she considered the proposition but had no explanation. Whatever Rayna's connection to the Galuth painting, it was apparently a mystery to her as well. "I don't know. I suppose. I don't look in mirrors often." I pictured mirrors covered during shiva. "She is familiar to me in some way, but she looks more like one of my older sisters than like me."

"Are you close with your sisters, Rayna?" I asked, trying to draw out any thread of information.

"Maybe when I was younger. But they are all married now, and busy with their children. My family was making plans to marry me away too. I had no say. I would be forced." She became quiet. I didn't know what to say about this arranged marriage she had apparently escaped. For a moment, I thought she would cry, but she forced the pain away and began speaking. "This picture also resembles my youngest aunt. More so than any of my sisters, actually. But lots of girls look like this . . ." She seemed more interested in the sketchbook itself than in her own picture, and flipped forward through the pages. She stopped on a picture of Goldov, Roman, and Timur.

"Do you know those men?" I asked.

"This one looks familiar, maybe." She pointed to Goldov. "But it's hard to say. So many men come to visit my father." I wanted to ask more about her father, but she quickly turned the question around. "Is there a self-portrait of your father in here?" she asked. "You talk of him often, I want to know what he looks like. Does he look like you?"

"No," I said. "There's no picture of Alojzy."

I tried to ask Rayna about recognizing Goldov's picture again a few times over the next couple days, but any discussion upset her. She would change the subject, or not say anything. I didn't press the issue very hard. As much as I wanted to learn more about my own father and the men in his world, nothing was worth hurting Rayna.

| | ■

Around this time, I heard that Milton, the silent veteran, had died. As with Al's purported death, it was a rumor on Mendy's lips. In this case, Mendy had more detail.

"He burned up," Mendy told me. "I know a guy who lives in the same SRO. The fire department came in the middle of the night. The whole building was filled with smoke, but only one unit was destroyed: Milton's.

"Apparently, he left his hot plate on when he went to sleep. His whole place was filled with newspapers and books and junk—he was kind of a hoarder, I guess, though maybe some people would say that about me too—and it all went up. They found Milton charred in his bed. His neighbor, Richie, saw them wheel the remains out."

"Damn," I said. I hadn't really gotten to know Milton, both because of the communication obstacle and because he spent his time at Asher's table, which I avoided after listening to Asher's paranoid tirades, but I hated to hear about a man dying like that. "That's awful."

"Yeah. At least no one else in the building was hurt. He went down by himself."

"True. Do you think he's going to the potter's field?" I asked. "On Hart Island?" I remembered what Goldov had said about Al, and himself. Al could have died as easily as Milton had. If Al burned up in some residential hotel out West, where he was checked in under a fake name, and was buried in an unmarked grave, no one would ever know.

"No." Mendy shook his head. "It'll be the military cemetery on Long Island. He was injured pretty badly at the Battle of Khe Sanh.

I think that's why he couldn't speak . . . shrapnel to his chest and throat. Richie and Asher called the VA—Milton didn't have any family—and the military took possession of what was left of his body." I had known people who died before, but never so suddenly. Milton was an old soldier—just like Al. He had survived bombs and bullets. He had survived a war. Then he died one night, stupidly and without reason.

❚❙❚▓

We spent the Friday afternoon after Rayna moved in going through the stock for the weekend. I had given up my *shomer Shabbos* ruse, and explained that my skipping work on Saturday was a onetime thing. We moved the cart out into the hallway to give us room to work. Setting up a stepladder where the cart usually stood, I climbed up to look through the boxes that were stacked up high along the back wall. Rayna sat on the ground, in the open doorway, with a box we'd pulled off the cart.

We came to a box of books from the Classics of Western Spirituality line. These were big books, six inches wide and nine inches tall. Depending on the length of the text, they were anywhere from one to one and a half inches tall, and from about one to one and a half pounds in weight. Their heft made them feel full of knowledge. Being convenient collections of fairly obscure primary sources, they were big sellers with the college crowd, especially the grad students.

"Do we have an *Augustine*?" I asked.

"Yes."

"*Early Anabaptist Spirituality*?"

"Yes."

"*Nachman of Breslov*."

"Yes." She flipped through the pages. "He was the one who told the story about the boy and the girl in the forest?"

"Yes. No one knows how it ends. *Apocalyptic Spirituality*?"

"No. Hand that one to me."

"How about *Hildegard of Bingen*?"

"Hildegard? I'm looking for H-A-L-L. . . ?"

"No, Hil-de-gard. H-*I*-L." Sometimes Rayna had trouble with the spelling of words. To be fair, "Hildegard" was a strange one. I noticed she didn't have any trouble with the Classics of Western Spirituality books on Jewish subjects, which spelled the names out in Hebrew letters too. She was more comfortable with that alphabet.

"Oh. Yes. Go on."

"*Ibn 'Ata'illah?*"

"No."

"Here. *Abraham Isaac Kook?*"

"Yes." She studied his portrait on the book's cover. "Who was he?"

"Kook? A rabbi. In Palestine. He was like a Litvak and a Hasid at the same time."

"That's good."

"Yes. But also a Zionist."

"Oh."

"*Menachem of Chernobyl?*"

"No, we need that one." I handed it down to her.

"*Pyotr Gershon of Glupsk?*" She didn't answer. "The cover also calls him *The First Glupsker Rebbe?*" Still no response. I looked down. Rayna had her face in her hands, and I stepped down one rung so I could reach to touch her shoulder. "Rayna, are you okay?" She had run away from a religious household. Did her father study the teachings of the Glupsker Rebbe? What memories did the book trigger?

"Just dust," she said, shaking off my hand. "Nothing more than dust. No, we don't have a copy of *Pyotr Gershon* here. Hand it down." She took the book from me and shoved it in the box without looking at it. "Listen, Isaac, after these, should we take a look at the Penguin Classics?"

"Definitely. That's a good idea." She was learning the business quickly.

We worked hard for the rest of the afternoon. Our accomplishment was measured in the three empty water boxes we cut down and recycled when we were done. The street boxes were all fully stocked, the empty spaces stuffed with extra volumes of Vonnegut and Burroughs.

In the late evening, we walked up into the Village to buy some good bread from the Italian bakery and some olives, cheese, hummus, and candy from the market. These were the things we liked to eat.

We set up our food on a crate in the storage space. Before we ate, Rayna dug out two tea lights and lit them. She closed her eyes, raised her hands over her eyes, and began to make the blessings. She blessed the tea lights, our cheap red wine, and the Italian bread.

"My mother said the blessings in our home," Rayna said. "It's the only thing I miss since coming here." I thought Rayna was happy to be free of the yoke of observance, but I supposed you can only go so far. Besides, the controlling laws of Rayna's Orthodox family and her connection to the unseen were likely two distinct, and largely unrelated, things.

I was afraid the candles would set off the fire alarm, but they didn't. Everything was okay, and Rayna's Hebrew filled the space. The letters floated around the room, sanctifying it. Rayna's *Kabbalat Shabbat* did not feel like an empty ritual so much as a true conversation with angels. This room was our home, the Shabbos bride was welcomed, and the angels were sent away. They would return to their world while Rayna remained here with me. I wondered what Al would make of seeing his son, now grown, sharing a traditional Shabbos dinner in his storage space.

After Rayna and I ate dinner and the Shabbos candles burned themselves out, we sat on a bench out on Sixth Avenue, by the statue of General José Gervasio Artigas, the father of Uruguayan independence. The general stood with his hat in his hand. There were electric lights around the Artigas statue, and I read to Rayna from *Caravan of Cats*, a book we'd discovered in the storage space. She had been attracted by the cover of the slim, tall hardback, which portrayed, in the style of a Coptic Orthodox icon, a lion thrashing as it died from the spear sticking out of its chest. The book had been printed in England, but the publication information was strangely formatted and confusing, not to mention partly in Arabic, so I didn't know what to make of the book's origins. According to the note at the beginning of the book, *Caravan of Cats* was the translation of a work by Farid Shenouda, who was an assistant zookeeper at the zoo in Cairo in the first two decades of the twentieth century. Shenouda was from a devout Coptic family, but practiced his own personal religion, a form of atavistic animism. His few friends were British zoologists. He was killed by a mob loyal to King Fuad in 1922, possibly because of his colonial associations, possibly because of his fanatical antimonotheistic and antimonarchist beliefs, or possibly just for having the misfortune to be in the path of a violent mob.

Caravan of Cats is a book-length poem, telling the historical saga of the lions of the Near East, as seen from the perspective of the domesticated cats of Egypt. In the time of the kingdoms, the Egyptian lions—who are known as the "guardians of the Eastern and Western horizon"—live where the lush land meets the desert, and are admired from afar by their tamed and diminutive cousins, who keep the royal storehouses free of vermin. As the desert grows, the realm of the lions shrinks, and the prides dwindle. The pharaohs hunt the few remaining lions to extinction. Amenhotep III kills over one hundred lions in one day hunting, shaming the families of the court cats who will be mummified in his tomb. The last lion of Egypt dies out in the desert, not from a king's arrow but of starvation. Her flesh is torn apart by the hated and cowardly jackals.

Lights whipped past us on the avenue, and we huddled close on our bench as I continued reading.

In time, the cats of Cairo hear tell of the lions of Judea. A caravan sets out to the east, crossing the Sinai and entering into Gaza, where they are fed and housed by the monks of the Monastery of Saint Hilarion, some of whom even knew the secret language of cats. Taking leave of the kind humans, the Cairo cats head north along the coast to Judea, where they meet the lions of Judea on the banks of the Jordan River. This tribe is made up of lean Asiatic lions, who are much smaller than the Barbary lions of Egypt had been, but strong and proud nonetheless. Alas, these prides perish too, with the onslaught of the European crusaders. In the end, it is left to a humble mouser of Saint Catherine's Monastery of Mount Sinai to put the history of the Levant lions down on parchment, and his account is the foundation of the book we now held. I had been attracted to the book as a novelty, but as I read on, I became more and more invested in the cats' quest. I knew what that was like, to go in search of a lion. The cats hated their domesticated status, and wanted to run with true hunters.

After I'd read to Rayna about the lions for a while, we came back inside and went to bed. It was early, not quite ten o'clock yet, but we wanted to be ready early the next morning. We nestled together, like we did every night. Her hair fell across my face, and I kissed her on the back of her head. She rolled toward me and kissed my face. We kissed on the lips, eagerly but shyly, like kids in the back of a movie theater, for a couple minutes, then Rayna pulled back. She gave me one last quick kiss and rolled away, her back facing me.

"Good night, Isaac," Rayna said, cuddling back toward me. I put my arm around her.

"Good night, Rayna."

Soon I was asleep, dreaming I was a lion running along the Nile with a lioness. An elbow to the gut ripped me back to the waking world. My eyes opened, and I tried to make sense of the blows. Rayna was fighting against me. She struggled to throw my arm off, nearly wrenching it from its socket, and scratched at my face, moaning with fear like someone suppressing a scream.

Before I knew what to think, I was defending myself, fighting back, pushing her away from me. Had I done something to her in my sleep? Had I rubbed against her? Tried to mount her? No. No. I didn't believe I had. We were still in the same position, more or less, that we had been in when we went to sleep: I on my side, she curled up in front of me, cupped in my arm, though now she was twisting toward and away from me. I had fallen asleep with my arm draped over her and hadn't moved. Things had only changed for her. My arm was not holding her any longer, but holding her down.

Her eyes were half-open but I could tell she didn't see my face. Who was I to her? Her murderer? The man who had thrown her from the Sea Beach Railway? I had woken up in her nightmare. When ghosts dream, are they back in their real world? But she wasn't a ghost. How could I think of her that way, when her nails were digging into my face? This terror went far beyond any ghost story. I grabbed her arm. She fought harder. Whoever I was, I was now a man who grabbed her arm, restrained and shook her. She sat up straight and opened her eyes, recognizing my face now.

"What's going on?" she asked.

"Nothing," I said. "I think you were having a bad dream. It's still night." She blinked, disoriented, and lay back down. If she didn't remember where she'd just been, it was best to let it go for the moment. We couldn't ignore these matters forever, but for now, I was just happy that her nightmare had passed. I moved away, so I was not touching her in any way, and closed my eyes. Soon we were both back to sleep, a deep sleep, thank God, where neither of us dreamed.

The next morning, Rayna seemed to have no memory of struggling or even waking up. She kissed my cheek, and smiled at me.

I wanted to talk to Rayna about what had happened, but I didn't have the words. Rayna had been fighting for her life. It was more than just a regular nightmare. I didn't know whether I had done something wrong or whether she'd remembered something from her past, from her family's home. Al used to dream about war, and scream in the apartment. When he closed his eyes, he was back in combat. I remembered this from both our family apartment in Manhattan and Al's apartment in Sheepshead Bay. Then again, there was the ever-present unanswered question about Rayna's appearance in the sketchbook. Her response to the book had clarified nothing. I couldn't rule out the role of the unseen.

"Rayna," I said, while we ate our breakfast of crackers and jam, "do you believe in ghosts?" It was the most direct thing I felt comfortable saying.

"Oh yes," she said.

"Really? Have you met any?"

"Many." She wasn't teasing or telling a story, but relating her lived experience.

"What is it like for them?" I asked. Maybe she could tell me what it was like for her.

"They are in pain," she said. "Deep pain. Because people are supposed to move on. They are supposed to live, and die, and live again. They are old, and then they are little babies. It is a good thing. It is said that Moses is with us in every generation." I thought of the woman from Galuth's painting. Maybe Rayna was not her ghost, but her soul reborn again. How much of our faces were purely physical, and how much were they a reflection of our souls?

"However," Rayna continued, looking sad, "some people can't move on. They are stuck. Maybe they did something bad, but more likely someone else did bad things to them. And they are in pain, and confusion. They can't find their way into a new life."

"You've met people like this?" She nodded. "Back home?"

"A few. But even more when I came to the city. I'd wander around by myself, and meet so many of these spirits. One morning I met a woman spirit sitting on a bench in Union Square. She had a long white dress, and her eyes were only the white parts, no pupils. She told me she had been waiting on the bench for someone since 1946." So Rayna sat and conversed with ghosts. And I sat and conversed with Rayna. I didn't know what to think or believe about all this. Akiva and Aher had shared the same experience but understood it differently. Neither interpretation was more true.

"Don't worry, Isaac." Rayna's face brightened. "We won't become like that. We will help each other forward. Come, give me a little kiss. Then I'll plug in the electric pot, and make us some tea, and we'll get ready for the day."

12

THE BOOK TRADE PICKED up as the weather became warmer. Tourists and undergrads wandered the streets, looking to spend money. On weekends, every bookseller I knew came out to sell. Mendy was always out. Asher put less effort into his business since Milton's death, and Roberto was a pretty erratic seller, but they both rarely missed a sunny weekend day. Steve Lesser had not gone to California after all, and renewed his presence on West Fourth. Jersey Steve was working pretty consistently as well, and on weekends his wife came into the city with him, their van packed full of stock. Hafid was always set up in his usual spot, and his girlfriend, Soon-ok, would sometimes work with him, in addition to selling her own homemade political buttons.

There were no women who sold books by themselves on West Fourth Street, though I heard there were a few farther east, on Astor Place and on Avenue A. I only really knew what happened on West Fourth Street; the punky East Village booksellers had their own world, as did the exclusively African American booksellers on Sixth Avenue, and the art-book sellers in SoHo. There were bookselling strips in

Harlem and Williamsburg too, but I had never visited them. None of those places appeared in Al's sketchbooks. They weren't on my map.

A few others hung around West Fourth but didn't sell their own books. Eye, who still referred to me as either "Baby Edel" or "the boy," often assisted Mendy. Sonya and Lionel hung around what everyone called "the plaza" drinking beer. The plaza was actually just a public alley running from Fourth to Bleecker that NYU had appropriated, bricked over, and filled with tables and chairs. The streets had parried the university's thrust, and the park inhabitants soon claimed the plaza as their turf too. Lionel in particular preferred the plaza to the park, because a punk-rock singer whose band he had roadied for in the '80s was now a fixture in the crackhead scene in the park's southeast corner, and Lionel said he had listened to enough of the man's bullshit for one lifetime. When Sonya was drunk—which was every afternoon—she was likely to do some singing herself, usually old hard-rock and hair-metal songs.

Lionel worked for most of the booksellers at one time or another—he had been in the Coast Guard, and was very good at tying knots—but it depended on how early in the day he got drunk on Steel Reserve. He could turn mean, but Sonya was always good company, no matter how drunk. She liked to brush and braid Rayna's hair while Rayna cleaned and priced books. We were selling a lot of books, and had to keep getting new stock ready to put out on the table. Rayna was shy about interacting with the customers, but she liked working with the books.

We picked up quite a few tricks from the other booksellers, to make the old books seem newer. Cleaning them with rubbing alcohol was only the first step. If the corner of the cover was separating, you could glue it back together. If part of the cover was bent or tearing, you could reinforce it from the inside with clear packing tape. Most paperbacks are perfect-bound, which means they are glued together at the spine, not sewn. When the pages started to fall out, you could just glue them back in. It was best to use a wide-gauge syringe to apply the glue. If any part of the cover was rubbed white, you could touch it up with a colored marker. This was Rayna's favorite task. Sometimes she went beyond just a touch-up; I had started noticing small angels and birds hidden in the background on the covers of various books.

As consuming as the work was, I continued scanning the crowds for anyone else from Al's sketchbooks. No luck. My search needed to be more focused. Though I'd found Rayna on the streets while selling, that strategy wouldn't yield further results. I called Roman again, but he had no news and told me to have faith. He also asked if I was going to be out selling that Saturday, and if so could I do a favor for a friend. Of course I agreed.

Rayna and I were particularly busy on Saturday afternoon. We hadn't sold any of the expensive books I'd brought out in the morning—three different full translations of *Remembrance of Things Past* (or in one edition, *In Search of Lost Time*), Reich's *The Function of the Orgasm*, an Aleister Crowley tarot deck—but the West Fourth Street standards were flying off the table at a rate of twenty books an hour. Kerouac, Tom Robbins, Bukowski. Kids who were new to the city picked up *Bright Lights, Big City* and *Slaves of New York*. Suburban women picked up Jodi Picoult novels for the train ride back to Jersey. Many young NYU students believe there is a place for them in the theater; Sam Shepard, Edward Albee, and Lee Strasberg pranced off the table. Rayna worked as fast as she could to keep stock on the table. I even offered to pay Sonya to help, but she said she'd rather focus on her drinking. Later in the month she might relent, but for now she still had money on her EBT card.

"I'll give you ten dollars," a professor type said in the early afternoon, tossing a bill on the table and gesturing to a stack of paperbacks he'd assembled, which was easily worth twenty.

"You'll give me?" I growled. I had spent most of my life listening to teachers, professors, and rabbis. But the street was not their domain. The street was my domain. I was earning my place and authority, day by day. They couldn't talk down to me here. "You'll give me?" I repeated. "It's not an issue of what you'll give me, but of what I'll take. And I ain't taking your shit. Get the hell out of here."

"Don't you want to make a sale? Don't you want my money?"

"*Feh*," I said. "I'll do without it." Money was important in Al's world, but respect was more important.

"Damn," Sonya said, after the professor had slunk off. "You sounded just like your old man." I couldn't help but grin.

Sonya, Lionel, and Eye went off at two thirty to get a meal at the Jewish Center. Eye didn't like having to pass through a metal detector to get inside, but they all agreed it was the best free meal in the area, much better than the Methodist church or the soup kitchen on the West Side. I was happy to see Sonya leave. She was fun but distracting, and by that time of the afternoon, tourist traffic was in full swing. Rayna and I had books to sell.

Later in the afternoon, a woman pulled her BMW up by the table and jumped out, leaving the motor running. She wore a fancy cream-colored suit, and had short, spiky hair.

"You're Roman's man?" she asked me.

"Yes," I said. "I am."

"I thought so. You actually look kind of like Al, the guy who used to handle these things." She smiled when she said his name.

"Have you seen Al recently?" I asked. She shook her head.

"No. I was hoping I'd see him today, as a matter of fact, until Roman told me I would be dealing with a replacement." So she didn't even know he was missing. "Anyway, here it is." She pulled an envelope from inside her blazer, and handed it to me. The sealed white envelope was about a quarter-inch thick, and had no writing on the outside.

"Someone will come for this later this week. Thanks. I gotta go before I get a fucking ticket. Tell Al Dani says hey." She hopped back in her car and drove off.

"Who was that?" Rayna asked.

"Just someone who knows my father," I said. "But she doesn't know where he is either."

That night, while Rayna was washing up, I inspected the envelope more closely. The contents were flexible, and felt like a stack of paper. It was a bit too wide to be cash. American cash, anyway. I held the envelope up to the lantern light, but couldn't see any words or images, only a dark rectangle, and resisted the impulse to steam it open with the electric teakettle. I needed to pass these loyalty tests, and would hold on to the envelope until someone came for it.

I was proud to contribute, to earn my keep, to show that I could take care of business. Most importantly, Timur needed to know that I could keep my mouth shut. My goal was to understand about my father, about the way he lived. If he was loyal to Timur, then I would have to be loyal to Timur as well. Dani was another direct link to Al, even if she didn't have any information. I was making connections, but I needed to figure out how to use them to move forward.

A few days later, a man came by the table to retrieve the envelope. He said he'd never heard of Al.

I I ∎ ▩

When Rayna and I arrived on West Fourth Street early the following Sunday morning, we saw Mendy standing on a milk crate like a statue of Aegeus, his beard blowing in the wind, his eyes fixed on a distant point.

"Mendel," said Rayna, "are you unwell?"

"What? Oh. Rayna. Izzy. Good morning."

"What's wrong?" I asked.

"The police are destroying Roberto's books. See?" Down at the far corner, men in green sanitation uniforms were throwing Roberto's books into the back of a trash truck. Roberto had no storage space; in the evenings he wrapped a tarp over the table, fastened it with packing tape, and took his chances. The jaw of the truck came down and crushed six boxes' worth of paperbacks.

"His books!" said Rayna. "They can't do that to his books."

"Yes, Raynele," said Mendy. "I'm afraid they can. They shouldn't be able to, but they are."

"But it's wrong."

"Yes," Mendy said. "But these people don't care. I mean, look, the Nazis in Germany. They burned all the books. Then they burned all the people. Guys I grew up with . . . the things they did in Vietnam, they burned people too." I pictured policemen tossing Al's body in the back of a garbage truck. "To sell books, that's a First Amendment thing. But the Constitution, that's more paper for the trash truck."

"We can't do anything about it?" I asked. "There's no legal recourse?"

"There were some lawsuits by a group of vendors in the '90s. So now, in New York, sometimes you can have your First Amendment rights. Unless they throw the lawsuit papers in the trash truck too." Mendy took off his glasses and cleaned them on his dirty undershirt. "That's why NYU security waits until the books are unattended, and calls the city to send the sanitation guys. This way, it's not written up as a vendor issue, with tickets issued, and a voucher for the seized merchandise." Mendy hated college professors, but he often sounded like one. "If your books are vouchered, they send them to this storage facility in Queens where you can go claim them. Theoretically. It's the same place bicycles go, when the police clip locks. They're classified as seized property, so there are some personal property rights still intact with that. But if they decide to call it refuse, rather than merchandise, then it's no longer an issue of personal property or a First Amendment issue for them. Then it's a waste disposal issue. That's how they always saw it from the start, I guess."

"So what can we do?" I said. I'd grown up thinking I had rights. Mendy would have called that "class privilege." My father, who had endured the indignities of both communist Poland and service in the IDF, had tried to disabuse me of this notion, but Long Island provides a powerful illusion for its inhabitants.

"We can't do anything. The First Amendment offers you nothing. It is predicated upon the Second Amendment, which also we don't have. Gun control is not a right-wing/left-wing thing. It's a rich/poor thing. Us working people, they took our guns from us, now they can take our books. I remember when Mayor Lindsay banned rifles." I was no longer following everything Mendy was saying. He gestured with his arms as he spoke. "I couldn't believe the trade unions didn't protest. Ludlow, for God's sake! Rockefeller killed two dozen people when the miners' union tried to fight back. They would have killed more if the miners didn't have rifles." Mendy was agitated. His milk crate was a soapbox. Many street people were like this, even the saner ones. They fixated on one thing and went on and on about it, hour after hour, day after day.

"You don't have to look so far to see the slaughter. Go two blocks that way"—he pointed up toward Washington Place—"and you'll find the old Triangle Shirtwaist Factory. *Twelve dozen* dead. They've always taken our labor. That's why they hate us booksellers. Because we don't work for them. They can't stand to leave you with nothing of your own. Nothing."

"But still," said Rayna. "They should leave the books alone."

"Yes," said Mendy, hopping down to the sidewalk. "They should."

A curse had been cast on the street. By three in the afternoon, we'd only made forty dollars and decided to pack it in. Mendy stuck around.

Two days later, I saw Roberto walking down Fourth Street from Sixth Avenue.

"Something happened to your stuff, man," I told him. "The other day." He was walking with his head up, like he was enjoying the warm sunshine on his skin. From the way he looked, I guessed he hadn't heard, and I wanted to head him off and break the news before he got to his corner. "They're all gone."

"Huh? Oh, my books." He took off his sunglasses. When he turned toward me I saw that there were deep scratches on his right cheek. For some reason they were half covered with scotch tape and pieces of tissue, not Band-Aids. Evidently, there were other struggles in Roberto's life aside from some lost stock.

"Yeah," he said with a shrug. "Snap, crackle, pop." He said it like a joke, but he didn't smile. It occurred to me that there could be a deep anger or despair bubbling just under the levity and indifference. You can never tell what's going on inside a person.

"You're not upset?" I asked. I would be livid. There would be no hiding it. It wouldn't even be anger, but a complete destabilization. If our books were suddenly gone, I felt Rayna and I might disappear as well, just like Al had.

"I guess I could be upset," Roberto said. "I mean, yeah, it sucks. But hey, easy come, easy go." It was true, Roberto's books were for the most part curb salvages. He hadn't put much money into acquiring his stock. He found what he could, sold what he could, and ditched the rest. He didn't hoard and catalog books like I did. But Al had walked away from his good stock without looking back. Maybe when you had no choice but to walk away, you did.

Roberto noticed Rayna and winked at her, but she looked away. He looked pained. I was afraid that Rayna had offended him, but it was probably just the loss of his books.

"What're you going to do now, Roberto?" I asked.

"Oh, shit, I don't even know. I guess maybe it's about time I headed back down to Florida. I got a sister down there. I ain't seen her in two, no, three years. I hope she's still living in the same place." His comment reminded me that I hadn't seen my own sister for well over a month. "I don't know, though. I really don't know." He surveyed the street and the park, then put his shades back on. He stuck out his hand. "Well, if I don't see you." We shook hands, and he bopped on down the street. I never did see him again. The streets were like that. People were there, and then they were gone.

〡❙❚■

My own books spent their nights safe and sound with us in the storage space, thanks to Timur and Roman. The business was going well enough to become self-sustaining and cover the storage costs, but I didn't see any reason to sever ties with them. If anything, I needed to actively strengthen my ties with Timur and Roman.

The next time I called Roman, he thanked me for this most recent favor, and said he was glad I called, because he had just recently heard some information of interest to me. I waited with bated breath for him to speak.

"I have heard that Al left town by bus from Port Authority three months ago." Finally, a sighting! It wasn't a current one, but it made me feel less like I was chasing shadows.

"Who did you hear that from? Can I talk to them?"

"Just a mutual acquaintance whom I spoke to. He gave Al the ride to Port Authority. Edel had his one suitcase with him. He was vague about where he was headed, but said he'd be back in town soon enough, when things 'calmed down.' The man didn't know anything else, and he doesn't like talking to strangers. But I promise you, I'll keep my ears open."

"Fine." I was frustrated Roman hadn't pushed the lead further and I suspected he was holding something back. Why couldn't I talk to the witness myself? But I didn't want to seem ungrateful for this morsel. And I was happy for further confirmation that Al was alive, that he had just skipped town for a minute and was coming back, sooner or later.

"While I am keeping my ears open for you, Izzy," Roman said, "perhaps you can keep your eyes open for me."

"Absolutely." This sounded like a fair exchange.

Roman gave me the street names of four drug dealers, including Malachi, asking me to keep track of when they were in the park, and how active they seemed to me. He didn't refer to them as drug dealers on the phone, but I understood what he meant.

I knew three of the men by name, and Sonya pointed out the fourth to me. I made sure to take note every day of which dealers were in the park. The four men Roman had asked about were working almost every day that I was, and doing a good amount of business.

I repeated the few details Roman had given me about Al's departure over and over in my head. The timing made sense; it would have been right after Al mailed the postcard to me. He left with one suitcase, which meant he either left quickly or didn't intend to stay gone long. Or both. It did sound like he had left in a rush, especially if he was asking for a ride at the last minute. This fit the theory that he was running from someone. But there was still something I was missing. Even if Roman wasn't actually keeping something from me, surely more information could be gained from the story. I needed to talk to the driver. All the more reason to keep currying Roman and Timur's favor.

Asher reappeared on West Fourth Street that week, after an absence of ten days or so. He usually walked by me without any acknowledgment, but today he walked right up to me. His eyes gripped mine completely.

"I was up in Central Park," he said. "Up there in the park, near the pond and the path and the path and the pond. I was all set up."

"You were selling up there?" I asked. Sometimes booksellers tried out different locations where there was no established market, but also no competition.

"Selling. Yeah. Selling everything. The people walked by, they looked at me. They looked at, you know, what I had, they didn't understand what I had. All these things. For my mother."

"You were selling things for your mother?" I didn't understand what he was talking about.

"What the fuck do you know about my mother, man? I mean, who told you about her?"

The paranoia flashed in his eyes for a moment. "Look, man, the shrine. Okay, it was a shrine for my mother. I built it up for her. But I wanted to be pure, so I sold some things. Some other things are left. I need to get rid of all of them." He began to pull objects out of his pocket. A handful of pens. Some string. A piece of fabric that looked like it had been ripped off his flannel overshirt. Then he pulled off the shirt, almost losing his balance as he worked each arm out of its sleeve, and threw the whole thing on the ground. He tried his pockets again, but nothing was left. "There's no money. You can't have money. You can't. You can't handle it. And you have to rent your shirt."

"Rent your shirt?" I wondered if Asher had ended up on the street because he was insane, or if his years on the street were what had driven him insane.

"Rent it? Fuck no. Sell it! Give it away!" He reached his hand into one of the holes in his Lynyrd Skynyrd T-shirt and pulled, ripping the shirt nearly in half. His hand got tangled up in the fabric. Frustrated, he pulled the whole shirt off and threw it on the ground. Standing bare-chested, he proclaimed, "I have to go to my storage space and get the rest of her stuff." His unit was in the same facility as mine, up on a higher floor. "I have to get rid of all of it. It all has to be pure for her. I'm going to sell everything. All these things. For my mother. I'm going to build her a shrine. I haven't slept for two days. I don't sleep. You sleep on the floor, by the coffin. No mattress allowed. I have to build the shrine. For my mother."

"Asher," I said. "Maybe you should get some rest before you try to build anything."

"What? What?" He looked at me sharply. The loop had been broken, for a moment, and I felt guilty for interfering. "What the fuck do you want, Al? Always with a dumb question or a smart comment." So he thought I was Al. It pleased me to think I'd stepped so fully into my father's shoes that others mistook me for him. But this was only true in Asher's confused mind.

"Don't tell me to go to sleep, Al. Don't tell me what to do. I can only sleep on the ground. I have to rent the garments. I'm sitting shiva for my mother. I don't care if you don't respect tradition; some of us do. I'm going to build my mother a shrine. Up at Central Park. Are you paying your respects?"

"Yes," I said. "I pay my respects to your mother."

"Asher," Rayna said. She had shied away when Asher first approached, but now she stood beside me. I didn't know if she'd ever spoken to Asher before. "I know you are sad. But this is not the right way to mourn. If you are sitting shiva, you need to be home with your family. Your mother does not want you in the streets like this." Rayna stared over Asher's shoulder, at something I couldn't see. It seemed she could actually see Asher's mother standing there, and was listening to the ghost's words, not just guessing about the dead woman's desires. I felt, once again, that the afterlife was Rayna's domain.

Asher looked at Rayna and blinked. His mouth opened, then snapped shut. He picked a few objects from his pile, stuffed them into the pockets of his shorts, and tied the ripped Skynyrd shirt around his head like a turban. He looked at Rayna, then at me, his eyes filled with confusion. Then he turned and headed off through the plaza, toward West Third Street.

"May God comfort you," Rayna said, as he walked away, "among the other mourners of Zion and Jerusalem."

Mendy came over and asked what it had all been about.

"He was really worked up," I said. "Manic. Freaking out."

"Yes," said Rayna. "He was sad because his mother died. He's sitting shiva. Or he's supposed to be. His behavior can be forgiven, in these seven days."

"The thing is," said Mendy, "Asher's mother has been dead for three years."

I went and sat down beside Rayna on the curb. There were tears in her eyes. I wondered if it was just that Asher's behavior had upset her, or if the encounter with the spirit world had drained her. Maybe she missed her own mother, who she'd mentioned the first time she lit Shabbos candles. I imagined my mother dying but didn't feel like crying, much less like going crazy and tearing up my clothes. Did this mean I was coldhearted or that I didn't have a very good imagination?

"This is bad," Rayna said. "He should let his mother go."

"Maybe he's sad about Milton," I said. "He lost his only friend. Maybe that pushed him over the edge, and he's confused." What would I do if I lost Rayna?

"Maybe that's so," she said. "But then he should let his mother go, and mourn for Milton."

I felt guilty about not speaking to my mother in so long. It wasn't because I was too busy; I had made a decision not to talk to her. She was no longer part of Al's world and had made a dedicated effort to make sure I wasn't either. If I talked to her, she would pull me back when what I needed was to pull close to Al. Though I wasn't talking to my family, they felt close because I kept seeing them in Al's sketchbooks.

Asher's junk was still lying on the sidewalk. The crumpled flannel shirt looked like a dead dog lying on its side. I understood why my mother felt the way she did about Al. He hadn't been a good husband. I once asked him about his relationship with my mother, when I was fourteen or fifteen. Why had she kicked him out? Or why had he left? Didn't he love her? Didn't he love us? Where had he gone when he finally left?

"After your mother and I were split up?" he said. "I went upstate and worked at the Selkirk train yard." We were eating onion rings at the Thessaloniki Diner in Sheepshead Bay. "These railroad jobs are very hard to get in America, but my old rasar—that would be like master sergeant in the U.S. Army—had become a big shot with Zim Shipping, working out of Virginia headquarters, so he called in a favor for me with his contacts at Conrail." Al's stories always had a hookup, a connection to make things happen. I wished I had a connection like that now, to put me in touch with Al.

"Let me tell you what it has been like: one time, they have us cleaning up a derailment just about thirty, forty miles south of the yard. Engineer fucked up, went off the rails. It was tankers mainly, that they had been pulling, and there were pools of spilled chemicals all over the ground. A lot of it was bound for the Fisher-Price toy factory. They were still manufacturing the toys in America. They were still a couple years from going over to China." Alojzy picked up three onion rings and shoved them in his mouth. He chewed them for a minute, then washed them down with the last of his beer and continued talking.

"It was the middle of the night, in nowhere upstate New York, but from somewhere comes this scruffles dog. Stray, no collar. He trots right up and starts drinking from one of the pools. We chased him off, but he keeps coming back. He had these big eyes, and these big floppy ears.

"I chased him off as far as I could. 'Yallah, kelev. Yallah yallah.' But we are in full protective gear, and in my hazmat suit, I couldn't run so well. I felt like I was a cosmonaut running on the moon.

"And this dog. He was running with me, nipping at the baggy legs of the suit. He thought we were having fun, playing games. Finally, I hit him in the side of the ass with a rock, and he ran off to the top of a hill. Not a hill, just a little rise, but out of reach of my rock throw.

"He lay down low—not resting, but prone like a sniper—and looked back at me. He had the most betrayed look on his face. You don't think of a dog as having such strong expressions on his face. But let me tell you,"—my father gestured at me with his empty beer bottle—"when your mother found out I cheated on her, the look on her face was not half as devastating." I didn't like hearing my father say that, even though it was really the answer to the question I'd asked, or part of it. I knew that Al had hurt Ruth. Even though I didn't like what Ruth's choices meant for me, I knew she hadn't made them out of cruelty, but out of self-preservation. Al's story didn't end there.

"I went back to work. I could not worry about a stray dog's hurt feelings. We had work to do. A derailed train to clean up. This is a six-thousand-ton train, a dozen tankers ripped open, thousands of gallons of chemicals spilled. We came back the next night, and that dog was lying there, dead."

13

REPOINTING IS THE PROCESS of renewing mortar joints in masonry construction. It's necessary, from time to time, because the mortar goes quicker than the stones. I didn't know this until the contractors began to repoint the big red blocks of NYU's Bobst Library. The scaffolding slowed foot traffic on West Fourth, but that was preferable to having the stones fall on our heads. I kept watching the dealers in the park; their business didn't slow at all.

The repointing work started on a Monday, and was still going on Thursday. Rayna and I sat on the curb with Sonya, listening to one of her tales of woe. She and Lionel had been planning on sleeping on the subway the night before, but Lionel drunkenly pissed on the platform, right in front of a cop. He had some warrants for open containers, and got taken to the Tombs. Too scared to fall asleep by herself on the train, Sonya spent the whole night sitting up awake.

"Why don't you go take a nap in the park?" I suggested.

"Nah," Sonya said. "I'm too wired now. There's no point in trying to sleep. Listen, I'm a Quaker. But sometimes I think about murdering that idiot. I'll put rat poison in his Steel Reserve."

One of the masonry workers approached the table as we were talking, and awkwardly pretended to survey our selection. When I came over to see what he was after, he pulled a thick folded manila envelope from a side pocket of his tool belt and jabbed it at me.

"What's this?" I asked, not reaching for it. Roman hadn't said anything to me about passing on another envelope. If it was something else, I wanted to be careful.

"It's a scam," said Sonya. "Or a subpoena. Subpoena servers like to put on disguises. Don't touch it."

"Is it a subpoena?" I asked him. I didn't know what I could be subpoenaed for, but it seemed like a possibility. Maybe the storage space was evicting me? Maybe I was being sued by the family of the kid who went insane from the acid? Maybe Al was being sued for something, and they didn't know where to serve it? Could he be running from something as mundane as a lawsuit? Maybe it was a grand jury subpoena.

"Don't speak English," the worker said with a thick Slavic accent.

"*Govarish po Rusky?*" I tried.

"Look," he said, in English. "I'm not involved. I'm just to give you this." He jabbed the paper again, and I took it. "I go back to work now."

Could this be a message from Al? Had he heard that I was selling on West Fourth Street, and found a way to send me a package?

I left Rayna to watch the table and went off into the park to open the envelope. Whatever this was about, I didn't need the news broadcast all over the street. I ripped the paper eagerly.

Inside the envelope was a cell phone. Was Al only a phone call away? In the bottom of the envelope I found a slip of paper that read, "Call Roman. Number in phone." My heart sank when I saw that the name was Roman, not Al. Still, it could be something worthwhile.

The contacts only listed one number, and it didn't have a name listed. I pressed "call."

"*Allo.*"

"Roman," I said. "It's Izzy."

"I know. I have this number. It's absurd I had to buy you a phone to get in touch with you. It is pay-as-you-go, so no name attached, but still, be careful what you say on a cell phone."

"Okay. Thank you. Was there something you wanted to talk to me about?" It must be something urgent if he didn't want to wait for my periodic phone call. Maybe Al had been located? Maybe this *was* a message from Al, in a roundabout way.

"Yes, of course there is. You might be willing," Roman asked, "to do a larger favor for us?" No message from Al, and no news of Al. Fine. At least it was a chance to further develop my connection with Roman and Timur.

"Absolutely," I said. Roman had not gone to such lengths to arrange the previous, smaller favors, so this had to be something more important. I was pleased to have the chance to prove myself to the men who had known my father. I wanted to show that I was as strong and reliable as he was, and would do any job that he would do.

"Good. I am glad. I happen to be coming through the area this afternoon. But I would prefer not to be seen too near the park. Can you get away from the books for a few minutes?"

I was eager to hear about this "larger favor." There were intrigues afoot. I had speculated about blackmail and fraud when I held the files. Goldov had referenced Al's involvement in buying and selling something illicit. Timur mentioned art at the restaurant. It could be anything. The true natures of the other favors were obscured by layers of paper and cardboard. There was going to be a conversation about this one, though. The covers would be opened.

At three p.m., I left Rayna to cover the table, and went to meet Roman in the spot he designated, a bench on LaGuardia Place next to the statue of the old mayor himself. Roman had a cap pulled down over his face, but his bulky figure was hard to miss.

"Izzy, thank you for meeting me." He didn't rise to greet me.

"My pleasure." I sat down, and we shook hands.

"How is business today?"

"It's going fine."

"Fine. Good. I won't keep you long, then. I asked you about some men, about ten days ago."

"Yes."

"And?"

"They have all been in the park almost every day. They seem to be the main guys selling, in fact. Lots of customers. They start earlier than any other dealers." Roman nodded.

"This was my understanding. Thank you for helping to confirm it. You see, because of the police attention, no one can keep their stuff in the park itself." I nodded, thinking about Malachi sending Merlin off on his bicycle. "So the stuff is kept in spots on Sixth Avenue, and the men come to get it from there.

"As in any business, there are rules. The problem is, the man that runs one of these distribution points, a newsstand, does not want to play by the rules anymore. He has tried to cut the usual supplier—a friend of ours—out of the equation. The men whose name I gave you are no longer buying from our friends, and yet they are still well supplied. We have had eyes on the newsstand itself, but your eyes in the park help confirm this also." Roman's eyes darted around, making sure no one had come within hearing distance of us. "And all this is no good. When things are upturned like this . . . it causes problems for everyone, not just the supplier losing money. It causes chaos. Is bad for everyone in the park. Do you follow?"

"Sure," I said. "I'm with you." Everyone had a set of rules. The police had the state's law. Religious Jews had halacha. Roman was talking about a law of the streets, now. A code amongst criminals. I didn't know this set of rules was different or better than any other, but if it was the law Al followed, I'd try to follow it too.

"Good. Now, this is where you come in. Listen closely. No, no, put the pen back in your pocket. Don't write this down, just remember. Tomorrow morning, you will leave your storage space earlier than usual." It made me uncomfortable that he knew what my normal departure time was, but it was no secret. "Be on the corner of West Fourth Street and Sixth Avenue at five a.m. You got all this?"

This was the moment when I could have said, no, I didn't get all this. I would not be on that corner at that time. I didn't want to know about the drug business. I didn't want to help faceless people stay in power. But then, I had already made my decision about the situation, without even realizing it, when I agreed to watch the dealers, and report on their actions. Maybe I had made the decision even earlier than that, when I moved into the storage space.

"Got it," I said. Tough guys were making moves, and the drama would unfold with or without me. Better with me. I wanted to know every hidden thing and see how the strings were pulled. I had come this far and wasn't going to back out now, not like I had all those years before.

"When you see the newsstand catch fire," Roman said, "call the police from the pay phone there." Fire. So it was arson that I was agreeing to. This was serious. "Do not use the cell phone, use the pay phone. It's one that still works. We checked. You know how they say 'see something, say something'? Tell them about the fire. Tell them you saw the culprit. This is a picture of his face." Roman took an old leather wallet out of his jacket pocket, and flipped it open to show me the driver's license of a man named Suhaib Abdul-hak. He was thirty-five, with black hair, light brown skin, and a little mustache. His most noticeable feature was a scar across his nose and left-hand cheek.

"Tell them that the man ran right past you. Very close to you. He stopped to look back at the fire, and you got a close look. Got it?"

"Yes."

"Then, you must do one last thing. Leave this bag on the sidewalk after you make your call." Roman picked up a black backpack by his feet and held it open for me. Inside was a crumpled red track jacket, a gasoline can, and some rags. "Mention on the phone that the man was wearing this red jacket." Roman tossed the wallet inside the bag, and handed it to me. I took it. I was holding the evidence to a crime that hadn't been committed yet.

"Okay," I said. "Got it. I'm good to go. But I'm just wondering: Why me for this?" I understood why I was willing to go along with this plan, but I didn't understand why I had been chosen for the job. Didn't Roman and Timur have closer associates they could trust with this task? Couldn't the actual arsonists plant the evidence?

"You don't want to help us?" Roman's expression was fierce.

"No, like I said, I'm in. It's no problem. You and Timur have helped me. With the bill, and with my search for my father. I'm sure you'll continue to help me with that. I'm just wondering why you trust me with such a task? Don't you have other people you can rely on?"

"Is there some reason it shouldn't be you, Edel's son? Some reason we shouldn't trust you?"

"No," I said. "There's not. Of course there's not." Since they were trusting me, I needed to see what I could get from them. I pulled the sketch of the dead soldier out of my pocket. I had ripped off the picture of Roman and Timur—it would be too much to show Roman a picture of himself—so only the soldier remained. "By the way . . ." I tried not to sound too eager. "I found a sketch my father made. Do you know this guy?" I handed him the scrap. He inspected it closely, then nodded.

"He was a friend of your father's from Israel. His name escapes me. I don't know what ever happened to him." He handed the picture back to me, giving the impression he didn't want to touch it any longer than he had to. Once again, I suspected Roman knew more than he was saying. But I'd pushed enough, at least until I completed the task at hand.

"Thanks," I said. "I should get back to my books."

|❚❚■

I told Rayna that I was going out early the next morning because someone was stopping by on their way to work with some books to sell.

"Don't you want me to go with you, Isaac?" she asked.

"No, it's okay. I can handle the cart myself, and you can sleep until the usual time. We'll leave you the small luggage cart packed with some more books to bring out later in the morning." She gave me a curious look, like my story didn't quite make sense, but she didn't press the issue.

Just before leaving at four a.m., I paused to watch Rayna as she slept. She was beautiful. Her unbraided hair was unfurled across her face. I wanted to wrap my fingers in her long hair and kiss her. I wanted to make love to her. Mercifully, I was usually too physically tired to think much about sexual urges. And right now, I had a job to do.

I wasn't used to being out quite this early. It was still pretty dark, and there wasn't much traffic except for a few stray taxis and work trucks. Hafid's tables were out when I got to West Fourth, but that was only because he'd left them out the night before. I set up my own card tables, then unloaded most of my boxes and placed them under the tables. There wasn't really time to put out my books, and I was too anxious to engage in the task anyway. I was getting ready to be an accessory to a drug-related arson. Besides, my books were safer packed away than out in the open, as they'd be unattended for a while. Leaving one full box on my cart for ballast, I placed the nearly empty box with the black backpack in it on top.

I knew exactly how long it would take me to get over to Sixth Avenue, but I left early and rushed over, and had to spend ten minutes standing on the corner, pretending to fix the ropes on my cart. The newsstand stood on the avenue, slightly up from the corner of West Fourth and across the wide sidewalk from the closed movie theater. It was basically a green metal hut, with a corrugated green gate pulled down over its window.

The sun hadn't risen yet, but the street is always fully illuminated in Manhattan. The only other people around out on the block were a delivery man bringing crates of soda into a deli on a handcart, and a couple of electrical workers from Con Edison checking something on a utility pole. There were a few people on the other side of the street, including some early commuters coming out of the train station and someone in a red smock unloading stacks of free newspapers from a cardboard box, but they weren't close enough for me to see their faces.

The soda delivery man closed up the back of his truck and drove off. The Con Ed guys were finished, too, and started messing around with the tools in their own truck. I kept my eyes on the newsstand, trying not to be too obvious about it. The two Con Ed workers walked over to the newsstand. One held a pair of bolt cutters, and the other held a duffel bag. So these were Timur and Roman's guys. They were shielded by their truck, so no one across the street could see them. Even someone coming up my side of the street would most likely have their view blocked by the newsstand itself. The guy with the bolt cutters nodded at me, to show he knew who I was, then clipped the lock of a small door on the newsstand's side. His partner slid inside with the duffel and came back out a moment later. They jumped in their truck and took off.

Even though I was waiting for it, I was still surprised when the newsstand burst into flames, just as the Con Ed truck pulled out of sight. I heard a thumping sound—more like rushing water than an explosion—and flames shot out the vents at the top of the newsstand. Within thirty seconds, the entire top of the structure was burning. The fire was the brightest thing on the dim morning street.

I looked around. A group of people who had just emerged from the subway across the street stood watching the fire. Their eyes were fixed on the flame; no one seemed to connect it to the Con Ed truck. By the time I started breathing again, the truck was out of sight. A man came rushing out of the deli and squirted at the flames with a bottle of spring water. The quarter I'd been clenching in my fist was slick with sweat. I popped it into the pay phone slot.

I dropped the bag, and booked it out of there before the fire department arrived. The sirens became audible just as I crossed Thompson Street. I went ahead and set my books up even though it would be a few hours before customers arrived, and tried to read more from *Knickerbocker Avenue*, which I had put aside when Rayna moved in with me.

Arturo is thriving in the military. His hard work and dedication are noted by his superiors, and he is sent for training at the 5th Special Forces Recondo training camp at Nha Trang, where they assign him to the elite LRRP platoon of the 101st Airborne. Arturo soon sees brutal combat against the Viet Cong in the DMZ. After receiving a promotion to the rank of sergeant, Arturo signs up for a second tour of duty, during which he distinguishes himself as a squad leader on daring nighttime raids into NVA territory.

I was having trouble focusing, and only made it through fifteen pages of Vietnam before I ended up just sitting on the curb with the book on my lap. I had been excited to be involved in the plot of the story Roman told me, but until I saw the flames, it was just that, a story. When I saw the paint peeling and the metal buckling, I saw how real it was. Again, I came to the question of why Roman and Timur had involved me. Hopefully this meant that they trusted me and knew they could count on me. And of course, the location made me a logical choice. But still, why couldn't someone else—anyone else—have called in the anonymous 911 tip? I half feared that it was a setup, and they just wanted to draw me in and get my hands dirty so they could control me. But stronger than my fear was my hope that it was a test, that they wanted to make sure I was truly trustworthy before they trusted me with my father's whereabouts. Even beyond that, I harbored a hope that my father knew about the situation, and would receive an accounting of my actions from Timur.

Surely there were other, more pragmatic reasons that I had been chosen for this task. Timur, as the shot caller, was undoubtedly far away from the neighborhood when the arson went down. Roman probably was too. The 911 operators used some sort of call tracking; it would be highly suspicious if a crime in Manhattan was reported from Brooklyn. The actual arsonists could have made the call, from a burn cell phone or the pay phone, but if they did and it was traced to them, there would be questions about what they were doing there. They must have been out on a fake job. And that was assuming that at least one of them was even a real Con Ed worker. As it was, the truck was just part of the scenery.

If the call was somehow traced to me, through a store security camera or something, I could easily explain that I was on my way to set up for the day, and happened on the scene. I was just a witness at the right place at the right time. Roman had wanted a perfect witness, who would indicate the offending party, without leading to any other theories. This all made sense—but it also meant the police might come talk to me. I was jittery all day long, waiting for them to arrive.

Mendy showed up on the street about an hour after me. I was happy for the distraction.

"You're out rather early today," he said.

"The early bird gets the worm," I said.

"So they say. I don't know much about birds, myself."

My first sale of the day was a copy of I. B. Singer's *Lost in America*, a tall hardcover with thick, glossy pages. The special paper stock was necessary to accommodate the color illustrations by Raphael Soyer. Because of the book's superior physical quality, and the fact that it was out of print, I was able to get twelve dollars for it.

My father had been fond of this book. Maybe not fond, but accepting. He usually dismissed Singer as "Jew fairy tales" for nostalgic Americans. "Like your mother," he said. "They want old-world Jews without smells of old world or of Jews." But he had liked this book. He said it was the only one where Singer tried to tell the truth. He didn't like the pictures though, too sentimental. As far as countrymen went, Alojzy liked Conrad more than he liked Singer, especially *The Secret Agent* and *Under Western Eyes*. He read all the books by Polish exiles, enjoyed the poems of Sydor Rey, and had great respect for General Anders, who led the Polish march from Russia to Tehran in 1942. Al had read Anders's thick memoirs more than once. Anders and his men marched from Poland to Israel. I connected my narrative to Al. He connected his narrative to these men. Were we all part of the same long thread?

Rayna joined me on the street around ten in the morning.

"Are you well, Izzy?" she asked. "You seem jumpy. In fact, you are acting like me."

"No," I said, "I'm fine."

While Rayna watched the table, I went to call Roman.

"It's done," I said. "No problems." I was sure that the men in the Con Ed truck had already told him this, but I felt a need to speak out loud about what had been done.

"I don't know what you are talking about," Roman said. "But very good."

The sun was out that day, but the cement was strangely cool. People gossiped about the newsstand fire. The collective assumption was that a kerosene space heater had probably caused it. News vendors loved to use them, and they were notoriously dangerous, especially around stacks of paper. These things happened all the time. Milton was a prime example. I parroted the theory.

Business was slow, as it was a Friday. Still, it had been a long day for me, and I was exhausted by midafternoon. Two yeshiva bochers were out on the street, stopping people and asking them if they were Jewish. Like all eager young Lubavitchers, they wore battered fedoras on their heads, in imitation of their dead rebbe, Menachem Mendel Schneerson. They had been given the afternoon off from class to increase holiness in the world by cajoling secular Jews into performing sacred rites.

I was intimately familiar with the Lubavitchers, because they had a Chabad house at Oberlin. The house was maintained by a young rabbi and rebbetzin from New York who hosted Shabbos dinners and study sessions for curious Jewish students like myself. I'd attended many of these, and learned a lot of things. The rabbi had taken it upon himself to familiarize us with foundational Jewish texts. I found it hard to stay interested in Mishnah, or anything relating to the minutiae of religious law and observance, but I was entranced with the volumes of the *Midrash Rabbah*, which offered story upon story about biblical characters. I was also interested in the rabbi's accounts of the Hasidic masters. He was an ordinary man from Queens, but he had a legacy that stretched back for three centuries.

One story that had always stuck with me was how the fifth Lubavitcher Rebbe had reacted when a tsarist officer put a revolver to his head. "That scares a man who believes in one world and many gods," he said, "but it doesn't mean anything to a man who believes in one God and two worlds." This fascinated me. I didn't want to be someone who was scared of a police interrogation—like the one that might still be coming because of my 911 call. I couldn't quite convince myself there was nothing to fear in this world, but I did believe in another one beyond this one. I didn't completely understand, though, why we should have absolute faith in the next world. Yes, it existed, but what if a third world existed beyond that one? And yet another world beyond that? Maybe a person should just choose a world and live in it.

The rabbi at the Chabad house had been generally tolerant of my questions, even encouraging, until the night I showed up for Shabbos dinner tripping on acid, and made a scene explaining to everyone that

I had seen angels myself, and could teach the rabbi a thing or two about holy mysteries. The next evening, after sundown of course, he called to say that I'd scared the rebbetzin, and was no longer welcome in their house. The excommunication didn't bother me so much as the fact that when I came down, I couldn't actually remember having seen any angels. Now that I was in the streets, seeing real ghosts and real flames, these antics were embarrassing for me to recall.

The yeshiva boys approached our table. Rayna gave them a wary look, and told me she had to walk off for a bit. They must have reminded her of the boys in the community she had fled from. Maybe they reminded her of the boy she was supposed to marry.

"You are Jewish, maybe?" one of them asked me. I was wearing my Yankees cap over my kippah. I thought about lying and saying no, so they'd go away, but I found that I very badly wanted to tie tefillin. Not because I needed spiritual solace, but because the ritual was ordering, and my mind was disordered with anxiety.

"Wonderful! What's your name?"

"Izzy."

"Your Hebrew name."

"Right. Yitzhak."

"And your mother's name?"

"Ruth." As always, Alojzy's name didn't seem to matter to anyone.

Bernie had taught me how to tie tefillin. It was not a daily ritual for him, but he did do it occasionally. I had found it intriguing at first, but fairly rote, and soon lost interest. Al, thanks to scientific communist indoctrination, found all such rituals superstitious and absurd. At the Chabad house, though, I'd learned that for the tying of tefillin to be truly meaningful, you have to tie the straps in such a way that they make the Hebrew letter shin—ש—on your hand. On the parchment in the tefillin boxes are letters written in ink, and you must write a letter on your skin to bind them to you. The story of the world is written in letters, and you must become part of that story.

I held out my arms so the yeshiva bochers could wind the straps. After they had helped me tie myself up, I covered my eyes to pray. I tried to feel the elation, the feeling that I was connecting myself to something higher. Mostly though, I just felt the tight leather straps binding my skin and thought of the man whose name I bore, and how he must have felt so long ago, up on Mount Moriah. Trusting his father so much as they walked up the mountain. Then beginning to wonder why they carried no animal to sacrifice. Slowly piecing the terrible story together. Then seeing the knife rise above him.

|| ■ ■

The next day, Mendy showed me an article in the *Daily News* about a news vendor named Suhaib Abdul-hak who had been arrested on suspicion of staging the firebombing of his own newsstand. There was a picture of the burned newsstand; the metal structure was still standing, but had twisted, blackened, and collapsed inward. The article, which was only a few sentences long, offered no clear motive. An eyewitness saw Abdul-hak fleeing the scene, and he was picked up shortly after the arson. Evidence found at the scene connected him to the crime.

The paper also had an article about Andrew's firm—Haber Simson—being under investigation by the SEC. Apparently, they had been lying to their clients about returns. I didn't know enough about the business world to know if this was a routine thing or a serious issue. Andrew would have to explain it to me the next time I saw him. At the moment, I was too fixated on Abdul-hak's story to spend much time on a business article.

The police had never come looking for me, and now that Abdul-hak had been arrested, I guessed they never would. If they had collared Abdul-hak for the crime, they had no reason to believe anything more complicated was afoot. An economically struggling news vendor wanted an easy way out of his lease. Or if he owned the newsstand, then he wanted the insurance payout. Either way, I'm sure the police had connected the dots. An open-and-shut case. If Abdul-hak had some far-fetched alternate story for them, it was just because he was trying to save his skin. They weren't going to waste time following up on it. Whatever trace of drugs or criminal activity had been present was carried out in the duffel bag long before the fire inspector showed up. Probably Abdul-hak had decided his safest bet was to make a false confession. What was he going to do, tell the police rival drug dealers targeted him?

"This surprises me," said Mendy, shaking his head.

"How so?" I asked. What did Mendy know about the situation? Was it as secret as I thought it was?

"Well, I know Abdul-hak, a little. Nice guy. He always seemed very proud of his newsstand. You'd see him out there, touching up the paint. He came here from Yemen, with the dream of being a business owner. An aspiring petty capitalist. He always talked about opening up a corner store or small grocery, but the newsstand was his first step. I can't imagine he'd do this to his own place.

"But you never know," Mendy continued. "Maybe he was in debt over his head, or there was some other situation. I know he'd had his ups and downs in business. I think he had his fingers in a few things, other than the newsstand. You never know what's going on with people."

"No," I said, feeling slightly guilty. "You never know. Who's to say what happened?" I hadn't thought about the man's story or dreams when I framed him, any more than Al thought about the lives and dreams of the Syrian soldiers when he had to call in the air strike. He couldn't afford to. I wanted to hold on to my and Rayna's little home, I wanted to find my father, and I wanted to stay in the good graces of these scary men who knew him. I took care of me and mine. This stranger's life was not my problem. Abdul-hak wasn't just a hard-working immigrant; he was also a drug dealer. He knew the rules of the game. I was learning them myself. The guilt began to leave me. I did what I had to do. There was no looking back.

14

THE STORAGE UNIT SMELLED of rubbing alcohol, and glue, and old paper, and my sweat, which hardened into my clothes when I came in from pushing the cart. The stiff, oily cloth rubbed against my skin as I walked, leaving my thighs and armpits painfully chafed. I kept smelling gasoline and smoke on my clothes, though I had to remind myself it was from all the car exhaust on the street, not from the newsstand fire.

Rayna also smelled of sweat, though her scent was more womanly. In such close quarters I couldn't deny the reality of her corporeal form. What I saw and heard could be illusions, or astral manifestations, but her smells were real.

It wasn't that we weren't sanitary. I kept a big bottle of Dr. Bronner's castile soap on hand, which we used as toothpaste, shampoo, and regular old body soap when we washed up in the restroom sinks. The harsh soap dried out my skin, and my desiccated hands were rubbed raw from pulling the ropes tight when I tied the boxes to the cart.

We used a lot of rubbing alcohol to keep the books clean and shiny and to clean up any food spills. Our bed was very close to the floor.

At night my sweat dried on my skin, binding my skin to the nylon of the air mattress when Rayna's tossing had pulled the bottom sheet away. My big nose, hanging off the edge of the mattress, was just two inches from the alcohol smell of the floor. It made me nauseous and it also made me want a drink. But better alcohol on the floor than cockroaches swarming, hiding in the pages of the books.

We were in dire need of a cleaning day, so we trekked uptown to my sister's apartment the Tuesday after the newsstand fire. Rayna had been living with me for over three weeks, and neither of us had showered during that time. The last time I had been up to Becca's was more than a month ago.

Rayna didn't seem very comfortable with the subway system. She hadn't left Boro Park by herself very often until she ran away. The elevated train line was a site of death in Galuth's painting; the subway tunnels were connected to Sheol in Rayna's account.

"The train can be disconcerting," she said, when we were settled in our seats on the 6 train at Spring Street.

"Yes," I agreed, though I had been riding it my whole life, and found it much less disconcerting than driving a car. But Rayna probably didn't know how to do that, either.

We stayed on the 6 local at Union Square, rather than scrambling for the 4 or 5 express. Passengers piled in and surrounded us. An overweight businessman was pressed against Rayna's right side. She held her laundry bag tight with her right hand, and on to my arm with her left. If I went to jail for the arson, or anything else, Rayna would be left alone. I could handle the incarceration; I would keep my head down, and read. They have to give you a Bible, if nothing else. Freedom of religion. But I would feel terrible for abandoning her.

Seeing Rayna's discomfort on the train reminded me of riding the subway the first time I tripped on acid, and how it had felt strange for a long time afterward. This was during my junior year of high school, not too long after I turned down Al's offer to go west with him. I told Rayna the story as we rode uptown. She knew, vaguely, that people did drugs—she saw junkies and crackheads in the streets everyday—but she didn't know what LSD was, specifically, and I had to explain it to her.

"I had never been able to get any acid in the suburbs, so I went into the city with two guys I hung out with, Mike and Adam, because Adam had an older brother at NYU who could hook us up. We took the Long Island Rail Road into Manhattan and went down to his dorm on Third Avenue. We all chewed two tabs but nothing happened, and we sat on the edges of the two dorm beds. We smoked a couple bong loads with Adam's brother's friends to bring us up. It still felt like nothing was happening, but I guess we started to come up or at least get rambunctious because they kicked us out."

The train came to Grand Central, and passengers poured off. People going to the Upper East Side, to East Harlem, or to the Bronx were still on the train, but three-quarters of the riders had been heading to Midtown. Rayna seemed to breathe easier once the car was less crowded, and no stranger was sitting too close to her. She still clutched her laundry bag to her chest. Mine rested on the floor of the car.

"We headed back to the subway. The day was a bust and we figured we'd just get the train back home. I picked a busted yellow plastic radio up off the street by Union Square. Mike and Adam made fun of me for carrying a piece of garbage around, but to me it was beautiful and giant, like a boom box from a real live 1970s ghetto, and I could actually see the music notes coming out of the speaker. On the subway, I realized I could control the speed of the train with the volume knob of the radio. For that moment, I had complete power over my environment. I made the train go faster and faster, then slowed it down." Our own train sped up. The conductor announced it was going express, and the next stop would not be until Eighty-Sixth Street.

"We were all peaking by the time we got off the train at Herald Square, and instead of going to Penn Station we ended up walking all the way up to Central Park, where there was slush on the ground and our feet froze. We were too gone to understand that the feeling was coldness. We spent the next three hours running through the Ramble, believing we were being pursued by the police." The same, paranoid feeling of being pursued by the police was with me again, and had been for the past four days since the fire.

"Were they really chasing you?" Rayna asked.

"No," I said, "it was just in our minds. We all believed it, though. It was real to us."

Becca's apartment had a nice shower with a big shower head, a sliding glass door, and a dial so you could get the water to just the right temperature. The shower felt wonderful after weeks of washing up with a sponge in an industrial sink at the storage facility. There was a combination washer and dryer next to the treadmill in the little alcove where I slept when I first came back to the city. The machine was small, but neither Rayna nor I had very many clothes to wash.

I wasn't a huge fan of the Internet or the TV, and was glad they weren't a part of my daily life, but after being on the street, it was fun to put on a music channel and check my e-mail and the news on Becca's desktop computer. I had several e-mails from my mom and sent her back a brief note, saying that I was fine, that I was working at an independent bookstore in the Village, and dating a nice Jewish girl. Rayna knew what TV and the Internet were, but she'd never really used either before. She was excited by them, but she also remained a little suspicious. Overall, Becca's apartment in the sky offered a refuge from the street. We were far from all the problems down there.

There was an e-mail from Becca too, time stamped from right after I moved downtown.

She had also left a note for me on the kitchen table, dated ten days ago. That's the kind of thing you could count on Becca for, to date a note so you'd know when it was written.

Izzy—

I don't know when you will see this, but I missed you when you stopped by the other time, and I'm sure you'll stop by at some other inconvenient time.

I did get your postcard, but didn't know where to write back to. Anyway, hello, you don't use your e-mail?

There are extra clean towels in the closet, but please put them in the hamper when you are done.

What are you doing? Where are you staying? I don't know exactly where you are. Leave the address of the bookstore so I can come by if I get a chance. You are still working there, I presume?

Call me. Don't call this number, I'm never here. You have my office number, I think, or just call my cell. But first, call Mom, she's worried.

I thought you were going to stay here longer than you did. I hope you didn't feel run off. You know you're welcome here.

—Becca

Even though Becca was just laying it on thick in her note, I did feel badly about mooching off her apartment and then ignoring her, so I called her office. She was busy, and only had a minute to talk, but we made plans to meet for dinner the coming Monday evening. She said Andrew should be able to come too, and to my surprise I found myself looking forward to seeing both of them.

Rayna was taking a long shower, surely enjoying the feeling of hot water on her skin. The newly constructed building always had hot water, so you could stay in the shower as long as you liked.

While our clothes dried, I sat on the couch with a towel around my waist, reading *Knickerbocker Avenue*. When Arturo returns to Brooklyn, he is a different man. No longer interested in the quiet life of a baker or store proprietor, he joins Don Niccolo's crew. Applying the violence, efficiency, and leadership skills he gained in Vietnam, Arturo quickly establishes himself in the organization. Niccolo is impressed with the increased revenue that comes in under Arturo's watch, and Arturo rises to become Niccolo's chief lieutenant. Niccolo's former lieutenant, Agastino, is not happy with this shift, but when he and an accomplice try to shoot Arturo, Arturo kills them both with his bare hands. Having secured his position, Arturo marries Niccolo's daughter, Isabella. Don Niccolo holds a lavish wedding feast for the young couple, inviting the entire neighborhood.

As the '70s go on, Bushwick changes. Many of the old Italian families and businesses move to Queens or Long Island, leaving only the poorest, roughest Italian families. Black and Puerto Rican families move into the neighborhood, bringing with them teenage gangs that have no respect for the old Italian organized crime networks. Newer Sicilian immigrants begin to move in as well. The Sicilians have none of the older mafiosos' objections to peddling heroin, and sell it through the street gangs.

I heard Rayna open the bathroom door. Out of the corner of my eye—the part not on the page—I saw that she was brushing her hair.

"What story are you reading?" she asked.

"This same crime one, from before." I looked up at her. She wore one of Becca's purple towels around her body. Her head was tilted to the side as she struggled to get the knots out of her long, wet hair, and the side of her neck stretched taught and smooth. Her breasts were normally suppressed in her high blouses, but now I could see the shape of them, full and flush, threatening to tumble out of the top of the poorly wrapped towel.

Rayna and I frequently kissed and hugged now, and held each other's hands. At night, we would often kiss passionately for a few minutes, but it never went further than that. We never got naked, let alone had sex. It was clear that Rayna didn't want to do that, at least not yet, though we never explicitly discussed our physical relationship. I didn't exactly understand the problems that Rayna had left behind, but I understood the limitations of our relationship, and didn't want to ruin what we had. But then I saw her in the towel and was overcome with the most lustful thoughts.

Rayna turned so she was facing me. What she saw was plain. She stepped toward me, and I stood up. Our bodies were being drawn together. Then Rayna jumped back and ran into the bathroom, slamming the door shut behind her. It was three-quarters of an hour before she came back out, fully dressed. "I was cutting my hair," she explained. This was evident; her hair had been hacked unevenly shorter. We folded the laundry together in silence, and headed back downtown.

ı ı ı ı

The next day, the weather radio forecast a thirty percent chance of rain. "Chance" meant how much of a chance were we going to take by going out on the street. Best-case scenario, the thirty percent would be enough to scare off other sellers, but not enough to actually rain us out, and we'd have more of the market share. Worst case, a storm would come too quickly for us to cover our books with a tarp, and the rain would ruin them. When I asked Rayna what she thought we should do, she shrugged and said we should wait.

We hung out for a while outside the storage space. By the time we knew it wouldn't rain, it was too late to go out on the street and get a full selling day in. After a while, Rayna said she was going to go take a walk. I'd given Rayna a set of spare keys I found in the storage space, so we didn't have to worry about coordinating anymore. I worried about Rayna when she went out by herself, and wondered where she walked. Each time she walked out the door, part of me was afraid that I'd never see her again. But she could go where she wanted.

I decided to sort through a box of books I'd bought off a woman a couple days earlier. They had been her late father's, and she'd sold me the whole box for twenty bucks, which was a good deal considering the books were in excellent condition for their age. There were a few I knew I couldn't sell and would have to throw out—no one wanted old legal books, they became outdated quickly—but at that price it was easier to just buy them all and recycle the junk.

The box had several Jewish-interest books from the '70s: Koestler's *The Thirteenth Tribe*, a psychology book about the *Akeda*, analyzing Isaac as a victim of child abuse, and a memoir by a sabra who'd served in the Haganah. The man has some never fully explained falling-out with the Haganah leadership, and is marked for execution in 1946. The hit squad, made up of his old comrades, comes to his flat in Jerusalem, but he manages to escape to Cairo, where he lives until the 1953 revolution, when he has to escape again. He goes to Mexico City and from there, eventually, to Cincinnati, Ohio, where he lives under an assumed name. In constant fear that Mossad agents will come for him, he purchases firearms and keeps his eyes on the windows and doors.

Was that what life felt like for Al, wherever he was hiding? He had to be somewhere. If he'd taken a bus from Port Authority, where had he ended up? Most likely in some city to the west. Chicago? Las Vegas? A smaller city, like Bismarck, North Dakota? Was he relaxing with a new, local girlfriend at a bar, or nervously gripping an SKS he'd bought at a gun show, peeking out through the motel-room blinds? Could he imagine me waiting for him here?

I fell asleep reading, drifting into a dream. The images were in and out, but the emotion of the dream, the strong feelings of constriction and fear, stuck with me when I woke. Was there a reason I had these feelings, or was the book lingering in my subconscious? I thought often of Akiva and Aher, but I understood Ben Zoma, who could never make sense of what he'd seen and lost his mind. I tried to order the images in my own mind. Rayna left, and eager IDF volunteers from my high school battered the door. Terror filled me, and I couldn't move. A life raft bobbed in the ocean. Was I on the raft, or watching it from land? How did these things fit together?

I decided to go out for a walk too. A couple of Zoya's girls were folding shirts in the corridor, but Zoya herself wasn't around. Mendy was sitting on the concrete loading dock outside the storage space. His luggage cart, with cardboard boxes and plastic bags strapped on as always, rested beside him. He looked lost in thought. I thought about walking by and letting him be, but I needed to talk to someone. "Mendy," I called out from several feet away so as not to startle him.

"Izzy," he said, looking up. "How you doing?"

"I'm okay. You decided to sit out the iffy weather too, huh?"

"Yeah, you know how it is. I made a decision—it's all subjective, I mean, it's more your own comfort level than a meteorological reality—I made a decision not to go out. Not to risk it. The weather radio was saying thirty percent this morning. Other times, in the past, I might have gone out in those kind of conditions. But not today."

"Yes," I said, "I wasn't prepared for battling the elements today myself." I sat down next to him on the edge of the loading dock.

"I'll say." He examined my face. "You do look a little—forgive me for saying so—thrown. Everything's all right?"

"Yeah. No. Everything is actually fine, I think. I was asleep . . . sometimes when I wake up, it feels like it takes me a long time, maybe all day long, to figure out which parts were the dream and which parts were real life. If that makes sense."

"I know exactly what you're saying. Only, I wouldn't be so quick to assume that this part is the real life, and the other one is the dream."

"Ha."

"Well, it could be wishful thinking on my part. You know, I often hope that there's something I'm missing. That things are better than how I experience them. Listen: last night, I thought about killing this guy, I really did." He stopped talking, his face clenched up on the line between sadness and rage.

"Nu?"

"See, I was walking around, maybe ten o'clock, which is unusual for me, so late. But I was walking around, and I wanted to buy a cream soda. So I walked into that little store up there, on the corner of Bleecker. And there was this group of guys standing in front of the cooler talking, so I had to ask them to move. But they just stopped there. I thought they didn't hear me, but then one of them said, 'Why do you need to go inside there? So you can steal something?' I knew I heard that, but I thought maybe I heard wrong. I said, 'Excuse me, what did you say?'

"And he went, 'Oh, I think you heard me.'"

"That's messed up. What kind of guys were they?"

"NYU-type guys. Clean-cut. Maybe a little older than college . . . the NYU law school is right there, probably they were law school guys. That would figure."

"I can picture them," I said. It was easy. I thought about the night less than two months earlier, when I'd gone out with Andrew and DC and the others, how DC had been rude, even cruel, to the beggar. In my silence, I'd supported DC. Now I saw myself in the crowd that had mocked Mendy and felt guilt. But then I imagined myself growing old and becoming like Mendy, being mocked by guys like Andrew and DC, and felt ashamed.

"It hurts me," Mendy said. "I've lived in the Village over thirty years, and the neighborhood has changed around me. And I don't belong there. I'm not welcome. Where else could I go, though? The old Italian men are dead, their kids are in the suburbs. The old bohemians, the old queers, the old freaks . . . my old friends: they drank themselves to death, or they killed themselves, or they died of AIDS. Their apartments went market rate, and these assholes moved in.

"All I wanted was a cream soda. I know how I look, and I had my little cart." He patted the luggage cart's handle like it was a dog's head. "But what the hell gives them the right to do that to me? Or anyone? Huh? Why would they do that?" It seemed like he really wanted an answer. For a minute I felt like he'd seen through me, that he knew I could have easily been part of that group, if I'd made a different turn.

"I don't know, Mendy. I really don't know why people do what they do. But you said something about almost killing someone?"

"I was pissed. I went . . . they use this expression, 'saw red.' That's literally how I was. I was almost blind, and just seeing the color red. The way your father used to get." I noticed the past tense. Mendy was convinced my father was gone. To him, Al was just another dead friend, one more body on the heap. I was the only one that maintained faith. "I was gonna fight this guy. He said, 'Bring it on, old man.' Oh, I was gonna bring it on, that's for damn sure." I could see the switch coming over Mendy, as he relived the moment. That beautiful old anger. That pure street violence that no amount of gentrification could do away with.

"But his friend was just a little bit smarter than him. He took a look at me, saw the fucking plain murder in my face, and he said, 'It's not worth it, Bobby, he's got less to lose than you do.' Which is true, though he said it in this dismissive kind of tone, so they could save face. I would've liked to shove his face in too. So they dragged him outside. And I was so mad, I forgot to even get my cream soda."

"Damn," I said.

"It reminds me of when I used to live on the Lower East Side, in the '60s. There was a group of tough guys, real hoodlum types, that hung out in what we used to call a candy store. I know it's different now, but back then, around Rivington Street, it was real rough, a real drug kind of neighborhood. But this group of guys, they'd mess with me every time I came down the street, to the building where I lived. I don't know if it was because I was white, or more the way I looked, in terms of long hair and dirty clothes and all. Or maybe they were just bullies. But one day, I just had enough. I was walking down the street and before they could come fuck with me, I walked into the candy store and said, 'Listen. Next time you guys wanna start with me, you're gonna have to kill me. 'Cause otherwise, I'm gonna kill every fucking one of you.'"

"What happened?"

"Nothing. I walked out. They never messed with me again."

"They didn't call your bluff?"

"Who was bluffing?" Mendy shrugged. He was standing up now, his shoulders were loose, ready to swing.

"You would have killed them?"

"Then, the way I felt then, yeah, I was ready to kill them."

"They could have killed you."

"Sure." He nodded. "Sure they could have. Absolutely. I'm a little surprised they didn't, thinking back on it. But, you know, there aren't as many killers out there as they'd have you believe. Most people, they talk a certain way, but I don't think they'd necessarily cross that line. It's easier now, with the guns. But still. Back then, they probably would have had to stab me. Which they might have done. But most people don't really want to stab a person to death." I wondered if Mendy would stab someone to death himself, or if it was just anger talking. He was tough, though; he'd survived out in the streets a long time. Probably he could stab someone to death, if he felt threatened or disrespected enough. I didn't have to wonder if Al could stab someone to death, only if he had.

The sketchbook picture of the dead soldier flashed in my mind. What was Al sorry for? Had Al killed this man? But they were fellow soldiers. Friends, Roman said. Had Al failed, allowing him to be killed? But the man had made it to New York, if Roman met him, so he wasn't killed in the war. I wondered if I could kill someone, if

I could stab or shoot them, to save myself or someone else. I hoped I could, if I had to. "My father fought in a war," I said. "Two wars, technically. I don't know if he killed anyone. Not everyone in a war does. But I think he did."

"I wouldn't be surprised if that were so," Mendy said. "You know, I didn't see eye to eye with Al about that military stuff. Because he was a conscripted soldier, and I was a draft dodger. I wasn't going to go kill people in Vietnam. They kept me locked up for sixteen months because of that." So Mendy's political speeches weren't just talk.

"But I understood what it was, to be a soldier. Because I had some friends—I won't say me, but some friends—back then who believed it was okay to kill people if it meant you could save a lot of other people from being killed. One of them was a good friend named Diana . . . she died on West Eleventh Street." He took off his glasses and rubbed his eyes. "I was supposed to go see her there. But by the time I got there, the whole town house was gone. I'm not going to say anything more about any of that." Mendy was talking about the famous Weather Underground explosion I'd read about at college. Two activists had been building a bomb, with the intention of attacking a dance at an army base in New Jersey. The movement had moved from peaceful protest, to sabotage, to attempted mass murder. The bomb exploded in the bomb makers' hands, killing both of them and another friend who was in the house. Mendy would have been the fourth victim. He had his secret war stories too.

"Well," I told Mendy, "I'm glad you weren't there. I'm glad you're alive." He could have been stabbed to death. He could have been blown up. It was dumb luck that he was here talking to me.

"Thank you. But am I?"

"Are you alive?"

"No. Am I glad I'm alive? Am I glad I lived another thirty-five years since then?"

"Oh. Aren't you?"

"I don't know." He thought about it for a moment, then shrugged again. His boney shoulders stuck out from his wifebeater; the shrug was full and genuine. "I guess so. I mean, I don't think I want to die.

If I did, I could have thrown myself in the river by now. Or in front of a train. But I didn't give a fuck, that day in the candy store, or most of those days in prison. I still don't, really. I felt like that when I was a little kid. Someone would pick on me, or make a comment, and I'd lose it. And since that time . . . I don't know that anything's changed. I feel just about the same as I did when I was nine years old. Nothing has changed. Nothing has been gained. I don't understand other people or myself any more now than I did then."

"You haven't gained any wisdom?" I asked.

"No, I don't think so. I don't know if I learned anything in all this time of being alive."

He turned to face me again. "I understand, maybe, that you're asking for yourself as much as for me. Like you want me to tell you that you will grow wiser, that some of the dust will clear from your eyes. I hope it does, Izzy, for your sake. I do. But me, I got off on a wrong foot somewhere—before I can remember—and I never got on the right one. Since then, I've just lived the days."

I said good-bye to Mendy, and went and treated myself to some pesto pasta salad at an artist café up on Spring Street. Artist cafés were cheap a long time ago, but now they're expensive, designed for kids who have their parents' credit cards and don't really understand how much money things cost. The two art students in front of me in line were talking about a pair of white jeans one had just bought for two hundred and fifty dollars. I stood behind them in my pants, which had once been a light gray but were now smeared with soot and tar from the street.

The pasta salad was good, though, and came with a chewy bread-stick. It was seven dollars, but the fact of the matter was that the money in my pocket was my dad's too, and a year earlier I had been subsisting on a student meal plan Bernie paid for, so I wasn't different from the hip artists and students in the café, except that I smelled worse and none of them talked to me. I was somewhere between them and Mendy, but I didn't know exactly where.

Mendy's stories troubled me. Not the violence—I could accept violence—but that nothing came of any of it, that no one seemed to become wiser, or less angry, or less afraid. I saw my world as a story moving forward, but for Mendy, the world was a collage, snippets pasted together with no sense of narrative or progression.

Back in the storage space, I sorted through the box from that morning. I puttered around for a bit, and got a few other things done. When I lay down for the night, Rayna still hadn't come back home. I was worried. She had been gone a long time.

Some time later, I woke up and saw Rayna sitting on a crate, staring at me. My eyes took a moment to focus, and at first Rayna appeared hazy. I rubbed my eyes, to make sure she was there, and I wasn't dreaming again. She was real. Her legs were crossed, and she leaned back against the wall, with her arms folded over her stomach. I was still getting used to her short hair.

Her eyes were puffy, like maybe she'd been crying.

"Rayna." I sat up. "When did you come in?"

"A little while ago. I didn't want to wake you. I was sitting here thinking."

"What were you thinking about?"

"The *Megilat Esther*. Do you know it?"

"Yes, I've heard the scroll read on Purim. I know the story." When was Purim? It must have passed us just a few weeks earlier. It was a commandment to hear the whole scroll read. I remembered sitting in the Chabad house at school, half drunk in a clown costume, listening to the rabbi's voice go up and down.

"The scroll is not the whole story," Rayna said. "What it says in there is true, about who Esther was and what she did, but there are other things that happened, that they didn't want to write down in the scroll." What was Rayna trying to tell me? What things had happened?

"Can you tell me about them?" I asked. She nodded.

"Yes, I want to." She came and sat down next to me on the mattress.

"Esther had heard what had happened to Queen Vashti when she refused King Ahasuerus. Ahasuerus made sure everyone in the kingdom knew. So when Esther was chosen to go live in the castle, she wasn't happy. It was scary for her. She was a slave, under the control of a eunuch called 'Hege, Keeper of Women.' She had to come when Ahasuerus demanded." I recalled Rayna talking about her family wanting to marry her off to a man.

"Her uncle Mordechai said he was protecting her. He said he would protect his family. But he was just fighting with Haman. He didn't do anything to help Esther. In fact, he used her, like a chess piece. A well-positioned little queen carved out of stone." Rayna's voice was growing stronger and more confident as the story went on.

"So she escaped. She made a rope of the fine silk bedsheets, and climbed out the window of the castle. She made her way back to the Jewish neighborhood in Sushan, and went to live with her childhood sweetheart, a *sofer* named Shahin. They lived in the back room of his shop, in a room piled high with half-finished scrolls. He loved to write the lines of scripture, and she loved to watch him work." I looked around the storage space. Not all stories were direct allegories, but she seemed to be describing us and our surroundings.

"Shahin was kind to Esther, whom he called by her old name, Hadassah. They ate yogurt with honey, and held each other close. But Esther could never be truly happy with Shahin, as much as she cared for him, because every night when they lay down she remembered being summoned by Ahasuerus to his bedchamber. Even if she never saw the king again, she would always be under the control of him and Hege." Did Rayna suffer through such painful memories, every night? What tyrant had forced himself on her?

"What's worse," Rayna said, gesturing with her arms, "Esther knew she *would* see the king again. She knew there was nowhere in all of Persia she could hide. Every night, she waited for the king's Immortals to storm the shop, burn the scrolls, and take her away.

"In the end, though, it wasn't the warriors who came for Esther, but her uncle Mordechai, who was an old *frum* Jew. Everyone in the community respected him. He was worse than the Immortals, because he came under the guise of kindness, not violence. He convinced her she had to return to the king's palace, to be an advocate for the Jews. Under Mordechai's direction, she had the king murder five hundred men in Sushan. She had him hang all of Haman's sons. She had him kill people in other cities. She was covered in blood. But she still had no true power. She was still summoned by the king at his whim. That was her fate." This seemed to be the end of it.

Rayna sat on the crate, staring at the floor.

"But maybe," I said, wanting to find some hope hidden in the story, "Maybe Shahin—"

"No," Rayna said, shaking her head. "Stop. There is no more to it. That's the whole story. Shahin is the one who wrote the *Megilat Esther*, at Mordechai's request. Maybe he believed that was what he had to do as a Jew. Or maybe he wanted the honor of composing a new scroll, instead of just copying as a *sofer* does. But if he had something else to say, something to add to the story, he could have written it into the story then. He didn't. He meant well, at least at first, and he loved Hadassah, but he was part of it all in his own way." When her story was finished, her eyes dropped to the floor. I didn't try to speak again. Rayna was telling me about her life, and I needed to try to listen. I thought of the *Megilat Esther*. How could a person know which stories were real, and which stories were written to cover up other stories? I knew that what Rayna was telling me was real. She was filled with pain and fear. She looked up, and we sat with our eyes locked for a moment.

"You can hug me now, Isaac," she said. "I want you to hug me, and hug me tight. But please don't kiss me. Not right now." I held Rayna close, and felt her tears on my bare shoulder. I kept trying to make sense of her story. She was telling me that I hadn't done anything wrong. But she was also telling me that she would continue to suffer because of the wrongs that had been done to her in the past. I wished I could make it better somehow. But she had just told me I couldn't.

15

WHEN I FIRST MENTIONED dinner with Becca and Andrew, Rayna said she'd be happy to go. Becca and I made plans to meet at a diner in Midtown, near her office. But when the time came to go on Monday night, Rayna refused to leave the storage space. She was apologetic, but said she couldn't bear to go to a restaurant and meet new people. I had to go without her.

I got to the diner before Becca and read *Knickerbocker Avenue* while I waited. When Don Niccolo refuses to change with the times, Arturo goes behind his back, importing his own heroin from Southeast Asia through his military contacts. Arturo's violation of mafia code and chain of command angers Don Niccolo and his counterparts in the other families. At the same time, the Sicilians are angry that Arturo is undercutting them in the local heroin market. After Niccolo attempts to censure Arturo for his activities, Arturo meets with the Sicilians, and convinces them to murder Niccolo, in exchange for a heroin supply deal. Once Don Niccolo is deposed, both the old-guard Italians and the Sicilians acknowledge Arturo as the new don of Bushwick. Little Arturo from the bakery shop is now king of Knickerbocker Avenue.

"Hey, Iz," Becca said, sliding into the booth.

"Hey," I said, "good to see you."

"You too, Izzy. Sorry I'm a few minutes late."

"No, it's cool. I'm sorry it's been a while. I've been working."

"You don't have to tell me. That's how we are. We're hard workers. Work comes first. We learned that from Mom." It was true—our mother always held down at least one job when we lived in the city, and she never missed a day of work. Even after we moved in with Bernie, who made plenty of money, she always worked.

"I guess so. Andrew couldn't make it?"

"No. It was kind of weird, actually. He said he'd be here when I talked to him Sunday. But then I called him when I was getting ready to leave the office this evening, and he'd completely forgotten about it. He sounded really hyper and stressed, and then said he couldn't come." She opened her menu.

"That's too bad. He's having a rough time at work?" Even at the nightclub, he and Jason had argued about figures. And I'd read in the paper about his firm being under investigation.

"Yeah, it seems like it. Hard to say for sure, though, because he's pretty private about it. But I have my own work to worry about."

"Well, tell him I say hi."

"I will. He likes you. Anyway, I was hoping you'd bring this girl you mentioned?"

"Rayna couldn't make it tonight. You'll meet her though."

"I hope so. What does she do?"

"She's working with me." Becca closed her menu and dropped it on the table.

"And what exactly are *you* doing?"

"Selling books."

The waitress came and took our orders. Our mom had worked as a waitress when Becca and I were kids and Alojzy still lived with us. We'd sit in a booth like this one and draw on paper place mats with crayons.

"So you're selling books?" Becca said. "At a bookstore downtown?"

"Yeah."

"Which one? I know there are a lot of little ones in the Village still. Maybe I can come visit. I don't have time to get downtown too often, but if I have a chance . . ."

"It's actually a freelance sort of thing, not at a store." Becca glared at me. I was being evasive, but I didn't want Becca to know I was working in the streets.

"Freelance. Right. You sound like Alojzy, always trying to explain away his little hustles. That's what you mean, a hustle."

"It's honest work. But yes, actually, it's Alojzy's business. I'm just running it until he gets back. Or until I find him."

"What do you mean, 'gets back'?" Becca looked shocked. "You think he's alive?"

"You think he's dead?"

"That was my understanding. Mom thinks so. Someone told her he was."

"Goldov. I met him. I think he's a liar."

"Whatever. The real point is, I don't think about Aojzy at all."

"He's our father." The waitress placed two cups of coffee on our table.

"He was supposed to be. But he sucked at it. Then he fucked off. Mom raised us. Bernie helped a little at the end, he's a good guy, but Mom mostly did it herself. It was easier when Alojzy was gone, because he couldn't blow Mom's money on his schemes. If Alojzy's alive, and he shows up tomorrow, I won't talk to him, any more than I'll take the time to talk to any other random bum off the street." Becca was wrong. Yes, what she was saying was true, from one perspective, but she didn't understand Al's side of the story.

"Becca, I want to show you something." I reached into my backpack, and pulled out one of Alojzy's notebooks. I knew the order of the pages, and quickly found images of us uptown as kids. I looked down at a picture of Becca as a serious child, and looked up at the face of the serious woman she'd become. "I found this in a storage locker full of Alojzy's stuff." I pushed the open book across the table to her.

She stared at the images for a moment before they registered and smiled involuntarily. Then she regained control and forced the smile off her face. She flipped the book closed and slid it back to me.

"There's more stuff in there," I said.

"It's okay. I get the idea. Thank you for showing me this. But I have you, and I have Mom. Alojzy's not a part of our family. It's been that way for a long time. Mom has Bernie. Next year I'll get married, and we'll have Andrew in our family too. We don't need Alojzy, or his sentimental memories. I have my own memories."

"Like what?" I didn't know what Becca remembered about Alojzy.

"Well, just to choose one, do you remember that day that he was supposed to watch us in the evening after school, but he got arrested?"

"No." I had no idea what she was talking about.

"I was in maybe fourth grade, so you would be in what, first grade? Is that right? Anyway, Alojzy was supposed to come by the school in the afternoon to walk us home, because Mom was working. But our neighbor, old Mrs. Almanzar, was there instead. She said Alojzy had been arrested outside the building—she didn't know for what, but she had watched the whole thing from the stoop. As he was being cuffed, he asked her to come get us, I guess so the school wouldn't call Child Protective Services. No one could get ahold of Mom; this was before people had cell phones. So we had to go sit at Mrs. Almanzar's house all evening and listen to opera records and eat, like, bowl after bowl of flan until Mom came home from work.

"Mom was frantic when she came to pick us up, crying and hugging us tight. We stayed up all night on the couch together, watching TV. Mom cried half the night. She'd been working all day, and she didn't know what Alojzy had gotten into. Then he came in the door in the morning, with a box of donuts, like nothing had happened, and didn't understand why Mom was so mad. 'Coppers took me to the Tombs,' he said. 'Those guys always got it in for me. But a night in jail never hurt no one.' He didn't see that it had hurt Mom. Or us."

Our food arrived. Becca had a Caesar salad, and I had an egg salad sandwich and some soup. We didn't talk much as we ate.

"Have you talked to Mom lately?" I asked, when I was done eating. "How is she doing?"

"You can call her and ask for yourself. Actually, no, you can't right now. She's at some sort of two-week-long retreat up in Taos. Some sort of meditation-creativity thing with no cell reception."

"That's good. She'll enjoy that."

"Yeah, I think so. I'd kill myself if I had to go on something like that, but she's doing what she wants to do. I think her free, younger life got cut pretty short, marrying Alojzy and getting pregnant with me. Having to take care of us and trying to provide a stable environment and all that. So it's her second chance now, to do all the art stuff she always wanted to. It's good for her."

The waitress came with the bill.

"Take your time," she said. The diner seemed to mainly function as a lunch spot for Midtown office workers, so it was pretty deserted in the evening.

"Izzy, I'm sorry," Becca said. "I wish I could stay longer. But I have to get home and do some work." I felt guilty about neglecting Becca for the street, and here she was apologizing for neglecting me for the office.

"You work too hard, Becca," I said.

"I know. But I'll make money now, while I have the chance, and put something away. You don't know what's going to happen." She reached for the check, but I grabbed it from her.

"My treat." I pulled out my cash roll to pay.

"You don't use a debit card?" Becca asked, incredulous. She worked for a credit-card company, after all.

"No," I said. "Cash is cleaner." I made sure to leave the waitress a good tip.

Becca and I walked to the train together, going our different ways on the platform.

It was still early when I got home. Rayna was sitting in the storage space, cleaning some books. She came over and gave me a kiss.

"How is your sister?" she asked.

"She's fine."

"I'm sorry I couldn't go."

"It's okay. Her fiancé didn't come either, some sort of work troubles, so it was just Becca and me."

We lay down to sleep. It wasn't very late, but the weather was supposed to be really nice the next day, and we wanted to get an early start. Rayna gave me another kiss when she lay down. We kissed for a few minutes, then Rayna rolled over and spooned back close to me. I rubbed her shoulders a bit, then slid my hand under her shirt. I went to sleep with my hand on her breast. Since Rayna told me the story about Queen Esther, some of the tension was gone, and we had become more physically affectionate.

||∎

The weather forecast held the next day. As soon as the table was set up, people started buying books. It was all we could do to keep up with the demand. I was happy to be busy.

An apartment-building super named Armando sold me a box of books. This wasn't uncommon; supers often had to clean out apartments when someone died or was evicted. The box was mostly English-language novels with some German, Hebrew, and Yiddish books at the bottom. I paid thirty bucks for the lot. Armando didn't try to negotiate; he just said "cool," put the ten and the twenty in the pocket of his tan coveralls, and headed back west.

Rayna took out the Yiddish books and started to read through the titles. Even though her hair was a good bit shorter now, it still blew in her face, so she kept it back with a denim headband while we worked.

"This book is called *Masoes Benyamin Hashlishi*, by Mendele Mocher Sforim," she explained. "It says that it's the story of a man's travels." She read Yiddish better than English. In English, she sometimes had to stop and sound out words, but her Yiddish was fluid and natural. "This one is *Gedankn un Motivn—Lider in Proze*. Ideas and poems. *Krieg Ein Zeik*. More poems. *Der Sheydims Tants*. It involves demons, I don't want to look inside."

During the late-morning lull, she took a small Yiddish book with a red hardcover binding out of the box and went off to read it by herself on a bench in the shade. When she came back to help with the table at the start of the lunchtime rush, I asked about what she'd been reading.

"It is a little storybook," she said. "It involves a girl who lives in a village with a blacksmith father, and three mean blacksmith brothers. They are cruel to her. Only, she finds out that they aren't her true family."

"How does she find out?" Rayna was adding up the price of a stack of books. She waited until she'd finished and told the customer the price before she answered.

"She sees a vision of her true family in a bowl of water, when she is doing the washing."

"So what does she do?" I asked.

"She goes off, through the forest and up the mountains, to look for her true family."

"Does she find them?" Rayna shook her head.

"Not yet. So far, she only gets the glimpses in the water. But I didn't finish reading."

When the afternoon lull came, I was ready for a break. Rayna and I sat on the curb and drank lemon seltzer. We were back on our feet every few minutes though; a steady stream of customers kept up all through the afternoon. Before we knew it, the after-work rush came upon us, consuming us with work, and it went on like that, through dinnertime and into the evening. A couple of tourists tried to snap photographs. To them, we were classic and picturesque. We all hid our faces. Our lives didn't belong to them.

At night in storage, Rayna counted our money. She was better at keeping records than I was, and copied the numbers neatly into photocopied tables. It was largely because of her bookkeeping that business was going so well. She said that our take for the day was two hundred and twenty-seven dollars, which was more than I'd been expecting.

We went on doing well. We were busy all day long when we were on the street, and we spent our days in storage working on inventory. We sold a good deal of Al's back stock, and had to constantly be on the lookout for books to buy. Occasionally, we stopped by apartments to buy books from people who were moving or who had inherited the books from a previous tenant. We kept the good books to sell and left the others on the curb, to be scavenged or recycled.

Business dipped for a week in late April, when the students were gone for spring break, but then in early May they started buying books for their final papers. More and more tourists appeared on the street. The weather got warmer. We stood out on the street in the sun and sold books.

❙❙ ❚ ■

"What are you reading?" Rayna asked, as she came into the storage space with groceries one rainy afternoon. The light spring showers had been enough to keep us off the street. We didn't have a refrigerator, and mostly ate from the deli, but we kept a few things like fruit, peanut butter, and bread on hand in a small plastic cooler.

"I'm not reading, actually," I said. "I'm looking through one of my father's sketchbooks." I hadn't shown her the books again, since she failed to recognize herself in the Galuth painting, but I hadn't stopped looking through them on my own. Since the newsstand arson, I'd begun to scrutinize the images of Roman and Timur in particular more and more.

"This little boy is you!" Rayna said, looking over my shoulder. She was delighted to see me as a small child.

"Yes."

"So this with you is your mother? And your sister, Becca?"

"Yes, that's right. Can you take a look through the book?" I asked. "Maybe you'll recognize something. I don't know what everything is." She took the book, hesitantly, and flipped through the pages, blushing at the pictures of the naked woman. As the images became more violent, her expression changed to one of fear.

"I don't recognize anything," she said. "Your father has lived a very scary life."

"Yes, he has. I don't know if it's been scary for him. But it would scare anyone else. It would scare me."

"Everyone gets scared, Isaac." Her fingers traced the clouds of smoke like she might push through the page, into the world of the drawings.

"I guess that's true. I mean, that's probably why he ran away, and why he's hiding somewhere. Because he's scared of something. Maybe something in one of these books."

"When he comes out of hiding, he's going to return here?"

"I believe so. I hope so."

"So he could appear here at any time?" She looked frightened.

"Sure. But there's nothing to be scared of. He's my father. He always looked out for me. He'll look out for you too. He'll like you." She nodded, but looked unconvinced.

A few days later, Rayna handed me a crumpled flyer.

"Isaac," she said, thrusting the piece of paper into my hands, "look." It was folded into four quarters, and had apparently been in her pocket for a while.

"What is this?" I asked.

"It was stapled to a temporary wooden wall, for when they build something?"

"Like around a construction site?" She nodded.

"I got it two days ago, on a walk. But I wasn't sure if I should give it to you." I unfolded it. At the top of the photocopied flyer, the following words were written by hand in thick black marker:

Madame Yemaya will answer all your questions.
Am I on the right path? And what is my destiny?
Psychic Readings — Astrology — Tarot Cards

Underneath was a photograph of a woman wearing a long white robe. She gazed toward the camera. Her long black hair and some sort of jeweled tiara framed her face. She looked familiar, but I couldn't place her. At the bottom of the photograph was a West Village address.

"In your father's picture books is a nude woman. I blushed when we looked at her."

"Yes?"

"It's the same woman. I recognized her from the wall, then. But I went and got a flyer the next day to be sure." We took out the sketchbook, and held the psychic's photograph next to the face of the reclining nude. Rayna was right. Al and Madame Yemaya were intimately acquainted.

"Why did you wait two days to show me this?" I was annoyed.

"I don't think you should go find this woman."

"Because she does black magic?" King Saul fell because he visited the Witch of Endor, to summon the spirit of Samuel, the seer and leader who had anointed him as king. Saul knew what he was doing was wrong, but he needed the guidance of Samuel's prophecies. When Samuel rose, with other spirits at his side, he was angry, and told Saul that his action had cost him the throne. Divine favor passed from Saul to David. Coming from the religious world, Rayna feared the occult. I thought of Andrew, and wondered how he was faring with his conjuring.

"No." Rayna shook her head. "Not just that. I don't think you should go searching so much. Things are okay. We are all right here. We are safe. You want to upset everything for yourself. You'll tear open your own world. I felt guilty lying to you, not showing you the flyer. But I wish you would just throw it away now that you've seen it." I understood that she was afraid our little world would collapse around us when I found Al, and I wondered if she was right. Maybe I had misinterpreted the signs in the beginning, and the postcards were leading me to this place, to my new vocation and my life with Rayna, and I was supposed to be focusing on what was in front of me, rather than chasing more shadows. This was an appealing thought, but ultimately it felt like an excuse, a cop-out.

"If there's a chance to find my father, Rayna, I have to look."

On the next overcast day, a Thursday, I left Rayna at the storage space and went to Madame Yemaya's storefront, on Carmine just off of Hudson Street. The place was tiny, but the neon sign made it easy to find. Madame Yemaya sat inside at a small table, reading the *Daily News*. She looked tired. She was draped in scarves and beads, but they were all carefully arranged so that her ample breasts were largely exposed.

Seeing me hesitating at her door, she jumped up. She held me with her big black eyes until she could get close enough to grab my hand and pulled me inside.

"Come in! Come in! You have a question? You have a problem? Madame Yemaya will help you out! You look like you are very much troubled." Her accent reminded me of old vampire movies. "For you, I will only charge ten dollars for a reading." She pushed me down into a chair, and took her own seat, without letting go of my hand. "I can see you are a troubled young man. I can see that you are adrift on a raft in a sea of mysteries. I can see you chase ghosts into their graves. I can see you must change—"

"Look, I'm not here to have my fortune told."

"No? I see." She put her other hand on top of mine and leaned close. "What is it you are searching for then? You do not have questions about the future? You are looking for a mystical experience in the present?" Her words were accompanied by ornate hand gestures.

"No, I actually wanted to talk about Alojzy Edel." She dropped my hand on the table and cursed in Spanish.

"What the fuck is this?" she asked. "Does he owe you money too?" She took out a pouch of tobacco and began to roll herself a cigarette. "I can't help you with that." Romania was gone from her voice, replaced with the South Bronx.

"No, he doesn't owe me anything. He's my father. But I found a picture of you—several pictures, actually—in his sketchbook, and I wanted to see how you knew him."

"A picture of me? You mean those nudie pictures of me he loved to draw. Christ. He loved my body. But you're a little pervert, ain't you? No wonder you wanted to hold my hand when you came in here." She licked the edge of the rolling paper.

"No, I didn't. I'm not. I just want to know how you know him?"

"I lay on the bed and let him draw my naked body. So how do you think I knew him?"

"You were his girlfriend, you mean?"

"Ha. Sure. I guess you could call it that." She lit the completed cigarette and took a deep drag. "The funny thing is, I was actually dating his best buddy, Simon."

"Simon?"

"Yeah, a painter. Russian dude."

"Oh. Semyon? Goldov?"

"Yeah. I called him Semen. Ha!" She slapped the table. "He didn't like that, made me call him Simon. But then he brought Al around." Yet another reason for Goldov to hold a grudge against Al. "Biggest mistake he ever made. Because the minute I met Al, man. What a man. I'd do anything he told me to. Just anything. So when he told me to forget about him, I did that too." She took another drag on the cigarette, exhaled in my direction. "He's missing. Or dead. He's dead."

"He is?" My heart started beating faster. Was this the truth? Or just the same rumor continuing to circulate? "How do you know he's dead?"

"I'm a fucking psychic. And not for nothing." She laughed. "No, I don't know what the hell ever happened to that asshole." So there was nothing to her words. "But it seems like you don't either, or you wouldn't be here asking me questions. He's dead to *me*, either way."

"Oh. Well, I just haven't seen him for a long time. And no one seems to know where he is. So when I recognized your picture on your flyer, I thought maybe you had an idea about where he'd gone."

"I wish I could tell you something about that. But at the same time, I also really don't care. He was just a con man who turned my head with his pretty muscles and sweet words. And believe me, he wasn't the first or the last to pull that trick." Everywhere I looked, people were tearing Al down. I didn't know how he'd look to me when I finally found him. "Oh, don't look so sad, puppy dog. *Mira*, I never knew nothing about my own daddy. He left my mother and went back down to Puerto Rico when I was two years old. I never saw him again. No problem. I didn't go looking. Matter of fact, you can leave, and I'll never have to see you again either."

"Before I go, I was hoping I could ask you about this other sketch, of another of Al's friends . . ." I had brought along the photocopied picture of the dead Israeli soldier in my pocket, in the hopes that one character from the sketchbook could lead me to the next.

"Sorry. Your time's up. Now let me get the twenty-five you owe for the reading."

"The sign says fifteen. And you said ten."

"The past costs more than the future." I paid the woman her money and left. I hated to admit it, but part of me wished I had listened to Rayna and not visited this woman. Al seemed to be retreating farther from me, not moving closer.

16

"DID YOU LEARN ANYTHING from the fortune-teller?" Rayna asked me when I returned to the storage space that evening. She was trying her best to express interest, to make up for keeping the flyer from me. I wasn't mad at her.

"The fortune-teller is a former girlfriend of Al's. But they broke up a long time ago. She doesn't know anything."

"I see."

"But this man Goldov, his name keeps coming up. You said he looked familiar in the sketchbook, when you looked before. Can you look again?" Instead of responding or acknowledging the question, she went over to the other side of the storage space, and started taking out some new books and the book cleaning supplies.

"Please, Rayna?" After a moment, she sighed and put down the rubbing alcohol and paper towels. I took out the book featuring Goldov and the Galuth Museum most heavily, though I avoided opening to the study of Rayna's face.

"This man, here." I pointed him out. She studied him for several minutes.

"Yes. I'm pretty sure he has been to see my father. Quite sure. But I don't know anything else. You have to understand, my father is very respected. Many, many people come to see him. Every day they come, for advice, or for a blessing. Or for permission to do things."

"Your father is an important man," I asked, "a rabbi?" She nodded.

"Yes. A rebbe." Her insistence on that term implied that he was a Hasidic leader, not just a regular rabbi. "People respect him so much. He is a great man. But there are . . . hypocrisies. He sees things as they are supposed to be. To be around him . . . is to have a weight upon me."

She slammed the book shut, and pushed it away from her with both hands. When she turned toward me I saw that she was silently crying. I took the sketchbook from her, and put it back in the box. I scooted next to her, and put my arm around her.

"It's okay," I said. "We don't have to look anymore." She didn't say anything. "I know you came to the city to get away from your father and his world, Rayna. And I don't want to make you think about that if you don't want to. It's just, I came down here to find my father. It's been two months, and I'm not any closer."

"I know you miss your father, Isaac," she said, slowly. She held on to my hand. "But talking about my father won't help. Nothing good will come of that. We have to draw lines between us and the world. Let things be as they are. Please."

"I'm sorry, Rayna. Forget about the sketchbooks. Let's get something to eat." She wiped the tears from her face with a handkerchief.

Hours later, Rayna was reading aloud to me from one of the Yiddish poetry books we'd gotten from Armando. I didn't understand the language, but I liked hearing Rayna say the words.

Her voice was interrupted by a ringing.

"What is that sound?" Rayna asked nervously.

"It's just the cell phone," I said.

"I didn't know you had a telephone in here."

"It belongs to the people who lease this space for us. My father's friends. I keep it charged in case they need to talk to me." I hadn't pointed Roman and Timur out in the sketchbook, because Rayna didn't need to know anything about criminal activity.

"Oh," she said. "The ones you helped so early in the morning. The day of the fire." So Rayna was more observant than I gave her credit for.

By the time I got the lantern turned on and found the phone, it had stopped ringing. The phone beeped again, and a text on the display said, "Call Roman ASAP." I climbed over to the business side of the storage unit and pressed the call button.

"Isaac," Roman said. "I appreciate you calling me back at such a late hour."

"No problem."

"We also appreciated the favor you did for us a few weeks ago."

"Don't mention it." I spoke casually, though I'd obsessed about the arson, and its possible repercussions, for days afterward.

"Very good advice. Remember that yourself. In any case, we have something else going on tomorrow night, and we are man down, due to an unfortunate turn of events. Normally I would turn to the Edel in such a situation. As he is not available, it occurred to us that you could step in. I should add that this is not a favor, this is paying job. You will be well compensated."

"Absolutely," I said. The opportunity to step directly into my father's shoes was more of an incentive than the money. Whatever was happening was illegal, but I had already crossed that line with the arson. In for a penny, in for a pound. And to tell the truth, it had been exciting when the newsstand burst into flames. "Tell me where and when." Roman gave me the details, and we said good night.

After I hung up, Rayna gave me an inquisitive look.

"Is everything all right, Isaac? Do they need us out of this space?" She looked frightened at that thought.

"No, no, nothing like that. My father's friends just need some help with something else tomorrow night," I told her. "Nothing is wrong. It's just business."

"Don't go," she said. "Please. I don't want you to go." I didn't want to upset Rayna any more than I already had. But I wasn't ever going to punk out again, like I had when I was a kid. More importantly, I wasn't going to pass up on a chance to follow deeper into Al's world. This was a job he would have done. I had to do this.

Roman had said that he would pick me up the next night at nine p.m. in a white Honda Civic. I waited on the corner of Varick Street, and when he pulled up, I got in without a word. He just nodded at me, then zoomed down Varick toward Canal Street. We went straight across town on Canal, then back up to Delancey and over the Williamsburg Bridge.

On the bridge, Roman turned to me and spoke. "This is a real hoot for me, you riding there in the passenger seat. I think of the times Al has rode with me. And now I have Edel Junior here."

"He's ridden with you a lot?"

"From time to time." I hoped Roman would offer a story or two, but he didn't.

"But I mean, it seems like he's worked with you guys often."

"Certainly. He has been someone we can rely on. The man who was supposed to be coming on the job tonight is not so reliable. He got into argument at a club last night. Some drunken nonsense over a woman. He slashed other man's face pretty badly with a broken glass, and called me from Brooklyn House of Detention.

"Timur did not want to postpone the job, and we discussed who could be brought in as a last-minute replacement." Evidently, Timur going out on a job himself was not an option. He was the don; he didn't get his hands dirty. "Like I said on telephone, I wished I could call Al, but since I couldn't we call you. You have proven reliable enough. So far." So all the favors I'd done for them had led to something. I had shown that I could be trusted.

"Well, I'm glad you called," I said. Roman just grunted in response. After a while, he said, "You are wondering where we are going."

"I am," I admitted.

"But you did not think you should ask?"

"No."

"You were correct." I grinned, but Roman did not.

"The former Brooklyn Navy Yard is now devoted to private commercial facilities. One of these facilities consists of warehouses, climate and humidity controlled for preservation of artwork. Collectors, galleries, and even museums store art there. Some of these pieces of art are quite valuable." He turned down a side street. "Another reason I called you: Timur remembered you saying you have some knowledge of art. Not every hooligan can be trusted with something as delicate as a painting." I was glad to hear this. I was afraid that my continued contact with Roman didn't get me closer to Timur, and any higher-level information. It was good to know that Timur was thinking of me, and that I was performing a task he valued.

"First stop." We pulled into an open warehouse in deep South Williamsburg. Two men were waiting for us. Roman greeted them without making any introductions. They both had Jamaican—or some type of Caribbean—accents. They wore well-used work clothes, and I got the feeling from their tired faces and rough hands that they were actual workers, not gangsters.

Roman and I changed into new Dickies coveralls that he took from the trunk of the Civic. Roman still looked like a gangster. God knows what I looked like.

"You guys clear on the plan?" Roman asked the men.

"Plan, chief?" the older one asked, playing dumb.

"The plan. Nu? What is your understanding of what is happening tonight?"

"The plan, chief, is that my partner and I go in, and we do our job. Which is strictly HVAC. Make sure everything is in order with the system. This is a routine check, as is done every month."

"And?"

"And I am telling you, by way of a heads-up, that for safety reasons I will have to cut the electricity for the area exactly eight minutes after we enter, and that the electricity will stay off for exactly fifteen minutes. This includes the electricity for the lights and the security cameras. Who knows what goes on in the dark? I only see the section of vent in front of my flashlight. Same goes for my partner here. We are very focused when we work."

"That is the right way to work," said Roman, nodding.

"What should I do?" I asked.

"You will do as you are told."

We all climbed into the Jamaicans' HVAC truck, them in the front and Roman and me in the back. The guy in the passenger seat put on a Brooklyn Tabernacle Choir CD, and no one talked after that. A few minutes later, we pulled up to the front gate of the Brooklyn Navy Yard. Our driver showed a work order and ID to the lone guard, and we were waved in without any scrutiny. I thought about the Con Edison truck on Sixth Avenue. For that matter, I thought about myself and all of Zoya's Russian girls pushing our carts, and the construction worker who delivered my cell phone. Timur understood that workers, especially immigrant workers, were invisible in New York City, and that he could dispatch them to take care of his illicit business without anyone ever noticing.

We reached the old red brick warehouse where the art was kept, and entered just as easily. Inside, it wasn't all that different from the storage facility where I lived. The same track lighting, the same cold cement and thin carpet. The same rows of steel doors. The only differences were that the doors here had key panels instead of padlocks, and this place was air-conditioned.

When the other guys got the electricity cut off, Roman took out a large LED flashlight, and led us down the row until he found the unit number he was looking for. He had a couple security codes written out on a scrap of paper, and he got the door to pop open on the second try. Inside, about a dozen paintings sat on a metal rack. They were contained in bulky wooden storage frames that were clearly not display quality, but allowed enough space for the paintings to be wrapped in polyurethane without having the wraps actually touch or constrict the paint.

"I'll go grab the dolly," Roman told me, handing me a smaller LED flashlight from his coverall pocket, "while you locate the painting. Oil painting, on canvas of about one hundred forty centimeters by about ninety centimeters. The subject is Jewish, a rabbi. But expressionist, not normal like the portraits in Judaica shops and lawyer offices."

I was worried that I wouldn't be able to find the right painting—this was the only discreet, independent task I had been given—but when I came to it, just a peek under the plastic wrap was enough for me to see that it was as Roman had described it. The rabbi was on his knees, with his face turned up toward the sky. His face was dark, with straight creases. His mouth hung open, and his large brown eyes searched the cosmos. His beard, made of loose swirls of gray and black paint, wilted down to his chest. His talis was pulled tight over his head, not for ritual reasons, but out of a need for shelter. The black night was mosaicked with stars that looked like uncut white, blue, and purple diamonds, and filled the whole background. The painting reminded me of Galuth's work, though this image was sparser, less complex, than the picture of the woman falling from the train tracks.

Roman came back with the cart, and together we carefully slid the painting down onto it. The painting was light, and we could have carried it by hand, but it felt safer to rest it on the middle of the dolly than to risk bumping the corner of the painting in the dark. As it was, we had to be very careful going around the corners of the narrow aisles with the dolly in the dark. The old oil paint was already cracking, and the canvas probably couldn't take too hard of a bump without some flaking off. I could see why Roman had wanted to bring a helper along.

"This way," he said, directing me to a corridor that led into another, nearly identical room of storage units. We stopped in front of one, and Roman typed in another number from the sheet.

"We're not carrying it out?" My heart had been beating faster, in expectation of the moment when we broke the picture out of the warehouse, under the nose of the armed guard.

"No," Roman answered. "Some art handlers will come and carry it out next week in a crate. It will be a routine, legitimate job for them. They will have a work order. No one will pay any notice. But enough questions. The lights will be on in five minutes. Let's get it in there." Just like that, before I even understood that the heist was happening, the heist was over. The lights snapped back on, and ten minutes later, we were walking out the front door, empty-handed, telling the guard to have a good one.

After we'd dropped off the HVAC guys and were driving back to Manhattan, Roman took a half-full pint bottle of Sobieski vodka out of his jacket pocket. He kept one hand on the wheel and managed to unscrew the cap with the other. He took a long slug, lowering the bottle's contents by a good three-quarters of an inch. I wondered if this was a victory ritual, or if Roman had been nervous about the job. He offered the bottle to me, and I took a sip. When I handed it back to Roman, he drained the rest and tossed the empty bottle in the backseat. Maybe he drank like this every night, and was just waiting for work to be over so he could get to it. The vodka put Roman in a more talkative mood.

"You weren't raised by Al, huh?" I wondered why he asked this. Did I not seem like Al's son to him?

"Not really. Only when I was very young."

"I know how that is. I left my parents at the age of twelve to go to special gymnasium school."

"A gymnasium? Like, a preparatory school?"

"No, like a school that is a gym, where you work out and do athletics. I was a strongman. I mean, really, a real strong guy. I am still, actually, but then, oh buddy. So you know how some people go to university? Or like your papa, he went to the arts institute? I went to the weight-lifting institute." We turned up Bedford Avenue. The street was full of Satmar families. For some reason, Hasidic families always have their kids out on the street in the middle of the night. I wondered if the family Rayna had run away from was like these families.

We crossed back over the Williamsburg Bridge.

"You know," Roman said, "your father likes to go out and have a good time."

"I guess he does."

"You ever been partying with the old man?"

"No. I was too young to drink the last time we spent any time together."

"Too young to drink . . . I'm not understanding." He looked over at me with pity in his eyes.

"I mean, too young to go out drinking. I was a minor."

"Oh." He shrugged. "You too young to drink now?"

"Nope."

"Well, let's pull over and wet our whistles, then?" Apparently, once Roman started drinking, he liked to keep going. "There is a place I like on Avenue B."

"That sounds fine to me." I knew Rayna was at home, worried, but this seemed like a good opportunity to learn more about Roman, and hopefully about Al as well.

"You know what they said when I first came to New York City? Alphabet City: first you come to Avenue Awful, then Avenue Bad, then Avenue Crazy, then Avenue Dead. Now it's all changed. No thanks to me. Ha ha! But I like the changes, truthfully. Nice place to get a drink, now."

We went into a bar called the Sack. There were high-backed stools at the bar, and overstuffed chairs upholstered with animal-print fabric elsewhere in the room. The place was very dark, even though there seemed to be bright lights everywhere. We sat at the bar and Roman ordered us each a shot of vodka. He offered a toast to my father. Then we got another round and I offered a toast to his family. Then Roman proposed a toast to the family of the bartender, who was so kind in keeping the shots coming quickly.

"I was always a strong boy," Roman told me. "Even before I went to weight-lifting institute. One time, I was ten years old, and I came home with my mother to our apartment in Odessa. We couldn't get up to the staircase, because these three drunks passed out in front of the door. Me, I just picked them up and moved them out into the court-yard, far away from the door. I stack them neatly, one on top of the other, like firewood. Because I was still a good boy, then.

"I liked it there, you know, in Odessa, when I was a boy. People talk about how terrible communism was, and they are correct. But there was niceness, when I was a kid. There were no more purges, everyone had enough to eat. You lived with your parents in apartment. Everyone lived with their parents, in the identical apartment. You came down into the courtyard and played with your friends, who wore the same sweaters as you to keep warm. Then you went upstairs and ate the dinner.

"I come here, it's whole other world. Everyone is in their own world, actually. In Brooklyn, black thugs walk around with unloaded pistols in their belts, trying to lecture you from the book of Corinthians. Pakistani mosques make the call to prayer from megaphones. Hasids ask you on the corner if you are Jewish. Some of them want to circumcise you. Some of them want to sell you stolen laptop computers. You know what I mean?"

"I do," I said. What he described wasn't really the America I'd grown up in, but I'd always seen glimpses of it through Al, and now it was a world I was really starting to see, being on the street every day.

"It's funny about Hasids though. I talk to them a lot, for business. Mainly Glupskers, but Satmars, Skverers, all these syndicates. Sects. What have you. They are an odd bunch. I am Jewish too, you know?"

"Yeah?" He didn't look Jewish. Maybe it was the muscles.

"Oh yes! I came here as 'refugee status' and everything. It's just, you know, there wasn't ever anyone around to show me how it is to be Jewish. What to say, or do, like a Jew. Timur is from an old Bukharan family; he knows all rituals and everything. But me, I never got to learn any of it. I never learned any of the, you know, the book."

"The Talmud?"

"No. The book."

"The Torah?"

"That's the one. You see, my parents, maybe they didn't know much about it either. I didn't have any grandparents . . . there were not many people from the generation of the Great Patriotic War around."

"Your grandparents died in the war?"

"No, I don't think so. My family is family of thieves. A long line of Odessa Jew thieves. You know about Odessa Jews? When Tsarina Katerina built her great port, she insisted there be some Jewish smugglers there, so it could be a real respectable port. She had to pay the Jewish smugglers to smuggle in the Jewish smugglers. Probably, my grandparents were all sent to the gulags for attempted profiteering. But I couldn't say, really. No one ever spoke about it.

"Another round, bartender! To the dead Jewish thieves of Odessa! To the tsarina!"

The bar was spinning, and my face felt very hot. Roman ordered more shots immediately after we finished the ones in front of us. I had lost count of the rounds.

"A drink to your father's memory!" he said. It wasn't until after I drank the shot down that I realized he had said my "father's *memory*," not my "father," or my "father's health." Did he actually believe my father was dead? Did he *know* my father was dead? Had the liquor caused him to forgo a farce? Or was that reading too much into the ramblings of a drunk man?

"Roman," I said. "Have you been in touch with the man who drove my father when he left town? I'd like to meet him." I was tired of being kept at arm's length.

"What's that?" He squinted, trying to place what I was saying. "Oh, yes, the man who drove him to Grand Central. He left town as well. Hasn't been around. I'll let you know soon as I hear from him."

"Sure. Thanks." Before it was the bus station, now it was the train station. Roman could have been getting his facts mixed up because he was drunk, or he could be making them up as he went along. My only actual confirmation that Al was alive was Roman's story. I had not talked to the "witness" myself. It wasn't even clear he existed. And even if he did, my 911 call was proof that people would lie for Roman and Timur.

"I have to get going," I said, but Roman grabbed me by the shoulder and forced me back onto my stool.

"More shots!" he shouted. "Many shots for my friend and I!" He started buying shots for people around us as well. I finally managed to slip out as Roman was trying to lift a giggling blonde girl over his head.

When I left the bar I was so drunk I couldn't walk in a straight line. I stopped to wretch into a trashcan, but nothing came up. I wanted to lie down on the street and go to sleep, but I forced myself to walk all the way across town to the storage facility.

I stopped for a slice of pizza and a liter bottle of water, and forced myself to drink all of it. Between the grease, the water, and the spring night air, my head started to clear a bit.

Rayna was awake when I made it back to the storage space. She sat in bed, with the lantern on.

"Why are you still up, Rayna?" I asked.

"I was worried about you. I knew you were doing something bad with those men. I was afraid you would disappear, like your father did."

"No, no. I'm fine, Rayna. Everything is fine, Rayna."

"Are you sure? You sound strange. You keep saying my name."

"I'm a little drunk. But not so much as earlier. I just need to drink some more water." She handed me the jug, and I took a long drink.

It was warm in the storage space, and the alcohol made it feel even warmer. I took off my pants, and came and laid down on the mattress. I cuddled up to Rayna, and lay with my head on her chest.

"Everything is really fine?" she asked again.

"Yes. There was no problem with the business thing. Only . . . only my father's friend said some things that made me think he thinks my father is really dead. I don't think he is. But what if he is . . ." I hated that my faith was wavering. I hated that I was letting myself doubt that I'd find Al.

"You don't know what you don't know, Isaac. You are a good son either way." Was I? I didn't think my mother would say so. What would Al say? I was maintaining his name on the street, and now in the criminal world. I believed that was worth something. What did Rayna know, or understand about what I was doing? Or did she just mean that I was a good man? Was I a good man? Could I be a good son of Al's and also be a good man, or were those two different things?

We lay on the mattress for a few minutes without speaking. Rayna leaned down and kissed me on the forehead. I pulled her down toward me and kissed her on the lips. She started kissing me back.

As soon as we started kissing, my erection pushed up through my thin cotton boxers. Rayna put her hand on top of it, gave a few tentative strokes, then gripped it tightly through the fabric.

"Are you sure you want—" I was surprised, but excited.

"You don't want me to?"

"No, I do, I just don't want you to if you don't—"

"No, I want to. I was afraid you were gone. And now I'm happy you're here in my hands." I didn't say anything else. She slid her hand into my boxers. Her hand felt good, after so many nights and weeks of forbearance, and I wasn't going to say anything that would make her stop. We were both quiet for a few seconds while she tugged, then I started breathing heavily, and came quickly, inside my shorts.

We started kissing again, and I dipped my fingers into Rayna's panties, just under the waistband. She pulled back for a moment, then pressed forward, and I pushed my hand down further. We kept kissing while I fingered her. After a few minutes, she came with a shudder.

Rayna pulled my hand away from her, and turned away from me on the mattress. She made a little sniffle, and it dawned on me that she was crying. The thought that I had done something to hurt her was terrifying to me.

"Are you okay?" I said. "I didn't . . . I'm sorry if . . ."

"No, no. It felt good. It's good. It's just . . . a lot."

I thought about trying to comfort her further, but I didn't know what else to say. I went to the bathroom to wash myself off and put on a clean pair of boxers.

By the time I came back to our space, Rayna was asleep. I kissed the back of her neck, and closed my eyes. I saw the swirling background of the painting we'd stolen, but no figure in the center. I had come down from the adrenaline of the crime, the buzz of the vodka, and the excitement of fooling around with Rayna. I was exhausted. I couldn't dwell on Roman's words. He was drunk, boisterous, and full of shit. I couldn't forget his words either. All I knew for sure was that Rayna was here with me. I took solace in that.

17

RAYNA AND I ARRIVED on the street three mornings later to find Mendy's cart standing unpacked in his spot. I looked around for him and saw that he was sitting on a bench in the plaza talking to a man wearing a wool cap low down on his ears. Their backs were facing me, and I couldn't really make out anything about the guy besides the hat, but a stack of large-format books stood between them on the bench, so I assumed Mendy was making a deal with him.

Mendy glanced back to check on his stuff, and saw Rayna and me.

"Oh, good morning!" He stood up. "Our mutual friend here was looking for you." The other man rose slowly. Something was so familiar about his broad frame and his achy movements. Had my father finally returned? I had been wrong to doubt. I stepped toward him. No, this man was too short. He turned around and I saw his face. It was Goldov.

"Izzy," he said.

"How have you been, Goldov?" I said, coldly. I had been suspicious of Goldov's motives since our first meeting, when he harped about money, but after hearing Yemaya's story about the love triangle between her, Al, and Goldov, I knew that Goldov was completely untrustworthy.

The fact that he seemed to be friendly with Mendy even made me a little unsure about Mendy—despite the fact that Mendy was one of the kindest men I'd ever met. But like Mendy himself had said, you never know what's going on with people.

"Unwell, to be honest," Goldov said, answering my greeting as if it were a genuine question. "My lungs, you see. But don't worry about me. I've survived worse. So. Rumors are true. You have taken over Pan Edel's book business."

"Yes, I have."

"Like father, like son." I shrugged. I didn't know if he meant it as an insult or not. "Chip off old block."

"I guess so," I said.

"And does this mean you have taken on his business debts as well?" Goldov remained steadfast in his position on Al's disappearance. I was no longer so sure of mine. Why did I see Roman and Goldov again and again, but no glimpse of Al?

"Children shall not be put to death for their fathers," I said.

"*Shto?*"

"Is that why Mendy said you were looking for me?"

"Eh? Oh, no, no. I was only making joke about debts. Come, step to the side with me so we can speak more privately. Excuse us for a minute, Mendy." Mendy turned his attention back to evaluating Goldov's art books, while Goldov and I stepped into the secluded corner of the plaza behind NYU's ornamental shrubs.

"It is actually I who am paying you today," Goldov said. "You see, I come up primarily for Mendy to take a look at some books I had to sell, but also to deliver this to you." He reached into his pocket and pulled out a white envelope. "From our common associate, Roman." Roman had said that he would send me compensation for the Navy Yard job once he received payment from the job's client, but Goldov was a surprising courier. I took the envelope and put it in my pocket.

"I understand you helped arrange a recent acquisition for the Galuth collection," Goldov said. Of course. The painting of the rabbi actually was a Galuth. If I had trusted my eye, I could have made this connection for myself. "Our collection extends beyond what is displayed in the gallery. I handle payments, and other details, for the museum's benefactor. Roman knows that I am coming up here to meet with Mendy, so he asked me to deliver your portion of the fee directly."

"I see. Well, thanks. I appreciate you bringing me this." Goldov wasn't listening to me anymore. He was too busy staring past me at Rayna. She was turned away from us, putting our books out on the table. I didn't like the hungry way he looked at her, as if he had some claim on her. I wanted to hit him, to tell him he had no right to look at her.

"Who is that young woman?" Goldov asked.

"Just a friend of mine. No concern of yours."

"She looks familiar to me." I tensed with fear. Rayna had seen Goldov in her father's court, so he could have seen her there too. Rayna fled her father's house because bad things had happened to her there. The other night, she had become distraught at the mere mention of her father. I didn't want any part of her father's world finding her. Did the old painter really request blessings from rabbis? It seemed out of character, but I didn't know the man very well.

Another possibility occurred to me. Goldov lived with Galuth's painting, after all, and saw it every day. If Rayna bore as much resemblance to the actual painting as she did to Al's sketch, then of course she looked familiar to Goldov. This was actually much likelier, as Goldov was in constant contact with the painting. Regardless of why he recognized her, I didn't like for Goldov to dwell on the question, or pry into my life. As much as I wanted answers, it was more urgent to keep Goldov away from Rayna.

"She just has one of those faces," I said.

"Perhaps." He bit his lip, but it didn't seem that he was able to place her. This was a relief.

"Goldov," Mendy hollered. "Are we going to make a deal on these books, or what?" Goldov walked back to Mendy, and I went over to Rayna.

"Who were you talking to?" Rayna asked. She didn't seem to have seen his face closely enough to recognize him, but she was curious about my conversation. I considered telling her he was the man from the sketchbook, but I didn't see any reason to frighten her. She was the one who had wanted to shut the sketchbooks, to not pursue these connections. It wouldn't be right to lie to her, but I didn't need to go out of my way to upset her either.

"He works with my father's friends, from the other night. He used to work with my father. Can you do me a favor? Can you go to the store and get us some black tea?"

"You don't think I should finish with this box first?"

"Could you go now? I need the caffeine." I wanted to make sure Goldov wouldn't get a chance to come over for a closer look. Rayna put down the box, and went off toward the deli on Broadway. Before she returned, Goldov concluded his business with Mendy and left the street.

❘ ❙ ❚ ■

My cut from the heist turned out to be sixteen hundred dollars. I thought Roman had said that I would be getting an even two grand, but it was possible that I was mistaken, or that Roman had exaggerated, or spoken imprecisely. Either way, it was a hell of a lot of money for moving a painting from one closet to another.

I didn't call Roman to confirm I'd received the money, or to verify the amount. I didn't want to talk to him or Timur at all. There was a strong possibility that they had been lying to me about my father all along. That didn't necessarily mean that my father was dead, or even that Roman and Timur, or at least Timur, didn't know where he was. It did mean that I couldn't trust them.

Rayna and I took a couple days off from the street to enjoy the unearned money. I was happy for the break. It was almost summer, and the streets were getting hot. A brawl broke out at the Cage—the fenced-in public basketball courts on the corner of Sixth Avenue and West Fourth Street, across from Abdul-hak's still-shuttered newsstand—and two teenagers got stabbed. Tempers were running short up and down West Fourth Street. Mendy got in a shouting match with Jersey Steve—as near as I could tell, over something that happened four years earlier—and Hafid got into a shoving match with a customer from out of town. I had begun to feel less and less comfortable reading on the street, even light crime books during the afternoon lull, for fear something would go down when I wasn't watching my back, and I hadn't been able to finish *Knickerbocker Avenue*. The night after Goldov paid me, I stayed up late reading.

Arturo's reign as don lasts less than a year. The military police seize an important heroin shipment at McGuire Air Force Base. Arturo hears clicks on the line, and sees suspicious vehicles patrolling the neighborhood. The local precinct is on Arturo's payroll, but whatever is happening is clearly a federal operation that the NYPD hasn't been apprised of. Sicilians have been arrested and deported, and Arturo fears that they have given information on his operation. He begins to suspect his own lieutenants. After all, he betrayed his don when he was a lieutenant.

As the net closes in, Arturo and Isabella decide to flee to Asia. They pack their suitcases, bringing enough cash to live in luxury on a Thai beach for twenty years. The feds are waiting for Arturo at the airport. He is prepared to shoot it out with them, but when he realizes that his sweet Isabella has led him into a trap, the fight goes out of him. Arturo accuses her of being disloyal, but Isabella says she was acting out of highest loyalty; she has sacrificed her true love to avenge her father's death. *Knickerbocker Avenue* ends with Arturo, now old and gray, baking bread in the prison kitchen.

Rayna looked at the money suspiciously, but she already knew I was involved in something shady, and I soon convinced her to help me spend some of it. For the first time, we went to an actual restaurant together, a nice old Italian place in the West Village. We ate olive salad, marinated eggplant, and pasta with white sauce, and drank a bottle of good red wine.

Rayna bought two new dresses, more brightly colored than the dark ones she'd worn threadbare, and convinced me to buy myself a shirt, purple fabric with darker purple buttons and a stiff collar. I also bought myself a herringbone newsboy cap, which looked a little more dignified than my dirty Yankees cap. I bought Rayna a bouquet of Japanese irises, and we walked all around lower Manhattan feeling light and unbound.

I remembered a time when Al had made a bunch of money—I have no idea how. He and my mother picked Becca and me up from school in a rented car in the middle of the day, and took us down to the Jersey Shore. Becca and I ate handfuls of saltwater taffy, and rode a roller coaster over and over. My parents sat on the boardwalk, drinking beer out of big Styrofoam cups.

They were happy that weekend. This was why people did crime, so they could live the good life while others were slaving away. I didn't know if I wanted to work with Roman again, but I didn't think I'd been involved in my last heist. Maybe I'd still have a chance to go on a job with Al.

Rayna and I spent the whole day after our shopping trip lying in our bed in the storage space. We drank a bottle of champagne and fooled around. We still stopped short of actually having sex, but we grew more comfortable being unclothed around each other and touching each other's bodies.

"We haven't been outside all day," I said in the late afternoon.

"It's fine," Rayna said. "It's happy in here. We don't have to leave, just yet."

"Yes," I agreed. "Let's stay here a while longer." I wished that we would never have to leave that place. I think she wished that too. We could be married, and make a pledge to love and protect each other forever. We would finally consummate our union. We wouldn't need anyone else. We could spend our whole lives together.

⁙ ■

Our first day back on the street after our little vacation, I noticed a black SUV with tinted windows parked on West Fourth, between

Thompson and LaGuardia, with the engine running. The vehicle was there when we got out in the morning, and took off about twenty minutes later. The windows were so dark I couldn't see who was inside. I didn't think anything of it, especially; I just took notice of it like I took notice of everything that happened on West Fourth Street.

"They look like cops," Mendy said, when the SUV drove away. He had noticed them too. "Or even feds. Like they were waiting to snatch someone up. Someone they heard maybe hung out around here."

"Guess they didn't see their guy," I said.

"Guess not. I hope they never do, for his sake, the poor bastard. Hey, you heard about Eye, right?"

"No." Come to think of it, I hadn't seen him around for a week or so. "He get arrested?"

"Yeah. I heard it from Sonya. He's at Rikers. Got caught selling subway swipes. Apparently he had a bench warrant out for something else, and he got jammed up for thirty days."

Rayna came back from the store with orange juice and buttered bagels. After we ate, we had to finish getting the tables set up.

It wasn't until later, during the late-afternoon lull, that I started to feel nervous about Mendy's words. The presence of cops had always made me feel uneasy, long before I'd gotten into drugs, let alone become a bookseller. Maybe that was a trait I'd inherited from Al. He was not what you would call a fan of the police. Even as a kid, I'd come to school and start sweating when I saw the security guard. If he turned toward me, I would assume that I had done something wrong, and someone had turned me in for it.

My fear about the cops in the SUV was much less abstract. I had been happy to get paid for the warehouse job. Less because of the money itself—though Rayna and I enjoyed our paid vacation—than because of the feeling that I was becoming a true hustler, and was involved in something real. When I finally saw Al again—in this world or the next—I'd have a good story to tell him, one where I was a character, not just a narrator. I could show him I understood what his life was like. The flip side of this was that I was now culpable for something real. West Fourth Street was where Goldov had given me the money; it was possible that some detectives were onto the warehouse theft, and tracked it back to me through Goldov.

I had been involved in framing Abdul-hak too, even though I had thought of myself as more or less a bystander in that situation. Maybe the arson squad was second-guessing their case against the news vendor. Maybe they had footage of me making the 911 call, and decided to watch me rather than question me. This was just paranoia; no one in the NYPD cared if an immigrant's newsstand burned down. But maybe it wasn't actually cops in the SUV; maybe the rival dealer Abdul-hak was involved with had decided to make a serious play for the park. And while Roman's words had made me fear that Al was dead, they were just the mutterings of a drunk man, and the most likely scenario was still that he'd had to flee some threat. Maybe the men in the SUV were that threat.

Rayna must have noticed that I was a bit distraught, because she came and sat down beside me on the curb. She took my one hand in both of hers, and put her head down on my shoulder. I put my arm around her. All the anxiety left my body, and I was no longer afraid of the police or gangsters or anything else. There was no real reason to think the SUV had anything to do with me. It could be ICE, looking to snatch up some noncitizen street vendors—most of the hot dog guys in the neighborhood were from Egypt, and several other food vendors were from South America—or it could be a security detail, making preparations for a foreign dignitary's speech at NYU. Maybe some NYU kids had gotten in over their heads with a drug dealer. Maybe some rich NYU student just thought it was cool to get the windows of his SUV tinted. There were plenty of police and criminals in the streets, but none of that was our concern. We had each other, and we'd be fine, as long as the world left us alone.

We had a good day of selling. Restless young feet were getting ready for their summer travels. I sold all my Kerouac novels, several Steinbecks, two *Electric Kool-Aid Acid Test*s, and one copy each of *The Powwow Highway*, *Burn Collector: Collected Stories from One through Nine*, and *Bound for Glory*. A woman preparing to study abroad in Italy bought *The Stones of Venice* and a thick Italian–English dictionary. We filled shopping bags with beach reads. Classes were starting to end, and a few students came by to sell us their books from the semester. Rayna was still a little shy about interacting with customers, but when it came to buying books, she was a good haggler, and got us some deals. I didn't know how the seasons went on the street, but I hoped our good fortune would last through the summer.

That night, Rayna and I sat outside under the Artigas statue. We shared a bottle of blackberry brandy, and she read Yiddish poetry to me. I was starting to pick up some words from Rayna. "*Libe.*" "*Toyt.*" "*Khaloymos.*"

"That poem sounded nice," I said. "What was it about?"

"There is a man, and he's speaking to a woman who is far away from him. He was traveling, on his way back to her, but he's caught in the snow, and he knows he's not going to make it. But as he freezes to death, he sees her approaching. She comes to him. To save him. It seems real, the way the poem says it. But then in the spring the villagers find the man's body. The woman was just a hallucination. He died alone in the snow."

"That's sad," I said. Rayna laughed.

"All these poems are sad." She gave me a kiss on the cheek. "Don't let them make you sad." It was getting late. We strolled back across the street, hand in hand.

An SUV left the parking lot as we came back to storage. It looked like the same one from earlier on the street. I had to admit, after a minute of intense paranoia, that it was dark out, and that furthermore, I didn't really know anything about SUVs or how to recognize them. On top of that, I was a bit drunk from the brandy.

"Is there something the matter?" Rayna asked. "You seem nervous."

"No. Everything's okay. I'm just seeing things." I didn't need to burden Rayna with my unfounded worries.

We went inside and went to bed. We still had a bit of the honeymoon feeling from our days off from the street, and we kissed and cuddled for a bit.

"*Zise khaloymos*," Rayna said. Sweet dreams. We went to sleep happy. I don't know if I dreamed or not, but I slept contently, with my arm around Rayna.

Several hours later, Rayna shook me awake. Both of her hands gripped my one arm, and I thought that she was back in the world of nightmares again. But when I opened my eyes, Rayna's were already wide open.

"Do you hear them, Isaac?" I did. Our door was creaking, no, more than that, straining. Some invisible force was trying to muscle itself into our world. I wrapped my arms around Rayna and we huddled close in the far corner of our room.

The door snapped open and two men pushed in. The motion-activated hallway lights had clicked on, illuminating the invasion. Al's locks had stood strong, but the first man in the door—a bear in a black hooded sweatshirt—had popped the hinges with the crowbar he carried. The man behind him was much smaller but wore the same black pants, black sweatshirt with the hood up, and black beard. Instead of a crowbar he held a semiautomatic pistol. These men were clearly not police.

"He's not here," I told them. "He hasn't been here for a long time." These men had to be looking for Al. These were the people he had fled from.

They ignored me. The big guy came over and grabbed Rayna with his free hand. She didn't scream; she was strangely silent. I shouted "no," and tried to pull her back, but the smaller guy leveled the big, black pistol at my face and I let go. I'd foolishly tucked Al's gun away in a box when Rayna moved in, so it wasn't at hand now. Rayna started to stay something, but the guy holding Rayna pressed the crowbar across her throat, and she shut her mouth. He tossed her over his shoulder and stepped out of the storage space. I heard two sets of footsteps slap down the hall, and realized that a third guy must have been standing watch outside.

The smaller guy backed out of the room slowly. He held the pistol with two hands for stability, and kept it trained on my face until he left.

I listened to the sounds of his sneakers hitting the thinly carpeted concrete as he ran down the hallway. Even after they had disappeared, I sat frozen for a moment, afraid of what I would encounter when I stepped out the door.

Snapping out of it, I dug Al's .22 out from the box. I started for the back door that the men had evidently exited through, but it occurred to me that they might be expecting that, and would ambush me when I stepped outside. I circled around to the front corridor, winding past the bathrooms and out onto the loading dock. I got outside just in time to see the black SUV peeling out of the parking lot. Without stopping to think, I fired a shot at the SUV's rear tire. The .22's pop was barely audible in the vast city night. The round slammed into the pavement. The SUV was gone. I ran out to the street, but I didn't even know if they'd gone straight on Hudson or turned down Spring. Rayna's nightmares were real. Demons had carried her away in the night.

I didn't know what to do. Back inside, I splashed cold water from the water fountain on my face. I took a long drink. I said *shehakol*, the blessing over water and other nonalcoholic beverages, as best I could remember it, because there is a Lubavitch teaching that if you are in grave danger you should pray *shehakol*. Nothing will happen until you are done, and by then, help may be on its way. I finished praying, but no help came.

I knew I needed to do something. I needed to act to find Rayna. The clock was ticking as I sat paralyzed, doing nothing but praying and moaning. Time was slipping away from me, the story was going forward, and I couldn't control the outcome. I wished for the power of *kefitzat haderech*—the juggling of time—that the Hasidic masters had possessed. The thought brought back a sudden memory—or flashback—of that first acid trip, when I could control the speed of things by turning a knob. I saw myself slowing everything down with the turn of a knob, so I'd have time to think. The image passed as quickly as it had come, and I was no longer on the train, but alone in the storage facility.

Real pursuers had come for Rayna. The men were gone with Rayna before I could react. The SUV zoomed off into the street. Wishing I could turn a knob and control time wasn't going to make it so. There was no knob to grasp. I wrapped my hands around the grip of Al's sawed-off rifle and shook back and forth. If anyone was watching, it might have looked like I was davening. But no one was watching and I wasn't praying anymore. I wanted to get high, higher than I'd ever been, and forget all about this situation. But I owed Rayna more than that. I couldn't retreat into fantasies, memories, dreams, or stories. I needed to find out what had really happened, who had taken Rayna, and why. I needed to know where they had taken her, and how I could get her away from there.

This was clearly not random. We didn't live in a farmhouse with lit windows facing the road. These men knew all about our secret living arrangement. They knew which of the hundreds of doors to open. They'd been stalking us in their SUV. They'd watched us working, and they'd watched us coming and going from our storage space.

I'd initially thought the men were looking for Al and, when they couldn't find him, decided to target Rayna and me. That didn't explain why they'd taken Rayna. Maybe they thought I could contact my father, and taking Rayna gave them leverage. But then why not say something to me, or even torture me, to see what I knew? My next thought was that this was my fault. Something I'd done for Roman and Timur had angered someone. Maybe Rayna was being held ransom until the Galuth painting of the rabbi was returned to its owner? Again, why had that not been expressed to me? So maybe nothing was wanted from me, and the threat had come from Rayna's world. It did seem like she was the target. The men had long beards; they could have been Hasidim.

Whoever it was, I should have found a way to fight back. I should have been holding the gun when the men came in. My bullet should have struck the big man's face, not the floor of the parking lot. Because of my failure, Rayna was being held by violent men. When she first came to sleep in my storage space, I told her that she would be safe. It wasn't true. Now I needed to set things right.

BOOK 3

The Binding of Isaac

18

I NEEDED HELP. IF Al was going to reappear, this would be the time for him to do it. I needed *his* help. His connections. His scheming. His calm. His strength. As hard as I listened, there were no footsteps outside the door. Al wasn't coming. Help would have to come from elsewhere.

Calling the police was obviously not an option. I tried Roman several times, but he didn't pick up his phone, or respond to my texts. If Rayna's kidnapping had to do with fallout from their business, Roman and Timur would know who was behind it. If it had to do with one of Al's hustles, then Roman and Timur probably had some ideas. They had been holding back on that subject, but they would have to talk now. Even if it had to do with Rayna's family, or another angle I couldn't see, Roman and Timur might be in a position to help me. Roman had said he did a lot of business with Hasidim. And Goldov, who did business with Roman and Timur, knew Rayna's father. Roman and Timur would know something. And frankly, I didn't know where else to turn.

The minutes and then hours slipped away, and I was doing nothing. I punched the dangling storage-unit door five times in quick succession, bruising my hand and further denting the metal.

The front desk opened at five a.m. I told the guy on duty that I had damaged the door with a moving cart the night before. He gave me a hard time about it—to be fair, a cart had clearly not popped the hinges—but I was eventually able to assure him that the hefty repair charge added to my bill would not be disputed. It would be easier to settle that with Timur later than to raise the suspicions of the management now and get the police involved. The facility gave me the temporary use of a smaller storage unit to lock my stuff in, and I spent the next two hours transferring everything into there. This new storage space was big enough to pack all the stock into it, but had no room left to set up the mattress. That was okay; I didn't feel safe sleeping here now, anyway. This new unit was just a storage space, nothing more.

Having to move the boxes down the hall was good, because the work kept me from flipping out completely. It was a rainy day, mercifully, so I didn't have to deal with a bunch of street vendors getting ready for the day. Mendy usually came by around seven thirty or so to work on his stock on days he didn't go out and sell. I didn't want to face him, to have to explain what had happened. Time was still slipping away.

At seven o'clock, I decided to try Roman again. If I couldn't get ahold of him, I could go down to Coney Island and grill Goldov, though that hadn't been too productive the last time I was investigating a disappearance. I'd set out to find one person I loved, and now two were missing. I was losing ground. The only other thing I could think to do was go down to Boro Park, and ask where I could get a blessing from an important rabbi. That probably wouldn't work out too well. I didn't even know Rayna's last name.

This time, Roman picked up the phone.

"Izzy. I got your messages this morning. I was planning to call you back." This made me angry. What had he been doing in the meantime? Didn't he understand how urgent the situation was? Rayna was in danger. I needed to know what he knew, though, so I didn't see any percentage in starting an argument.

"Do you know anything?" I demanded. I knew I sounded frantic, but I didn't know how to keep my cool in this situation. "Do you have any idea who's behind this? I need to do something to help her."

"For now you should keep calm, and just lay low for few hours. We have a lead on the situation—I do not believe things to be dire—but I need to speak with some people before I can tell you anything certain about your friend's whereabouts."

"What lead? Enough with the mysterious shit. Tell me what the hell is going on."

"Izzy, do you want my assistance or not? I'm doing best I can to help you."

"Okay," I said. I still had to play by the damn rules. "I need your help."

"I'm sure you understand that this is not a conversation for the telephone. And as I said, the situation is still coming into focus. Can you meet us later at Kutadgu Bilig? You know where I mean? Sayyid's restaurant, in Brighton, where we first met? Come at noon. I'll be sure to have some information for you by then." I agreed, and hung up.

On my way out, I stopped back by the new storage unit and put my cash, Al's sketchbooks, and a couple changes of clothing into a backpack. I interrogated the parking lot attendant, but he hadn't come on until six a.m.; the lot was self-service at night. The closest stores were over on the avenue. Only the bodega had been open all night, and the clerk hadn't seen anything unusual. If an SUV sped by, he hadn't noticed it. I wasn't getting anywhere on my own.

I walked for a while, ending up at West Fourth Street without meaning to. For the rest of the morning I sat in a deli I knew, drinking coffee and searching through the sketchbooks. There were more answers in here, answers to everything, if only I could decipher them. Al was haunted by a dead Israeli soldier. The soldier was connected to Roman and Timur, who were connected to Goldov, who was connected to Galuth, who was connected to Rayna. But how exactly was she connected to Galuth? There were hard facts I was missing.

"Rayna," I said out loud, "where are you?" I searched for her in the pages, but knew she was somewhere in the world, afraid and likely being mistreated.

The hours passed, somehow, and then it was time for me to get on the B train to Brighton. When I got to the restaurant, Timur and Roman were at their table in the back of the otherwise empty room. I was too upset to eat any of the food they put on my plate, but I did knock back two glasses of vodka in quick succession. Timur seemed uninterested in addressing the issue at hand. After greeting me, he asked if Goldov had given me my money. He said that I had done a good job, and there might be more work for me in the future. The first time I had been invited to Timur's table, I thought that it was incredibly kind of him. Now it just seemed cruel, like he was playing with me.

"I appreciate that," I told him, losing my patience. "I do. But you know I want to talk to you about what happened last night to my friend Rayna. I'm very worried about her. I need to find her. Have you heard anything?"

"I can tell you," Timur said, "that there is no reason to worry."

"Why not? Do you know where she is? Is she okay? Tell me."

"You are close to the girl, Isaac?"

"Yes. Very close. That's why I'm so worried about her."

"Do you know much about her background?" Why was everything a question? I needed answers.

"Not specifics, but I have a general idea."

"Do you know who her father is?"

"She doesn't like to talk about him much, but I know he's a big rabbi in Boro Park."

"That is correct. In fact, he is the grand rebbe of an important Hasidic dynasty, the Glupskers. They are one of the smaller groups in Boro Park, but they are growing, and very well connected. The Glupsker Rebbe is very influential, and very respected. He has been searching for his daughter since she ran away. When he learned of her location, he sent his sons to bring her back to him. Apparently, they did so rather roughly, but they were merely concerned brothers." So

I was right about those *Hasidische* beards. Surely Rayna recognized her own brothers. That's why she didn't scream. She had been about to say their names when one of them put the crowbar to her neck. I was happy to have some sort of confirmation about where she was, and I was happy to know she wasn't being held by gangsters or killers. Everything Timur was saying squared with what I already knew about Rayna's background. But as I also knew that awful things had happened in her own home or community, I was not greatly relieved.

"So you know where she is?" I asked. "You can help me get to her?" For months, I had been building up goodwill with Timur in the hopes of finding Al. But I was willing to cash it all in now to find Rayna.

"Maybe you did not hear me correctly. They are a well-connected group. Her father is their leader. He has been reunited with his missing daughter."

"Yeah, I heard you, but what does that—" Timur held up his hand, signaling silence, and I obeyed. I hated myself for it, but I obeyed.

"You should be grateful that he is a holy man, and not vindictive." Holy man? All I knew was that his daughter had run away from his oppressive home, and that he had sent thugs after her. That didn't sound very holy to me. "Otherwise, you would have quite a bit to worry about. I would not be able to protect you. As it is, you are not to worry yourself about this Rayna anymore."

"But she was kidnapped."

"No. It was simply a family matter. No one was wronged."

"I was wronged! She was wronged." I banged the table with my fist. "This is all fucking wrong." Timur was calm. He understood the situation fully. How exactly had he come by this information? "Tell me this, Timur: How did you find out these details so quickly? When did you know this was happening? What did you have to do with this?" Timur gave Roman a nod, and before I understood what was going on I was pulled up out of my chair, and walking out the door with Roman.

"What's the idea?" I said. "He hasn't answered my questions."

"You have gotten overexcited," Roman said. "And forgotten who you were talking to. Perhaps too much to drink, or just the stress you are under. What you need is some fresh ocean air." I knew that Timur was the don, and that he expected to be treated with respect. But I needed to find Rayna.

Roman steered me up onto the boardwalk, where we sat down on a bench facing the water. After a couple minutes of me stewing with my fists in my pockets, and Roman staring out at the waves, he spoke.

"When I had been here for seven years, I had enough money to bring over my papa. I hadn't lived with him since I was twelve years old, but always he was a good papa to me. I was making money. I had my big condo upstairs in the Oceana with more room than I needed. My mother was dead, my father was all alone in his Odessa hovel. The situation was worse and worse there. I applied for a family reunification visa, spent a few dollars to push it through the system, and brought him over.

"We get along okay. He was happy to be here. But I am busy doing jobs for Timur all the time, and my father is past an age where he makes friends. He started to wear a yarmulke, because of the freedom to do so"—Roman gestured at my newsboy cap, knowing what was underneath—"but he doesn't have the patience to sit at the Chabad house and learn. All he did was walk up and down Ocean Avenue, walk up and down Brighton Beach Avenue, walk up and down boardwalk. When his knees act up, he had to stay in the apartment all day and watch the Russian language channels, or the wildlife channel.

"One day he was walking on Neptune Avenue, and a parrot starts following him down the street. Honest! A little green parrot, strolling behind him. It followed him for blocks. Finally, he sees the parrot isn't giving up, so he picks it up, puts it on his shoulder like a pirate captain, and brings him home. Now he is happy. He has something counting on him, something to take care of. Something to feed. They are the best of friends. They sing dirty songs together.

"The Jewish service, they send aide. To look in on my father, make sure he takes the medicine for his diabetes, this sort of thing. He doesn't care, he doesn't want someone telling him what to do. The old aide, he had a deal with. She never showed up to work, but when the service called to check, he'd say she was there. Then she'd come by and give him a kickback from the wages. I take care of the old papa, give him everything he needs, but it makes him feel good to have his own deals, you understand? Be a little bit independent. But this woman, I guess she ran too many scams and got fired. So they sent a new aide, last week. She comes in, her first day, and says, 'Oh my God, my parakeet Barbara! She escaped out my car window on Neptune Avenue! I thought she was dead!'

"My father said, 'Oh no, you are mistaken, this parrot I purchased at the pet store a year ago. I can see your mistake, though; parrots often look very similar to each other.'"

"Did she believe him?" I asked.

"I doubt it. But what could she do?"

"Can you tell me where I can find Rayna and her family, Roman?" Why was Roman telling me this silly story? Was he drunk so early in the day? Did he think that I believed he was my friend? It was nice for him that when he needed to be reunited with his father, he paid some money and made it happen. What the hell did this have to do with my problems?

"I am telling you about parrot," he said. There didn't seem to be any point to this. I didn't need a story. I needed help.

"I have to go now, Roman." I stood up.

"Sure. So long. But, Izzy."

"Yeah?"

"If the woman comes back seeming like she means business, I will tell my father to give the parrot to her."

"Won't he be lonely?"

"Most likely. But he has been lonely before. Besides, I can buy him a new one at Pet World on Avenue U. It's what, a couple hundred bucks? What the fuck do I care? Or I'll buy her the new one. It's just a bird."

Roman didn't give a fuck about me. He didn't care that Rayna was gone, and he didn't see why I cared. He didn't care that Al was gone. He wouldn't care when I was gone. People were just animals to him; they could be bought and sold. I walked away.

"Don't do anything stupid, Edel," Roman shouted after me.

ı ı ∎ ∎

I now knew Rayna was somewhere in Boro Park, so when I left Roman I rode the D train from Stillwell Avenue to Fifty-Fifth Street, the heart of the neighborhood. As soon as I got off the train, I knew the trip would be fruitless. I walked around the sad streets, passing produce and fish markets piled high with days-old merchandise. Yiddish signs mocked me with their impenetrability. Above one business on Thirteenth Avenue was a sign shaped like a giant wide-brimmed hat. The store window beneath it was filled with all manner of black hats and *shtreimels*.

I passed under two mulberry trees, but all the berries had fallen to the sidewalk. The pavement was covered with red stains from their juice. There is only a week or so to harvest mulberries—after they ripen but before they fall—and I had missed it.

Groups of women with scarves tied tight around their heads pushed baby strollers down the sidewalks. Men in long black coats rushed by on business. They all eyed me suspiciously, and I didn't try to approach any of them with questions. People would close ranks around their rebbe, and no one would tell me anything. There was no way to know which of the hundreds and hundreds of brick homes held Rayna.

I had gotten all I was going to get out of Roman and Timur. Goldov would know how to find Rayna's father, but I needed to figure out how and when to approach him. I needed to come back to Brooklyn with a plan. For the moment, I didn't know where to go.

When I packed my bag and left the storage space, I didn't have a clear idea of how things would progress. Roman and Timur were supposed to help me. I had thought that I might stick around with Roman and Timur for a while as things played out. I had a vague idea that I would rescue Rayna. Maybe things would be resolved and Rayna and I would be able to come back to our storage space, with its restored door. Maybe we'd have to run away from the city together. Considering the way things had gone in Brighton, that still might be a possibility.

I didn't want to go back to the storage facility. There was no room for me in the new, smaller unit. The front desk clerk had said it would be a few days before a new door was installed on my old unit. Even then, I didn't really want to go back to a place that belonged to Timur. Aside from the chance that Roman and Timur might be annoyed enough with my disrespectful behavior to come hassle me, or cancel the unit, I didn't want to keep living off their charity. Hanging around West Fourth Street was always an option, because it was my home turf and I was comfortable there, but everyone would ask me where Rayna was. And if Roman and Timur did want to hassle me, they could find me on West Fourth Street as easily as at storage. I felt hunted, even though I was the one doing the hunting.

The best option was to head up to Becca's place. No one would hassle me there, and I would have a respite from the streets. Becca was family. She'd take me in, no matter what. If Rayna was able to run away from her family again, she would eventually try to find me up here; she knew where Becca lived, and she knew I'd go there sooner or later.

19

THE DOORMAN WAS AT his post in the lobby of Becca's building, with the phone to his ear. He neither welcomed me nor moved to stop me. His gloved hand lowered the receiver to its cradle, and his eyes followed me across the lobby to the elevator. I banged on the buttons. They lit up but the door didn't open. The light was stuck on floor nine. Becca's floor. The nine did not decrease to an eight, even after several minutes of waiting. The uniformed man continued watching me. I walked over to the door that led to the staircase. The staircase felt secure; it was made of steel and cement to withstand fire.

When I got up to Becca's floor, my tired arms pushed the heavy fire door open slowly. This turned out to be a good thing: as soon as I had it open a crack, I saw that the whole hallway was full of cops. A uniformed officer was holding the elevator door open. No wonder the elevator hadn't come. Another uniform and two guys in suits were carrying out cardboard boxes from Becca's apartment. I pulled the door closed as quietly as I could.

Roman and Timur must have tipped off the police about how I was involved in the theft of the Galuth painting. Would they know

Becca's address? Well, why not? Timur had eyes everywhere. It made sense: they didn't want me around to cause trouble for them with Rayna's father. They may have even promised Rayna's father they'd deal with me for him. Maybe I'd been a sacrificial lamb all along, and they'd made sure that the painting and the arson could be pinned on me, and me alone. Why else had Roman even brought me to the Navy Yard? I wasn't sure what evidence the police thought they could find in Becca's apartment, but if they were investigating art theft, they could have tossed Becca's work files to see if they could find a financial connection.

Then again, Rayna's father could have sent the police after me himself. Maybe he told them that I was the one who kidnapped Rayna, that I was the one who had hurt her. She might have been coerced into giving up the address.

Regardless of who called them, the police were here now. And if the police knew about Becca's apartment, they damn sure knew about my storage space. Not that I could get that far, anyway. The doorman had seen me, and had probably already tipped the cops off that I was in the building. There was no escaping. I could give them a run around through the different floors, but what would be the point?

Taking a deep breath, I stepped out into the hallway. The last plainclothes cop was about to step into the elevator with the rest of his cronies. I walked up to him. He turned and stared at me.

"I'm Izzy," I said. The guy blinked. "Edel. Isaac Edel." He stared for another moment, trying to place the name.

"Oh. Okay. Well, this is the last of it. We're done in there. You can go in." With that, he stepped into the elevator. Becca emerged from her open apartment door just as the elevator was closing.

"Izzy? Christ. About time you showed up." Even though it was evening, she looked like she did when she put herself together in the morning. Her makeup was fresh and unsmudged, and not a hair was out of place. She wore a navy blazer and skirt. It was a formal outfit, like something a person would wear if they had to go to court.

"Becca. What's going on? I thought . . . I thought they were here for me."

"For you? Why would they be here for you? No, don't answer that, please. I don't want to know. I have enough crap on my mind."

"Then what's going on?"

"They were gathering evidence on Andrew."

"On Andrew? Why?"

"Don't you watch the news?"

"No."

"Andrew was arrested last night for fraud. I guess he fucked up the funds he's been managing far worse than anyone knew." She was speaking calmly and evenly, but I suspected that was a mask she'd put on, along with her outfit. Her words surprised me for a moment, but Andrew himself said he was doing black magic. It made sense that something had gone wrong. I had seen the article in the paper about his firm being investigated. "I assumed you heard about it, and that's why you were here."

"No. I'm just here." I had been planning on explaining to Becca about Rayna's situation, and why I couldn't stay downtown, but now I decided not to. She had enough to worry about.

"So you are. Well, come inside then."

I followed Becca through the door of her apartment, pulling it shut behind us. She walked into the kitchen, and I sat down on a stool on the living room side of the counter that separated that room and the kitchen. We were in two different rooms, but could see each other.

"If I had known about this," I said, "I would have come sooner."

"I know, Izzy. I know. Are you hungry? I'll make you a grilled cheese." She was already pulling things from the fridge.

"That's okay. You have enough on your mind, you don't have to cook for me."

"No, I want something to do. I had to just stand around for the past day and watch these people tear my apartment apart. Andrew didn't even have much of his stuff here—he has his own apartment after all—but they went through every inch of the closet he keeps here, and all my shit as well. I took a personal day from work, but I wish I hadn't. I'd rather be working." She unwrapped the block of cheese as she spoke, then started slicing it.

"A grilled cheese would be great," I said. Becca used to always make me grilled cheese for dinner. There was a time when we were old enough that the two of us could be left home by ourselves, but I was still too young to use the stove, so it was on Becca to cook for me. Al was already gone, and my mother worked late. She had gotten a position as a secretary at a law firm soon after he left. I think she met Bernie through that job. It was a step up for her, but she often got stuck at the office when her boss was preparing a case. We were to stay in the apartment, with the door locked, until she came home. Becca was twelve or thirteen, I think; the only things she really knew how to make were macaroni and cheese and grilled cheese. Her secret was that instead of oiling the skillet, she buttered the outsides of the slices of bread. I don't know where she learned this trick. Other than that, she kept it pretty simple: thick slabs of cheddar, a couple thin slices of tomato. I have tried the buttered-bread method myself many times since, but have never gotten it right, and always burn the bread. She grilled the sandwich quickly and deftly, then put it on a plate and placed it in front of me. She'd only made the one sandwich.

"Aren't you hungry, Becca?"

"No, I'm not hungry. I'll just have some tea." I ate the sandwich while she put the kettle on.

"What's going to happen to Andrew?" I asked her.

"I guess they'll send him to prison. I mean, not *prison* prison; just some country club prison in Connecticut or something. He'll be okay."

"How much time do you think he'll get?" Regardless of what he did or didn't do, Andrew was a nice guy, and I hated the idea of him being locked up for years.

"I don't know. It depends on how mad the SEC is, and what all comes out in the investigation. A year, or maybe two? I don't really care."

"What do you mean? You don't care what happens to him? Isn't he still your fiancé?"

"No. I hope he doesn't have too bad a time of it, but I'm not waiting any amount of time. An engagement is a promise about the kind of life you're going to live with someone. Committing imprisonable felonies breaks the promise." She put two coasters out on the counter.

"So he's guilty?" This question was worth asking; it was always possible that the higher-ups were pinning everything on him.

"He didn't say as much, but yeah, I think he's guilty. Over the past year, there've been times when he's seemed stressed, really stressed. Not normal work stress—Lord knows I know what that's like—but a crazed kind of stressed. And when I'd ask him about it, he'd be kind of paranoid, combative. So I knew something was wrong, something was off at his work."

"You didn't have any idea what it was, though?"

"I didn't really want to know. I know that sounds cold. I know you think I'm cold and mean. I know you probably feel sorry for Andrew. But I have my own worries, my own career. I'm a twenty-six-year-old female in a corporate environment, with a dozen employees directly under me. I have to be on top of my game. I love Andrew, but I couldn't take on his problems too." She put a tea bag in each of our mugs. "When the police came and got him—we were out at dinner together—he seemed relieved. Like everything had been building to that outcome, and he was ready for it. He told me he was sorry. Then they took him away."

"And that's it then? You're just done with him?" She nodded.

"Andrew isn't a bad person. I don't condemn him. I don't hate him. I love him. I—look, fine, I'll tell you this, embarrassing as it is: I was kicking and screaming, when they came for him last night. I shouted at the agents, and I tried to claw their faces. They had to hold me back." She was getting angry, just relaying the story. She paced around the kitchenette. I was proud of Becca's defiance, and ashamed that I hadn't kicked and screamed at Rayna's brothers.

"Then they brought me straight back here to start the search. I guess they thought maybe I was covering him, after seeing how I wanted to protect him from being arrested, and that I might destroy evidence if they let me come home alone.

"So I was awake all night while they searched my apartment. And my clothes were all messed up, and my hair was all messed up. I was crying and my makeup was all over my face. I fell asleep in my clothes, sitting on the couch, and slept maybe two hours, while the investigators milled around me. It was humiliating. Then I looked in the mirror, and I thought, I am not doing this shit. I am not letting this dude's bullshit destroy me. So I showered and got dressed, and that's that."

"Just like that?" I asked. This whole story had unfolded within the past twenty-four hours. But I knew Becca, and if she had made this decision, she would probably stick by it.

"Yeah. Just like that. I'm trying to have it be just like that. I'm so worried about him. Of course I care what happens to him. I don't want him to go to prison! He already tried to call me from jail this evening. And I need to talk to him, to know he's all right. But I refused the call. I declined the collect charges. If he calls here again . . . ask him how he's doing for me."

"Sure. But why can't you ask him?"

"I can't talk to him. I won't. Because if I talk to him, he'll probably convince me he's being railroaded. And I'll stick by him like a sucker." She looked out her big window. "I don't want to be like Mom was, wasting half my life in love with a fuckup who's in and out of jail. I promised myself I'd never be like that. In high school and college, I dated thugs, bad boys, fucked-up guys. But I don't want to be that damaged girl, replacing her con-man father with a con-man boyfriend. So I tried to find a nice preppie guy. And he ends up being a hustler too." She shook her head. "I can't get away from being like Mom with Dad. But I keep trying."

"That's so bad?" I said. "We'd never have been born if Mom hadn't been with Dad." I thought of a line from the Talmud that went something like, "It would have been better if you'd never been born. But since you were . . ." And then everything else comes. The kettle whistled. Becca went and turned off the stove, and brought the kettle out to pour the water into our mugs. She sat down across from me.

"I'm glad you're my brother, Izzy. I don't know if I'm glad Alojzy was our father. He was so cruel to Mom. Don't you remember?" I thought of the story she told me in the diner. How many of those was she holding?

"No." Things were bad when he was gone, not when he was there.

"You were too young to remember."

"No. I remember. I remember them dancing in the kitchen."

"Sure. They'd dance for a song or two, when one he liked came on the radio. Some corny '70s rock song. But don't you remember him shouting at her, and punching holes in the kitchen wall?" She looked over at the clean condo wall, as if there would be a hole in that one too.

"No. But I hurt my hand that same way, arguing with Mariam, the girl I dated at school. It's one of the reasons she broke up with me." Toward the end there were a lot of tense nights, with the two of us stoned and on edge in her room, getting into argument after argument.

"Don't be so proud of that." Becca glanced down at my purple knuckles. I'd forgotten about the storage-unit door that morning.

"I'm not proud. I'm just telling you. Don't you remember going down to the Lower East Side? On Sunday afternoons? We'd go to the Ukrainian diner on East Twelfth and eat pierogi?"

"Yeah. He always had to go see that creepy guy, Oleg, on Second Avenue. The apartment smelled like cat piss and cigars. He'd look at me weird. Call me a 'pretty girl.' Put his hand on my head. I hated it there. Alojzy always had to give him some envelope. I don't know what they were involved in. Some sort of gambling thing, maybe?"

"Probably. But don't you remember that afterward he would take us to that bodega next door, where they made egg creams? And we'd each get a chocolate egg cream in a little plastic cup? Then we'd go up to Tompkins Square Park?"

"I don't know what he was thinking, bringing kids around all those junkies that hung out there."

"No one ever messed with us. We just swung on the swings. Don't you remember that he was so strong he would stand behind and push both of us, one with each hand? And his left arm was just as strong as his right arm, so we were always neck and neck? And we went so high? And then he'd suddenly grab us off the swings, one arm each, and hug us close as we screamed?"

"Yeah. I do." She didn't elaborate. Her face was a mask again, and I didn't know what memories, good or bad, were playing out behind it. "Drink your tea," she said.

We were both exhausted. Becca put some clean sheets out on the couch for me, and went into her bedroom. I wondered where Rayna was sleeping. Was she back in her old bedroom at her father's house? Or did they have her locked up somewhere so she couldn't escape? It was strange that we had lain down in our storage space together last night, but by tonight we'd both ended up with our families again. Rayna was a victim, and Andrew was a white-collar criminal, but I felt as if they'd both been dragged away by the same dark force. The same force that had taken Al. It would take Becca and me next.

I lay on the couch and thought about how kind my sister was to me, despite her troubles. The thought surprised me, because I'd spent so long with an animosity against her in my heart. One time, not long after we'd moved to Long Island, some older guys jumped me on the way to the bus stop. We had started at our new school right after Christmas break; when this happened, there were still islands of dirty snow left between the roads and the sidewalks. The two guys came up behind me and started jabbing me in the back with a lacrosse stick. That was one thing that I noticed when I moved to the suburbs: everyone was always carrying lacrosse sticks. They kept poking me and calling me a "faggot," and I kept stumbling, but I didn't turn around. Finally, they whacked me really hard across the legs and I fell down. They gave me a few good kicks that knocked the wind out of me, and I couldn't get back up. One of them pulled out his dick and took a long piss into a pile of snow. They picked me up and rubbed my face into the piss snow.

A while later, I saw Becca hanging out with those same guys at the mall. I waved but she ignored me. That wasn't the only time she did something like that, and I'd held on to every incident. I know it wasn't easy for her. The fact that she was a little older than me when we moved out there meant that she missed shared bonding experiences like Hebrew school and first sleepovers. It also meant she had a

little city sexiness in her step that made the suburban girls feel threatened. I didn't know what it was at the time; I wouldn't have thought
to attach the word "sexiness" to my sister. I just knew that she was
always looking for a fight, and it felt like I was usually the one to take
the beating, one way or another.

There were other things, though, that I ought to have held on to as
well. I don't know how many of those grilled cheeses she'd made me.
And I remembered one time, right before we moved to Long Island,
when we were at a car dealership. Our mom was spending a lot of
time going back and forth between our apartment and Bernie's house,
and she decided she needed a car of her own. Bernie probably helped
her with the down payment.

She went into the office to sign the paperwork, leaving Becca and me
in the waiting room. The salesman had given each of us a big orange
lollipop to keep us occupied. I was so excited to eat the lollipop, beyond
excited, desperate to taste the sweetness. But when I pulled open the
plastic, the candy shattered somehow, just shattered into a dozen little
pieces that fell to the carpet and gripped the dirty fuzz.

About a month before he left for good, Al had borrowed a car from
a buddy and taken us all driving out in New Jersey. We made a whole
day of it, going far out into the country. We stopped at a roadside produce stand, where my mom bought fresh vegetables and Becca and I
got to pet a big dog. We got ice cream from Dairy Queen and everyone
was having a nice time. My mom was laughing, and my parents were
getting along. Then, out on the turnpike, a truck kicked up a rock. At
first we thought it was just a little nick, serious enough to send Alojzy
into a fury of trilingual curses, but minor enough that my mom could
still calm him down. But as we drove, the crack spread. Two rays of
the tiny star spread slowly and evenly, curving out in opposite directions. As the crack grew, Al's rage grew inside the car. By the time the
glass was divided by a giant S, the rage was choking us. No one spoke.

And when he left, no one said a word then either. No explanation
was provided. He was just gone. I asked Becca, but she said it wasn't
any of my business, and not to bother Mom. Becca probably didn't
know either; she was just upset and holding it together. I think that

was when she learned to act cold and collected all the time. Maybe she learned it from Mom, who was holding it together too. Everyone had to hold it together except for me. I got to cry in the waiting room of a car dealership.

I cried for a long time. My father was gone, and the crack was spreading through everything. A little while later we'd be gone too, to Long Island. Even the little token of sweetness they'd offered me was ruined by the spreading crack. What Becca did next was so strange. She took her own lollipop, unbroken and unwrapped, and handed it to me. The messed-up thing was, she always liked lollipops so much more than me. She genuinely likes sweets, the way I like vinegary things. But she handed me that lollipop, said she didn't even want it. I grabbed it from her and stuck it in my mouth. When my mom came back out of the salesman's office, Becca didn't say a word about what had happened.

20

I REACHED FOR RAYNA, but didn't find her lying next to me. When I opened my eyes, I saw that I was in Becca's apartment. Whatever happiness I had felt in my dreams dissipated as the real world asserted itself. Rayna was gone. She had been kidnapped. I hoped that no one was hurting her.

Becca had already left for work. She would rather be busy than sit around the apartment. I needed to get busy too. Not knowing where else to start, I used Becca's computer to search for information about the Glupsker dynasty online. Surprisingly, they had their own website. It had a bit of Yiddish text on it, blue on a white background. The only sections in English were a page to donate tzedakah with a credit card, and a form where you could request a fifteen-minute audience with the rebbe.

I kept searching. There were a few sites in Hebrew and Yiddish that I couldn't read, and one or two in English about Jewish charities. A couple of *Daily News* articles mentioned the Glupskers in passing, in relation to local Brooklyn politics. A blog called *The Spinoza Spin—* written by an anonymous, bitter, ex-Orthodox man—mentioned the

Glupskers, along with two other dynasties, in a long post about the cover-up of sexual-abuse scandals at religious schools. There had been two serious allegations relating to Glupsker schools in particular, but the Brooklyn DA's office had declined to pursue either case. The blog's author connected this to the Glupsker Rebbe's endorsement of the incumbent DA during every election. The Hasidim voted as one uniform bloc. I didn't doubt the allegations for a moment. Rayna had run away from terrible things. She had tried so hard to tell me she needed help, but I hadn't wanted to hear.

The University of Pennsylvania's website had a reference to a dissertation titled *Pyotr the Maggid: The Appropriation and Transformation of Slavic Folktale, Christian Parable, and Extra-Dynastic Hasidic Tale within the Glupsker Tradition*. A few books came up on shopping sites. Most of them were in Hebrew or Yiddish. The only major English translation of Glupsker writings seemed to be the same out-of-print Classics of Western Spirituality volume that had upset Rayna. I couldn't remember if the volume was still in storage or if we had sold it. Either way, I didn't see how getting lost in more tales would help me find Rayna.

There was a brief stub on the history of the Glupskers off of the "List of Hasidic Dynasties" Wikipedia page. All it said, really, was that they were a dynasty that had begun in Poland in the nineteenth century, and whose followers were now divided primarily between Boro Park and Jerusalem, with a few others living in Montreal. Below, it gave the rabbinic lineage of the dynasty, starting with Rebbe Pyotr Gershon of Uman (b. ?, d. Glupsk, 1823) and ending with Rebbe Shmuel Langer (b. 1956, Brooklyn). Rayna's father. I tried to imagine Rayna as a little girl, sitting on a rabbi's lap. In between the two rebbes was a long line, cutting diagonally down across the screen: Rebbe this of Glupsk, Rebbe that of Glupsk. Pyotr, who only had daughters, appointed his son-in-law, Zalman Langer, as his successor. The position had been passed down through the Langer line ever since. Scattered along the timeline were little notes of miracles and pogroms. The article briefly mentioned a rebbe's daughter who had defied her father, and disappeared to America in 1919.

The only citation given at the bottom of the page was an article by Joseph Jacobs from the 1906 *Jewish Encyclopedia*. The article itself wasn't online, but there was a set of the encyclopedias down at the public library on Forty-Second Street.

The night before, Becca had strongly encouraged me to give my mom a call. I decided I would do that before I headed downtown. Bernie picked up the phone, and said Ruth wasn't home.

"But, Isaac. It's been a while. Your mother has been worried about you. Have you been all right?" I had never really talked to Bernie on the phone, but I guess he wanted something to tell my mother in case I didn't call back.

"Yeah, I've been okay." I didn't want to tell my family about Rayna, and everything that had happened. The situation was hard enough to deal with, without feeling like I had to justify it too. It was easier to just say I was okay.

"And Becca? She's holding up all right?"

"I think so. It's hard to tell. She always has a tough front."

"That's true."

"But hey, Bernie, you're an accountant, can you explain this Andrew mess to me?"

"Well, I don't know all the details, of course."

"But generally."

"Generally: Andrew had quite a bit of success early on in his career—too early in his career—and was subsequently given a responsibility he could not handle. People entrusted him with funds, expecting him to continue to deliver large returns. What he delivered instead were losses. Rather than owning up to this, he put an astounding amount of time and energy into creating the illusion that the profits were continuing. This is known as fraud. Unfortunately, the longer Andrew continued with this fraud, the more people were motivated to entrust him with even larger sums of money."

"And he lost those as well?"

"Yes."

"So he's guilty."

"It certainly looks that way. Of course, there could be factors we don't know."

"In one of your books, that I read, they talk about Gershom Scholem."

"Yes?"

"And the Hasidim called him 'the accountant.' Like an accountant knows more about the rich man's wealth than he does, but can't spend any of it, so it's not worth much."

"Yes. That was a metaphor. For his relationship to spiritual wealth."

"I understand that. But still, it involves a description of the position of an accountant."

"Well, yes, it does. Andrew isn't an accountant, strictly speaking. But I see the connection."

"How come you became an accountant, Bernie?" Why did people like Bernie and Andrew think it was good for men to sit in offices and type numbers, while people like Al and me thought it was better to go out into the streets? Not that Al had ever had much of an opportunity to sit in an office.

"An accountant, specifically? Primarily, because I had a professor who encouraged me in that direction."

"Okay. But generally."

"Generally speaking, I wanted a good, clean job. My father, from the day he came to this country, he was scrapping and hustling, and he never got himself settled. He always had a scheme, and he never got ahead. I didn't want to have to lead that type of life."

"Where did your father come from?"

"Poland."

"Like my father."

"Yes. I suppose you and I have that in common."

"But he was older. He must have been a Holocaust survivor?"

"Yes. He was never in a camp, but he was in the ghetto in Lodz. He made it out somehow." The word "somehow" landed heavily.

"How come you never mention him?"

"I don't have all that many good things to say about the man. And there's not much value in speaking ill of the dead."

"Well . . . he was a survivor, though."

"Yes. But you know, it wasn't necessarily the good ones that survived."

"You think the survivors were the bad ones? That they were guilty of things?"

"Some of them. I think some of them survived by stealing bread from the others."

"And you think Andrew is a bread stealer?"

"I don't know that I'd say 'bread stealer.' None of us know how we'd act in that situation."

"But you think he's guilty?"

"Yes, I do. But that doesn't mean I think anyone else is innocent."

"What about the dead ones?"

"Maybe the dead ones. But I doubt that too."

The phone rang a few minutes later. I thought it might be my mother calling back, but it was Andrew. Speak of the devil.

"Aren't you in jail?" I asked.

"No. You sound disappointed."

"Of course not. I'm glad you're not in jail, I just thought . . ."

"No, it's cool, Edel. I know it's a weird situation. I'm out on bail. But I'm pretty restricted. House arrest, with the ankle monitor and everything. They froze my bank accounts. I had to surrender my passport."

"How did you post bail if they froze your account?"

"My mom bailed me out. She had to put her condo in Florida up as collateral. I didn't want her to do it. My stepdad didn't want her to do it either. But she did it."

"I see."

"Yeah. I guess your sister's not home?"

"She's at work. She went back today. You could try her cell phone."

"I have. She's not taking my calls. She won't even send me to voice mail; she just clicks 'answer' then clicks 'end call' immediately. I tried to leave a message with the receptionist at her office, but I didn't get the feeling she was going to pass it along. So I thought maybe I'd leave a message on the voice mail at the house here."

"Do you want to hang up and call back, and I'll let it go to the machine?"

"Nah. She doesn't want to hear my voice. Anyway, what're you up to today, Izzy?"

"I'm on my way to Midtown. I have to check something at the reference library."

"Well, that's not too far from me. I'm on Forty-Sixth past Ninth. Maybe you could stop by?"

"I don't know, man." Andrew and I weren't that close. I didn't know why he wanted to see me. Maybe he wasn't really close with anyone. He seemed tight with DC and the others, but my college buddies had disappeared pretty quickly when I got in trouble. Or maybe he just wanted to talk to Becca's brother, because he couldn't talk to Becca. She *had* wanted me to find out how he was doing. I hated to do anything that would distract me from trying to get to Rayna, but I owed it to Becca to help her if I could.

"Fine," I said, "I'll come by after I finish at the library."

After I got off the phone with Andrew, I caught the 6 train down to Grand Central, and walked down to the main library on Fifth Avenue. The stone lions reminded me of reading *Caravan of Cats* with Rayna. I'd spent months standing outside NYU's Bobst Library, never once being permitted entrance. Now, I walked up the marble steps of an even grander library, and entered with ease.

A reference librarian directed me to the *Jewish Encyclopedia*, which took up an entire long shelf. According to the Joseph Jacobs article, the founder of the Glupsker dynasty was indeed the enigmatic Rebbe Pyotr, who appeared in the Berdychiv region of Ukraine sometime around 1812, eventually settling in the shtetl of Glupsk. He had traveled up from the town of Uman, and appeared to have spent some amount of time in Salonica and other parts of the Ottoman Empire, though there was no evidence he ever made it to *Eretz Yisrael*. His enemies claimed he was a secret Frankist, but his followers maintained he was a disciple of Nachman of Breslov, who founded no lineage. No real evidence existed for either claim. Pyotr's beard was thin, and no one knew why he had a Christian name. Still, everyone agreed he was a man of great piety, as well as a mesmerizing storyteller, and he attracted many followers. He was heralded as the author of one legendary book, though no copies remained in existence, and no one knew what the nature of its contents was. Stories and sayings of his were collected by his disciples after his death.

While I was at the library, I searched the electronic card catalogue for R. Galuth. Maybe there were some plates—or at least a mention— of his work in some forgotten art history textbook. The only thing that came up was a book called *My Loves and Losses in Greenwich Village* by Moses Bodenheimer, which lived across the street at the Mid-Manhattan Library, the smaller circulating branch.

I found the volume on the fifth floor of the circulating branch. It had been rebound in red library boards, and the thin pages had turned brown. No one had opened the book in a long time. The last circu- lation stamp was from 1972. Bodenheimer appeared to have been a bohemian poet who haunted Greenwich Village in the 1920s and '30s. According to the inside flap of his book, he was murdered on the Bowery in 1954, and the memoir was released slightly later that same year. In the beginning were a few of his poems, which were full of ecstatic bohemian lyricism, and personified concepts such as "Youth" and "Beauty." Many of the book's short chapters were titled with the name of the cultural figures that they discussed. One of them was titled "R. Galuth":

Galuth was that most curious of creatures, a Greenwich Village painter who painted more than he drank or bragged. What's more, he never chased after models or any other young women. Nor young men for that matter.

I had admired some of his canvases at a local gallery, and we became friendly. Always, though, Galuth kept me—and everyone else—at an arm's length. Rumors abounded about him (the Village was a village indeed, in those days!).

He simply appeared in New York one day, saying little more than that he had come from Europe. He made references, occasionally, to Paris. Some said that he was the son of a Hasidic rabbi from the

Pale, and had rejected tradition for art. Others said that he was a deserted officer from the kaiser's army.

He spoke gently, wore fine suits, and showed no signs of being able to grow a beard (which, for a rabbi's son, would certainly be most strange!). Some said he was a homosexual, others that he was a hermaphrodite. He would lock himself away in solitude for days at a time, painting, and this only added to his mystery.

One evening, by chance, I found myself on the fire escape outside his fourth-floor studio. I had been enjoying an evening of wine and romance with a young lady when her "husband"—a bull-dyke cab driver built like a dockworker—came home earlier than expected. I managed to escape out onto the fire escape and across the roof, wearing just my trousers.

I realized that I had come down the side of Galuth's building. An unprecedented chance to observe the mysterious painter—how fortuitous!

What I observed was more complex and more beautiful than anything that could be contained in rumor.

Galuth lay naked, posing on the couch. I could see that she was indeed a woman, and a comely woman at that. Truly, a muse any artist would be blessed to have! Then she stood, and as she walked her body tightened, contracted, and, while her parts did not change, she assumed the masculine gait of the Galuth I met in the street. He stood at his easel, painting the ghost of his female self that lingered in front of his eyes. After a time, she returned to the couch. Then he, in turn, returned to the easel.

This mesmerizing dance went on and on throughout the night, the masculine and the feminine, the *Adonai* and the *Shekhinah*, coming together only on the canvas.

I read through the passage three times. It was intriguing, though clearly fanciful. The idea of Galuth being female, as well as a Hasidic rabbi's child, was interesting. There was that reference online to a Glupsker Rebbe's defiant daughter. Was Galuth that daughter? Had she passed as a man, to make her way into the secular world and across the ocean? If so, was this a survival mechanism, or had Galuth truly identified as male? Assuming Galuth really was born as a Glupsker Rebbe's daughter, then there was a tangible connection between Galuth and Rayna.

Bodenheimer's account of the male painter's intertwinement with his female muse was clearly based on his own sentimental eroticism. Still, maybe the idea of the rebbe's daughter being the subject of some of Galuth's paintings held some truth. If this was the case, the woman falling from the train could be a self-portrait. It made sense, then, that I could see a strong family resemblance between the woman and Rayna. It also made sense that Rayna had said the woman resembled her sisters and aunt.

I looked up at the clock. I'd lost track of the time, and was late to go see Andrew.

When I left the library, I walked across town to what used to be, and was once again, called "Hell's Kitchen." This route took me through Times Square. Times Square had supposedly been completely sanitized in the '90s, but the street vendors never went away. Up here, I wasn't a vendor, only a passerby or potential customer. The hawkers' spiels filled my ears. Men with Arabic accents offered all-beef hot dogs for two dollars each. Looking for something sweet? That same two dollars will get you a bag of honey-roasted peanuts. New York's finest gourmet nuts. Hot hot hot. Get them now. Okay, friend, you got it. Cashews, three dollars. You look street-smart. What's your name? Street-smart guy like you could dig my mix CD. Five dollars, I'll even sign it for you. Well come on, son, I already wrote your name. Take a photograph with the Naked Cowboy. Take a photograph with the Naked Cowgirl. Take a photograph with Elmo, for the kids. You look so handsome, with New York City as your backdrop. A photo not enough. You need portrait drawing. Ten dollar. Your brother wants one too? Sure he do. Tell you what, two for fifteen. These are not caricatures, these are portraits. This woman is a true artist. She went to the Central Academy of Fine Arts in Beijing.

Past Times Square I came to Eighth Avenue, an avenue still full of old drunks, dive bars, and peep shows, thanks to the looming influence of Port Authority, the largest bus terminal in the United States of America. Eighth Avenue was the kind of place where Al made sense. I hoped I might see him coming from the bus station to the bar with a duffel bag on his shoulder, but it didn't seem likely.

Once I crossed Eighth, I was firmly on the West Side. Hell's Kitchen. I read in a true-crime book that the last Irish gang in the neighborhood, the Westies, supplied the union labor for the construction projects that gentrified the area and drove out the remaining working-class Irish families. Everyone is devoured, but usually people devour themselves, and there's no one else to blame.

It was a warm day, and old men were drinking beer outside Andrew's building. Andrew had mentioned that the lower floors were filled with the residents of the SRO that had been here before the luxury rental building was built. Keeping the SRO inhabitants on had been a stipulation of the deal that allowed the developer to build on the property. The old men would eventually die, and their apartments would go market rate. In the meantime, the type of life my father had lived and the type of life that Andrew lived were only separated by a flight of stairs.

Andrew opened the door in sweatpants and a New York Islanders jersey. I was a little taken aback, as I'd never seen him dressed so informally. During the workweek, of course, he wore suits. Lounging around Becca's apartment on the weekend, he wore khakis and polo shirts.

"Hey, Edel the Kid. Thanks for coming by." We clasped hands.

"Sure. My pleasure. How are you doing?"

"You know. Been better." He shrugged, and turned back into the apartment. "Come on in." I followed behind, noticing the bulky monitoring device just below the elastic ankle band of his sweatpants. The apartment had been remodeled recently, and Andrew owned nice furniture, but the place was a mess. Dirty clothes lay across the floor. New-looking sports equipment—a bag of golf clubs, a pair of roller blades, different sizes of free weights—was piled in the living room. A PlayStation 2 video-game system lay as far from a large television set as its cord would allow. There were books too. Not a lot, but more than I expected. Business textbooks. Pop-psychology books about "success." *The Great Gatsby*. Some Michael Crichton. Some Jack Higgins. *Tough Jews* by Rich Cohen. Two coffee-table books about Israel.

"I'd offer you a beer," Andrew apologized, "but I'm not allowed to have any booze in the house."

"That's okay," I said. "I mean, I'm okay."

"You want to go to the roof? I'm already going stir-crazy in here. And it's only the first day. I'm in for months of this. First I was locked up at the federal building for a day, now I can't leave this building. If I go past the front stoop, my ankle monitor triggers an alarm. I was running up and down the staircases this morning. You feel free, during moments when you're sitting comfortably, reading a book, but you're not free at all."

"A gilded cage," I said.

"Yeah. But having a job was sort of like that too. So whatever. It'll give me time to catch up on hobbies. Hey, do you know how to play chess?"

My father had taught me the rules of chess when I was a small child, but I didn't really learn to play until later on, in the Sheepshead Bay days. Al had a regular Sunday afternoon game with a guy named Jerzy, who worked at the horse stables by Prospect Park. We'd get off the F train at Fort Hamilton and walk across Ocean Parkway on the pedestrian overpass. Between the overpass exit ramp and the sidewalk was a line of four concrete chessboard tables with attached concrete seats, like the ones in Rayna's pigeon story. I don't know why the city had placed the tables there, and I never saw anyone else playing on them. It was like the space had been made just for Al. We would sit at the third table from the ramp, and play a few games while we waited for Jerzy. Al inevitably beat me, but he'd give me good advice along the way, to keep things somewhat balanced.

When Jerzy would show up, stinking of horseshit, I would move aside and give him my seat at the board. Jerzy was a Pole—an actual Polish Pole, not a Polish Jew—and he fancied himself something of a chess master. They would play a few games, and trade nips from a plastic bottle of Sobieski, shouting, "*Na zdrowie!*" Jerzy would say things like, "Ah, I see your plan! Nimzo-Indian Defense, and then move into a good old Queen's Gambit." It never seemed to me that Alojzy did have a plan, let alone one with a fancy name attached, but he generally won. After an hour, Jerzy's break would be over, and he'd trot back down the block to the stables. Every time, Al made the same joke about Jerzy needing to go take care of the cavalry horses, so they'd be ready for the charge against the tanks.

Up on Andrew's roof, there was a wooden picnic table with attached benches. Andrew put the chessboard on the table and we set up the pieces.

"It's funny," he said. "I hadn't played chess much since junior high, but with things getting so crazy over the past few months, it's been one of the only things that holds my interest." He won the first game easily. He toyed with me a bit, letting me take a few pawns and a knight and lead myself into a trap. I should have seen it coming.

"So, what happened, Andrew?" I asked, as I set up the board for the next game.

"I don't know. I guess your sister just decided . . ."

"No, I know about that. I mean, this thing you're arrested for."

"That thing. It's fraud. They're charging me with fraud."

"But are you guilty?" I knew better than to ask this inside, but I didn't think the building's shared rooftop could be bugged. The question had to be asked, for his and Becca's sake. Andrew could be innocent, framed by overzealous investigators, or superiors who needed a fall guy. If he was innocent, or even partially innocent, Becca had to know, so she could stand by him.

"Oh," said Andrew. He looked around, but we were all alone. "Yeah. I guess I am guilty. My lawyer told me not to discuss any details with anyone, until we have a plea deal signed, so I won't get too specific. But I mean, yeah, there's no mistake. I fucked up. I'm pleading guilty."

So Becca was right. Bernie was right.

"Why'd you do it?"

"It's not like I sat down and decided I was going to commit this huge crime. I just, you know, I cut some corners. To keep people happy. And it added up. See what I mean?"

"And before you knew it, you'd crossed the line."

"No. That's the thing. There is no line."

"I see."

"You do, huh? Have you ever committed a crime, Izzy?"

"Yeah."

"Right, that drug stuff."

"No. I mean, that too, but I also helped some guys steal something once. Something valuable." I wasn't going to go into specifics either.

"Oh. I see. How did it feel?" I thought back to when Roman and I slid the stolen painting into its new storage locker, how anticlimactic it had been.

"Like nothing. It was just work."

"Exactly." He moved his pawn, starting the match.

I was more conscious of my long game the second time around, and managed to put up a little bit of a fight, but Andrew still beat me in the end. He took the third game too, with a queen sacrifice.

"I have to be honest, Izzy, you seem more messed up than I am. And I'm the one facing prison time. What's the matter?" Andrew had been honest with me about his situation. I decided I would be honest with him about mine. Besides, I wanted to talk about Rayna. Her absence weighed so heavily on my mind, and though I hadn't wanted to explain it to my family, I needed to talk about it with someone. I would have liked to talk to Mendy, actually, but he was too connected to Goldov and the others. Andrew was barely in my world. He was the safest person to open up to.

"There's this girl. She means a lot to me. And now she's gone, and I have to figure out what to do about it."

"Becca said you were living with a girl downtown."

"Yes, that's her. Her name is Rayna. We did live together, for a little while."

"Where is she from?"

"Brooklyn. She's from a Hasidic family." I was afraid Andrew was going to make a joke about yeshiva girls gone wild or something. "She's back there now. Her family came and got her. She didn't want to go back." It sounded less horrible than it was, when I said it like that. I didn't know if I was softening things for my benefit, or for Andrew's.

"Was this the first time you ever lived with a girl?" His voice was surprisingly kind.

"Yeah."

"It can be hard."

"It was hard. I didn't know what to do." I told Andrew about what it was like between Rayna and me. I didn't get too deep into the details about the storage space or the abduction—I only trusted him so far—but I felt the need to try to explain how I felt about her. What it felt like to sleep beside her. What it felt like to know that she was gone from me, taken against her will to a place she didn't want to be.

"Izzy," Andrew said when I was done talking. "It sounds like she has serious problems. Like maybe she was abused."

"I know." I hadn't articulated the word "abuse" to myself, but I knew that Rayna had been sexually abused. The truth was, I had actively avoided acknowledging the situation. It was easier to think of her as haunted, rather than traumatized. I was sorry that I'd never really discussed any of it with her, except through parable. I was sorry I hadn't asked more questions.

"You probably shouldn't have been living with her. She probably needed counseling. She probably shouldn't have been living with anybody."

"I know. But we were doing the best we could for each other."

"You miss her?"

"Yeah. I do. And I worry about her. I don't think her family home is a safe or healthy place for her. That's the first thing. But I do miss her a lot."

"How long has it been since she's been back there?"

"Almost two days now. Is it weird to miss someone so badly so soon?"

"No. I miss your sister."

After an hour and a half, I'd lost five out of six games. I only took that sixth one because Andrew had become flustered talking about

Becca. It hadn't occurred to me that he loved her as much as he did. He was still a bread stealer, but he would have given half his stolen crusts to my sister, for whatever that was worth.

"Do you wish you'd done anything differently?" I asked him.

"I shouldn't have let you take my rook. But I wasn't paying attention." This was the second time Andrew had misunderstood my question. I didn't know if I was asking the wrong questions or if he was evasive by habit now.

"No. I mean, in general. These past months."

"Oh. Yeah." He leaned over the table, halving the distance between us, and resting the weight of his upper body on his fists. "I should have stolen more. I should have robbed everybody. I should have taken everything."

"I think you're right," I said. I was slowly beginning to figure out what I needed to do. I stood up. "I have to get going." It was time to get back to my search. The chess games had been helpful, though. I was figuring out what players were on the board, and how they were positioned. Now I needed to figure out what my next move should be.

◼◼◼

My mother got me on the telephone back at Becca's.

"Isaac. It's your mother, Ruth Fischer. Do you remember me?"

"Vaguely. How are you doing?"

"I could be better. My children are worrying me to death. One was betrayed by a white-collar criminal, and the other is running around doing God knows what." Part of me wanted to hang up the phone and not deal with her. The other part of me wanted to start crying and tell her all about Rayna. I didn't do either.

"I was working as a street vendor, earning some money. But I'm not doing that anymore."

"What is it you're doing now? Looking for some indoor employment I hope?"

"Yeah, I'm starting to," I lied. "I'm back here at Becca's for a minute, trying to sort things out."

"Oh. Well, it's good that you're with your sister. She needs your support right now. How is she holding up?"

"I don't know. She's doing fine I think. She's strong. You know that."

"I know she acts strong. I did the same thing, every time your father disappeared."

"Okay." I'd heard so many things about Al over the past few months. I knew he wasn't just like I'd remembered him. I was sure he would act as callously as Timur and Roman. But I needed to judge him for myself. I didn't want to keep listening to Becca and my mother knocking him.

"Andrew meant a lot to her. They were planning a life together. She was depending on him."

"I saw him today."

"I see. Have you told her?"

"No. But I will. She wants to know he's okay."

"Maybe she wants to cut him out of her life altogether. He's bad news."

"How are you doing, Mom?" She hadn't answered the question the first time.

"I'm fine, Izzy, I'm fine. It's sunny out here, and our neighbors are nice. I wouldn't go back to New York for a million dollars. I hate that you kids are there, and having such a rough time of everything. Take care of each other."

"We are." My mom talked on for another fifteen minutes, about the importance of siblings, and how she had forgiven Uncle Howard. She was still mad about the papercuts, but she didn't need them to remember her mother. Her monologue segued into the importance of starting a career, and how the decisions you make in your twenties impact the rest of your life. She told a long story about the daughter of a friend who had just been accepted to law school, but wasn't sure if she wanted to go or not. Lawyers would never be out of work, she pointed out—the situation with Andrew was a prime example of that.

After a while, I cut her off.

"It's good to talk to you, Mom, but I have to go. I have to go see about a job thing." I figured I'd leave her with that morsel.

"Fine. Go. Though, I thought after all this time you'd want to talk to me more."

||■■

When I got off the phone with my mom, I went back to the Glupsker website, and clicked into the form to request an audience with the rebbe. A calendar of available times popped up, and there were a couple open slots for the next day. I typed in a fake name and my e-mail address. If I was granted an audience, I could meet Rayna's father face-to-face. The time had come for direct confrontation. I refreshed my e-mail every ten minutes. After two hours, a message from the Glupsker World Council appeared:

BS"D

Dear Supplicant,

Per your request, you have been granted an audience with the Great Rebbe of Glupsk.

Your audience is scheduled from 11:15 AM to 11:30 AM tomorrow.

Rabbi Moishe Nemirov
Secretary of the Great Rebbe of Glupsk

I was going to meet Rayna's father. He would be a real person, not a dark weight. Rayna's world would no longer be an abstract place where she had been hurt, had escaped from, and had been dragged back to. The obstacles would come into focus.

I didn't know exactly what I was going to do. Should I make up a fake story, and try to find a way to stick around the Glupskers until

I found Rayna? Should I come barging in with guns blazing, and demand to see her?

At the bottom of the e-mail was an address. I looked it up on the map online. I had circled around the building the day before, without realizing it. Now I knew where to go. Now I would be granted entrance.

21

THE ROOM I WAITED in the next day was like the reception area of a dentist's office. People sat in matching chairs, stealing nervous glances at the closed door. Instead of a woman in flowered scrubs, the clipboard-wielding gatekeeper was a skinny rabbi with round glasses and a pointy red beard. He swooped around in front of the door to the rebbe's office, like some exotic pet bird who had been made trusty of the birdcage.

Two eager yeshiva bochers sat next to me. They sat upright on the edges of their seats, waiting for the red bird to squawk their names. Across from me was a fat man wearing Velcro sneakers and a pinstripe suit with no tie. He poked furiously at his wristwatch, and I realized that he had an old-school Casio calculator watch. Maybe the man was using the calculator to do gematria, to divine mysteries. He looked a little schlubby to be doing such work. Maybe he was one of the thirty-six hidden *tzadikim*. If so, he was well hidden indeed. No, he was probably a vendor of some sort, trying to determine what the rebbe owed him.

"Fischer," the voice called. "The rebbe will see you now, Isaac Fischer." That was me. When I had filled out the online form, I had used Bernie and my mom's last name, in case the name Edel sent up a red flag.

I was swept into the rebbe's office, and the door shut behind me. The room was lined with bookshelves. The black, pictureless volumes Rayna had spoken of. I was in Rayna's world. How close was she?

There was one picture in the room: the Galuth portrait of the rabbi that Roman and I had stolen. It was now in a tacky gold frame, with a layer of polished glass over the painting itself. I'd examined it closely in the warehouse; I knew it well, and there was no mistaking it now. This confirmed the theory that I had developed in the library. Galuth and Rayna were both members of the rabbinic Langer family. The rebbe traced his lineage back through previous rebbes; Rayna could trace her legacy back to Galuth. My search for my own legacy—my father—had brought me face-to-face with Rayna again and again: in the museum, in Al's sketches, then in person on the street. Now I had come to find her again.

"You have already wasted two of your fifteen minutes shuffling around and staring at my wall." I looked at the rebbe. His eyes were focused on documents on his desk, even as he spoke. His beard was still thick and black. A short-brimmed hat hung on a rack behind him, and he wore a large velvet kippah. "You must learn to make the most of your time on this earth, young man." His voice was firm and paternal. "Come, what can I do for you? Are you not here to ask me something? About a personal or business trouble, perhaps? About your studies?"

"That's a fine painting," I said, pointing over his shoulder. "I'd like to get one like it. Who painted it? Where did you get it?"

"It is a portrait of my great-grandfather." He answered without looking at the painting. "It was lost during the Shoah, but was recently returned to my family, by an anonymous donor. That's what you came here to ask me?" Asking about a stolen painting should have made the man nervous, but in his domain, the rebbe was the king. He was untouchable.

"No," I said. "I came here to ask you what you've done to Rayna. I need to see her."

He took his reading classes off, and looked up at me for the first time. "I suppose you are the boy. Edel. The peddler who was harboring my youngest daughter."

"Yes," I said. The way he said "harbored" made it sound like it was something illicit, a concealment. But I didn't object; it was the right word. I had offered her refuge, like a harbor offered a ship coming off a stormy sea. "I am Edel the book peddler. Where is Rayna? Is she all right?"

"Is that any business of yours?"

"Yes, it is. Tell me. Please. Where is Rayna? Have you hurt her?"

"Hurt her?" He seemed shocked by the question. "Of course not. She is my daughter. My youngest daughter. My most precious jewel."

"You send thugs to manhandle your most precious jewel?"

"No. I sent my sons to fetch their sister home. I do not want you to get the wrong idea. My daughter is safe, with family. Where she is supposed to be. She is to be married next month. She will be making a new home for herself and her husband, safe inside the hundred gates. Mea Shearim, *Yerushalayim*." Rayna had said that her family wanted to place her in an arranged marriage, against her will. Not only were they forcing her into the union, they were dragging her five thousand miles away from me. I couldn't let them do this.

"No," I said. "I'll . . . I'll . . ." What could I do? "I'll go there. To Jerusalem."

"I would advise against that. You will not be welcomed in that neighborhood."

"I don't care."

"Many zealots have come from America to Jerusalem, and lost their minds. No one is surprised when they disappear as quickly as they have come."

"But I love her." I did. Was that worth anything?

"You lust after her."

"No. It wasn't about that. We never had sex." I didn't think our juvenile fumbling counted.

"So she also claims. It does not matter. She has been matched with a young man—a righteous man, a student of mine—who has the humility to forgive her impurity. They are to be married very soon." I felt as if the rebbe had struck me across the face. It would have been better if I had fought her brothers, and been beaten with the crowbar.

"I should be the one to marry her," I said. Hearing that she would be getting married, that someone else would be living with her, eating meals with her, lying beside her at night, and protecting her made me jealous and angry. That was my role. Rayna and I had made a home together. If Rayna had to have a husband, I should be her husband.

"You? You fancy yourself a good match for my daughter?"

"Yes. I'm the only one that took care of her."

"You took care of her?"

"I tried."

"You tried? Really? That's so? Then why, when my sons came for her, did you let them take her?" I had asked myself this over and over.

"How did you know where we were?"

"We have many friends. One of them saw her working with you on the street." This was actually helpful; it narrowed down my list of suspects considerably. "Why did you not defend her?" the rebbe said. "Why did you allow her to be dragged away into the night?" I couldn't answer. I had no answer. Seeing this, the rebbe leaned back in his chair and clasped his hands together. "She will be protected now, by her husband."

"If I had a chance," I said, trying to justify myself, "I could live a good life and make a good husband for her."

"Perhaps that was true once. Or perhaps you did have chances, and squandered them. I cannot say. Either way, it is too late for you now. The evil is deep down inside you, and you will never be pure. Just go now." He waved me away with a pale hand, and turned his attention back toward his papers. "Please. Go. Return to your sick world."

"Can I leave a note with you? A letter, that you could pass on to her, so she knows that I came?"

"Certainly not. There is nothing you need to say to her. Leave. You are no longer part of our story." He wanted to blot out my name like Elisha ben Abuyah's.

My hand was on the doorknob when I stopped and turned back toward the rebbe. This might be my only chance to confront Rayna's father. I couldn't let myself be intimidated into wasting it and leaving without even getting my piece in. "What it was like between us is something you can't understand," I said. "It wasn't something to be sanctioned, or arranged. It was like something from an old tale." I wanted this man to know that what I felt for his daughter was real, that it went beyond the grime and physicality he had heard about. "She appeared to me on the street. Like it was meant to be. It *was* meant to be. We were both lost, and it was destined we should find each other. She was . . . like a ghost to me. An apparition. It was beyond the physical world."

"You are a foolish man. You suffer delusions. My daughter is just a girl. A troubled girl, but a girl. Ghosts do not walk the earth."

"My father is a ghost," I said. "He walks all over this city. I do too now."

"Your father was an *oysvorf*! He was a thug!" the rebbe shouted, as two bearded men grabbed me and began dragging me from the office. "There was nothing magical about him either."

⁞ ▮ ▪

Though it hurt me to leave Boro Park once again without having seen Rayna, I had to retreat to Manhattan for the time being. I went up to the roof of Becca's building with a bottle of brandy to think over the situation. Hearing the rebbe's marriage plans for Rayna had hammered home the urgency of the situation. I needed to act before she was sent away. Seeing the Galuth portrait in the rebbe's office not only confirmed Rayna's connection to the Galuth painting, but also clarified the connection between the Gluspker Rebbe and Goldov, and by extension Roman and Timur.

I opened Al's sketchbooks to Galuth's painting of the woman falling from the train. It had seemed to be a strange coincidence that I should find Rayna, whose face appeared in the sketchbooks, on West Fourth Street. Coincidences abounded only in crime novels, not in the world. But it wasn't actually a coincidence; it was *bashert*, preordained in heaven, that we would meet. Since the six days of creation, Hashem's attention had been devoted to creating couples. Rayna and I were meant to meet. We would have been pulled together across continents.

Or maybe not. There was ultimately a practical explanation to why Rayna's face appeared in the painting, one that didn't involve unseen forces, only a natural family resemblance. I had been eager to get to know Rayna because I recognized her face from Al's sketchbook, had, in fact, gone out of my way to forge a connection with her. Hundreds of pretty girls passed by my table. Many of them were runaways. I had searched for every face from the book; it was only a matter of time until I found one on the street.

The rebbe said that the informer saw Rayna on the street too. If he had said the informer had seen her at the storage unit, that would have pointed to Zoya, Roman, and Timur, but none of them were directly connected to West Fourth Street. Barring the unlikely possibility that a party unknown to me had happened to see Rayna in the Village, this implicated Goldov. I remembered how he had watched Rayna on the street the day he delivered my money. This wasn't to say that Timur hadn't been consulted about me and provided the unit number, after Goldov provided the lead.

What the rebbe said about Al was disturbing. In the heated moment, I had taken it as mere insult, born of frustration, and meant to further discredit my point of view. But as soon as I left, it started to bother me: Did the rebbe know Al, or at least know who he was? Like everyone else, the rebbe had used the past tense. I wondered about Al's connection to everything. He worked with Goldov, and he worked with Roman and Timur. He was just as guilty as the rest of them. Or he had been. Timur and Roman were the ones who convinced me that I was right to believe he was alive, but they were not trustworthy men. Goldov must have had some reason for writing to my family in the first place. He must have known something about Al's disappearance he didn't divulge. Goldov had been eager enough to tell my family that Al was dead. I hadn't wanted to listen to what Goldov had to tell me before. It was time for another visit to the Galuth Museum.

|▮▮■

I slept in the evening, then went down to the storage space at four o'clock in the morning to pull the boxes out of the small unit they were packed into. I'd gotten them pretty well organized when I shifted units, so I knew what was what. A lot of the space's contents were worthless, old radios and bits of rope and other debris, as well as books that wouldn't sell for very much due to their title or condition. No one needed all these paperbacks. I carted the junk out to the curb.

Al was not coming back. I was done maintaining a strange shrine, like Asher had tried to do for his mother. There was no more time to linger and avoid doing anything concrete to help Rayna. I needed to take drastic action. Burning this bridge was the first step. If I couldn't go back, I would have to go forward.

On the way back inside, I stopped at the front desk to inform the facility that my storage space would be empty by the end of the day.

"We can't refund this month's fee," the kid at the desk said. "Or next month's."

"That's fine," I said.

"It looks like you're paid up until the end of the year, though, so you will still have six months' rent refunded. Would you like us to mail you a check, or charge it back to the card?"

"Charge it back to the card." Timur could keep his money. I had now severed all my ties to him and Roman.

All that was left in the storage unit was the dozen boxes of books worth saving, which I carried down the corridor by hand to Mendy's storage unit. I could have left the boxes outside my vacated unit, or at least used the cart, but I wanted to pour my nervous energy into labor. When I was done, I took one of Al's old belts that I'd put aside especially for this purpose and ran it through the trigger guard of his sawed-off rifle. I fastened the belt diagonally across my neck and chest, so the gun hung down on my side, under my arm, and pulled on a loose sweater and a raincoat. Satisfied that the gun was fully concealed, I left the unit unlocked and went and sat down on one of the boxes to wait for Mendy. He was a man of routine, and I knew he would arrive soon.

"Isaac?" he said, when he turned the corner with his little luggage cart and saw me waiting. He came closer and the light snapped on. "Good morning." We shook hands. "I was listening to the weather radio on the way over. There's going to be rain today. Not just rain, a pretty big storm actually. I wouldn't recommend trying to go out today." He appraised my stack of boxes. "What is all this?"

"I'm out of the business, Mendy."

"I see. So you are. I didn't think you'd be down here forever. But I'm sorry to see you go."

"Thanks. I'll miss talking to you."

"Did you find what you were looking for?" he asked.

"Not really."

"Yeah. I didn't think you would. I sure haven't. Did you find a job in the straight world, or are you just taking off?"

"Just taking off." He nodded, and didn't ask any more questions. He didn't mention Rayna. Maybe he thought she left me, and it was a sore subject. "Can you use my back stock?" I said.

"Well, let's see. Let's see." He tugged on his beard with his right hand, and gripped his bent right elbow with his left hand. His eyes scanned the stack of boxes. "What did you want for it all? I mean, I'd have to see the titles, but knowing the general quality of your books . . ." I noticed he called them my books, not Al's. "I'm sure I could go four, four fifty."

"No. I don't need any money. I want to give them to you, Mendy." I was done with the buying and selling, and just wanted a clean break. But I also wanted to do something for Mendy. Since I came down to the street, he was the one person, other than Rayna, who'd been genuinely kind to me. I wondered if he had a grown son or daughter somewhere who he never saw.

"Oh. I see. That's very nice of you, Isaac. I know you mean it. But the thing is, there ain't really such a thing as a gift. Everything comes with an obligation. It's better to pay it off as it comes. So that people can part as friends, with nothing owed." I was happy that Mendy considered me a friend. He didn't use the word lightly.

"Tell you what," I said. "Give me fifty for the cart, and I'll throw in the books as part of the deal. To sweeten it."

"I meant four hundred only for the books. That cart is worth at least a hundred alone. On top of what the books are worth."

"The wheels are practically useless. The rubber is ground down, and one of the cotter pins is rusted in place; it'll be a hassle to get it popped off when you do replace that wheel. Half of the books are too esoteric to sell quickly, and we have to factor in your storage costs. Fifty for the whole lot is a fair price."

"Okay," Mendy said. "You drive a hard bargain. Usually people drive bargains in the other direction, but hey. Fifty it is." He slid me two twenties and two fives. Pocketing them, I turned to leave. I felt his hand on my arm and turned back toward him.

"Isaac," he said. "Take care of yourself."

❘❚❙■

I got the Q train down at Canal and rode it all the way to Coney Island. I spent the long ride looking through Al's sketchbooks. The images on the pages no longer seemed as foreign or as frightening to me as they had when I'd first encountered them. I'd been living with them for a little while now.

Stillwell Avenue was crawling with cops. As I passed through the terminal, I folded my arms to pin the gun to my side as tightly as I could. The police didn't pay me any mind.

When I got to the museum, I pounded on the door until I heard Goldov shout, "I coming! I coming! What is so urgent so early in the morning?" He pulled the heavy door open. "Oh. It's you. Edel's boy."

"May I come in, Goldov?"

"Why not?" He stepped back into the gallery and I entered, pushing the door closed behind me.

"Goldov," I said. "I have come to settle accounts with you."

"Oh? You are here to pay the money old Al owed me? Come on up. For this I have been waiting." He was already heading up the stairs to his apartment.

"I know you have." I thought of the note he'd sent my mother a few months earlier, and the comments he made the first time I came down to the museum. "But that's not my account to settle. I'm here because of what you took from me."

"What I took from you? I took nothing from anybody. Always people have taken from me. Go home, *malchik*, if you have nothing for me." We were standing in Goldov's kitchen now, surrounded by his terrible paintings.

I pulled the gun out from under my big sweater. Goldov watched with confusion as I struggled to unbuckle the belt with one hand. When I did get the gun free, and pointed the barrel at his face, his expression changed. I unclicked the safety with my thumb and held my pointer finger against the trigger. A thin layer of sweat instantly appeared between my fingertip and the trigger's flat metal surface. I had never pointed a gun at a human being before. I realized that it meant I was in control of the situation. I didn't need to be nervous or afraid anymore. Goldov did.

"Okay," Goldov said. "Fine. So maybe I skimmed a little off of what Roman gave me to give to you. A courier fee. Maybe I took more than I should have. It's still far less than what Edel owed me. But there's no need for guns. This is a civilized country. I'll give you your money."

"You're damn right you'll give me my money. But that's not why I'm here."

"I am not understanding."

"Shut up. You're the one who snitched to the Glupsker Rebbe. We both know that. You work for him. Galuth was the rebbe's great-aunt, or something. That's a self-portrait of her downstairs. The painting where she is thrown from the tracks."

"*The Sea Beach Line*, it's called."

"*The Sea Beach Line*. The rebbe is the benefactor of this place. He keeps one of Galuth's paintings in his office. I know because I helped steal it for him with Roman. Timur paid me two thousand for that, and you stole four bills. Quite a courier fee. You recognized Rayna on the street as your boss's daughter. And you snitched on her and me for what, a little bonus?" Goldov stood silent and motionless. "Nu? Nu?" Goldov let out a long, pained sigh.

"Fine. You know this is true. What do you need me to say? Galuth is the aunt of the *alter* rebbe. She is the great-aunt of the current rebbe. And the great-great-aunt of your little playmate, for that matter. Galuth studied Torah with her brothers. She outpaced them in her studies, even delving deep into the kabbalah. Deep into aspects of mysteries they could never understand. But a woman could never be rabbi, so she fled to Paris and became next best thing, a painter. The rabbis, they still respect her. If only in secret." There was reverence in his voice, and I could see that he respected her too. For all his faults, Goldov really loved Galuth. Then his face turned, became cruel.

"So you are not a complete moron. I work for the Glupskers. They are zealots, not lovers of art, but Galuth was one of theirs, and they honor her. At least the rebbe does. So I told my employer I am knowing where his daughter is. What of it? It was the right thing to do."

"The right thing to do? We were happy. We had our little world. We weren't hurting anybody. And you destroyed it for us." I jabbed the barrel of the gun in his direction as I spoke.

"What do I care about your happiness? Besides, your world, your little closet, the books you sold: that was all Edel's. He stole from me. He did worse to others. No joy is not built on someone else's pain. What do you think Alojzy did to obtain the favor of Timur in the first place?"

"He was loyal to Timur. To his organization. Even if they didn't deserve it."

"To be loyal to someone means to be betraying someone else. Alojzy's great act of loyalty, do you know what it was?"

"No."

"I thought not. A friend of his—a man from Israel who was trying to make a name for himself here in Brooklyn—made an overture to your father. They had served together in army, and he wanted Edel to come in with him as he made moves on Timur's operation. Edel pretended to go along with the plan, but only so he could inform on this man to Timur."

"So Alojzy saved Timur's life." Even as I defended my father, I knew Goldov was telling the truth. He was talking about the IDF soldier in Al's sketchbooks. The man was dead in Israel, dead in New York. Not dead from the war, but dead because Al had betrayed him. Goldov was telling me that my father was a rat—and Goldov would know a rat. The joke was on me; I was steadfast in my loyalty to a man who hadn't known the meaning of the word. My face flushed with shame.

"Sure," Goldov said, "you could say so, but what do you think happened to his army buddy? His old *chevre*, who he had fought side by side with. How do you think his other Israeli buddies thought about him after this? After he sold his friend out to that butcher? Are you proud to have his name? I would not be. I spit on your father's name."

Goldov spat on his own floor. I didn't care what my father had done; nothing gave Goldov the right to disrespect his name. I swung the rifle down toward his leg and pulled the trigger. The gun popped, and a disproportionately large flash erupted from the cut barrel. Goldov screamed out in pain. A black cat leaped out from behind a stack of canvases, and darted out the door.

"Do you think that I am a liar?" Goldov demanded, bent over. He held the wound and lowered himself the rest of the way to the floor. The fact that he was still speaking with such hostility meant that the small bullet had not hit an artery or anything important, but only embedded itself in the meat of his winter salami of a leg.

"No," I said. "I know you're not a liar." I worked the stiff bolt. The empty brass casing hit the floor with a little clinking sound, and I loaded another round into the chamber. I held the gun on Goldov with my right hand, and searched in my pocket with my left. I pulled out the photocopy of the dead soldier sketch that I'd been carrying around. The picture with the words אני מצטער hidden in the background. Now

I knew what Al was sorry for. "You are speaking of this man, right?" I held up the paper so Goldov could see. He squinted, then nodded.

"Yes. That's him. Ezra was his name." The last bit of legend I'd built around Al had been stripped away. I felt the loss acutely. If I'd been alone, I might have cried.

"Now tell me about what happened to my father. No one else will. He's really dead too, isn't he? You tried to tell me that last time. Tell me now. Did Roman and Timur do something to him too? I get that you bit your tongue when I asked before because you didn't want to cross Timur. But now you understand that I'll hurt you as badly as he will."

"*Ladno*," Goldov sighed again. Despite the stakes, it seemed that our whole interchange bored him. "Never should I have sent the postcard. I only wanted that maybe your rich mother would cut me a check. But I did not lie. Your father is dead, of a heart attack." It was true. I knew it was true. Al was dead. He wasn't coming back. "He was helping Roman with some job in Red Hook, receiving something stolen that had been smuggled from overseas, paintings or something of that nature. The excitement of the job was too much for his ticker, it must have been. Roman and his thugs threw Edel's body into the harbor. They couldn't call 911 to bring an ambulance to their crime scene. They couldn't carry a body nonchalantly off ship. So they tossed him in the harbor. Roman mentioned it to me, because I was the closest thing Alojzy had to a friend. I guess he thought I'd miss him." He looked up at me, to see if I was satisfied. I nodded. More than anything, it was a relief to finally know where Al was. "You do believe me?"

"I do." Goldov's account sounded true. Al ate horribly. He never exercised, and he never went to a doctor. He'd self-medicate with liquor, or occasionally with the black-market medicine that old women sold on Brighton Beach Avenue like it was dope. Roman himself had said that Alojzy was his go-to man for jobs like that, so it made sense he'd be in that situation. Roman wouldn't have thought twice about throwing Al in the water. Get another bird. Get another friend. Get another father. There were no great mysteries. Just the usual bullshit and suffering.

"And Rayna?" I said.

"What of her?"

"She's still in Brooklyn? They haven't rushed her off to Israel yet, or hidden her in Lakewood or Monsey or someplace? You seem to know what goes on with the Langer family."

"Yes, I believe she is." This was good news. I didn't know how I would have been able to follow her to Israel. "The whole family will depart for the wedding next week. Until then, they are keeping her under lock and key."

"Good. Now," I said, "I want my money. That hasn't changed." I pointed the gun at Goldov's face again. I didn't want to kill the man, but I knew that I would if I had a reason to.

He gestured toward a coffee can sitting amongst the paint tubes on the windowsill. I pulled out the wad of bills without counting them, and stuffed them in my pants pocket.

"That's my whole savings . . ."

"I don't care." This was no time for hesitancy, or second-guessing. I would take what I would take. I was different than Al, but I was just as tough. Besides, I was sure the old thief had money hidden in plenty of places. He would never starve.

Turning my back on Goldov, I went down the stairs. I listened for sounds that he might be making a move to call someone or attack me from behind—I wouldn't be surprised if the old man had a rusty Makarov tucked away somewhere—but I didn't hear anything. I stopped in the gallery and took a long look at *The Sea Beach Line*. Rayna flew in the air, just above death, for all eternity. She'd been flying there before she was born, and she'd be flying there still when she'd grown wide and blank-eyed, holding one brat against her hip and pushing two more down a narrow street in a double stroller. For a moment, I thought I could reach out and catch her.

But I couldn't. This was just a picture. It wasn't a window to anything real. I'd taken Goldov's money, same as Al would have. Same as Al had. But he wouldn't stop there and wander out misty-eyed over a painting. He'd have stayed on his toes, played every angle. I took a box cutter out of my pocket and cut the canvas from the frame. I rolled it up as carefully as I could, and tucked it under my arm.

I walked back up the stairs. Goldov was lying in the middle of the room, gripping a dirty rag to his bleeding leg. "Something else you need to take from me?" There was fear on his face; he wasn't mocking me.

"Yeah. I'm taking this picture, *The Sea Beach Line*."

"You know that the pictures do not belong to me. They belong to the Glupskers."

"Yes, I know. Tell your boss, the rebbe, that I'll be happy to trade him back the picture for a meeting with Rayna. I won't try anything. I'll come unarmed. He can send his guards or chaperones or whoever. But if I can't see her once more, I'm keeping her picture. Roman and Timur know the number to reach me at."

I went out onto the fishing pier to ditch the gun. It had served its purpose and was now just a liability; if a cop caught me with it, I would be going to Rikers. If the rebbe wanted to send his and Timur's people after me, one little .22 wouldn't be anywhere near enough firepower to make a difference.

Luckily, the pier wasn't too crowded, at least down at the very end. A couple of old men were fishing, but everyone else had packed it in. A small group of teenagers were hanging out, but they were coupled up, and too busy flirting and playing grab ass to notice anything an adult was doing. I managed to work the gun out from under my sweater and tossed it off the pier. The weight carried it farther out over the water than I'd expected, and for a moment it seemed to hover in the air.

Out of the corner of my eye, I saw a freighter moving out toward the Atlantic. The ship was moving quickly. I turned to watch it. My eyes were suddenly telescopes, and I zeroed in on two figures standing on the ship's deck: a man in his early twenties, and an older man pushing sixty. They wore thick work jackets, and grinned as the wind whipped their hair. The ship was three hundred yards away if it was a foot, but I could see the men with perfect clarity: Al and me.

He had not died. He had not been thrown into the harbor. He had been waiting for me at the docks this whole time. The postcard had told me what ship to board. We sealed ourselves inside a shipping container, and slipped past the Port Authority. We would spend the six-day journey bunking with the sailors, then be sealed back in the container before the ship landed in Rotterdam and was inspected by EU customs. The container would be offloaded onto a freight train, and we'd ride until we'd made it to Berlin, where Al knew people.

I heard a splash, and turned back just in time to see the gun disappearing beneath the surface of the water. I looked back up again, and the ship was gone too. There was no Al, and no escape. My father was gone. I had to see Rayna, before I lost her too.

22

IT WOULD HAVE BEEN best to stash the painting somewhere, so I wouldn't lose my bargaining chip if Roman and Timur or the rebbe's sons came after me, but I couldn't think of a safe place. Al used to stash things at the lockers in Port Authority and Grand Central, but they had all been removed after September 11. Andrew's apartment would have worked—his ankle monitor was the perfect alarm system if anyone came after him—but I didn't think he'd want to risk adding art theft to whatever charges he was already facing. Besides, he didn't really owe me any favors. *The Sea Beach Line* would have to stay with me.

I was almost back to Becca's apartment when the cell phone rang.

"Hi, Roman," I said.

"Jesus fucking Christ, Izzy. You stupid little bastard." He was angry, but there was also a note of respect in his voice.

"Goldov gave you guys my message?"

"Yes. We must speak, to straighten things out. Can you meet me at—"

"No," I said. "I choose the place." If Roman chose a location, he would likely have other guys waiting around to snatch me up when I tried to leave. Just like they'd snatched Rayna. I needed someplace open, public, and neutral, with plenty of entrances. "I'll be in the main branch of the library, on Fifth Avenue, at two p.m. this afternoon. In the Rose Main Reading Room. One of the tables on the north side."

"Fine. Hasta la vista, baby."

I went out again around twelve thirty to meet Roman. The temperature had not risen since the early morning, which was strange. It was dark and windy for so late in the spring. As I crossed Second Avenue on my way to the 6 train, a yellow cab speeding to make the turn onto Seventy-Ninth Street almost struck me and another woman in the crosswalk. The woman jumped forward; I pivoted around the front fender of the cab as it stopped short. I punched downward into the hood of the car with both fists. The full weight of my body was behind the blows, and I felt the metal dent.

"Fuck you!" I shouted, not looking back.

The cab, suddenly in less of a hurry, followed beside me down Seventy-Ninth. The driver was shouting and gesturing. I refused to give him the courtesy of turning my head to look at him. He was angry that I had hit his car, but I didn't hear any authority in his voice, only pleading.

I stopped and turned so my whole body was facing the street. The car stopped short, skidding forward so that we were neck and neck. I leaned down toward the window.

"If you get out of your car," I said, "I'll fucking kill you."

I didn't sound like myself. But I recognized the voice: it was Al, as I'd heard him in numerous street interactions in Brooklyn. He was gone now. It was time for me to stand up for myself. I looked right at the cabdriver, who was bigger than me, but a lot older and a little flabbier. I hoped he wasn't as crazy as I was. Maybe he was. Who knows what type of life he'd led in Pakistan or Bangladesh or wherever before he came here. Maybe his dad was dead, too. Maybe his dad's body had been thrown in a river. Maybe his girl had been kidnapped or arrested. People were thrown into secret dungeons all the time. I knew I wasn't special. It didn't matter. Right or wrong, I couldn't back down. "Drive away," I said. He shrugged and drove away. Probably he had kids of his own now, and couldn't risk it. Fuck him, and fuck his kids too.

I was in the reading room by one p.m., waiting at a long oak table, beneath the fifty-foot-high ceilings. Painted clouds blew across the wall behind me. There was no difference between inside and outside. I sat and waited. I didn't read.

Roman arrived at one thirty. As near as I could tell, he was alone. He looked both surprised and impressed to see that I was already there. He came around the table and slid in next to me.

"You know," he said, "you scared the shit out of old Goldov. Put some lead in his leg, eh? He thought you were going to put some in his head as well." My violence seemed to amuse Roman. It was strange to hear such a boisterous man converse in a whisper.

"Maybe I should have," I said.

"I guess you do take after your father, after all." I was loyal to my father. But he was not a loyal man. So I only took after him so much.

"Sure I do. Does that mean you're going to throw me in the harbor?"

"Goldov's been telling you stories." Roman spoke derisively, but he didn't actually contest the story's veracity. This was probably the closest thing I was going to get to an admission. In his mind it was justified; Al was no longer useful. Trying to get medical help for my father would have put Roman and Timur's operation at risk. So they tossed him overboard.

"You threw him away," I said. "Was he still breathing? Maybe he could have been revived."

"No. People don't come back, Izzy. Don't you know that?"

"Why did you and Timur tell me he was alive? Why did you guys string me along?"

"You believed what you wanted to believe. Your foolishness is not our responsibility." They had lied to me, but I recognized that his statement contained some truth. I had played myself.

"Fine, but why talk to me at all, or bring me into things? Why not just ignore me?"

"Your first call spooked Timur, so we had to check you out. We had to be friendly, get lay of the land." Roman wasn't going to say anything too specific or incriminating, now that we were on the outs, but I got his point. He had checked me for a wire before my first meeting with Timur. My family could have been working with the authorities, or could have hired a private investigator to look into Alojzy's death. Timur and Roman probably thought I was putting together a claim for a life insurance payout. Wining and dining me was just a way to make sure no one was looking into their business too closely. "And then when we saw you were such the puppy dog, so eager to impress, Timur figured we could use you. Anything we ask, you say, 'Absolutely!' You didn't even ask to be paid, most of the time, so long as we let you live in the closet." Roman was trying to get a rise out of me.

"Well," I said, keeping my voice calm and even, "that time is over."

"So it is. *Ladno*. You have the painting?" I nodded. "Where is it?"

"Somewhere safe." I hoped no one was ransacking Becca's apartment as we spoke. But that seemed unlikely; the apartment was in a doorman building, which had recently been under federal surveillance.

"Naturally. Timur thought we should beat it out of you. I thought so too. But the rebbe, he is a compassionate man. He is granting your request."

"I can see Rayna? Where? When?" Roman grinned, and I regretted my eagerness immediately. Once again, I was their goddamn puppy.

"The Galuth Museum. You will return the painting to where it belongs." This made sense. The rebbe wanted to meet on his own turf, on his own terms, but he didn't want me to come into the Glupsker community, with all its prying eyes. "Tonight, ten p.m."

"That's fine," I said, standing up. The agreement seemed genuine, but I still wanted to make sure to slip out first, so I could go through the runaround of the library's stone staircases, then cut through the gift shop and out the small north entrance before Roman or anyone else he had with him could follow me. "I'll be there."

| ▎▎▪

I didn't have a clear idea of what was going to happen that night, but I was filled with anticipation. I was going to see Rayna again. Back uptown, I went to the diner and ate a big meal of eggs, potatoes, and coffee, then went back to Becca's apartment and looked through all of Al's sketchbooks one more time. Now that I knew for certain he was dead, they took on a different meaning. They were no longer the volumes of an atlas, but more like history books. Leaving a sketchbook open on a drawing of Becca, my mother, and me, I picked up the phone and dialed my mother's number.

"Hello?"

"Mom."

"Isaac. How are you? Have you heard about the hurricane warning for New York City?"

"Not really." Mendy had said there was going to be a big storm, but I didn't realize it was anything as serious as a hurricane. "My friend mentioned something about it."

"Listen to the news. It's a big deal. And be careful."

"Okay. Look, I wanted to tell you something, Mom: Alojzy is dead."

"You know for sure now? You sound sure."

"Yes. I talked to the man who sent us that notecard. He gave me some more details, and then I spoke to someone who actually witnessed him die." Roman hadn't given details, but as far as I was concerned he had confirmed Goldov's account. "It sounds like he had a heart attack when he was working. He fell in the harbor so no body was recovered. But it's confirmed. He's gone." My mother let out a long wail. I could hear her heart snapping in two. I had to move the phone back from my ear.

"My poor sweet Ally," she wailed. "My poor Ally. And you with no father."

"I don't understand," I said. Wasn't I the only one who hadn't accepted that he was gone all along? "I thought you said you let him go a long time ago?"

"I know what I said, Isaac. And you're old enough to understand why I had to say it, over and over. But you don't think I ever really let him go, do you? He was the love of my life. I cried when I got the notecard from that man, and I'll cry twice as hard now."

"Thank you for calling, Isaac," she said, regaining her composure. "It's good to know for sure, even if it means we have to accept it. Have you spoken to your sister about this?"

"No, I haven't had the opportunity. I'll see her when she gets home from work this evening."

"Well, be gentle about it. She's not so tough as she seems. Thank you for calling. I have to go sit out on the *portal* now, and think a little by myself." Usually I was the one trying to get off the phone. My mother had had to deal with things by herself when Al left, and we were too young to help. She had an inner life I knew almost nothing about. "Wait! Bernie wants to talk to you. If Bernie is willing to use the telephone, it must be important."

"Okay. I love you, Mom." I heard the noises of people shuffling themselves. So Bernie had been standing right next to her. He must have come when my mom screamed. I wondered if he heard what she said about Al being the love of her life. But then, Bernie wasn't stupid, he must have known.

"Hello, Isaac."

"Hello, Bernie."

"Listen, when we talked the other night, I spoke very negatively about my father."

"Yes."

"One thing I should say, though, is that despite everything, I still said kaddish at shul for him when he died."

"You prayed for him?"

"Yes, I did. I said kaddish for him. For a year. It's a son's obligation."

"I'm obligated to say kaddish for Alojzy?" Spending two months performing Al's daily rituals wasn't enough. Tradition dictated that I also had to pray for a man who'd never prayed for himself.

"You have it verified now, that he's dead?"

"Yes."

"Then you should say kaddish. As long as he was only missing, it's taught that you should maintain hope rather than mourn."

"I did. I maintained hope."

"I know you did, Isaac. But now it's time to mourn. There's another prayer, the *El Malei Rachamim*, that is specifically for the deceased. But the mourner's kaddish—not that it's not for the dead, there are teachings that it helps their souls—is for the mourner too. For you."

Becca came home around four thirty in the afternoon. I was surprised; it was rare that she made it back before eight. She carried her laptop case in one hand, and a paper grocery bag in the other. I took the groceries from her.

"Decided to play hooky?" I said.

"No, they closed the office early because of the storm warning."

"I talked to Mom earlier. She mentioned the storm."

"That's good. It could be really bad. Have you been watching the news?"

"No. I've had other things on my mind."

"You should still pay attention to the world around you. I was going to mention it last night, but you were asleep when I came home. This storm started in the Caribbean, and did a lot of damage to some of the islands down there a few days ago. They thought it would dissipate in the ocean, but now it's coming up the coast, and it's probably going to make landfall in Jersey this evening. They don't know how bad it's going to hit the city." I put the groceries away in the cabinets and refrigerator while she talked. "It's way early in the year for a storm this bad. But businesses are closing, and they might even shut down trains in case the tunnels flood. There are warnings and advisories in effect. It's pretty crazy. I had to elbow some old bitches to get my hands on candles and milk at the store."

"We don't drink milk."

"I know, but in an emergency we might want it." She smiled. "Or you might want to make egg creams."

"True. Becca, I need to tell you something. Do you want to sit down?"

"You're making me nervous, Izzy." We sat down on the couch.

"What is it? Did you talk to Andrew?"

"I did, actually. I saw him yesterday. He's okay. He's under house arrest. He's going to plead guilty."

"I'm glad he's home," she said. "He looked all right?"

"He looked fine. But that's not what I wanted to talk to you about."

"No?"

"It's something else: I found out, for sure, that Alojzy is dead. I've confirmed it from a witness. He's really gone." Becca got up from the couch. She uncorked a half-full bottle of wine and poured herself a glass. She walked over to her huge window, and looked out toward the East River.

"Are you okay?" I asked.

"Yes. I'm fine. Thank you for telling me. It's good to know for sure, to not have the . . . question hanging over us." She drank her wine.

"Do you want to talk about it?"

"No. It's okay. I don't have anything to say about it. He was already gone. I've told you what I remember about him. They aren't happy memories. Have you talked to Mom? Do I need to call her?"

"I told her this afternoon."

"That's good. How did she take it?"

"She took it hard." Becca nodded, unsurprised.

"Anyway, I still have to get some work done, even though I'm not at the office." Becca took her laptop out of its bag. She set it up at the kitchen table, put her headphones on, and started typing.

After about twenty minutes, Becca pulled off her headphones and tossed them on the table. The jack snapped out of her computer, and music started playing from the speakers, the kind of radio rock my mom and dad used to dance to in the kitchen.

Becca got up and went over to the closet across from the bathroom. She rummaged around in the back, beneath the linens, pulling out a crushed pack of Marlboro Golds. I hadn't seen her smoke since high school, but apparently she still did, now and then, in secret. She flopped down on the couch and lit a cigarette. I was surprised that she would allow cigarette smoke in her immaculate apartment. She saw me watching her.

"Do you want a cigarette, Izzy?"

"Sure." I wasn't much of a smoker, but at college I often smoked spliffs that were half rolling tobacco. We sat on the couch and smoked in silence. The gray clouds gathered outside the window.

After a few hours, Becca asked if I wanted to order some Chinese food.

"We might as well get some delivery while we can," she said, "and save the groceries for when we need them. We'll just make sure to give the poor delivery guy a good tip."

"Actually," I said, "I have to go out tonight."

"Are you serious? Don't you hear the wind already? It's going to be dangerous out there."

"I'll be careful."

"This better not have to do with some scheme Alojzy left behind."

"No. It has to do with the girl I told you about, Rayna."

"I thought maybe you two broke up," Becca said. "I thought that's why you came up here so suddenly the other day. I should have asked, but with the Andrew thing . . ."

"It's okay. It's not that we broke up; her family forced her to go back home. She's with them now. But her home life, it's not a good one. She's . . . a victim. I need to intervene." I was already putting on my coat. Becca sighed.

"What's that you have with you?" *The Sea Beach Line* was under my arm. I unrolled the canvas and held it up under the overhead light.

"It's beautiful," Becca said, after a minute. "Is that the girl—Rayna?"

"No," I admitted. "I thought it was when I first saw it. It's actually her great-great-aunt. But they look very similar."

"You're going to take it out in the storm?"

"I have to return it to Rayna's father. I'm going to get a couple garbage bags from the kitchen, to wrap it up. And I thought I could borrow one of your yoga mat bags to carry it in? I have to take care of this painting."

"You have to be careful, Izzy," she said.

"Rayna might be in trouble. I need to see her. I'll be fine."

I got the 5 train at Eighty-Sixth, and transferred to the Q at Union Square. There weren't many people in the subway. Notices had been posted, listing the various service disruptions that would be going into effect over the next twelve hours. After eleven p.m., there would be no trains between Brooklyn and Manhattan. This didn't seem to matter. I couldn't picture my return to the city. I was just focused on getting to the Galuth Museum to see Rayna.

The wind whipped at my face as I walked from the Stillwell Avenue terminal to West Eighteenth Street. It howled like the tormented souls of the dead. I thought of Alojzy, lying beneath the water. Coney Island was always colder than the rest of the city, but this was ridiculous. It was May, but it felt like winter. I zipped up my raincoat so the collar covered my neck and pulled my knit cap down over my ears, but it didn't help much.

I got to the museum and knocked on the door. Roman let me in. In addition to Roman, I saw Timur and a couple tough-looking guys my age. The rebbe stood across the gallery, examining one of the smaller Galuth paintings. Rayna was nowhere in sight. My suppressed suspicion that this was a trap immediately resurfaced—what would stop them from beating or even killing me, and taking the painting?—but I didn't see why the rebbe would have bothered to come personally if that was the case.

"Isaac," Timur said. "You have the rebbe's painting?"

"Yes," I said, patting the yoga bag. "It's right here."

"Hand the bag to Roman. Slowly. Dima here will then pat you down. We don't want you putting any little .22 caliber holes in us."

"Wait," I said. "How do I know I'll get to see Rayna? How do I know you all are keeping your side of the deal?"

"Enough of this nonsense," the rebbe shouted. "Do as Timur tells you, and give me my painting. If I wanted to double-cross you, you would not be standing here. But unlike you, I am not a gonif. I am an honorable man. I would not go back on an oath. I said that you may see my daughter one final time, and you shall see her. Under my super-vision." I let Roman take the bag. The kid, Dima, patted me down, and indicated that I was unarmed.

Roman slid the painting out of the yoga bag, and carefully unwrapped and unrolled it. He and Timur laid *The Sea Beach Line* out on a worktable that had been placed in front of the painting's empty frame. I hoped I wasn't behaving like the people in the crowd, watching Rayna fall to her death at the mercy of these goons, and not being able to do anything about it.

It occurred to me that Goldov was nowhere in sight. Understand-able, considering how our last interaction ended. The rebbe pulled a pair of eyeglasses from his jacket pocket and leaned in close to the canvas. I sat down on the viewing bench in the middle of the gallery. Did the rebbe see the beauty in the painting, I wondered, or did he only want it back because he believed it belonged to his family? After a couple minutes of inspection, he was satisfied.

"This is indeed the original painting," the rebbe pronounced. It hadn't occurred to me to forge it, but forgery was likely a common practice in these men's world. "It is unfortunate that the canvas was cut out of the frame, but other than that the painting is undamaged. I am sure Goldov will find a way to satisfactorily mat and display it." He went over to the stairwell that led up to Goldov's apartment, and shouted something in Yiddish.

Rayna came down the staircase, followed by two young Hasidim. I wondered if they were the same brothers who had invaded our storage space. It was hard to imagine that these men in knickers, white blouses, black vests, and velvet kippot could have inspired fear in me, but it stood to reason that they were the same guys.

I wanted to run to Rayna, but making sudden movements wasn't a good idea. She came over to the bench.

"Hey, Rayna," I said.

"Hello, Isaac." I stepped forward to hug her, but she shrank back, gesturing to her brothers and father with her eyes. We sat down on the bench, with our backs to the rebbe and the others, so we could have at least a semblance of privacy.

Her hair looked different. It had been trimmed more evenly, and instead of being wild and witchy, it was combed straight, and pulled back with a thick headband. Over her black blouse was a gray cardigan, and beneath her black skirt were matching gray stockings. She had a large and slightly shiny handbag, which she clutched tightly on her lap. I watched her for a long moment. Her eyes didn't dart and dance anymore; they remained fixed. We had been separated for less than a week, but it felt like there were months between us.

"Rayna," I said. "I thought you were gone from me forever."

"I am gone from you. Now is just to say good-bye." We both spoke quietly, so the others couldn't hear what we were saying. I glanced over my shoulder. The men stood across the long gallery, smoking cigarettes and watching us.

"No. You don't have to be. I've gotten stronger. I can protect you now."

"So now you are a hero?"

"Yes. For you."

"Isaac. That is the thing. You are talking about a storybook hero. Always. We were playing as characters in a story." I barely recognized this voice as Rayna's. The nervousness was gone, but so was the sweetness. And when had I ever heard her speak the word "story" with derision? "You were playing your father. I was playing a free woman. We pretended a closet was a castle. It was a nice story, but stories end. Books are shut, and put back on the shelf."

"My father is dead," I said.

"I know. He was dead the whole time. I didn't understand why you pretended he wasn't."

"I couldn't give up until I knew for sure. You seem different."

"I am healthier. I am back on medication. You liked me better when I was a mess?"

"No. I like you regardless. But you don't seem healthier. You just seem . . . drugged up. Do you feel healthier?"

"I don't feel anything. It's better that way."

"But they hurt you." She glanced up at the men waiting for her by the door. "Someone did something very bad to you."

"Yes," she said, looking down at the floor. "Someone did bad things to me, for a long time. My father and the others didn't believe me. But they believe me now. It's being dealt with . . . there will be punishment." Rayna had run away because no one would listen to her story. I had listened to her. But I had never asked for details. Never pressed her for the whole story. I should have. "What happened won't affect me anymore," she said. "I am going to go far away from where that happened. I am going to live in Israel. As a married woman. With my own life, and my own home. I'll never have to go back to my father's house. Most important, I'll never have to go back to the Bais Glupsk School, or walk by it." So the demon had been a schoolteacher. Rayna looked back up at me.

"Rayna," I said. "I'm sorry I didn't ask who had hurt you . . . I was scared to know."

"It doesn't matter what was said or wasn't said. I won't think of New York at all once I'm gone. I won't think of you. And you shouldn't think of me."

"Think of me. Think of me always." I could accept Rayna leaving, if it was what she wanted, but I could not accept being blotted from her memory. I could not accept that there was no place for me in her heart. It meant there was no place for me anywhere in the universe. Rayna was still seated next to me, but I felt lonely, lonelier than I'd ever felt before.

"That is a cruel demand, Isaac."

"I don't care. I demand it. Israel is never the happy ending to a story, Rayna. It's not an escape from the world. My father thought it would be, when he was young, and then he was forced to become a killer. He was ruined forever." I was angry. Not at Rayna, maybe, but at everyone else. Well, at Rayna too. I wanted her to want to run away with me. I wanted another chance to fight her brothers. I knew it was hopeless, but I wished she would at least give me a sign that I should try. "All the rules your *haredim* follow are from the Babylonian Talmud, anyway. You might as well go to Iraq, if it's about living a religious life. The whole idea of Israel as a holy land is nonsense. New York City is a holy land."

"What does any of that have to do with anything in my life, Isaac? People don't do things because of ideas."

"Then why do they do them?"

"Because this is real life, and we have to do certain things to get through it." She looked at me, sadly. "Don't dwell on our story, Isaac. Just find a way to live your life. I'm not trying to be cruel. You were kind to me, and I want to be kind to you. And the kindest thing I can say is forget all this nonsense. Forget all these pictures and tales. Forget me. Go live a real life."

She stood up. I didn't.

"Rayna?"

"Yes, Isaac."

"When I first saw you, I recognized you from Galuth's painting. From the drawing of the painting."

"I know. You told me."

"I know now she was your ancestor. Your ancestor who ran away, and did what she wanted to do. But still, to me, it's a painting of you. It brought us together. It's sitting there, on the table. Will you look at it, once, before you go?"

"No. I refuse to."

"Why?"

"Because." She started crying. "Because if I see it, I will see what you saw, and I'll tumble right back into our world. I'll believe in it again." She turned away from me. "Father," she called. "We can leave now."

Rayna, her father, and her brothers filed out the door. She didn't look back. The black SUV was parked outside. Rayna's brothers got in the front. She and her father got in the back, and the car pulled away into the dark night.

I walked away without saying anything to Timur or Roman, heading down West Eighteenth Street to the boardwalk. Due to the weather, almost no one was out in the streets, and no one but me went up on the boardwalk. The wind came off the ocean like a derailed train. The cold wind didn't bother me; I was already completely numb. Huge waves crashed on the shore.

"Isaac. *Malchik. Malchik.*" I turned, and saw Roman approaching me at a brisk pace. "I want to speak to you."

"Why?" I said. "What else is there to say?" He was nearly upon me. I stopped walking, and leaned back on the metal railing that separated the boardwalk from the sand. He would catch up to me either way. I was wary, but not scared, exactly; the moment for a double cross had passed. But what more was required of me? Or did Roman want to approach me on his own accord, now that the situation was resolved? Maybe he wanted me to help with some crime.

"For one thing," he said, "I'd like to express that I am impressed by the way you handled this predicament you found yourself in. Such a pair of balls you have on you. I did not say so today at the library, and I did not want to say so tonight in front of Timur and the rebbe, but I am very proud of you. These men that even I fear, you think nothing of pissing in their faces. And for what? The chance to speak with a pretty girl." I didn't like the way he said "pretty girl."

He came up beside me, moving very smoothly for such a stout man. He had spent his life working with his body, and knew how to control it. "Alojzy would have been proud. I myself am proud of you as if you were my own son." He put his strong arm around my shoulders. I couldn't have moved if I wanted to, so I acted like I didn't want to. Surely Roman hadn't chased me out into the ugly, windy night just to compliment me. But he didn't seem to be mocking me either; he seemed genuine. What did he want?

"Do you have children, Roman?" I asked.

"No. Well, you know, I had a son. In Ukraine. I imagine he's still there."

"Maybe you should look him up, instead of bothering me. It's cold. I need to get back before the trains stop running." Roman's grip remained firm on my shoulder.

"Perhaps. But you see, I am here not on behalf of myself, but on behalf of the rebbe. He asked that I deliver a final message to you, after he is gone. I thought it better to wait until we were outside the museum, as it is very private." This didn't make any sense. If the rebbe had something to say, why didn't he say it himself? Was it something he didn't want his children to hear? "It is on the subject of sons, as a matter of fact. It is from the Torah, I believe. But I am sure it will not escape a learned young man such as yourself." Roman reached into his pocket for the message. Then he stopped and hesitated, a sad look on his face.

"Nu?" I said.

"Yes, the message. The rebbe says to tell you: 'If a son is disloyal and defiant, if he does not heed us, then thereupon the men of his town shall stone him to death.'" I tried to break away, but Roman was too strong. He pulled the screwdriver from his pocket and plunged it into my side. It really felt as if I had been struck with a heavy stone. "Thus you will sweep out the evil from your midst," I heard him say as I wilted to the surface of the boardwalk. "All Israel will hear and be afraid." And then, more softly, from somewhere in the spinning distance, just barely audible above my own gasping for air: "I am sorry, *malchik*."

23

I CAME TO IN a hospital bed. My brain was soggy and porous. Two other beds were packed into the small room with me, but we were separated by curtains, and I didn't know who lay in them. Behind the curtain I heard a stream of urine hitting a bedpan. A nurse spoke to the patient when he was done urinating, and though I couldn't make out the words, I flinched at her Russian accent.

After a while, a different nurse came in and explained my situation. This was Coney Island Hospital. Two policemen driving up the boardwalk in a patrol car, checking that the beach and surrounding area were completely evacuated before the storm made landfall, had found me and brought me in. I was lucky; they had apparently driven by me once without noticing, but on their return trip their headlight had landed on me for a moment, and I caught one of the policemen's eyes. If I'd stayed out until morning, I could have died of hypothermia or blood loss.

My left kidney was lacerated, though not too deeply. Roman had hit me pretty hard with a flathead screwdriver, but his aim had been a little high, and the edge of my rib had taken most of the impact. The doctors who had sewn me up wanted to keep me for a couple days of observation, until they could definitively determine that they wouldn't need to open me back up and perform surgery. The phone system was too overloaded to allow personal calls, but I gave the nurse Becca's contact information, and she said someone would call and inform Becca of my location and condition. After her brief explanation, the nurse had to move on. There were numerous car accidents and injuries related to the storm, and the hospital was understaffed due to employees not being able to make it in. The storm was just fully hitting Brooklyn now—we heard the windows rattling behind the heavy plastic curtains—and things were only going to get worse.

A few hours later, a detective came in to ask me some questions about the attack. I told him it was just a run-of-the-mill mugging.

"Coney Island isn't safe," I said. "I should have known better than to walk down there at night. Maybe a kid from the projects? I don't know. Doesn't matter now. It's done."

"So the attacker was young?" the detective asked. He was forty or so, with a shaved head. His polo shirt and jacket were damp. He wrote on a pad in a leather case, but the speed and arc of his pen strokes suggested that he was sketching or doodling, not taking notes. "A teenager?"

"I don't know. I didn't get a good look at the guy, because he came up beside me, quick, and he had a handkerchief over his face. Besides, it was dark. And rainy, you know?"

"All right. It was rainy. It still is. Normally bad weather keeps teenage delinquents inside. They'd rather play video games than get their sneakers wet. What race was this attacker?"

"I just told you, I couldn't see his face."

"What about his hand? What color was that?"

"He had gloves on."

"Maybe he did have gloves on. See, the officers that brought you in recovered a weapon. A flathead screwdriver with the point filed down sharp, like something from a prison. Your blood was all over it. And there were no fingerprints on the handle. But they could have been wiped, or the rainwater could have cleaned them."

"Okay."

"You don't seem very interested in this information."

"No."

"If this was a mugging, why didn't he take your wallet?"

"I don't know. You'd have to ask him. Maybe it was his first time. He'll learn."

"You aren't going to be very helpful, are you, Mr. Edel?"

"No. So you might as well go ahead and get the hell out of my room." The detective shrugged.

"Hey, it's no skin off my balls either way. You look pretty felony assaulted to me, but if you don't feel like being helpful, I'm just going to write it up as a misdemeanor and let it go."

A minute or two after the detective left, everything went black. I thought that I was passing out again, but it was just the lights. I was completely vulnerable. Anyone could kill me in the dark. The lights turned back on.

I pulled the IV out of my arm and stumbled out into the hallway. The ground was unsteady under my feet, and I had to lean on the wall as I moved. Down the hall, I found what I was looking for: an unattended nurse's cart. I rifled through it quickly, searching for a scalpel. No luck. There wasn't any particular reason for a surgical tool to be on a nurse's cart. I found a pair of scissors, like a nurse would cut bandages with. The serrated edge was pretty sharp. My gown didn't have pockets, so I slid the scissors into my sock. The excursion took all of my energy, and when I made it back to my bed I slept.

When I woke up again, a Hasidic man was sitting in a chair by the covered window, watching me. The first thing I saw was his long beard, black streaked with gray. I looked up at his eyes, trying to read his intention. Surely he was a Glupsker. How had he found me? Was he here to finish me off?

Pretending to be only half conscious, I slipped the scissors out of my sock under the sheets.

"Come closer," I said, speaking in an exaggeratedly raspy voice. "I have to say something."

The man scooted his chair forward and leaned in. When he was close enough, I grabbed him by his beard with my left hand and yanked his head toward me. I took the scissors out from under the covers with my free hand, and held the open blades to his throat. He seemed surprised, but not afraid.

"Why do you want to do that?" he asked.

"Did the rebbe send you to finish the job?"

"Which rebbe? What job? No one sends me here."

"Don't play dumb," I said. "The Glupsker Rebbe wasn't satisfied with Roman's handiwork? He wants more blood from me?"

"The Glupsker Rebbe?" The man blinked. "Do I look like a Glupsker?" On closer inspection, the man was dressed a bit more modernly than a Glupsker. He wore a normal-length suit jacket, not a long coat. His hat was a normal fedora, not short brimmed like the Glupskers favored. Still, one couldn't be sure. Roman didn't look anything like a Hasid—he was not only secular, but a muscleman—and he had done the rebbe's bidding.

"Okay," I said, lowering the pair of scissors, but keeping it in my hand under the covers, in case I needed to pull it again quickly. "Go sit back by the window. Out of reach." He complied. "So, why *are* you here, if no one sent you? What do you want from me? Are you a policeman or something?" I'd heard rumors that the NYPD had an entire Orthodox division, which filtered through the community. "I told that detective I didn't see anything."

"No, no, nothing like that. I am a rabbi. I do this as *avodah*, as service. When there are new patients with Jewish names—especially those who have no family or friends visiting them—I come to visit with them. To see that they are all right." The man had a slight Hebrew accent. My understanding was that Glupskers favored Yiddish, even in Israel, so this was another indication this guy was on the level.

"Well, you've visited me. I'm fine."

"No, you don't seem fine." He glanced at my battered body. "A man who is fine doesn't threaten a rabbi with sharp objects." I ignored his comment.

"If you're not a Glupsker, what kind of rabbi are you?"

"A Torah-observing one."

"Hasidic?"

"Yes, I'd say so."

"But what dynasty?"

"I was ordained here in Brooklyn, at the Lubavitcher Yeshiva. But I studied at other yeshivas in Israel, when I first came to Torah. I'm not an adherent of one rebbe, if that's your question." He smiled. "Certainly not the Glupsker Rebbe." I wondered why he didn't ask why I was so concerned about Glupskers.

"So you're a *baal teshuvah*?"

"Yes."

"You weren't raised religious?" Rayna had tried to escape the fold. She had almost succeeded. And this man ran right into the fold. A year ago, when I was reading holy texts at college, I could have imagined myself taking that path. But the opportunity for that in my life was now passed.

"No. I was raised without God. Pure Zionist. My family came from Iraq and Morocco. My Moroccan grandparents did folk things, rituals. My grandfather visited the graves of many *tzadikim* to ask for blessings. My grandfather from Iraq was a Marxist. He believed in the material world only. Yet even his Marx knew that material things would one day melt into air. My parents were good Zionists. I came to Torah on my own after the army. My name is Hayyim, by the way."

"But tell me about your family, Isaac." I hadn't told him my name, but I recalled that he'd gotten it from the hospital's admission list before he came here. They had gotten it off my ID. The detective had said my wallet was still on me when they brought me in. "Are they religious?"

"My mother and her husband observe certain things. They are not Orthodox, but they are not without faith. Regular American Jews, I guess. I think they belong to a Reform congregation in Santa Fe. I'm not sure." The rabbi nodded. "My father was different. He was without rules. My stepfather says I must say kaddish for my father."

"If you are a mourner, it is only right that you should recite the mourner's kaddish for your father. When did he die?"

"I don't know for sure. Within the past year."

"What was his name?"

"Alojzy. Alojzy Edel."

"What was his Hebrew name?"

"I don't know. I think he said in Israel he went by the name Assaf? I'm not sure."

"He lived in Israel?"

"Yes. He wasn't from there. But he served in the army."

"I see. Where is he buried?

"At sea. His body is under the water. It will never be recovered. I had an idea that maybe I could paddle a boat, or a rubber raft or something, out off the coast to where I thought he was. And recite kaddish like that."

"No, that wouldn't do." Hayyim shook his head back and forth. "You can't say it by yourself. It doesn't work like that."

"But it's between me and him."

"No. It's between you, and him, and Hashem, and the Jewish people. Perhaps you've heard the saying: 'nine rabbis can't make a minyan, but ten pushcart peddlers can.' You need to pray in a minyan. It can't be done in solitude." He looked at his watch. "It's almost time for maariv. You could come down to the chapel to daven with me and the other men."

"I don't have the strength to walk," I said. The trip to the hallway and back had wiped me out.

"I can get a wheelchair and push you." He smiled. "But you'll have to leave the scissors here."

The chapel was down on the third floor. There were about a dozen men in the room, all holding prayer books. Two old men were in wheelchairs like me, with non-Jewish attendants standing by to push them. Several men wore scrubs and kippot. Their skin ranged from lighter than mine to black. Some of them must have been doctors and some nurses, or technicians or aids of some sort. A Russian-looking man wore a security uniform with short sleeves, and I could see the faded, greenish tattoos on his arms. Beside him stood an Orthodox man in a three-piece suit and talis. He could have been an off-duty doctor, an administrator, or just a visitor. So these were the Jewish people. I took my place amongst them, and Hayyim placed a siddur in my hands. We faced southeast. I knew we were praying in the direction of Jerusalem—Rayna's new home—but I felt as if we were trying to make our peace with the ocean, where the storm had come from.

The familiar words of the Shema began. This prayer was soon followed by the silent Amidah, which I pulled myself up out of my wheelchair for. I remained standing for the mourner's kaddish.

May His great Name grow exalted and sanctified. The Talmud says that God spends a quarter of every day playing with the Leviathan. Perhaps they were playing now. Perhaps that's what the storm was.

May there be abundant peace from heaven. The harbor surged in the storm. There was no peace on land or sea. Alojzy's bones would be picked clean by now. The surging waters would tear his bones apart and scatter them.

May Hashem create peace for us, and all of Israel. I could let Alojzy go, so long as it meant the man could have some peace.

Amen. Do widzenia.

As Hayyim and I waited outside the chapel for the elevator to come, the power cut out again, and the hallway went dark. Strips of very dim safety lights came on along the edges where the walls met the floors, and machines continued to hum from rooms, but the hallways remained dark, and the elevator call lights stayed off.

"Isaac?" Hayyim said, searching for me with his voice.

"Yes, Rabbi?" After my experience with the Glupsker Rebbe, I spoke the word "rabbi" with less respect than I once had.

"Perhaps I might speak a word of Torah, to make the most of our time?"

"Fine." We had prayed maariv. Now we would have a *shiur*. I was in his hands.

"You know of your ultimate namesake, the patriarch Isaac? You know that he was bound by his father, Abraham, who was going to make a sacrifice of him?"

"Yes. Of course."

"When Isaac lay on the altar, he looked up at his father's face, and saw his father was truly ready to slaughter him. Abraham's eyes were filled with a dark storm. He was far from Isaac, and Isaac could not reach him with his own pleading eyes. Then the storm cleared, but Isaac didn't know why. He couldn't hear the voice of the angel calling out to Abraham, telling him to stay his hand. Only Abraham could hear that.

"After he was untied, and rose from the altar, Isaac turned away from his father. Abraham went back home, but Isaac left and went farther east, to study at the Academy of Shem and Eber. Shem taught his students the law, and he told them stories of the days before the flood.

"We learn later in Genesis that when Isaac was old he was blind. He could not distinguish his son Jacob from his son Esau. Do you know why this should be? Do you know how Isaac was blinded?" The rabbi waited for an answer.

"Perhaps he was just old," I said.

"No," Hayyim said. "Everything happens for a reason. There is always a cause and an effect. An action and a consequence." I flipped through the volumes of tales in my mind.

"Tears," I said. "Angels' tears." The story came back to me as I spoke. "Hashem and his angels looked down on Isaac on the altar. Isaac was facing up toward the heavens. The angels cried at his plight, and their tears fell into his open eyes. Blinding him." A related story said the tears had melted the knife in Abraham's hand. Now that I had been stabbed myself, I was less inclined to believe that such a thing was possible.

"This is a common explanation," Hayyim said. "It is related, amongst others, in Rashi's commentary. But it is just a story. One of the problems with it is that Isaac was not blind until much later. When Isaac first met his bride Rebekah, he saw her approaching from across the field on her camel, so he cannot already have been blind then.

"After Isaac was married to Rebekah, and their sons were born, he received word that Abraham was on his deathbed in Hebron. Isaac had not seen his father since the trip to Mount Moriah, but he was determined to see him once more before he was gone.

"Isaac arrived too late. By the time he made it to Hebron, Abraham had already breathed his last breath. His youngest wife, Keturah, had bathed his body, and laid him out in his linen shroud to await burial. When Isaac entered his father's tent, he asked Keturah to remove the cloth from his father's face. He thought he might learn something by gazing upon the dead man. Perhaps he could understand what happened so many years ago on the mountain.

"The moment the cloth was pulled back, and Isaac looked upon his father's face, he was struck blind."

It seemed like Hayyim was going to keep speaking, but just then the lights came back on. The elevator rumbled and the doors pulled open. If there was more to the rabbi's story—a moral or lesson—I didn't want to hear it. I didn't need anyone else interpreting a story for me.

"I think I can manage to get upstairs myself," I told him. I appreciated that Hayyim had brought me down to the chapel, but I still didn't feel comfortable letting a stranger stand behind me.

"You are sure? It's no problem for me to push you."

"I'm fine on my own." He released his grip, and I rolled myself into the elevator.

I was glad to see Hayyim disappear behind the doors, but felt anxious in the confined space. A few other people were inside the elevator with me, including two men who had been in the minyan. One of them, a nurse, helped me maneuver the chair out into the hallway on my floor, then left me to my own devices. Even without having to walk, using my arms to roll the chair's wheels took a lot of energy out of me.

When I finally made it to my room, I climbed out of the chair and went into the bathroom. My legs felt wobbly, and I had to lean against the wall while I peed. My weakness was probably tied to dehydration. A nurse would need to reinsert the IV into my arm. In the meantime, I leaned against the edge of the sink, and gulped some water from the faucet. I washed my hands and face.

I pulled up my gown and examined my injuries in the mirror. My whole left side was a mix of black bruises and red inflammation. The gash itself was longer than I expected, nearly a full inch. Roman had caught me at an angle. I would be in much worse shape if the shaft of the screwdriver had gone straight into my kidney. The emergency room staff had stitched the cut up with black thread.

So, I thought, this is how it happens. This is how a body becomes scarred. Al used to walk around the apartment with his shirt off. He always wore blue jeans, not ripped or dirty, but clean, bright blue jeans that he was proud of. He put his jeans and chains on right after he showered, but he'd leave his shirt off until it was time to leave the apartment. His torso was strong and manly, despite the gut. He had so many scars, all over his arms and shoulders and chest and belly. Some were thick and some were razor thin. Some had healed as raised, lumpy ropes, while others were flush with the skin around them. I asked my father about his scars once. He shrugged and said, "I have been cut. Is life. They will cut you too, boychik. You will bleed."

Acknowledgements

Thank you, as always, to Oksana Mironova for putting up with everything.

This novel began when I was in the MFA program at the City College of New York. I would like to thank everyone I met there, including professors Keith Gandal and Peter Trachtenberg, and my many talented peers.

Thank you to Corey Eastwood, Daniel Fishkin, and Will Crofoot for being insightful readers.

Thank you to Liat and Blaine for providing me with a tent in the woods when I needed to escape.

Thank you to Jonathan Mukai for the crabbing trips and the talks about the old street days.

Thank you to Peter Aaron for discussing spiritual matters with me. Thank you to Catherine Tung for discussing material matters with me.

Thank you to my editor, Michelle Caplan, who saw more in my manuscript than I did.

Thank you to the Nadler/Watson family for their ongoing support.

Peace to all the street vendors in New York City. I know it gets cold out there.